THE MANDEVILLE SHADOW

CALLIE LANGRIDGE

Storm
PUBLISHING

Ebook ISBN: 978-1-80508-297-2
Paperback ISBN: 978-1-80508-299-6

Cover design by: Eileen Carey
Cover images by: Shutterstock, Midjourney

Published by Storm Publishing.
For further information, visit:
www.stormpublishing.co

ALSO BY CALLIE LANGRIDGE

The Mandevilles Series

A Time to Change

The Mandeville Secret

The Mandeville Shadow

For Mum. With so much love x

PROLOGUE

NINETEEN YEARS EARLIER

'Do it, Kate. Go on,' Harry said from beneath the fort in the parlour, fashioned from two kitchen chairs and a sheet their mother said he might borrow from the laundry press.

Kate crawled in beside her brother. She sat cross-legged on the floor and blew on the jam in a tart she had been allowed to take hot from the oven. 'I don't want to,' she said.

'Go on, do your magic trick,' Harry persisted.

'It's not a trick.' Kate blew on the jam again.

'Well, what is it then?'

Kate shrugged.

Harry held out a small tin soldier. 'Dad said it belonged to someone in the family before it was given to him. Who was it, Kate? Who did this belong to? And why did they give it to Dad?'

Kate took a bite of the tart and shook her head.

'Go on,' Harry said, pushing the soldier at her.

Kate chewed slowly and turned her shoulder to her brother. She shook her head again.

Harry dropped the soldier into the box on the floor. 'Spoilsport,' he said. He pulled back the sheet and let it fall as he got to his feet outside the fort. Kate listened to his footsteps and to his voice in the kitchen. Followed by their mother's voice.

Kate let her hands fall to her lap. Beside her, the light from the parlour fire glowed orange on the white sheet. Kate peered at the soldier in the box. He lay amongst Harry's other toy soldiers. Some sat on horses. Others gripped lances beneath their arms, ready to charge. Others held guns.

Kate closed her eyes. Father had been away for more than a year. He had missed Christmas and her last birthday. In his letters, he always said how well he was doing and that he had lots of pals and the food wasn't so bad. He said she must continue to be a good girl at school and for mother, and that Harry must be a good boy until the war was over, when he would come home, and they would all be together again.

Kate squeezed her eyes tight. Not everyone that went to war came home. Just before the Whitsun weekend, a boy in her form had been called out of a handwriting lesson by the head-master. The rest of the class had heard his wail out in the corridor where his mother waited for him. Miss Forrester had explained to them later in the day that Ernest Lavery's father had been killed. And that they must all be very kind to Ernest when he returned to class, which wouldn't be for a few days.

Kate inched away from the box. The pictures she saw in her mind sometimes when she touched objects all seemed to be from the past. She might see an old woman who, from Kate's description, Mother recognised as an aunt of hers, patching a hole in the lace tablecloth that Mother liked to bring out on special occasions. Kate might see her grandfather digging in his garden before he gave his spade to her father. She might see the little boy who had owned the bicycle before it was given to Harry on his birthday and which Father had bought from a chap at work.

Kate peered at the soldier in the box again. He didn't look frightening. But she was afraid of him. She couldn't decide what object would show its history to her when she touched it or what she might see of its past. The images came to her like pages in a picture book. But they were pictures that moved. Mother called it her 'party trick' and put it down to the fact that Kate had always listened so intently to the conversations of adults, even when she was a very small girl. She listened and took everything in. And what with the photographs in frames around their house and the homes of their family, it wasn't surprising that Kate seemed to know about people she had never met.

Mother had a sensible explanation for everything. And Kate had thought it best not to say that she wasn't sure she remembered as much as Mother might think. And she never told anyone outside her family about what she saw. They might have thought she was making it up.

The light from the fire glowed on the soldiers in the box. As far as Kate knew, she had only ever seen things that had already happened. But what if, one day, she was to see something that was happening in that moment. Or that might happen in the future. She didn't want to hold the soldier that had belonged to her father. If she was lucky, she would see a picture of him playing with the solider as a child. But what if she saw more than that? What if she saw something awful so that she wailed like Ernest Lavery?

Kate gripped the tart so tight that it turned to crumbs in her hand.

ONE

THURSDAY 24TH OCTOBER, 1935

'Is Mum leaving this for the new people?' Harry asked. He picked up the small side table and showed it to Kate.

Kate pressed her finger to her lips and shook her head. With her eyes, she indicated to the floor above.

'What?' Harry said.

'Just be a bit quieter,' Kate whispered. 'Mum's finding it hard to talk about what she's leaving and what she's taking.'

'I've only got the van till six,' Harry said, and started for the parlour door, the little table between his arms. 'Mum will have to let me know what's to go.'

'Just ask me,' Kate said. 'And yes, that table's to go with you.'

Kate pulled back the curtains at the parlour window. She watched Harry carry the table out to the van he had borrowed from his work in Leicester. As a master carpenter, her brother might have a delicate touch when it came to turning wood, but he had always been clumsy with his words.

Kate let the curtain fall from her hand. Harry hadn't had to navigate the clearing of the house for the last few weeks, watching on as their mother removed treasured possessions and mementos from shelves and cupboards. Kate didn't begrudge him that. She had precious little else to occupy her time and it was good to be busy. To have something meaningful to occupy her mind as well as her hands. To not have to think too hard about what had happened and what would become of her.

Harry had been at their parents' house when it really mattered. When Mother first needed a shoulder to cry on and to make all the necessary arrangements. Kate helping now meant Harry could carry on with his work. He had a wife and two small children to support after all.

Every day for the last few weeks, Kate had sat beside Mother, packing ornaments, folding linen, wrapping a lifetime of building a home in newspaper and placing each item with great care into tea crates that were now on the van to be transported to Harry's home. It was a detached house where Mother would have her own room.

Harry's wife, Enid, was about the sweetest woman Kate had ever met. She had been so accommodating, saying how wonderful it would be to have her mother-in-law living with them. Enid looked after Mother as though she was another daughter. And Kate was glad for it. Glad that Mother had Enid to support her too. Enid telephoned at least twice a week to say how much Michael and Violet were looking forward to seeing their grandmother. And of course, it was no problem at all to have whatever possessions she wanted to bring. Didn't they have a nice big attic in which they could be stored? And Mother's new bedroom was large with lovely wardrobes Harry had made and it got the very best of the morning sunshine.

Kate ran her fingers down the curtain. Along with the table and chairs in the kitchen, the curtains in every room would be staying. The young couple buying the house had been thrilled with the lovely floral fabric. Fabric that Kate had helped her mother choose at the department store in Northampton to decorate each window of the brand-new house on the brand-new estate. Fabric they knew would complement the climbing pink roses Kate's father had planted to frame the windows when her parents moved into this home three years ago.

The stairs creaked out in the hall. Kate straightened her skirt as her mother came through the door. She was holding a small suitcase.

'I would have brought that down for you,' Kate said.

Her mother tried to smile. 'You've done so much for me already, sweetheart. I don't know how I would have managed all that had to be done without you.' As she said the words, her face crumpled. 'I'm sorry,' she said through a sob.

Kate took the case from her mother and placed it on the floor. Her mother took a hankie from her sleeve and covered her eyes.

'You've nothing to be sorry for, Mum.' Kate rubbed her mother's hand. 'Just think, tonight, you'll have Michael and Violet to fuss over. They'll be thrilled to see you.'

Her mother nodded slowly. She wiped her eyes. 'Will you be all right here on your own, sweetheart?'

'Don't worry about me, Mum. I'll sleep like a queen on the old campaign bed.' She pointed to the wooden box. 'See,' she said. 'Harry's set it up by the fireplace for me. I shall light a fire tonight and be toasty.'

'I'm so sorry the bed in the spare room has gone already. But the man who bought it was keen to take it straightaway.'

'I'll be fine, Mum. Honestly.'

'What will you do for your tea?'

'I've a tin of pilchards and some bread. And Harry's brought me his old camping pan to boil water and his old tin cup, so I shall have a cup of tea. I've a book I'm enjoying so it'll give me time to read.'

'And you're back to Sheffield tomorrow?'

Kate paused. 'That's right,' she said a little too brightly.

'It's been good of them to let you have so much time off. You've landed on your feet there. Your dad was so proud of you following in his footsteps...' As she said the words, her face crumpled again. Kate took her mother in her arms and felt the heave of her as she sobbed.

There came a cough from the door. 'You all right there, Mum?' Harry said.

Kate transferred her mother into Harry's arms so that she could retreat to the kitchen. Through the closed door, she listened to her brother gently soothe their mother. Kate leant against the wall. The kitchen was empty of every item that had made this house a home. No kettle on the stove. No teapot on the side. No teacups with their matching saucers waiting for a steaming brew to be poured into them. No Father reading his morning and evening newspapers at the kitchen table, sipping his tea as he regaled Mother with the cricket scores while she pretended to be interested. No Father jabbing at the reports of the loss of work in the north that was affecting his extended family in Yorkshire so badly. Where was the help from the government when it was needed? If it was happening closer to Westminster, they wouldn't be turning this blind eye to the depressed economy and the devastation it was wrecking on industries across the north. An honest day's pay for an honest day's work – that's what the working classes wanted. A chance to get a foot up the ladder. And if they fell on hard times, there should be a safety net to catch them and support them until they could get back on their feet. If they didn't have that, they would sink.

There was no Father with his passion for the working man and woman. No Father anywhere in this house anymore. Kate buried her face in the crook of her arm. Her mother hadn't seen any of the tears she had cried in the last two months. She had not and would not cry in front of her mother. She had enough to bear.

.   .   .

Harry placed their mother's suitcase in the back of the van. The thud of the closing door sounded so final. With Kate's help, he had managed to load the bedstead and mattress as well as the other small items of furniture, a variety of rugs and the dozen or so tea chests.

'Here, Mum,' Harry said, returning to the hallway, stamping his feet, and patting himself with his arms across his body, as though he could pat away the cold. 'Let me take that for you.' Their mother didn't resist when he slipped her handbag from the crook of her arm. He held it by the strap in both hands. Kate watched as Mother looked around the entryway as though trying to soak in every detail of the wallpaper, the staircase, the runner up the stairs held in place by brass rods. She wore her best Sunday dress and overcoat, her hat pinned to her hair with the silver pin their father had given her as a gift on their silver wedding anniversary. Harry shifted from one foot to the other. 'I'll take this to the van, then. I'll wait for you out there.' He leant and pecked Kate on the cheek. She knew he was glad to have his hands occupied. It meant he didn't have to embrace her. At thirty years of age, Harry was only four years older than her, but his way of showing affection had always been a light punch to Kate's arm or a joke made at her expense. 'We'll see you next month then, sis,' he said. 'Vi's looking forward to sharing her room with you for a couple of nights. Can't talk about anything else.'

'Tell her I'm looking forward to it, too.' Kate smiled.

Harry walked away down the path and got into his van.

Kate turned to her mother. Any words forming in her mind seemed too abrupt. How could she tell her mother to take a final look around before leaving for the very last time?

'I'm so looking forward to seeing you next month, Mum. And in just a few hours you'll see Michael and Vi. Won't that be a treat?'

It was clear that their mother had not heard a single word

Kate or Harry had said. And the words Kate spoke felt as hollow as the look in her mother's eyes. Her mind was no doubt three years away from this moment when she had crossed the threshold for the first time.

'It'll be all right, Mum. I promise.'

'We loved this place so much,' her mother said, still looking around, still soaking in details.

'I know.'

'They'll look after it, won't they?'

'The new people? They seem lovely. I'm sure they will.' Kate left a pause. 'Are you ready?'

Slowly her mother nodded. She walked to the front door. Kate followed her across the threshold, down the path and through the gate. The neighbours had all said their goodbyes the day before to save Mother the upset today. On the pavement, Mother turned to look back at the house. She put her palm to her lips, kissed it, and held it up to the window of the bedroom on the first floor. Kate felt her heart break even further.

TWO

After watching the van disappear up the road, Kate walked slowly back down the path and closed the door. Her footsteps echoed oddly on the bare floorboards. The fire her mother had laid in the grate that morning had cooled. Everything felt odd. Empty. Turning her back on the parlour, she pulled on her overcoat and brown beret and left the house. She collected her bicycle that leant on the wall beside the front door and wheeled it down the path.

The chill and the fog had settled in for the day and Kate paused to secure her scarf tight about her neck. She latched the gate and looked back at the house. That thing of bricks and mortar held her parents' every dream. Beyond the good health of their family, to own their own home had been the thing in life they wanted above all else. They had worked hard and saved hard. That house with its parlour, kitchen, two generous bedrooms, bathroom, and gardens front and back, might have been the pot of gold at the end of the rainbow; it meant so much to them. It was the reason for holidays to the coast not taken, extra hours worked, the elbows of jackets and knees of trousers darned and patched rather than buying new. The bank manager had agreed to the mortgage. As bookkeeper for one of Northampton's most successful shoe factories, it was clear that Father's position was stable and his salary regular. Kate's parents had chosen the house from the plans and visited from their rented terrace in Northampton regularly to watch the progress of the build.

But now, without Father's salary, the mortgage could no longer be paid. Even if Mother had been able to afford it, she would not have had enough left each month to buy groceries or pay the many bills that came with managing a home.

Kate closed her eyes briefly. Without looking back, she mounted the bicycle and pedalled slowly along the pavement, past a row of houses that looked just like her parents' house.

At the edge of the estate, the street met a wider road with a recently built wall running the entire length. The road was generally quiet but, with the fog, Kate decided to cycle on the pavement. She pedalled slowly, on the lookout for any pedestrians. The new housing estate soon gave way to open land. Mist clung to the grass as though a carpet of white had been laid out, and Kate followed the path beside the high brick wall. After two miles or so, she came to a junction which opened onto a green with a pond, a pub, a little grocers', and a Post Office. Turning right Kate cycled a short distance, past a neat row of cottages on the other side, much older than the houses on the new estate. Coming to a gate, Kate dismounted and rested the bicycle against the wall.

She had visited St Mary's many times in the last two months, but today the weathervane atop the fine spire was lost to the fog. Kate followed the path winding around the side of the church.

As with every visit, the sight that met her at the back of the church made Kate's heart sink in her chest. At the end of the rows of headstones and memorials peppered with moss and weathered by the years, were a collection of mounds. Simple wooden crosses marked the burials too fresh for a permanent memorial. Only once the ground had settled sufficiently could headstones be placed on the graves. Kate stopped before the mound of earth at the very end of a row and before a holly bush. Along with her mother and Harry, Kate had chosen the simple stone that would be placed there. She knew by heart every word that the stonemason would etch into its surface:

Joseph John Durrant
21/4/1880 to 25/8/1935
Taken too soon
Much loved husband, father and grandfather
Friend to all. Enemy of none

Kate knelt on the damp grass and arranged the petals of the flowers she had helped Mother place there the day before. 'Hello, Dad,' she said quietly. 'Mum's gone with Harry today. I think she'll get on just fine. You've no need to worry.'

Kate's voice caught in her throat. A hot tear forced its way down her cheek. She wiped it away, focusing on the tufts of grass that had begun to sprout through the surface of the earth. In the spring the mound would be flat and carpeted with fresh grass and perhaps the odd wildflower. New life from old. Kate placed her hand on the earth. 'I miss you so much, Dad,' she whispered.

'You're your father's daughter,' her mother had always said. There had been no jealousy or malice. It was a simple fact. Kate had inherited her father's dark wavy hair and brown eyes. As a small child she had liked nothing more than helping him work on his allotment when they lived in the terrace in Northampton with no garden of its own. When the weather was fine, she and Harry would join their father for long walks out in the countryside around Northampton, with a flask and box of sandwiches packed by her mother. They could walk for miles, surrounded by farms and woodland. 'Fresh air costs nothing,' her father would say. 'It belongs to no man and to every man.' Many was the Saturday afternoon that Kate had fallen asleep while the bus swayed on its way back to Northampton, resting against her father's shoulder until they got to the stop close to home. And many was the evening that she had sat beside him at the kitchen table as he read from the newspapers when he would explain the politics of the day to her.

When she struggled with her sums and long division, Father was always there to help. Along with gardening and keeping an eye on what politicians were up to, numbers were his passion. His talent for mathematics had seen her father side-step the life he was destined for and was the lot of his grandfather, father, uncles, brothers and cousins. A teacher had recognised a special talent in him and tutored and nurtured him through his school certificates so that college followed by an apprenticeship took him to a life in an office and not the pit face.

Working out a problem. Finding a solution. That was what her father had loved. It extended to how he dealt with life. When Kate found her beloved pet goldfish floating lifeless on the surface of the water in its bowl and didn't know what to do with its little body, it had been her father who suggested they bury it beneath his precious dahlias on the allotment so that she always had a place to visit. Her father had listened when she had something to say or a question to ask. And it was for him that she had taken up the role of receipts clerk in the accounting department of the largest steelworks in Sheffield. He felt that it was important for young women to gain their independence as far as they were able and be allowed to use their brains and intellect. The job in the steelworks was the lowest level in the accounting office, but it was a good job with prospects of advancement.

For a while Kate had toyed with training as a dressmaker as

she loved keeping up with the fashions. But it had pleased her father that she would in some way follow in his footsteps. He had arranged the interview for her with a friend he had known since his days at college. With her good school reports and her certificates, and the experience she had gained working in a large draper's in Northampton, they had been pleased to take her on. And she worked hard. Just like her father had taught her. 'You don't get anything for nothing in this life, Katherine,' he had so often said. 'You must work hard and look for opportunities.'

Kate stared at the bare earth. 'I didn't tell them, Dad. I just couldn't. Mum has enough to worry about without me. They think I'm going back to Sheffield tomorrow.'

How could she tell her mother that there was no job to return to? That she'd had to give up her room in the boarding house and leave all the other young women employed by the steelworks that she had befriended.

Being away from their homes and families, they looked out for each other and became good company. They went to dances in town, to the picture houses, and sometimes to the theatres. Sometimes in the company of young men but just as often as a group of female friends. In their free time in the summer months, a group of the girls would head off on the bus to the Peak District close by to walk in the hills.

Kate had settled into her life in Sheffield. The money in her pay packet each week was hers to do with as she pleased once she had paid for her board and lodging and put an amount into her Post Office savings account. She had shared a room with two other girls and a bathroom with four more and had become rather popular as she was always ready with her sewing kit to fix a hem or adjust a new skirt that wasn't quite the right size. She had even stretched to making some simple items when any of the girls had a special event to attend.

They had been a happy band, until the problems that had

been brewing around the world for several years visited themselves on the steelworks. Working as a clerk in the accounts
department, Kate had seen it approaching. When the exports to
countries around the world began to dry up, there had been less
money coming in and too much going out.

In the newspapers in the canteen at work, Kate had read
about the competition from foreign manufacturers which was
taking away so much business. She'd read about the marches
from northern towns and cities to London to protest the lack of
support for the ex-employees of the once thriving businesses.
On her trips home every other month, the desperate situation
had been her father's main topic of conversation over the
kitchen table. He had been horrified that any man or woman
should need to march on the capital to plead for help to put
food in their bellies. What kind of country had they become
that there was not food on the table for each person? Hadn't the
war taught them anything about the need to treat fellow
humans with dignity and respect, and see to it that the basic
needs of every man, woman and child were met?

Finally, the day came when the workers of the steelworks
were told it would be necessary to rationalise the workforce.
The single young women were first to be let go to save the work
for men who needed the money more.

Kate looked at the flowers on the mound of earth. 'What am
I to do, Dad?' she said. 'The new people are moving into the
house at the end of the week. I've nowhere to go. I can't ask
Harry to take me in, too. He has his own family to look after.'
Kate grasped a handful of the cold earth. For the first time in
her life, her father wasn't there to help her with a problem.

Nobody was there to see the tears she wept while she
searched the corners of her mind for a solution. She'd already
tried the accounts departments of all the local factories but
there was no employment to be found. She had only worked at
the most junior level and any role of that kind had been filled by

better trained and qualified people who had moved further south to look for jobs after finding themselves unemployed in the north. She should have been more diligent. She should have gone to night school to learn bookkeeping. She should have studied at weekends rather than gallivanting around the Peak District or stepping out arm-in-arm with the other girls, enjoying the entertainment that Sheffield had to offer. With more qualifications, she might have been able to secure a job. If she'd found a job with a regular wage, she might have been able to help Mother pay the mortgage so that she hadn't had to move out of her home.

Harry had desperately tried to find a solution to keep Mother in her house. He earned decent money but had no savings and lived month to month on his wages, supporting Enid and the children. At least Harry had a skill and a trade, which meant he was able to put a comfortable roof over their mother's head. Kate had no skill that anybody wanted. Nobody needed her labour.

Kate hung her head and stared at the patch of grass before her knees. Birds sang up on the hidden weathervane and called to each other from the trees surrounding the graveyard. If she could have one wish, just one, it would be to see her father one last time. She was alone. So very alone.

THREE

Kate stayed at her father's grave for as long as the cold would allow. When she finally got to her feet, she took a handkerchief from the pocket of her overcoat and wiped her eyes. 'I'll come back tomorrow,' she said, trying to smile. 'I'll try to sort out what I'm to do by then.'

As she stood, a robin flew by so close that Kate could almost feel its wings brush her cheek. It came to rest on a branch of the holly bush behind her father, cocking its head to look at her before flying just a few feet to sit on the top of a gate in the low wall just beyond the bush. The wall being only waist height, the gate was mainly hidden by green foliage and Kate had paid it no mind before. The robin flew up into the branches of a tree. Her curiosity piqued, Kate made her way towards the gate, the robin watching her every step. It was only when she was a few feet from the wall that the robin cocked its head one last time before taking to the wing and disappearing into the dense foliage.

It was a bit of a squeeze, but Kate was able to get behind the holly bush without it snagging her overcoat too badly. There must at one time have been a path. Why else would there be a gate? But whatever had been there was hidden. Unlike the neatly kept lawns around the church, the grass behind the holly bush was overgrown with tall weeds. The gate was clearly very old and when Kate pushed it, it let out a low creak and rust fluttered from the hinges into the long grass. She forced it open just far enough to pass through.

The other side of the wall was similarly overgrown. What was left of a path ran parallel to the low wall, but it was the woodlands that interested Kate. Picking her way through the tall grass and weeds, she came to the edge of a sea of trees. They stretched as far as she could see in every direction. She looked behind her. The spire of St Mary's was still hidden in the fog. A quick venture into the woods could do no harm. She had nowhere else to be.

Stepping into the trees, she was met with the smell of damp earth. It was the smell of the childhood walks in the woods with Harry and their father. She and Harry would collect sticks and stones from amongst fallen leaves to take home, competing to see who had the most or the best. Kate smiled at the memory. She walked further into the woods. It grew darker as the trees became denser, the foliage of evergreens blocking the path of any daylight to the forest floor. As she walked, Kate thought about what she should do next. She was fortunate to have savings in her Post Office account. But that would not last long if she had to pay for a lodging room or a guest house. With no income, it would soon dwindle. Harry or Mother might be able to loan her something. But that really would have to be a final resort. And it wasn't a sustainable option. They couldn't continue to help her. She had been financially independent for years. As much as she might finally have to admit that she needed their help, she would rather find her own solution to her troubles. Otherwise, what had the last few years in Sheffield been for? Her father's words played over in her mind. *Make your own luck.* She was trying so very hard, really, she was. But she couldn't pluck a job from thin air.

Kate picked up a stick. As she walked, twigs and dry leaves crunching beneath her shoes, she ran the stick along the bark of the trees she passed. She was glad of the memory of a happier time, of charging through woods with Harry, jumping over gnarled roots and dragging the biggest sticks they could find across the trees.

It wasn't until she had walked for quite some time, picturing Harry running ahead, that it occurred to Kate that this might be private land. Other ramblers might feel there should be no hindrance to where they were allowed to walk but breaking the rules had never sat well with her. She stopped and looked around. There was no sign of anyone else. More pressing than that was the realisation that she had no idea where she was or where she had come from. Kate dropped the stick to the ground. She spun around. There was no obvious difference to any part of this woodland. Every path away from the spot on which she stood looked the same. She pulled back her sleeve and looked at her watch. It was after three o'clock. What little daylight there had been would soon fade. Choosing a route that looked vaguely familiar, Kate set off. But after five minutes or so, she still recognised nothing. She stopped and looked through the trees. Setting off in a different direction, she picked up her pace until she was running. If she couldn't find her way back to the church, she might at least stumble across the wall that ran the length of the road from her parents' estate to the junction which led to St Mary's. She would be able to follow it to get back to the church to collect her bicycle. It might be a long walk, but it was better than being lost in this wood overnight.

Kate looked up to the sky visible between the orange leaves clinging to the branches of the deciduous trees. A pinkness broke through the white bank of fog. 'Red sky at night...' she thought. It might bode well for the day dawning tomorrow but for now, it was a sure sign that daylight was slipping away. Setting off through the woods, she picked up her pace, jumping over gnarled roots that broke through the brown earth. She dodged sharp, bare branches of bushes that rattled as she passed. It was a stupid approach. It wasn't an approach at all. It was blind panic. But she really could not be stuck in this wood when night fell.

Running through a cloud of her own breath, Kate changed direction. But this path seemed the same as the one she had just turned from. Changing direction again, she ran faster. She stumbled and tripped over an exposed root. Another took her by surprise, her shoe snagging, threatening to upend her. Had it not been for tumbling into a well-placed tree, she would have ended up on her knees.

Kate braced against the trunk, pausing to catch her breath. A plan. She needed a plan. To take stock and plot her next move rather than panic. Pushing away from the tree, she brushed dry bark from her palms. She took another deep breath and turned around. She looked, really looked along every route leading away. But the way the branches grew here was different from any other part of the wood she had passed through. What she had tripped over was not a root breaking free from the earth, but a branch reaching down from a trunk of one of two vast trees – the tree that had broken her fall and another no more than twenty feet away. Countless branches grew from each and rather than reach to the sky, bent down to the ground as though the weight was too much for the trees to bear. It created the feeling of a cage about her.

In the moment it took to realise that the arrangement of these branches was not an act of nature but the result of cultivation, Kate heard a noise. A crunch. She turned around. A man dodged one of the branches to join her in the cage.

'Hello,' he said.

Kate's heart punched at her ribs. She quickly looked him up and down. Like any young woman used to living in the city, she quickly weighed up any threat. With his country clothes, he seemed like he belonged here.

'I didn't mean to startle you,' the man said. He was young, possibly a similar age to her. He wore tweeds and a cap, like a gamekeeper might. He was tall and slender with a fair moustache. It seemed to Kate that the hair might be cultivated on his top lip so that he didn't appear so young since, like his hair, his complexion was fair and – so far as she could see – without blemish.

'You didn't startle me,' Kate said. 'Sorry. I mean, you did, but I'm... I was lost and it's getting dark. I was afraid I might not be able to find my way out... sorry...' she laughed nervously.

The man looked into her face. 'How did you find yourself in here?' he asked.

'I came through a gate in the churchyard.' Kate nodded in the direction of St Mary's.

'Goodness,' the man said. 'I don't think that gate has been used in years.'

'It was rather hidden,' she said. 'I was worried that it might fall apart when I pushed it open.'

The man smiled – just a small smile – but it was enough to chafe the edges from any fear Kate might have felt. He removed his cap and held out his free hand. 'Albert,' he said. 'Albert Morrison.'

Kate placed her hand in his and he shook it warmly. 'Katherine,' she said. 'Katherine Durrant. It's a pleasure and relief to meet you, Mr Morrison.'

'And you, Miss Durrant,' he said and then quickly added, 'Or is it Mrs?'

'It's Miss,' Kate said, a little surprised that he had decided to maintain formality rather than offering to use Christian names. Perhaps this formality was another way for him to appear older. Mr Morrison swept his fair fringe back from his face and placed his cap back on his head, adjusting it carefully so that it sat straight. 'We should leave,' he said, looking up. 'It will be dark soon.' He held out his palm, indicating the way. Kate followed him, ducking beneath a branch.

'These trees have grown in a very unusual way,' she said, glancing back once they were free of the cage of branches.

'They're yews,' Mr Morrison said as he walked beside her. 'Probably at least two hundred years old. There were once supports holding up the branches, so they formed a sort of pathway. It was probably quite the talking point to impress visitors. The land would have still been part of the Caxton estate then. There's a painting in the library of people picnicking beneath the branches in the middle of summer.'

'The library?' Kate said.

'Yes. In Hill House.'

She looked at the side of his face. Mr Morrison stopped and glanced down at her. 'You do know you're on Hill House land, don't you?'

Kate shook her head. 'Am I trespassing?'

Mr Morrison smiled. This time, he seemed to relax into it. 'Yes and no,' he said. 'There are many ancient rights of way through this land. You just seem to have veered off course a bit. You're not the first person to have found themselves wandering here quite by surprise.'

Breathing a small sigh of relief, Kate said, 'I'm sorry. I should have thought.'

'No harm done.' Mr Morrison nodded to a path. 'This way,' he said, setting off again. Kate followed and sooner than she expected, the trees gave out onto a path, with rolling parkland on the other side, the mist still clinging to the grass.

'Here we are,' Mr Morrison said, pointing to a truck parked a little further along the path.

'Oh no, really,' Kate said. 'I couldn't impose. Please just point me in the direction of the village and I can walk back to collect my bicycle.'

Mr Morrison looked to the darkening sky. 'It's no imposition.' He walked ahead and Kate followed. They arrived at the truck. It was the sort that had a cabin at the front for two people and an open back, covered with a tarpaulin. He opened the passenger door.

'Are you sure?' Kate asked.

Mr Morrison held out his hand. Kate took it and placed her foot on the wooden step, lifting herself into the cab. Mr Morrison closed the door behind her with a metallic thud. The inside was fastidiously clean and, like Harry's van, smelled of fuel and oil. Thinking of her brother made her think of her mother. Had they arrived in Leicester? How was Mother doing?

Kate became aware of the driver's door closing.

'Are you quite all right?' Mr Morrison asked.

'Pardon?'

'You're very pale all of a sudden.'

Kate shook her head. 'I'm fine.'

'Here,' Mr Morrison said. He reached into a bag on the floor of the truck and produced a flask. He removed the cup and unscrewed the lid. He poured steaming liquid into the cup and handed it to her.

Kate took it without question. She sipped the hot, sweet tea. 'Thank you,' she said. She made to hand the cup back, but Mr Morrison pushed it gently towards her. 'Have some more,' he said. 'My grandmother always says that a good cup of tea is the cure for most ills of the world.'

Kate took another sip.

'Better?' Mr Morrison asked. She could hear the note of concern in his voice. For the last few months, she had been the one to offer consolation. To offer care and compassion. To keep her emotions at bay. A tear formed in the corner of her eye. She brushed it away.

Without a word, Mr Morrison topped up the cup. Kate drank more of the hot tea.

For a few minutes they sat wordlessly. Between sips, Kate stared out at the path immediately before the truck. Anything further away was obscured by the mist and hidden by the fading light. Warm hands touched her fingers as the cup was removed. Mr Morrison opened the window and shook the tea leaves into the long grass before screwing the cup onto the flask and returning it to his bag.

'Your grandmother sounds like a very intelligent woman,' Kate said. She turned to see Mr Morrison smile.

'She is,' he said. 'If you tell me where you live, I'll drive you home.'

'I really don't want to be a bother,' Kate said. But looking out at the rapidly fading daylight, she hoped he wouldn't find it a bother.

'It really is no trouble,' Mr Morrison said, starting the engine.

The progress along the path was slow and rather bumpy. To Kate's left ran the woods. To the right was open parkland. Soon they came to a gated wall. Through the fog, Kate could make out a garden beyond and then almost immediately, they passed what looked like a yard. Peering closer, she could see from the cobbles and the size and shape of the doors that it was a stable yard. Pale light from a window at the end of the stable block vaguely illuminated the cobbles.

It occurred to Kate that she hadn't asked Mr Morrison why he had been in the woods. She was about to ask and to comment that it was a happy coincidence which had found him stumbling upon her, when the words she had been about to say were swept away by a sight emerging through the gloom. The stable yard gave way to the corner of a building. As they grew closer, the building grew in size and scale. And the rough path gave way to the crunch of gravel beneath the tyres.

Mr Morrison brought the truck to a stop on the gravel drive and turned off the engine. Kate craned her neck to take in the three-storey house. It was large and square. Light shone from the windows, in defiance of the gloom. Even in the encroaching darkness, it was clear to see that the house was built from white stone. The same white stone of the pillars forming a portico around the vast front door. It looked warm and welcoming on a cold October evening.

'This is Hill House,' Mr Morrison said.

Kate shifted her focus from the house to Mr Morrison. 'And you live here?'

He nodded. 'I do.'

'What a place to own.'

Mr Morrison laughed. It was kind and soft and not at all mocking. 'I live here,' he said. 'But I don't own it. I'm the estate manager for the Mandevilles. They are the owners. Not me.'

Kate still stared up at the house. Of course, that explained why he was in the woods. Doing some kind of checks, no doubt. 'I had no idea this house was here,' Kate said.

'You're not local then?' Mr Morrison asked.

Kate shook her head. 'My parents live on the Wilkinson Estate.' The words came so naturally. She couldn't quite bring herself to use the past tense to speak of her parents' house. 'They moved in when the house was new. I've never lived there myself.'

'But you're staying there now?'

Kate faltered. 'For the time being.'

Mr Morrison seemed not to notice her hesitancy. 'There are so many people on the estate and so many new faces to remember.' He looked around. 'It all used to be Hill House land, you know. The Mandevilles have gradually sold off parcels for development. It makes sense. These old houses aren't cheap to run. The money they raise from the sale of land means they can pay for the upkeep of Hill House.'

'And that's the reason for the long wall? It delineates their land.'

'That's right.'

'So, I *was* trespassing.'

Mr Morrison smiled. 'I won't tell if you won't.' It was a joke of sorts. The first joke he had cracked. Perhaps beneath the formality there was a sense of humour waiting for a chance to be let out. He put the truck into gear. 'You will have to tell me your address.'

Kate gave him the address of her parents' house and he drove slowly down the drive, flanked by trees. Kate turned back to look at the house over her shoulder. What a place it must be to live in. To have such a beautiful home.

Mr Morrison stopped at St Mary's and Kate watched in the mirror as he loaded her bicycle onto the back of the truck. He didn't pry into the reason for her visit to the church. Perhaps he thought her hobby was brass rubbing or flower arranging for the altar.

'This is it,' Kate said, and Mr Morrison brought the truck to a stop outside her parents' house. He left the cab and removed Kate's bicycle from beneath the tarpaulin.

'Thank you,' she said, taking the bicycle from him. He unlatched the gate and held it open for her.

'It doesn't look like anyone's home,' he said, looking up at the dark windows.

'No.' Kate swallowed. 'They're all out at the moment.' She pushed her bicycle into the front garden. 'Thank you,' she said. 'For bringing me home.'

'It was my pleasure,' Mr Morrison said.

Kate turned the key in the lock. Without looking back, she closed the door behind her and rested the bicycle against the wall in the hall, beneath the empty coat hooks. Still in darkness, she went through to the parlour. Holding back the curtain, she watched the lights of Mr Morrison's truck disappear up the road.

Kate pressed her forehead to the cold glass. A draught chilled her legs through her tights. She turned around slowly. With no fire or lamplight, the parlour was drained of colour so that everything was grey. She closed her eyes and pictured the Christmas tree in the corner less than a year ago. Silver strands glittered in the glow of the multicoloured electric lights Mother had selected at the department store in Northampton. Michael and Violet happily opened the presents their grandparents, parents and aunt had made or chosen for them to delighted squeals. A train set. A dress Kate had created from taffeta and silk bought from the draper's where she used to work, hand-stitching it every evening for two months in her room in the boarding house in Sheffield. The smell of a goose cooking floated in from the kitchen so that their mouths all watered. Along with her mother and Enid, Kate sipped a sherry. Harry and her father each had a pint of beer.

Kate's head dropped. Aside from her suitcase, the only thing left in the parlour was the campaign bed.

Crossing the room, she opened the front of the wooden case and pulled out the concertina of canvas that sat on a crisscross series of wooden legs. The front of the case became the end of the bed and the back, the headboard. It was a campaign bed used by an officer in the war. He had decided he had no further use for it and rather than see it burned on a fire, her father had bought it from him and brought it all the way home when he returned from France. According to Father, it hadn't seen much use as the officer mainly lived in a hotel in a town near the barracks.

Kate slumped onto the bed. As it took her weight, the legs lowered into place and the canvas became taut. Still in her over-coat and without removing her shoes, she curled into a ball and pulled the eiderdown over her. Mother had left it folded for her on top of the suitcase, along with a clean towel and her sponge bag. Kate pictured her mother's face. Father had been gone for months now, but until tonight, Mother had slept in the room that had been theirs, with the reassurance that he had once lived here and had loved this place. In her mind's eye, Kate saw Mother's final act when she left the house earlier. To kiss her palm and hold it up to the window on the first floor, as though sending the man she loved a final kiss to say goodbye.

Kate clasped the gold St Christopher she always wore on a chain around her neck. It had been her father's and he had given it to her on the day she left for Sheffield to protect her on her journey into her future. With her free hand, she clutched the eiderdown and buried her face in its soft folds.

FOUR

Kate woke with the first pale daylight outside. She sat up awkwardly, chilled to the bone, her stomach rumbling. She left the bed and eiderdown, knelt before the fireplace, and used the poker to shove grey ashes through the grate. Taking up the metal bucket Harry had left beside the fire, she poured a handful of coal onto the grate. She added the twists of newspaper her brother had left too. Still kneeling on the floor, she lit the paper.

With the flames licking around the coal, she shrugged off her coat and laid it on the bed. Kicking off her shoes, she collected the towel and sponge bag and took it through to the kitchen, where she had a wash at the kitchen sink. She brushed through her hair, staring out of the kitchen window. It was a dim morning, the daylight struggling to break through the heavy clouds.

In the parlour, Kate opened her suitcase and placed it before the fire. She draped the towel over the lid to dry and sat down on the campaign bed, looking around the room. Where once had been light and life, there was now emptiness and silence. In a few days' time, even this shell of a home would be closed to her. She wiped her face, pushed herself up from the bed, and considered opening the tin of pilchards, but wasn't sure her stomach would welcome it. In the kitchen, she brewed a cup of tea. Taking it back through to the parlour, she drank it sitting on the campaign bed, watching the flames of the fire. When she had finished, she checked her watch. It was just after seven o'clock. She looked down at her clothes. They were creased and not fit to be seen out in public, so she changed into a brown skirt and jumper. After pushing her feet into her shoes, she placed the guard before the fire. In the hall, she pulled on her coat and beret, and tied her scarf at her neck.

Kate breathed in the fresh morning air as she walked along the street, joining the road that ran parallel to the brick wall and the woods beyond. Being outdoors was a welcome relief and she always enjoyed the walk to the village.

The bells of St Mary's chimed eight o'clock as she passed the duck pond. A few other people were about. A postman on his bicycle cycled around the green and nodded to her. A couple walked their small dog outside the pub and smiled good morning.

Kate stopped at the Post Office. It had become part of her regular routine to check the postcards in the window at least twice a week, in the hope that amongst the neatly written advertisements for household goods for sale and piano lessons, there might be a card advertising a suitable situation vacant. She looked through the cards as the bell rang above the door and a paperboy emerged. His heavy bag of newspapers over his shoulder, he collected his bicycle from where it was balanced against the wall and cycled away. Another look through the cards and it was clear that nothing had been added since she had looked only two days ago. She turned to go into the Post Office to buy a newspaper and saw a familiar figure approach.

'Good morning, Miss Durrant,' Mr Morrison said. He lifted his cap briefly.

'Good morning, Mr Morrison,' Kate said.

Mr Morrison glanced at the window. 'Were you looking for anything in particular?'

Kate shrugged. She barely knew him; he wouldn't be interested in her troubles. 'Not really,' she said. 'I was going to buy a newspaper.'

Mr Morrison pushed his hand into the pocket of his jacket and pulled out a postcard. 'I thought I'd put this in the window before I head up to the house,' he said.

'Have you something to sell?' Kate asked. It was pleasant to have someone to talk to. Especially since it was likely she would be alone for the rest of the day.

'No,' Mr Morrison said. 'Mrs Mandeville is looking for a new housemaid. I said I'd put the card in the window for her.'

'There's a vacancy at Hill House for a housemaid?' Kate said.

Mr Morrison nodded. 'We're a bit short since some of the staff moved to Caxton Hall with Sir Charles and Lady Mandeville.' He looked down at the card then back to Kate. 'You don't know someone suitable, do you?'

Kate's mind quickly swirled around his words. 'I'm actually looking for work,' she said before she had even decided if it was a good idea.

'You are?' Mr Morrison said. A smile lit his eyes. 'Do you have any experience working as a housemaid?'

Kate thought quickly again. 'Not a housemaid exactly. But I worked in the largest draper's in Northampton for three years. So, I know customer service. And I know how to sew and fix if that's needed. And how to look after different fabrics. And I used to help clean the shop and keep it right.'

Mr Morrison tapped the card against the fingers of his free hand. 'That all sounds good,' he said. 'But you would need to speak to Mrs Mandeville to see if she's happy with your experience.'

Kate felt a grin on her face. 'When should I meet her?' she said. 'I'm free now.'

Mr Morrison seemed to think for a moment. 'It's quite sudden,' he said. 'But Mrs Mandeville is keen to hire someone as soon as she can. So yes, why not? I can walk you there now. If Mrs Mandeville can't see you this morning, you can come back another time.'

Looking down at herself, Kate realised that she wasn't dressed for an interview. But she would have to do. If she didn't take this chance to meet Mrs Mandeville, somebody might get in before her. At least she had made the effort to brush her hair and clean her face.

Mr Morrison pushed the postcard back into his pocket. He began to walk up the road, with Kate beside him. As they walked, Mr Morrison gave her details of the household. Kate made a mental note of everything he said, while summoning up details of her skills and experience that might be relevant to the role of housemaid. She also thought about where she might live. If their staff lived out, with her savings and a salary, perhaps she could afford a room in a boarding house. It wasn't likely that a housemaid would be paid very much but it might be enough. But if their staff lived in ... no, that would be too good to be true.

They crossed the road outside St Mary's and in just a few minutes passed through the fine gates in the brick wall that Mr Morrison had driven her through last night. In the daylight, Kate saw two golden lions on top of the gates, holding aloft a globe. And, at the end of the drive, stood Hill House. The sun had managed to break through the clouds and the white stone almost gleamed with its three floors of windows and the portico over the front door held up by two stone pillars.

'It's beautiful,' Kate said, looking around the drive at the woodland and parkland. 'I can't believe I didn't know it was here.'

'I suppose, since it's a private house, you wouldn't. Not if you don't live locally,' Mr Morrison said. 'The family have thought about opening it up a few days a year for public tours. But it's just an idea at the moment.' At the front of the house, Kate paused to look up at the windows and the portico over the front door.

'It is rather beautiful isn't it,' Mr Morrison said, standing beside her.

Kate nodded. 'It is.'

'This way,' Mr Morrison said. He guided Kate around the side of the house and past a conservatory. At the back of the house, hills rolled away into the distance. They came to a stop at a set of steps leading down from ground level. Kate followed Mr Morrison down and he opened the door at the bottom to let her through.

Kate stepped into a basement with a long corridor, white-washed and immaculately clean, with doors leading off to many rooms. It smelled like breakfast. Sausages and bacon and toast. Kate pressed her hands to her stomach as it growled.

'The kitchens are down here,' Mr Morrison explained. 'But we'll go up to the office where you can wait while I speak to Mrs Mandeville.'

Mr Morrison led the way along the corridor and up some stone steps at the far end. He walked with confidence and very quickly. Kate followed him along a windowless passageway with a set of bells high up on the wall. It occurred to Kate that if she got the job, it would be her duty to respond to their ringing. She was thinking about how she might remember the names for each room when Mr Morrison opened another door for her. She stepped through and came to a stop, her breath taken away. They had passed from the narrow passageway into the back of a grand entrance hallway. Paintings hung on the wood-panelled walls. Marble statues stood on plinths in recesses and beneath Kate's shoes was a floor of beautiful tiles in bronze and white with a pattern of flowers. Over their heads, a great glass dome let in daylight.

'Come and have a proper look,' Mr Morrison said. He held out his hand, indicating for Kate to head further towards the front of the hall. She walked slowly, taking in the details. So many doors led from the central hallway, and she caught glimpses of the rooms beyond – books on shelves, a billiard table, a comfortable looking room with sofas and chairs.

A huge front door led from a vestibule and a spectacular dark wooden staircase ran up the centre of the hall. It was decorated with carved birds and animals and fruit and covered by a deep red carpet.

Kate stopped at the huge fireplace at the bottom of the stairs. Two stone creatures playing musical instruments supported the mantelshelf. They looked like men but had the bottom half of what looked like goats. Above them, a coat of arms stood proud of the stone. It was the same as the decoration on the top of the gates at the end of the drive: two lions holding a globe between them.

'That's the Mandevilles' coat of arms,' Mr Morrison said.

Kate stared up at the lions. She thought back to the steel-works in Sheffield with its furnaces and flames and soot. Everything had felt black and dirty and heavy there. Here was lightness and splendour.

'I've never been anywhere as grand as this,' Kate said.

'You're taken with the lions?'

Kate spun around. A woman was standing at the entrance to the room with the sofas and chairs. She was a woman in her middle years as far as Kate could tell, but not as old as her own mother. She had glorious auburn hair and was very attractive.

'I'm sorry, Mrs Mandeville,' Mr Morrison said. 'I had meant

to speak to you. This is Miss Durrant. She's interested in the housemaid vacancy.'

'Oh, that's wonderful,' the woman said, smiling warmly. 'Bertie, would you mind letting Audrey know we'll have breakfast in the kitchen? The children are starting school a little later this morning and it makes sense to keep the mess contained!'

'Of course,' Mr Morrison said.

'Miss Durrant,' the woman said. 'Let's take a seat in the morning room beside the fire.'

Kate followed the woman into the room with chairs and sofas, nerves rising in her chest. She wanted to apologise for the intrusion but surely, she shouldn't speak unless spoken to.

'Please have a seat,' the woman said.

Kate sat on the very edge of a green chair. The woman took a seat on a pink sofa and smiled at Kate. 'Don't be nervous. I know this is all a bit grand, but we are quite normal. Why don't you take your coat off?'

'Thank you,' Kate said. She placed her handbag on the floor, slipped out of her coat and placed it over the arm of the chair. She removed her beret and tucked it inside the pocket of her coat.

'Now,' the woman said. 'Why don't you tell me your first name.'

'It's Katherine, your ladyship.'

The woman laughed softly. 'I'm not her ladyship. That's my husband's mother. I'm plain old Mrs Mandeville as I am married to Sir Charles and Lady Mandeville's son, Edward.'

'I'm sorry,' Kate said.

'It's an easy mistake to make,' Mrs Mandeville said. 'Now, why don't you tell me what it is about being a housemaid at Hill House that appeals to you?'

'Appeals? Well, it's a beautiful house. I mean, I've never seen anywhere like it. It would be such a privilege to work here.'

'And can you tell me a bit about the work you've done before?' Mrs Mandeville asked.

'I worked in a draper's in Northampton. I really loved the fabric and helping customers choose what would work best for what they were making. I did cleaning and tidying in the shop, too. Mrs Mathers, who ran it, always kept a tight ship. I wanted to be a dressmaker and Mrs Mathers said I might make a very good one if I put my mind to it, but my father...' Kate had been so involved in talking, and so reassured by Mrs Mandeville's manner, that she hadn't realised she had said quite so much and where it was leading.

Mrs Mandeville leant forwards. 'What is it, Katherine?' she said.

'I'm sorry.' Kate shook her head.

'You've nothing to be sorry about.'

Mrs Mandeville looked at her with so much kindness. But she couldn't tell her. This was an interview for a job, and she couldn't cry. She took a deep breath. 'I just feel a bit disloyal,' she said. 'You see, my father, he got me a job in the accounts office at a steelworks in Sheffield. It was a good job. With prospects.'

'But it wasn't where your heart was?' Mrs Mandeville said.

Kate shook her head. But remembering herself, quickly added, 'It came with a room in a boarding house, which was a rare benefit.' As she spoke, she could hear her father's words in hers.

Mrs Mandeville smiled again. 'And how long were you there?'

'Three years.'

'And is there a reason you left?'

Kate smoothed a crease from her skirt. 'They had to let lots of us go. They stopped making so much money and didn't need as many staff anymore.'

Mrs Mandeville shook her head. 'These last few years have been so hard for businesses.'

Kate nodded. 'They have.'

'And do you have an experience as a housemaid?' Mrs Mandeville asked.

Kate tried to remember all the things she had thought on her walk to the house. All the reasons she would make a good housemaid. It was likely that there would be any number of young women very keen to have a role in a house such as this, so she had to be convincing. 'I don't have any direct experience,' she said. 'But at the draper's, I had responsibility for a great deal of the cleaning. I swept and mopped the floors every day and it was a real job as there was so much fluff and so many threads from cutting fabric. I did the dusting too of all the shelves and had to keep the counters scrubbed clean and spotless so that no fabrics got dirty. And I've always helped my mother in the house. If I don't know how to do something I am a quick learner.'

'Well,' Mrs Mandeville said. 'All that sounds like you are very diligent. And three years at the steelworks shows such determination and loyalty to the company and to your father.'

Mrs Mandeville paused. Kate was worried that she was going to say that, in spite of her qualities, she didn't have the experience needed.

'I would be happy to do a trial period,' Kate said quickly. 'If you wanted to see whether I'm suited to the job.'

'That might be a good idea,' Mrs Mandeville said. 'But as much for you as for us. To see if it's a job you'd like to continue with. How would a trial period of four weeks be with you?'

Kate looked into Mrs Mandeville's face. 'I've got the job?'

Mrs Mandeville nodded. 'When can you start?'

Kate felt her pulse quicken. 'Today. I can start today.'

'Wonderful,' Mrs Mandeville said. 'And so you know who's here, there's me and my husband, Edward, with our four children – they will make themselves known soon! Apart from our oldest son, Tommy, he's away at university. But the rest of them are never far away and generally up to mischief. Charlotte – Mrs Kenmore, my husband's sister – lives here with her husband and their daughter. Then there's Audrey and Rosemary who you will work with. There's Elliot, too, who's the chauffeur and groom. And you've met Bertie. We all live here but we also have some staff from the village who come in to help with gardens and suchlike. Your duties will generally be cleaning and keeping us all in order. Perhaps with your skills you could also do a bit of dressmaking or mending. Then there might be some work in the kitchen, to assist. We really do work as a team and Charlotte and I help where we can with running the house. You'll get Tuesday off each week and every Sunday afternoon. How does that sound?'

'It sounds wonderful,' Kate said.

'And will you live in?' Mrs Mandeville asked. 'It will mean a little less in your pay packet each week, but we are generous with food and we've lovely rooms up in the attic since the roof's been fixed.'

'I can live here?' Kate said, almost unable to believe what Mrs Mandeville was saying.

'We would welcome you.'

Kate could feel her cheeks begin to ache from so much smiling.

'That's settled then,' Mrs Mandeville said, getting up from the sofa. 'Let's go down and tell the others the good news.'

Kate collected her coat and bag and followed Mrs Mandeville out into the hall. The sun had finally broken through the gloom and now streamed through the great glass dome. The bronze flowers in the tiles on the floor glittered. The marble of the statues in the recesses of the wood panelled walls shone. Mrs Mandeville walked beside Kate, telling her about the children who lived in the house. There was her daughter, Daphne.

She was fifteen and had it in her mind that she wanted to be a chef in a London hotel. She could often be found in the kitchen with her nose stuck in a cookbook or boiling or steaming something in a pan. Mrs Mandeville's son, Charlie, was ten and liked to spend his time making models from paper and bits and bobs he found around the house. 'I think he might be an architect when he's older,' Mrs Mandeville said with a smile. She put her hand on Kate's arm. 'And then there's Oscar,' she said with a little good-natured grimace. 'He's a bit of a handful. But you'll soon find that out.' The register of children was completed with Mrs Kenmore's daughter, Louisa, who was eight. 'Oh, and I'll ask Bertie to call you Katherine and you should call him Bertie,' Mrs Mandeville said. 'He's a bit of an old soul and likes things done properly. You'll get used to him. And he relaxes once he's got to know a person. But the rest of us aren't so... formal. If I had my way, I would have you all call me by my first name. I did try it, but Lady Mandeville almost collapsed!'

Kate nodded politely and made mental notes of everything. As kind as Mrs Mandeville seemed, she would surely be watching to see how Kate responded to what she was told and how she performed her duties.

Almost as soon as they entered the passageway with the bells, they were met with the noise of many voices. 'Ah,' Mrs Mandeville said. 'It sounds like breakfast is ready.'

Kate smelled the sausages and bacon that had greeted her on her arrival. She followed Mrs Mandeville down the stone steps, her stomach growling so loudly that she was glad of the voices, all speaking at such a volume that it was almost impossible to separate one from the other. She followed Mrs Mandeville through a door and into a kitchen. A huge sink and draining board sat beneath the windows, which were half below and half above ground. Along the opposite wall ran a vast black range with many ovens and a stove top capable of taking more pots than Kate could ever have imagined. Gleaming copper pans of all shapes and sizes sat on shelves around the range. Pans sizzled and steam belched from a kettle. Three women and a girl worked at the range, moving sausages and bacon around in a pan, seeing to some cooking eggs and a pot of porridge. And, at a huge table running down the middle of the kitchen, were so many people that Kate almost had to take a step back.

'Everyone! Everyone,' Mrs Mandeville called over the din, succeeding in silencing them. All eyes turned to Kate. She clutched her coat and bag and looked to the floor. 'This,' Mrs Mandeville said, placing her hand on Kate's arm, 'is Katherine. She's our new housemaid.'

'Thank heavens!' one of the women said. She hurried around the table. As she approached, Kate saw how kind her face was, with a nose that turned up at the tip. Her blonde hair was styled so that it sat on her shoulders, the fringe tucked behind her ear. She seemed to be about the same age as Mrs Mandeville, with very fine lines around her eyes that creased charmingly when she smiled. She held her hand out to Kate. 'Charlotte,' she said. 'Charlotte Kenmore. It's a great pleasure to have you here!' She looked to Mrs Mandeville. 'I didn't think we'd placed the advertisement yet.'

'We haven't,' Mrs Mandeville said. 'Bertie found Katherine for us.'

'What a stroke of luck!' Mrs Kenmore said. 'Well. You need to meet everyone then.'

Kate looked around the kitchen.

'Over there are Audrey and Rosemary, who assist us, like you will. They help us cook and clean and keep the place shipshape.'

The two young women with dark hair held back from their faces looked at Kate and smiled. One wore glasses, while they both wore black dresses with aprons tied at the waist. She guessed they were roughly the same age as her.

'That's Daphne,' Mrs Kenmore said to the girl with Audrey

and Rosemary. She was pushing some sausages around in the pan. She looked up. 'Hello, Katherine,' she said. 'It's lovely to meet you.' For Kate there was no doubting Daphne's parentage; she shared her mother's beautiful auburn hair and could have been Mrs Mandeville's twin with her pale, flawless complexion.

Three children sat in a row on the other side of the table. Two boys with red curls and a girl with blonde hair and a nose that turned up at the tip. They were all looking at Kate. 'That's Charlie and Oscar, and that's my daughter, Louisa. Say hello to Katherine, children.'

'Hello, Katherine,' they chanted in unison.

'Hello,' Katherine said. She noticed how her voice shook again slightly.

Mrs Mandeville leant into her. 'It's a lot to take in, isn't it?' she said quietly.

'It is, a little,' Kate said.

Mrs Kenmore pulled out a chair. 'Will you have a tea or a coffee?' she asked. Kate looked at her, knowing that her eyes were wide. Was she really being invited to sit with them?

'A tea would be lovely,' she said.

'Jolly good,' Mrs Kenmore said. 'Take a pew.'

Mrs Mandeville took Kate's coat and hung it on a hook behind the kitchen door. Kate sat at the table and placed her bag on the floor. Almost immediately, the hubbub started up again. The women at the range discussed the progress of the breakfast. The children chatted and laughed loudly at some story one of them was telling. The older boy had begun trying to stack cruets to make a tower and the smaller boy laughed uproariously when he pushed them down, spilling salt and pepper onto the table. 'Oscar,' Mrs Mandeville said to the smaller child. 'It isn't kind to spoil Charlie's fun.'

'Sorry, Mummy,' the little boy said with a smile that would no doubt melt any mother's heart.

Louisa helped Charlie assemble his building materials

again. Mrs Kenmore placed a cup and saucer before Kate. She poured tea from a huge pot before pushing the sugar and milk to her.

When Mrs Kenmore placed a plate before her and arranged cutlery around it, Kate looked down at the blue and white pattern. It was so like the crockery her parents had bought for their new house. And that had been sold the week before.

Mrs Mandeville took the seat beside her. She poured milk into Kate's cup.

'Thank you,' Kate said, stirring a spoonful of sugar into the tea.

Audrey, Rosemary and Daphne began putting dishes of food onto the table. Sausages, bacon, scrambled eggs, mountains of toast and a vat of porridge. They all sat down at the table – Audrey and Rosemary at either end and Daphne with the children – and the dishes were soon being passed around the table for everyone to help themselves. Mrs Kenmore, who had taken the seat on the other side of Kate offered the dish of sausages to her. Kate made to take the dish to pass it on to Alice. 'Help yourself first,' Mrs Kenmore said, nudging the plate towards Kate again.

'Are you sure?' Kate said. 'I don't mean to impose.'

'It's no imposition.' Mrs Kenmore smiled. 'Everyone needs a good feed in the morning.'

Kate took a sausage and placed it on the plate. With each dish that came around, Mrs Kenmore insisted Kate take something. Soon she had added two rashers of bacon, a pile of scrambled egg and two slices of toast. She watched everyone pick up napkins and place them in their laps. Kate followed. Her mother had taught her manners from the moment she could sit at the table. At least she wouldn't disgrace herself.

Mrs Mandeville placed the butter in front of Kate. She took a scraping to spread on her toast. She sliced into the sausage and took a bite. Her stomach immediately thanked her. She took a sip of the hot, sweet tea.

The mood around the table was lively. The children all spoke of their delight at starting school an hour later than usual as their teacher had an appointment to attend. They spoke about what they would do after school. There would be homework to be done but then plans were made to meet in the nursery for some board games as it would be too dark to play outdoors.

Mrs Mandeville and Mrs Kenmore spoke to Audrey and Rosemary about what housework was to be done for the day and what would be cooked for dinner.

From the conversations, Kate understood that the menfolk had taken breakfast in the dining room earlier that morning. Mr Mandeville – or Edward, as he was referred to – and Bertie were now out on estate business, visiting various farms. Mrs Kenmore's husband – Paul – was a doctor at the hospital in Northampton and had left early for work. Dinner for the family was always taken in the dining room. Kate tried to take in all the details of the household arrangements. She would be expected to remember them all and to play her part to earn her wages. But the noise was too great. In Sheffield, she had been used to the sounds of a factory and a workforce of hundreds, clocking in and out every day, the sound of boots on cobbles, the mechanical din of heavy machinery and trucks and the calling of many voices. But for the last two months, she had known only near-silence. Just her and Mother, sitting quietly, eating quietly, clearing the house quietly.

'You're not touching your food,' Mrs Mandeville said to Kate.

'Sorry,' Kate said.

'You don't need to apologise,' Mrs Mandeville said. 'It can be a bit overwhelming with so many of us. Do you come from a big family?'

Kate shook her head and took a mouthful of scrambled egg. She swallowed it down. 'I just had an older brother.'

'And were you close?'

'We were. When we were small. We still are really. But he's lived in Leicester for a few years now.'

'After breakfast, do you need to go and collect any belongings? If it suits you, we could have Rosemary make up your room today and you can move in this afternoon. How would that sound?'

Kate thought of the cold parlour with the old campaign bed, Harry's camping stove, the pan, and the tin of pilchards. 'I'd like that very much,' she said.

'Then that's sorted,' Mrs Mandeville said. 'I'm sure Bertie can arrange to have your things brought here.'

FIVE

After finishing the generous breakfast and helping with the washing up, Kate thanked the Mandevilles and their staff and left through the door at the back of the house.

At the top of the steps outside, she stopped to take in the view across the valley, to the grass and the hills beyond. The late autumn sun shone brightly now and there was even a bit of warmth to the day. Kate walked around the opposite side of the house to that which Bertie had driven them. How would he take to her calling him Bertie rather than Albert or Mr Morrison? She could hardly refuse a direct instruction from her new employer, could she? She looked at her watch. It was almost half past eleven. Mrs Mandeville had said that Bertie and Mr Mandeville were expected back at about midday. After their lunch, Mrs Mandeville would ask Bertie to collect Kate and her things from her house, so she should expect him at around half past one. Mrs Mandeville had suggested that Bertie drive her home too, but Kate had refused as politely as she could. She wanted to prepare everything alone and without the need to explain why she didn't want to invite him in.

. . .

Approaching the Wilkinson estate, Kate slowed her pace. All the way from Hill House, she had thought of her new job and having somewhere to live and how lucky she was. But the closer she got to her final destination, the more her thoughts turned in a far less cheery direction.

Smoke trailed into the sky from the chimneys of all the other houses on the street, warming parlours and bedrooms. But not even a wisp of smoke rose from the chimney above her parents' house. The meagre fire she had set in the grate that morning would have burned to nothing.

Kate unlatched the gate and walked slowly up the path. The sound of the lock catching as she closed the front door echoed around the empty house. In the parlour, she packed her few belongings into the suitcase and closed the clasps. She eased the campaign bed back into its box. Folding the eiderdown, she balanced it on top before placing Harry's camping stove on the mantelpiece. She had arranged for her parents' neighbours to store the bed and the other bits in their spare bedroom until Harry was able to visit again and take them to Leicester. But they weren't expecting to help her move them into their spare bedroom until the following Friday as the new people were moving in on Saturday. She couldn't ask if she might do it earlier as they would be at work by now. She would have to return one last time.

It was too cold to remove her coat, so Kate left it on when she went through to the kitchen. She could make a cup of tea on Harry's camping stove, but she didn't want to. She looked around, hoping there was something meaningful she could do to occupy her time while she waited to be collected. There was nothing. Mother had been over the house with a fine toothcomb before she agreed to get in Harry's van. Every room had been cleared and cleaned and polished. Save for her few belongings in the parlour and kitchen, anything in the other rooms was to be left for the new people.

Kate rested against the sink and looked out of the window. Bare canes were all she could see. Rows and rows of canes tied to each other with twine, waiting to find a use again come spring. It was late autumn, everything that her father had planted in the spring had died. There would be no new life curling around the canes, no new buds preparing to bloom in the summer sun.

Kate pulled out a chair and sat down at the kitchen table. She held her hand above the tabletop and closed her eyes. She paused, then gently pressed her palm to the wooden surface. Instantly so many images fought to present themselves to her. Full of colour and life. There were breakfasts eaten at the table in this house and, before that, breakfasts in the small terrace in Northampton. She saw Christmas last year with Mother's best tablecloth and the goose cooked to perfection. All her family sat around and laughed and talked and said how it was the best Christmas dinner yet. Kate moved her hand. Now she saw herself sitting at the chair on the opposite side, her father beside her. His evening newspaper spread out, he was explaining the news of the day to her. Even further back she went. Still in Northampton, she had been sitting at the table shelling peas for Mother. There had been a knock at the front door. Harry had answered it and then the kitchen door flew open. Her father, still in his uniform, had dropped his kitbag on the floor and grabbed first her mother and then her and Harry, and held them so tight. After three long years at the Front he had come home to them.

Still with her eyes closed, Kate moved her hand. And still the memories came back in flashes. She saw them as clearly as if she were sitting in the picture house watching Clark Gable or Fred Astaire and Ginger Rogers dance across the screen. If her mother were here, she would say these were simply memories attached to an item. In this case, the kitchen table Kate had known all her life. They were just the things she could recall of events that had happened. But they were so very real. She could smell the roasted goose. Taste Mother's silky gravy on her tongue as she savoured each roast potato. Hear the lard sizzle in the pan to fry eggs for breakfast. Feel the peas pop from their shells and see her fingers turning green from the pods. Taste the tender sweetness that burst between her teeth when her mother said she could try a few before they were cooked – always such a special treat. Feel her father's arms around her and the smell of his uniform like nothing she had ever smelled. Like oil mixed with wax and earth, like she was inside a tent. And if she let herself, she could hear the words spoken. Hear every sound and feel every sensation.

Kate pulled her hand away from the table. Clutching it in her lap, she stared at the grain of the wood. This table had been the scene of Harry asking her so many times to do her party trick, handing her an object she had never seen before to tell him the history of it. She could never control what she was able to tell. The thoughts simply came, and she relayed what she felt or saw behind her closed eyes. If it was able to be verified, she was always correct. Always.

Kate rubbed the palm of her right hand with her thumb. Outside the house, it never happened. She could touch anything. She could touch everything. And no images came. No sensations of tastes or sounds. But each time she stepped foot inside her parents' new home, it started again. Just like it always had in their terrace in Northampton. In the last few weeks, while helping Mother clear the house and pack, she'd had more experiences than ever before. Even before her mother had relayed the history of each item she passed to Kate to wrap in newspaper, Kate knew what she would say. What had been given as a wedding gift and by whom. What Mother and Father had received as anniversary gifts or had bought themselves.

Kate rubbed her palm again. Despite what Mother said, she knew that these were not always memories. She could be handed an object she had never seen before and know its history or events attached to it. As a child, she had tried to believe that what she saw came from her mind as her family believed it did, that she had soaked up information from what people said around her and stored it away. And she played along with that explanation of her party trick. Her mother had always liked to talk about her possessions when she fastidiously moved her feather duster and polishing cloth over them. It was possible that, armed with that information, and with an imagination that liked to picture things, Kate could somehow summon up the history of particular objects when she was asked to perform her trick. It was possible that it wasn't magic or a skill. It was a talent of memory. Her mother had always said that from a babe in arms, she had remembered everything she was ever taught. Her father said she had a watchful nature, taking everything in. Once she learned something, it was never forgotten.

Kate sat back in the chair. Here, in the kitchen, in the cold light of day, these logical explanations seemed plausible; what she saw or sensed was simply a replaying of what she had learned or gleaned. When she spoke of long-dead relatives who had owned items or given them as gifts, it was because she had overheard them talked about. But she knew it wasn't that simple.

A knock at the door made Kate jump from the chair. She looked at her watch and ran into the parlour. Grabbing her suitcase, she took it through to the hall. She would come back when she was able to take the remaining things next door.

Kate opened the front door only enough to step outside with her suitcase. Bertie was standing on the path looking up at the house. He smiled when he saw her.

'So,' he said. 'You got the job.'

'On a trial,' she said.

'Mrs Mandeville was very impressed with your experience

in your other jobs. She thinks the skills will easily transfer to the role of a housemaid. And Mrs Mandeville is always keen to give people opportunities.'

'I'm very grateful to her,' Kate said.

Bertie smiled again. 'I've been told, in no uncertain terms, that I am to call you Katherine, rather than Miss Durrant. So, you must call me Bertie – everyone does.'

'Are you happy with that?' Kate asked.

'Of course. Especially now that we are to work together.' Bertie took the case from Kate and looked at the house again. 'I remember these being built,' he said. 'Anthony Wilkinson – a great friend of Mr Mandeville's – bought the parcel of land from the Mandevilles and built the entire estate. Over the centuries, this has been both Hill House and Caxton land. Your family were wise to buy one of the Wilkinson's homes. They really are top quality.' He looked to Kate. 'Should I speak to your father and mother, in case they have any questions about your new job and want reassurance that you'll be taken care of?'

Kate shook her head. 'No, thank you. They're not in at the moment. Should we go?' She followed Bertie down the path. She would rather not speak about what had happened to her family recently. It would be too painful to have to have to relive it with all the people she would meet in her new role. And she was sure that she would not be able to talk about her father without crying, for his death and for the memory of his final days, which filled her with so much guilt that she felt she might drown in it.

At Hill House, Kate once again followed Bertie down the steps at the back and into the basement corridor. The only sound now was the low chatter of a couple of voices. Bertie placed Kate's suitcase outside the door to the kitchen and followed her inside. Two of the women from earlier – the women wearing black dresses and aprons – were scrubbing down the table and the sides.

'Were you introduced to Audrey and Rosemary?' Bertie asked.

Before Kate could answer, Rosemary stepped forward.

'Course we were, Bertie,' she said, dropping her cloth into the sink. 'Mrs Mandeville brought Katherine down to take breakfast with us.' She manoeuvred around the table, wiping her hands on her apron. She took Kate's hand in hers. 'We're so glad to have you here.' She smiled and shook Kate's hand warmly. 'And in case you forgot, I'm Rosemary. And her over there by the sink is Audrey. But I call her Aud.'

Audrey pushed her glasses back up her nose. 'It's good to have you here,' she said. 'There's more than enough work to keep the three of us occupied. And you'll have to excuse my sister, she is a silly heart. Always has been, always will be.'

Rosemary pulled a face and Audrey tutted at her. Audrey was clearly the eldest. She was rather serious looking with dark straight hair pulled back into a tight bun. Rosemary, on the other hand, was a little less neat, her apron slightly crooked. Her hair had a bit of a kink and sat on her shoulders with the fringe escaping the clips holding it back from her face.

'Have you worked here long?' Kate asked.

'On and off for the last ten years,' Audrey said, taking up a cloth and scrubbing at the table again.

'Mrs Mandeville had us come when we were still at the orphanage,' Rosemary added. 'To train us up. You were fifteen, weren't you, Aud, when we came permanent?'

'Permanently,' Audrey corrected, still scrubbing at the table.

Rosemary raised her eyebrows, before continuing. 'So that would have made me thirteen. Nine years we've been here then.'

Kate had been right; the sisters were just a few years younger than her.

Bertie coughed.

'Oh, sorry, Bertie,' Rosemary said, with a laugh in her voice. 'Were we ignoring you?'

'I should be going,' he said. The side of his fair moustache dipped as he frowned ever so slightly. 'I have work to attend to. Will you see Katherine to her room and acquaint her with some of the responsibilities of the job?'

'Of course, Mr Morrison,' Rosemary said, in a voice slightly mimicking Bertie's formal tone. 'We shall acquaint Katherine as you request.'

'Very good,' Bertie said, a little furrow in his brow. He turned to Kate and lifted his cap slightly. 'I hope your first day is successful,' he said.

Kate smiled at him. 'Thank you.'

Rosemary waited only a moment or two after Bertie left before laughing. 'Honestly,' she said. 'Why does he have so many airs and graces? "*I hope you find your first day successful, Katherine*",' she said mimicking Bertie's way of speaking.

'Stop it, Rosemary,' Audrey said, speaking softly and looking towards the wall as though following Bertie's path along the corridor. 'You shouldn't tease him so.'

'Well...' Rosemary said, dragging out the single syllable. 'He asks for it. Do you know, Katherine,' she said, turning to Kate, 'he's the son of a lady's maid and a footman. From the way he goes on, you'd think he was royalty.'

'Stop gossiping,' Audrey said. She placed her cloth down on the table and glanced at the clock on the wall. 'It's a bit early for tea,' she said, 'but Mrs Mandeville said we should offer you refreshment when you arrived.'

'Thank you,' Kate said. 'How can I help?'

'Cups and saucers are on the dresser,' Audrey said, collecting the kettle and taking it to the sink. 'Spoons are in the drawer.'

Kate tucked her beret inside the pocket of her overcoat and

hung it on the hook behind the door, along with her handbag. She wanted to show willing straightaway and demonstrate that she was keen to work.

Rosemary took the sugar bowl from the dresser and placed it on the table. 'So, what brings you here?' she said as Kate took down three cups and three saucers.

'I was let go from my job in a steelworks in Sheffield. There wasn't enough work for us all.'

'What?' Rosemary said, her eyes wide. 'You worked making steel?'

Kate laughed and placed the saucers on the table. 'No, I worked in the accounts department.'

'And where have you been living?'

'I've been staying with my parents. They live on the Wilkinson estate.'

'Blimey, that's a bit swish.' Rosemary raised her eyebrows in surprise.

'Not really,' Kate said. 'It's one of the small cottages, not one of the big houses.'

Audrey had been filling the kettle. She turned off the tap and placed the kettle on the range. 'Stop badgering Katherine,' she said to her sister. 'And get the milk.'

Kate placed each cup in its saucer. She should really tell the truth about her parents. But she preferred to imagine this version of the world. With them still in their cottage, smoke billowing from the chimney and a rosy light in the parlour window.

Kate joined the sisters to sit at the kitchen table. Audrey poured the tea and began to run through some of the duties that Kate could expect to undertake, with regular interruptions and embellishments from Rosemary. Kate nodded, taking it all in.

It was Rosemary's job to lay the fires in the occupied rooms and to keep them fed throughout the day. But Kate would help with that now. There would be cleaning, and dusting and they had quite a good system which meant that they were able to clean each room every week. There were beds to change and bathrooms to scrub and the whole of the downstairs to sweep and dust and polish and mop. The laundry was sent out – which was a blessing – so they only had the job of emptying the hamper of clean clothes and linen when it was returned. Audrey took charge of the preparation of the meals. The family generally took meals upstairs in the dining room but, like this morning, the women and the children would sometimes eat breakfast in the kitchen. It was Rosemary's job to lay the table and take the food up to the dining room and Kate would start to help with that in time.

'It sounds a lot,' Audrey said. 'But we work hard and get on with it. With you here, it will make it a sight easier. And Mrs Mandeville and Mrs Kenmore help us when they can. We're lucky that way. They don't stand on ceremony. We've no footmen, but Elliot, the groom, helps with fetching and carrying of things like coal and helping with deliveries and the outside cleaning and maintenance. Bertie helps, too, and he brings in others from the village to assist when it's needed.'

'Is that how it's done in all big houses?' Kate asked, sipping her tea.

'This is the only house we've ever worked in,' Audrey said. 'It's the Mandevilles' house so they can do what pleases them.'

'There's no housekeeper now, Katherine,' Rosemary said. 'Mrs Mandeville lets us use the housekeeper's room as our very own parlour. There's an old desk in there but it's not used as Mrs Mandeville and Mrs Kenmore do the household accounts. None of the family bother us in there and there's some comfy chairs and a nice fireplace. There's even a little table and chairs so we can take our evening meals in there if we like.'

Audrey stood and picked up the teapot. 'I need to get on with peeling the carrots for dinner,' she said. 'Rosie, show Katherine to her room, would you.'

Kate stood too and helped clear the tea things. 'Would you like me to wash them?' she asked.

'No,' Audrey said, tapping the tea strainer on the side of the sink and rinsing the leaves down the drain. 'Mrs Mandeville wants you to have the time to settle in this afternoon. Come down at four and you can help with dinner.'

'Will we have our pudding in the parlour tonight?' Rosemary said. 'I can set the fire later. And can we read those magazines Mrs Kenmore left for us.'

'I should think so,' Audrey said. 'Now go on, show Katherine to her room. And be quick about it.'

Kate took her coat and handbag from the hook and was about to collect her suitcase when Rosemary ran into the hall and picked it up. 'Honestly, I can manage,' Kate said.

'Make the most of it,' Rosemary said. 'You won't get room service again.'

Kate followed Rosemary into the corridor. 'Come along, slow coach!' Rosemary laughed. Kate picked up her pace and caught up with Rosemary at the bottom of the stone steps.

'Don't mind our Aud,' Rosemary said. 'She's very serious but her bark is worse than her bite. I'll give you the grand tour of the basement tomorrow. There's not much to see. We mainly use the kitchen and the parlour. Makes sense to keep rooms closed if we're not using them. I'm so glad Mrs Mandeville got a refrigerator for the kitchen. It means we don't have to go into the cold larder every day. It's bitter in there! I swear I grow icicles on my nose every time I go in.'

Kate laughed as she followed Rosemary up the steps. They reached the top and she saw the bells high up on the wall. 'Will I be expected to learn all of the bells and what rooms they're for?'

Rosemary shrugged. 'Not really. They don't ring much. Just the dining room and morning room when the family is ready to eat or want some tea. I can't remember the last time we were called to a bedroom. They see to themselves generally. This way,' she said, pointing in the opposite direction to that which Bertie had taken Kate earlier.

Rosemary continued to chat away as she led Kate further along the passageway and up the first flight of stairs of a stone stairwell with no windows and lit by a series of unshaded bulbs. Kate took hold of the wooden handrail. Rosemary didn't even pant as she made her way up. 'You'll get used to this,' she said, glancing over her shoulder at Kate. They stopped on a small landing where the staircase twisted. Rosemary nodded to the outline of a door in the wall. 'First floor,' she said. 'That's where the family bedrooms are. I make their fires up in the morning. Aside from making up the beds and cleaning once a week, that's about all we do in their rooms.' She carried on up the next flight of stairs. 'Elliot leaves the coal on this landing for me. He'll leave the coal for you too. You'll do the fires downstairs in the library, morning room, billiard room, dining room and hall. There's also the office corridor. I'll show you that later.'

Finally, the staircase gave out onto a larger landing. 'This is us,' Rosemary said. They were in an attic corridor, the floor covered in dark green carpet and the walls papered with a pretty red floral design. Windows ran the length of the slanted ceiling and on the opposite side were a series of doors.

Rosemary carried on. She nodded to the first door. 'That's our Aud's,' she said. 'The second is mine.' Stopping just short of the third, she said, 'And this is you. I closed the door to keep the heat in.'

Kate pushed the door open and stepped inside. For a moment she lost the power of speech. The wallpaper from the corridor carried on in the small room. There was a bed, a chest of drawers, a washstand with a washbowl and jug, a small table and chair, and a nightstand. A green rug covered the floorboards and green curtains hung at the window. An eiderdown covered in pink flowers sat plump on the bed. Kate took a step further into the room. A fire had been lit in the small, black hearth and on the mantelpiece above sat a few books.

'What do you think?' Rosemary asked, placing the suitcase on the floor.

'I never imagined anything so... pretty,' Kate said, still taking in the details of the room.

'When we first came here, the roof leaked. And these rooms were riddled with damp!' Rosemary said. 'We used to sleep in rooms in the basement. When the roof was fixed, Mrs Mandeville had these rooms decorated. She says that since the staff give a good day's work, they deserve a good night's sleep. There's a scuttle of coal out on the landing. We tend to make up the fires in the morning and then come up an hour before bed to pop a few more coals on. Aud says we shouldn't take advantage. We likely wouldn't get any coals with another employer!'

'It's so lovely,' Kate said.

'There's a bathroom next door. Mrs Mandeville had that put in, too. And it's even got a lav. No pots under the bed for us!' Rosemary said with a laugh. 'Me and Aud have our baths on our days off. It's such a treat. Right! I'll have to love you and leave you. I've my duties to be getting on with. I'll see you in the kitchen at four.'

Rosemary closed the door on her way out and Kate stood before the warmth of the fireplace, looking around again. She hadn't had her own room since leaving the terrace in Northampton. In the boarding house, she'd shared a bedroom, and every morning there was a fight for the bathroom with all the girls wanting to get washed at the same time. Baths lasting longer than five minutes had become impossible since there was always a knock on the door with someone needing to use the lav.

From what Audrey and Rosemary had said, she would be expected to earn her salary. And there would be plenty of opportunities to show how hard she could work. Thinking of the sisters down in the kitchen made Kate smile. Audrey was so serious and a little stern. It was probably best to try to stay on her good side as she seemed to be in charge and appeared to be the type of woman who might be difficult to impress. Rosemary was so different to her sister, with her quips and funny ways. There was no mistaking she was younger when she pulled faces behind Audrey's back. She reminded Kate of how she had been with Harry when they were small children. Always full of mischief. Always a very capable annoying little sister, even when Harry and she were quite grown up. But that had all changed when she moved to Sheffield.

Kate glanced at her reflection in the mirror. Everyone had to grow up at some point. And she had been twenty-three years old after all. But it had seemed so abrupt at the time. Mother and Father had moved from the terrace in Northampton to their new cottage and she had left the draper's to take up her new role and move into the shared room in the boarding house in Sheffield. When she stayed with her parents for Christmas or Easter, it was always on the campaign bed in the parlour, since Harry, Enid and the children took the guest room. For three years, she hadn't had a room of her own. Or a home. Not really.

Kate ran her fingers along the brass bedstead. In the space of just a few hours, she had gone from no job, no home and no hope, to this. She crossed to the window. The view looked down to the drive and across the treetops to the spire of St Mary's. She was within walking distance of her father.

Kate pressed her forehead to the cold glass. A familiar sensation that was with her in every waking hour cast a long shadow across the joy of the day. In her desperation to keep her job at the steelworks when others were losing theirs, she had not visited her father when he had suddenly taken ill. She had telephoned him from the boarding house, and he had told her not to worry. He would be right as rain in no time and Mother was making an incredibly proficient nurse. Kate had been relieved that she hadn't had to ask for unplanned days away from the office. If the managers were looking for people to let go, she wanted to give them as little reason as possible to choose her. She knew her father would understand, and she would see him just as soon as she was able. The very next day, she had been called into the supervisor's office with half a dozen other girls to be told that their services were no longer required. At the boarding house that afternoon, Harry had telephoned to tell her that Father had passed away from the failing heart he had kept from everyone for many months.

Kate put her hand to the glass. 'I'm so sorry,' she said. 'I'm so stupid and selfish.' All her life, she had tried to do the right thing. To make her parents proud of her. Even going to work in Sheffield when all she had really wanted was to stay at the draper's. But when her parents had needed her most, she had failed them.

Turning to the bed, Kate opened her suitcase. She removed a silver frame wrapped in her silk slip for safekeeping. The frame held a photograph taken to celebrate Harry's twenty-first birthday. Posed in the photographer's studio in Northampton, Kate sat beside her mother with Harry and their father standing behind them, in their best suits and ties. Kate looked down into her father's face. He smiled back at her. 'I promise to try to make you proud of me now, Dad,' she said. 'I'll work so hard for the Mandevilles.'

Kate placed the photograph on the mantelpiece beside the books. She held her hands out to the fire, feeling the warmth on her palms before unpacking her clothes into the chest of drawers and placing the suitcase under the bed.

She folded her nightdress, tucked it beneath the pillow and placed her alarm clock on the nightstand. Sitting down at the small table, she took the notepad from her handbag. She wrote a letter to her mother, telling her not to be shocked but that she wasn't going back to Sheffield. She hadn't told her before as she

hadn't wanted to worry her. But Mother wouldn't have to wo
after all. She had a fine new job at Hill House that came with a
room and board. It was a trial for now, but she would work her
hardest to convince the Mandevilles to keep her on. And best of
all, she would be able to visit Father on her days off. She knew
Mother had been fretting about him being left alone but she
didn't need to fret any longer.

Placing her pen aside, Kate looked down at the notepad.
Was it dishonest not to have told the Mandevilles about her
father's death and her mother having to move away? She wasn't
ashamed of what had happened to them. But she was ashamed
that she hadn't rushed to her father the moment she had heard
of his illness. That she hadn't been there when her family
needed her. And that she hadn't been able to sit with her father
before he left her forever.

Kate slipped her hand inside the neck of her jumper and
took hold of the St Christopher. She closed her eyes and
grasped it tight. It was all she had left of her father.

SIX

When Kate left her room, she paused to look into the bathroom. It was small, tiled all in white and spotlessly clean. Just beyond the bathroom, a long green curtain split the corridor. Pulling it back, Kate found that it covered a door. There were two glass panels in the door but whatever lay beyond was in darkness. She cupped her hands around her eyes and leant in close to the glass. There was just enough light coming from the windows behind her to see that the corridor continued and appeared to run the full length of the house. From what Kate could make out, there was no carpet on the other side and the walls were plain rather than papered. She tried the door handle. It was locked. She narrowed her eyes. As it occurred to her that it was an odd thing to do – to partially close your eyes in the hope of seeing better – she saw a movement. She stepped back. Someone must have come up the stairs and what she had seen was the reflection of them. She looked behind her. She was all alone. Slowly she turned back. The corridor beyond the door seemed still. Even so, a cold blast rushed down Kate's back, snagging every vertebra on its way. A sensation took hold of her and wouldn't let go. It felt like dread. It felt like foreboding. Kate put her hand to the wall to steady herself. She closed her eyes. She was tired. It had been a strange day and her exhausted mind was playing tricks on her. She was in the attic of a big old house and her imagination was taking her to the films of creepy old houses she had seen at the pictures. From what she had experienced of Hill House so far, it was full of kind people. It felt safe and like a home. Opening her eyes Kate made herself look at the door. She saw it for what it was: a means to separate a disused part of a corridor from the occupied side. Nothing more. She pulled the curtain back across and a stillness returned. But that didn't stop her reaching for the light switch so that a series of bulbs came to life and lit her way along the carpeted end of the corridor, and down to the kitchen.

The sisters were already in the midst of preparations for dinner when Kate joined them in the kitchen and delicious smells filled the air.

Audrey looked up to the clock. 'Tea?' she said.

'Let me,' Kate said. 'You two look very busy.' She filled and boiled the kettle, took the cups and saucers and spoons from the dresser and found the tea leaves in the caddy. When she opened the door of the refrigerator and took the jug of milk from a shelf, a gentle coolness came out to greet her. She would have liked to explore how it worked; at home the milk and cheese were kept on a cold stone in the pantry. But she didn't want to show her ignorance to Audrey, so closed the door and placed the jug of cold milk on the table. After pouring the tea, she sat down with the sisters as they took a break in preparations.

'Everything all right with your room?' Audrey asked.

'Perfect,' Kate said, cupping her tea. 'It's so much nicer than I imagined it might be.'

'The Mandevilles are good people,' Audrey said. 'We're very lucky to have them as employers.'

Rosemary took a biscuit from the barrel Audrey handed to her. She placed it on her saucer. She took a sip of the tea and her eyes widened. 'Ooh, that's a great cuppa, Katherine,' she said. 'If it's up to me, you can stay.'

Kate smiled. Rosemary handed her the barrel and she took a biscuit. She bit into it. It tasted of butter and vanilla.

'Our Rosie made them,' Audrey said, taking a bite of her own biscuit. 'She might be a silly heart but she's a grand baker.'

They drank their tea and ate another biscuit each, Kate enjoying the chatter between the sisters as they planned an afternoon of baking the next day. 'I'll do some jam tarts for the children's tea and some scones for the grown-ups, they always go down well,' Rosemary said.

Talk moved on to the order they needed to place with the grocer's the next day. When the tea was finished, Kate insisted on clearing away. With the washing up done, she joined Audrey and Rosemary in peeling potatoes and top and tailing a colander of green beans.

Remembering the envelope on the table in her room, she said, 'Is there any way I can post a letter from here? I'd like to send it to my mother.'

Audrey popped the beans into a pan of water. 'Leave it on the post tray in the hall in the morning. Elliot collects the post each day and takes it to the Post Office in the village.'

'How will I pay for the postage?'

'Ask Bertie,' Audrey said. 'He'll know.'

'We've never had to send a letter,' Rosemary said, adding more beans to the pan.

'Oh, yes, I'm sorry,' Kate said. Of course, they came here from an orphanage, they had said earlier.

'No harm done,' Audrey said and pushed her glasses up with the heel of her hand.

'Will Bertie and Elliot come for their dinner tonight?' Kate asked.

'We won't see hide nor hair of them,' Rosemary said. 'Elliot cooks all his meals for himself in his rooms in the stables. He might come in for a spot of tea, but that's about it. Bertie has one of the cottages down by the gates. He has his lunch here but takes his breakfast and dinner elsewhere.'

Audrey got up to tend to the custard on the range, making sure it didn't catch and burn. Kate continued to peel the potatoes and Rosemary left to lay the table upstairs. Within twenty minutes she had returned.

Kate watched what the sisters did and took in whatever they said. She wanted to learn everything and regularly glanced at the clock to see at what time each task was undertaken. The activity in the kitchen ran like clockwork.

She watched how Audrey tended the beef stew and dumplings in the oven. There were eight people to feed upstairs and the three of them down in the kitchen. There was so much food, but Audrey made the preparation and cooking look easy. Every so often she opened the oven to check on the stew and apple crumbles. On the range, the lids of two pans rattled as potatoes boiled in readiness to be mashed. She watched as Audrey put on two smaller pans – one of potatoes, the other of beans. At just before half past five, Audrey drained the potatoes in the smaller pan and added butter and milk. Kate helped Rosemary lay three places at the table, with three glasses for water. Audrey served them each a plate of stew with the mashed potatoes and beans. Kate sat beside Rosemary with Audrey opposite and closest to the range, to keep an eye on the food. Audrey said grace and Kate joined the sisters in eating the meal. She closed her eyes as the beef melted on her tongue. She was hungrier than she had realised and everything tasted so delicious.

'Where did you learn to cook like this?' she asked Audrey.

Audrey nudged some potato onto her fork. 'Mrs Randal was the cook here. She taught me all her recipes. She went to Caxton Hall with Sir Charles and Lady Mandeville. She cooks for them in the dower house now.'

'The Caxtons are cousins of the Mandevilles,' Rosemary added. 'With all the children, it was a bit noisy for Sir Charles and Lady Mandeville here! That's why their cousins offered them the dower house to live in. It's very grand. Probably not much smaller than this house. Sir Charles' sister, Mrs Hart, lives with them. I think they prefer it a bit quieter. They are getting on a bit.'

'Hush,' Audrey said. 'That's no way to talk about Sir Charles and Lady Mandeville.'

Rosemary pulled a face and took another mouthful of food. Kate decided to eat her stew and save herself any sharp words from Audrey.

After the meal, Audrey had Kate wash their crockery and pans so that Rosemary was free to arrange a series of serving dishes on the table and fill them with water from the kettle to keep them warm.

At half past six on the dot, a bell rang out in the hall. Audrey transferred the stew, potatoes and beans to the serving dishes. Rosemary placed each on a trolley she had wheeled into the kitchen. After a few minutes, she returned.

'Aren't those pots heavy to carry up the stairs?' Kate asked.

'It's a good job we have a dumb waiter,' Rosemary said. 'Otherwise, those stairs would be plastered in casserole I dropped.'

'Next to the stairs,' Audrey explained as she stirred the custard. 'Rosie loads it down here. Sends it upstairs where she has another trolley waiting to take it into the dining room.'

'They serve themselves,' Rosemary said. 'Mrs Mandeville and Mrs Kenmore prefer it that way. Apparently, years ago, it was all grand dining with a Swiss chef, a butler and lots of footmen to serve. Imagine that! Mrs Randal started cooking for them after the war.'

The bell rang again, and Rosemary jumped to her feet. She loaded the trolley with the crumbles and the custard that Audrey had transferred to jugs. Rosemary soon returned with a trolley of rattling dishes, which Kate washed while Audrey made pots of coffee. The bell rang again, and Rosemary put the coffee, milk, sugar and a jug of warm milk for the children on the trolley. She wheeled it away and Audrey wiped her hands on her apron.

Rosemary was soon back. 'That's it then.' She smiled. 'Just the tidying away and setting up for breakfast before we go to bed.' She looked past Audrey. 'Are we having some of that crumble then?'

'Go and see to the fire,' Audrey said. 'Take Katherine with you.'

Kate followed Rosemary along the corridor. It was cold now and she was glad when Rosemary opened a door to a room where they were met by a rush of warm air.

They were in a lovely parlour with a dark sofa and two armchairs. A desk sat in one corner and a table in another. It felt like the parlour of the old terrace in Northampton. Small and dark, but homely. Two pottery dogs stood watch from either end of the mantelpiece and a clock ticked reassuringly between them. The walls were decorated with prints of countryside scenes of hills with sheep and cows. There was also a print of three Labrador puppies asleep in a basket. Rosemary knelt before the fireplace to heap extra coals on the fire.

'Pull the curtains, would you?' she said. 'Keep the heat in. This basement can get perishing in the cold weather with these stone floors.'

Like the kitchen, the windows were high in the wall, half above ground and half below. Kate took hold of the heavy curtains. Just beyond the path above, she saw the dark night sky briefly before pulling the curtains to.

The jingle of cutlery signalled Audrey's approach. She entered the room holding a tray and closed the door behind her with her elbow. She balanced the tray on the edge of the table and set three bowls down, with spoons and a jug. Rosemary was soon in her seat and Kate waited for Audrey to take a seat before sitting down.

Audrey passed around the steaming jug of custard and Kate closed her eyes again on tasting the buttery crumble, sharp yet sweet apples, and creamy custard. After finishing their pudding, Audrey said that they should leave the tidying up until later. Kate joined the sisters in the comfortable seats before the fire, taking the empty chair. Audrey poured them each a cup of cocoa before removing some knitting from a bag by her feet and Rosemary handed Kate a magazine from the pile on the small side table, explaining that Doctor and Mrs Kenmore took lots of magazines and left them in the housekeeper's parlour when they were done. 'Mr Mandeville leaves the newspapers for us, if you'd prefer,' she said.

Kate opened the magazine, but it lay unread in her lap. She listened to the rhythmic clicking of Audrey's knitting needles and the swish of the pages of Rosemary's magazine. The heat from the fire warmed her eyelids...

'Katherine, Katherine.' She heard a voice as though from a distance. Someone was gently shaking her by the shoulder and taking the magazine from her lap. 'It's half past nine. We're turning in.'

Kate came abruptly to her senses. 'I'm so sorry,' she said. She got to her feet to clear the table. But it had been cleared already. 'Can I help tidy upstairs?' she asked.

'All done,' Audrey said. 'You were dead to the world there.'

'I'm so sorry.'

'It's been a lot to take in for one day, I should imagine,'

Audrey said. 'And you'll be busy tomorrow, so you'll be glad of that extra bit of sleep.'

Kate followed Audrey and Rosemary up the stairs. They walked briskly, the cold from the stone floor and walls bitter about them. On the landing at the very top of the stairs, Audrey took two black dresses and two aprons from a cupboard. She handed them to Kate. 'They're freshly laundered,' she said. She looked Kate up and down. 'You're roughly the same size as Mary who these belonged to. They should fit.'

They said their goodnights at their doors, Audrey reminding Kate that she should be ready to work at six o'clock sharp. Rosemary got up an hour earlier to lay the fires in the family's bedrooms. Kate would be expected to lay the fires in the ground floor rooms, where the family spent the day.

'Good night,' Kate said. 'And thank you for being so kind to me today.'

Rosemary laughed. 'We'll make you pay us back tomorrow through your hard work.'

Audrey raised her eyebrows. 'Take no notice,' she said. 'Good night, Katherine. God bless.'

Kate hung the dresses on the hook behind her door. She undressed quickly, laying her clothes on the back of the chair, and pulling her nightdress over her head. She set her alarm clock to half past five to make sure she was awake early. She held the clock to her ear to check that it was ticking before placing it back on the nightstand. She switched off the light and slipped into the crisp sheets, too tired to consider brushing her teeth. There was still just enough warmth in the fire to take the chill from the air and she pulled the eiderdown around her.

Alone, her thoughts were finally able to wrap themselves

round the events of the last two days. Had she not pushed open
that gate at the back of the churchyard, she would never have
found the Mandevilles and been brought to Hill House where
the employers were kind and generous. Had she not followed
that robin, she would not have found the gate. And had she not
visited her father, at this very moment she would be in a
campaign bed in a cold empty room. Alone. Instead of in a
house so full of people and life. She hadn't realised how much
she had missed gossiping and chatting about everything and
nothing. At Sheffield, there had hardly been a moment's silence
in the boarding house, except in the few short hours when they
had all been asleep. She wasn't one for gossiping herself, but she
quite enjoyed listening to the chatter of others.

Kate nestled her head into the pillow. Good fortune had
intervened to place her in Bertie's path for him to guide her
from the dark wood. She smiled at the thought of seeing Bertie
in the entwined yews. He was probably a similar age to her. But
in so many ways he seemed older, in his manners and his bearing. And in other ways he seemed so young, with his fair moustache and the way his cheeks grew pinker if he was a little
embarrassed or unsure. He was so unlike the men at work and
at the dances in Sheffield. They were tall and broad and rather
gruff, in a way she had always found a little off putting.

As her mind tried to find sleep, Kate suddenly came to at
the thought of the locked door out on the landing. She put her
hand to her chest and felt for her St Christopher. There was
nothing beyond that door except an abandoned corridor.
Nothing to be scared of. Kate clasped the St Christopher and
closed her eyes. Not for the first time, she pictured her father,
handing it to her, closing his warm hands around hers. 'It'll keep
you safe,' he said. 'On all of life's journeys and adventures.
Whenever you wear it, always know that I am with you.'

Kate squeezed her eyes tighter. Never in her life had she
wished to see the history of an object. The images simply came

to her. But in the last few months, she had wished that this piece of gold might show her something of her father. To see him moving and speaking and full of the life that had been taken from him.

The sense of loss gripped Kate's heart. She held the St Christopher tighter still. She should have been there for him in his final moments. She should have been there to say goodbye and tell him how much she loved him. She had failed him when he had never failed her.

Kate swallowed back a tear. Her father had always hated to see her sad. She would not cry now. And the best way to make him proud would be to work hard and earn her position here.

SEVEN

SATURDAY 26TH OCTOBER, 1935

Kate was first down to the kitchen. It was still dark outside, and she turned on the light to find that all was still and tidy and clean. She opened the metal coal trap beside the range and filled the scuttle. The fires beneath the stoves and ovens were still alight and she added only enough coal to bring them to life rather than smother them. She licked her finger and placed it briefly on a plate. It sizzled reassuringly. Filling the kettle, she placed it on the plate and took three cups and saucers from the dresser.

The clock on the wall struck six o'clock and Audrey entered the kitchen. 'You're enthusiastic,' she said. 'I'm pleased to see it.'

Kate smiled and poured boiling water onto the tealeaves in the pot. 'I didn't want to be late on my first day.'

Audrey took a jug of milk from the refrigerator and placed it on the table. She looked Kate up and down. 'That dress isn't a bad fit,' she said.

Kate looked down at herself. If she could get her hands on a needle and some thread, she would add darts to the bust. It was a little generous around the waist, too, but tying the apron tight sorted that. 'Who's Mary?' she asked. 'You said the dress had belonged to Mary.'

'Mary was a maid here on and off for years. She was teaching at the village school three days a week, so worked here a few days and had your room before you.' Audrey took three spoons from the dresser drawer and placed them in the saucers. 'She's been headmistress of the village school since September and lives in the little house next to the schoolhouse now. She doesn't have time to help anymore.'

Audrey took a seat and Kate sat beside her.

'She was a maid at Hill House and is now a headmistress?' Kate said as she poured the tea.

'The Mandevilles believe in helping their staff get on in life,' Audrey said. 'I never thought at this age, and from where me and Rosie started, that I'd be running a kitchen and most of a house. Mind, I'm not complaining.'

Kate stirred a spoonful of sugar into her tea. 'And do you enjoy it?'

Audrey pushed her glasses up her nose. 'I don't mind it. But in the summer I was helping in the gardens. The gardeners from over at Caxton Hall come and look after the land when it's needed. I was learning from them. I think that's where I would like to be if I can.'

'And is that a possibility?'

'Mrs Mandeville says she will look for a new cook and maid come the new year, so it might be.'

The kitchen door flew open. 'Is there one in the pot for me?' Rosemary asked. She pushed a strand of hair away from her eyes, leaving a black trail of soot up her face.

'Get yourself washed and I'll pour you one,' Audrey said.

Rosemary turned on the taps and scrubbed at her hands with a nailbrush.

'Don't forget your face,' Audrey said.

Rosemary washed her face and roughly dried it on a towel. She sat down, her cheeks glowing.

'We'll have these then I'll show you the fires that need making up on the ground floor,' Rosemary said, heaping sugar into her tea. 'I'll help you today but tomorrow you'll be on your own.'

Audrey took a pad and pencil from a drawer in the table. With Rosemary's help, she compiled a list to be telephoned through to Pennymore's. It was the grocery needs for the next week to be delivered on Monday.

'Put some extra turnips down,' Rosemary said.

'Turnips? Why?' Audrey asked.

'It's Halloween on Thursday,' Rosemary said.

'Of course.' Audrey scribbled on the pad. 'We've plenty of apples in the store. We've got enough candles, too.'

Clearly reading the confusion on Kate's face, Rosemary said, 'We always do Halloween at Hill House. Doctor Kenmore's American and it's quite the thing there. He always leads on the game of bobbing for apples where the children get very wet. Elliot's mother was Irish, and he likes to scare the children with his folk tales. He doesn't usually have much to do with the children but on Halloween, he'll help them make jack-o'-lanterns and put them around the house. Those scary faces at every door and window are enough to turn your hair white! And there's a terrific smell of burning vegetables for a few days after!'

'Jack-o'-lanterns?' Kate said.

'It's an Irish tradition, so Elliot says,' Rosemary explained. 'Ghosts can come through to the living on Halloween, and the faces carved into the turnips scare them off. What is it that Elliot calls Halloween?' Rosemary asked her sister. 'Something Irish.'

'*Samhain*,' Audrey said. She pointed to the clock. 'It's half past six. Time you two were upstairs. I'll clear this.'

Kate followed Rosemary through the cold basement corridor. At the bottom of the stone steps they stopped, and Rosemary opened a cupboard. She handed Kate a long, thick apron and two fabric oversleeves that she had to put on over the sleeves of her dress to protect her frock from the coal dust. Rosemary collected a bucket containing a dustpan and brush, and Kate followed her up the stairs, along the stone corridor and into the grand hallway. It was still dark – the sun wouldn't show its face for some time – but the moonlight coming in through the glass dome high in the ceiling gave enough light to see the beautiful features of the hall.

'We stay quiet when we're down here,' Rosemary whispered. 'And we don't put the lights on until we're in a room. Some of the bedrooms are just at the top of the stairs and we don't want to disturb the family.'

Kate followed Rosemary and tiptoed across the mosaic tiled floor. They came first to a dining room. Rosemary handed the bucket to Kate and collected a scuttle of coal waiting outside. Once inside the room, Rosemary closed the door and turned on the light. The panelled room had a dining table running down the centre and a sideboard at one end.

'Elliot leaves the coal outside each room for us,' Rosemary said. 'I think he must do it in the middle of the night. We never see him.'

Kate joined Rosemary in kneeling before the fireplace. She watched how Rosemary carefully cleaned out the fire, discarding the ash in the bucket and the amount of coal Rosemary added and how much kindling. 'Each scuttle should have enough in it for the day,' Rosemary explained. 'We come back every hour or so to check the fire's still going. If we ever run low on coal, we just let Elliot know and he brings more.' Once the fire took, Kate followed Rosemary out, closing the door behind them. Next, they entered the morning room where Kate had been interviewed by Mrs Mandeville. Rosemary let Kate try

making up the fire. Once she was satisfied with Kate's handiwork, they moved on to a magnificent library with shelves of
books, some feet high and some mere inches tall. They shared
the task of making up the fire in the library. Out in the hall,
Rosemary nodded to a door beside the library. 'That's the
billiard room,' she said. 'It's kept closed most of the time. We
only do the fires at the weekend really or when the men want to
use the room in the evening. They usually just stick to the
library.'

Kate followed Rosemary through a door beneath the grand
staircase, into an area with a very different feel. The ceiling
was lower, it was narrower. Half a dozen doors led from a corridor. 'It's storage mainly,' Rosemary said. 'This is where a
guest's luggage is brought before being taken upstairs. And
there's a sink in that room where you can fill your bucket for
mopping the floor.' At the very end of the corridor, they
entered an office. Two desks were squeezed into a room clearly
meant for one. They sat amongst shelves of boxes and ledgers.
Paintings hung on the walls, scenes from a hill and splendid
buildings. Rosemary knelt at the hearth and began cleaning out
the grate. 'This is where Mr Mandeville and Bertie work from,'
she said.

Kate knelt beside Rosemary and scooped coal into the grate.

'You should have seen this room before,' Rosemary said. 'Sir
Charles collected all sorts of masks when he was a young man
on his travels, and they were all hung on the walls. I never liked
to come in then. I felt like I was being watched the whole time!'

'Where are they now?' Kate asked.

'Sir Charles had them moved to his office in the dower
house over at Caxton Hall,' she said. 'Good riddance to those
masks, I say. I'm just sorry for Mrs Randal and Sally if they ever
have to go in there!'

'Mrs Randal and Sally?' Kate asked.

'The cook and Lady Mandeville's lady's maid. They used to

work here but went across when Sir Charles, Lady Mandeville and Mrs Hart moved there. Bertie's grandmother and mother.'

'Bertie's grandmother and mother?' Kate said.

Rosemary turned to her. 'I could swear there's an echo in here,' she laughed. 'Bertie's family has lived and worked here for so long. His father was a footman, but he died in the war when Bertie was still a little boy. Sir Edward's brother died, too.' Rosemary set a match to the paper and sat back while it took, humming a little tune. She spoke as though the death of a father was as commonplace as setting a fire in a hearth. Perhaps it was a reaction to growing up in an orphanage. Kate wanted to give Rosemary just five minutes of her father's love to know what it felt like. Instead, she touched Rosemary's warm, dirty hand. 'Thank you,' she said. 'For being so welcoming.'

Rosemary turned to her. 'You know, Katherine, I'm so glad Bertie found you in the woods. You might only have been here a day, but I've really taken to you. Audrey feels the same, I can tell. Although she would never say as much.'

'She is very serious, isn't she?' Kate said.

'She'll get more friendly when she gets to know you,' Rosemary said. 'She's just had lots of practice at being a very bossy big sister! She's barely a year older than me but treats me like a child!'

'I'm sure it's because she cares,' Kate said.

'I suppose so.' Rosemary placed the pan of ashes into the bucket. 'Come on,' she said. 'We should get washed up and ready to help with breakfast.'

The family were to take breakfast in the dining room, so Kate helped Audrey with the cooking. She took charge of making the porridge and coffee, while Audrey cooked the bacon, sausages, and eggs. With the various serving bowls and dishes delivered upstairs by Rosemary, and after almost three hours of work,

Kate was glad to sit down at the kitchen table with Audrey and Rosemary to enjoy a bowl of porridge followed by tea and toast.

After breakfast, Kate waited at the bottom of the dumb waiter to collect the trolley Rosemary had filled in the dining room, and she transferred the dirty crockery into the kitchen. She was up to her elbows in soap suds, scrubbing a frying pan, when Rosemary returned with the news that the whole family was going out for a walk to make the most of the crisp autumn morning. They would stop into the dower house at Caxton Hall to take lunch with Sir Charles, Lady Mandeville and Mrs Hart, so wouldn't be home until at least three o'clock. Just in time for tea. 'I've never known anyone like to walk as much as they do,' Rosemary said. 'And take so much air!'

When Kate followed Rosemary up the stairs to clean, the great hallway was ablaze with colour in the sunlight flooding through the glass dome. Kate placed the mop and bucket down on the tiled floor beneath the staircase. Rosemary tasked Kate with checking on the fires while she disappeared into the office corridor.

Kate was on her knees, adding coal to the fire in the morning room, when Rosemary returned pulling a contraption.

'Ta da!' Rosemary said.

Kate got to her feet, wiping her hands on her dirty apron. 'Is that a vacuum cleaner?' she asked.

'It is!' Rosemary looked proudly down at the silver cylinder. She pushed the plug into the socket in the wall and showed Kate how it worked and how it saved so much time, with no need for sweeping. Kate watched, enthralled, as the machine whirred and sucked at the carpets. She was used to helping her mother take the rugs outside on sunny days to beat until they were free of dust!

With the demonstration over, Rosemary moved from room

to room, the mechanics inside the vacuum cleaner making quite the noise as Kate mopped the tiled floor in the hallway. In the small vestibule, she opened the front door to shake the doormat. Out on the gravel beneath the portico, she shielded her eyes and looked up at the sun. It really was a glorious morning. On a normal day she would have gone for a walk and stopped in at the Post Office or the grocer's in the village to collect some flour for Mother. There would be no more of that. Not now she was working again. She looked over her shoulder into the hall. Hill House was far more beautiful than the steelworks. She breathed in deeply. The air here was clean and smelled of leaves, not smoke and soot.

After a brief break at midday for lunch, the sisters began preparations for an afternoon of baking. Kate headed back up the stairs with a feather duster, a cloth and a tin of beeswax. The tasks ahead of her for the afternoon were relatively clean, so there was no need for the dirty apron and sleeve protectors.

Kate emerged from the door at the back of the hall. It was silent. No people. No vacuum cleaner. No chatter. She placed the beeswax and cloth on the floor and made her way around the hall, taking in the details as she dusted the frames of the paintings hung on the honey-coloured wood panelled walls. There were so many portraits, of children, adults and animals. Some of the sitters wore wigs and were dressed in clothes that she recognised as satins and silks. The painting was so fine that it felt if she touched the fabric, it would be soft. Other paintings were of hillsides with cows and sheep. Close up the skies were purples and pinks and blues, but when Kate took just a step back, the colours merged to become the normal colour of the sky.

In recesses in the panelling, marble statues stood on plinths. Like the creatures holding up the mantelpiece, there were many fantastical creatures. One took the form of a human on top with the legs of a goat. He was playing some kind of musical instrument, like pipes. They had learned some Greek and Roman mythology at school, and if she remembered correctly, this was Pan.

The tick of the long-cased clock at the back of the hall and Kate's shoes on the tiles were the only sounds as she crossed the hall. She stood beneath the glass dome and looked up, smiling at the autumn sun shining on her face and the fire in the hearth warming her. The fire that she had set that morning. She was doing an honest day's work. A day's work that her father would be proud of. She looked towards the vestibule. Beyond the front door was the drive and the woods which hid that little gate in the wall that led to the churchyard. She was closer than she had been at her parents' house and on her days off, she would be sure to go and spend time with her father. But, in order to have days off, she needed to do her work. She placed the feather duster on the bottom step of the grand staircase and was on her way to collect her other cleaning things when a painting beneath the stairs made her stop. It was different to the other paintings. It was larger. Probably life-sized. It was of an army officer on horseback. He wore a blue uniform with a scarlet plume to his golden helmet. His boots gleamed in the stirrups of the black stallion on which he sat. And in the background was Hill House.

'Captain Thomas Mandeville,' a voice said over her shoulder. Kate spun around.

'Oh, hello,' she said, 'Sorry. I should be working. I was just looking around.'

'It's quite right that you should be acclimatising yourself with your new surroundings,' Bertie said. 'How is your first full day going?'

'Good. Thank you. Audrey and Rosemary have been very

kind and very thorough in helping me understand what I need to do.'

'I'm glad to hear it,' Bertie said. He smiled. He looked younger even than before. He wore no hat as he was inside, and he ran his fingers through his fringe, pushing it back into place. He looked towards the painting. 'It's a very good likeness,' he said.

'You know him?' Kate asked.

'When I was a very small child. He was so kind. He used to carry me around on his shoulders, letting me pretend to be Wellington while he was my trusty steed.'

Kate looked at the side of Bertie's face. There was real fondness in his eyes as he studied the man in the painting. 'Where is he now?' she asked.

Bertie's eyes dipped slightly. 'He died. In the war. In August 1914.'

'I'm so sorry,' Kate said, mortified that in trying to be friendly, she had been overfamiliar. She wanted to say more to Bertie but was afraid of what might come out of her mouth. She might mention his father. It was probably no secret that he had died but she wouldn't want Bertie to think she had been gossiping with the other staff. Especially as she had barely been here a day. His family's history was his and only his to tell.

'Captain Mandeville was incredibly brave,' Bertie said. 'He sacrificed himself and saved many of his men.'

'I'm sure they are very grateful to him.'

Bertie smiled. 'I'm sure they are.' He swept his hair back from his face again. The action broke the melancholy. 'So, what tasks do the sisters have you doing today?'

'I helped prepare breakfast this morning,' Kate said. 'I'm responsible for making up the fires on this floor each morning, I mopped the hall floor and now I'm to dust the bannisters and wax the handrail of the staircase.'

'Goodness.' Bertie rocked back on his heels. 'They are keeping you gainfully employed.'

'I like to be busy,' Kate said.

'I could tell as much when I first met you.'

'Really. How?'

'There was something about your efficiency.'

'My efficiency in getting lost in the woods, you mean!' Kate laughed. Then abruptly stopped. She was being overfamiliar again. But Bertie's response was to laugh, too.

'That's true,' he said. 'Perhaps I was mistaken.' His cheeks grew a little pinker.

'May I ask you a question?' Kate said.

'Of course,' Bertie said.

'The creatures holding up the mantelpiece. What are they?'

'Fauns.'

'Oh yes,' Kate said. 'Of course.'

'And the instruments they are playing are a flute and a lyre.'

'I see.' She smiled.

'You have an inquisitive mind,' Bertie said. 'And that reminds me,' he added. 'I have something to show you. I won't keep you long. This way.'

He headed to the library and Kate followed. They passed the bookshelves and crossed to the far end of the room.

'There,' Bertie said.

Kate stopped beside him and looked at the picture in a frame above the fireplace. It wasn't like the paintings in the hall. It looked almost as though it had been drawn in pencil. Kate recognised it immediately. It was the yew trees. But in another time when supports held the branches up. There were fine ladies and gentlemen sitting at tables beneath with a feast spread out before them.

'When is this from?' she asked, taking in the ladies' dresses and the food on the table.

'Early eighteen hundreds, I would say,' Bertie said. 'Judging by the clothes.'

'What a thing it must have been to have a picnic under the boughs of those trees,' Kate said, studying the exquisite details. When Bertie didn't answer, she turned to find him looking not at the drawing, but at her.

He quickly turned his attention back to the art. 'Yes,' he said, 'I'm sure it would have been.' His cheeks grew pink again. To spare his blushes, Kate pointed out some other aspects of the picture. Bertie nodded and explained details of how the landscape around the trees looked now. Kate listened but couldn't help glancing at him every so often.

Finally, Bertie scratched his cheek. 'I should let you get back to your duties,' he said. 'I'm afraid I've kept you too long. Audrey will have my guts for garters if I interfere with the running of the house.'

'We wouldn't want that,' Kate said, holding in a smile. 'Guts really do best when they are in their correct place.'

Bertie paused for a moment, before laughing. 'I couldn't agree more,' he said.

Kate laughed, too. Perhaps he wasn't quite the stick in the mud she had first thought. But she shouldn't be too overfamiliar and risk having him think her foolish or regret suggesting her for the job.

'I have some paperwork that needs my attention,' Bertie said, leading the way back out into the hall.

Something inside Kate felt a little sad that they were about to part. 'Rosemary is making scones,' she said quickly. 'For tea this afternoon. She said that you sometimes take tea. Although not breakfast or dinner as you live in a cottage by the gates.' The words came out so rapidly and Kate couldn't seem to stop herself. Was she being indiscreet? Should Rosemary have told her so much about Bertie's living arrangements? Would he be cross?

'I am partial to a scone,' he said. 'I might just pop down to the kitchen later to avail myself.'

Kate had to hold in a laugh again at his old-fashioned turn of phrase. 'I'll be getting on then,' she said. With a final nod, Bertie turned and pushed through the door beneath the stairs leading to the office corridor.

Kate collected the cloth and beeswax. She placed them on a step and took up the duster. Making her way up the scarlet carpet, step by step, she let the duster glide over the surface of each carving in the bannisters, paying particular attention to pushing the feathers through the gaps in the details: the birds, the fruits, and the animals. She was soon at the top of the stairs, overlooking the hallway. Corridors ran off to the left and right with doors leading away to the family bedrooms. In the wall on the landing, she saw the outline of a door. It was panelled at the bottom and papered at the top, mimicking the wall in which it stood, just like the door at the back of the hallway downstairs. From its position, Kate guessed it to be the doorway to the stone staircase that she passed each time she went to and from the attic.

Making her way back down the stairs, Kate let the feathers of the duster glide over the carvings once again. At the bottom, she paid particular attention to pressing them into every detail of the pineapples topping the two newel posts.

The clock struck half past one. With the family due to return at three o'clock, Kate wanted to have the dusting and polishing finished in plenty of time to be downstairs again before their arrival, although Rosemary had said the family really didn't mind them getting on with their work while they were around.

Kate removed the lid from the tin and placed it carefully on the mantelshelf so as not to get it on the carpet. Taking a good scoop of the wax, she stood on the bottom step. With her free hand she reached to place her palm on the handrail to gauge how much polishing it might need. But the moment her bare skin made contact with the dark wood there was a flash. She was hit with the salty, briny scent of the sea. She felt herself rocked as though on a wide ocean. Men called to each other. A man high up in a crow's nest shouted to men on deck and those scaling the rigging. The sky was dark. A storm was coming in. Seagulls screeched overhead. The men's voices called in desperation. Battening down the hatches. Spray hit her cheeks and the deck creaked beneath her.

Kate snatched her hand away. She collapsed onto the bottom stair, her heart thumping. In the hall, the sun shone on the bronze tiles. It sparkled across the marble statues and lit the people and animals in the paintings. Kate gripped the edge of the stair. Why had that happened here? And why now? Why had she seen a ship? She shook her head but couldn't shake away the smell of the sea. She gripped the edge of the stair tighter. This didn't happen. She didn't see images when she touched an object outside her parents' home. And it had been so real. As though she was standing on the deck of that ship tossed around in the angry waves.

Kate closed her eyes and rubbed her temples, breathing deeply. She pushed herself up. The cloth she had been clasping fell to the carpet. Stooping to collect it, she saw that it had left a waxy stain on her crisp white apron. She had been trying so hard to be proper and had fallen almost at the first hurdle. With her shoulders slumped, she placed the cloth on the handrail. It felt as it was, a piece of wood. She began to rub at the grain. With the buffer of the cloth, she was safe. For now, at least.

With the dusting finished, Kate returned to the kitchen and asked Audrey whether she might have a piece parchment paper. She took the paper through to the housekeeper's parlour where she had set up an ironing board and had an iron heating on the fire. She slipped off her apron, covered the waxy mark with the paper and pressed the iron over the top. The wax transferred from the apron to the paper; it was clean again. She screwed up the paper, threw it onto the fire and tied the apron back around her waist.

When it was time for afternoon tea, Kate sat at the table in the kitchen, staring into her cup.

'They're long days to get used to,' Audrey said, sitting down opposite her.

'I'm not too tired to work,' Kate said quickly, sitting up straight. 'Should I go up and help Rosemary lay out the tea for the family?'

Audrey placed a scone on a plate and pushed it towards her. 'You've done a lot today already. If you wanted to take a few minutes to go to your room—'

'Honestly, no,' Kate said, afraid that this might be some kind of test that she needed to pass to prove how hard she was able to work. 'Put me to use,' she said. 'That will perk me up.'

'You're a good worker, I'll give you that,' Audrey said. 'Now eat up, sugar is good for giving you more energy.'

Audrey returned to the sink and set about peeling a pile of potatoes. Kate didn't want Audrey to think she wasn't up to the tasks of her new role. And if it hadn't been for the shock of seeing that ship, she would still be alert and ready for the next job.

There was a knock at the already open door. 'Is there a scone going spare?' Bertie asked, hovering in the doorway.

'Of course,' Audrey said. 'Tea?'

'Thank you,' Bertie pulled out a chair and sat at the table.

Audrey dried her hands on her apron but before she moved, Kate got up. She collected a cup and saucer and a plate from the dresser and placed them before Bertie. He put a napkin in his lap and poured his own tea. He offered the pot to Kate when she sat down, but she shook her head. He took a scone from the dish on the table, split it in two and added butter and a spoonful of jam to each half.

'You've done a fine job on that staircase, Katherine,' Bertie said, stirring his tea. 'Mrs Mandeville commented on it when the family got back.'

He took a bite of his scone and smiled. 'You know,' he said. 'I really think these are better than the scones Monsieur Gotti used to make when I was a boy. But don't tell Rosemary.' He took another bite and made an appreciative noise.

'My sister has a high enough opinion of herself already,' Audrey said. 'If she thought for one minute that she was a better baker than a fancy Swiss chef, her head would swell so she wouldn't fit through that door any longer.' She held the peeler out to the kitchen door.

Bertie and Audrey laughed. They laughed easily together, just as Kate did with Harry. It was familiar. And it made sense. Bertie and Audrey would probably have known each other for years and since they were still children. Perhaps, for the sisters, Bertie had taken the place of an older brother. He was the son of a maid and footman and the grandson of a cook. No doubt he and the sisters understood each other and their lives.

Bertie and Audrey continued to chat about the running of the house and Audrey's plan to polish all the silver before Christmas, which would be on them before they knew it and she wanted everything to be just so. The familiarity and love they had for Hill House shone from their conversation. This was their home. And had been for so long. They surely knew every inch of this house and much of its history.

'I was wondering,' Kate said when Audrey put the kettle on to boil again, in case more tea was wanted upstairs. 'When I was polishing the handrail, I thought how it looked a bit like the wood used on a ship. My brother's a carpenter,' she added quickly, hoping that made it sound less ridiculous. 'So, I'm always a bit interested in different woods.'

Bertie wiped his mouth and moustache and placed his napkin on the table. 'You have a good eye!' he said. 'A lot of the timbers in the house were from a ship. When it was broken up, the timbers were sold. The wood from the captain's and officers' quarters were used for much of the decorative detail around the house. It was quite a common practice.'

Kate thought of the men shouting to each other in the rigging and crow's nest. 'It wasn't a wreck, was it? Nobody was hurt on it?' She couldn't bear the thought that anytime she touched timbers around the house, she might be faced with the image of a long-dead sailor.

Bertie shook his head. 'No, it was a clipper, going to and from India with cargos of tea and beer. It was damaged in a storm but managed to limp back to Southampton.'

Kate closed her eyes briefly. At least there had been no disaster attached to the wood. No lost souls left to cry out, looking for someone to hear them.

'Are you spinning us a yarn?' Audrey asked. 'How would you know so much about an old ship like that?'

'The clipper belonged to the Caxtons,' Bertie said. 'When Sir Charles' ancestor, Thomas Mandeville, built this house, Lord Caxton sold him the timbers. Thomas Mandeville was married to Lord Caxton's daughter, so he gave him a good price. It's all catalogued in a ledger in the office. The original Thomas Mandeville kept scrupulous records when he had this house built.'

Audrey smiled. 'Have you heard from the current Tommy Mandeville recently?' she asked. There was a softness in her voice that Kate hadn't heard before. And it was matched by Bertie's smile.

'I received a letter from him last week,' he said. 'He's having a whale of a time at Cambridge. Mind, I'm not sure how much studying he's doing!' Bertie raised his eyebrows and Audrey laughed. 'He asked me to send him his penknife. I've no idea why – up to some mischief, no doubt – but I found it in his room and posted it at the beginning of the week.'

'Oh,' Audrey said. 'That reminds me. You wanted to post a letter, didn't you, Katherine?'

'Only if it's no trouble,' Kate said. 'I'm happy to pay for it, it's just that I don't know when I'll get a chance to go to the Post Office in the village.'

'Just leave it on the post tray in the hall,' Bertie said, getting to his feet. 'The Mandevilles don't mind us posting a letter or two. It won't go until Monday though; I hope it's not urgent...'

'No, it's to my...' Kate was about to say that it was to her mother. But Bertie thought her mother and father were still in their house on the Wilkinson estate. 'I'm posting it to my brother's house. To let him know how I'm getting on.' It wasn't a lie. It would go to Harry's house. It was addressed to Mrs Durrant, which was Enid's name, too, so it wouldn't be suspicious if anyone saw it on the post tray.

'Elliot will post it on Monday morning,' Bertie said. 'If you'll excuse me, I'll take my leave. But would you thank Rosemary for me for the scone, Audrey?'

Kate looked after Bertie as he left. The half-truth she had told about the letter sat heavy with her. 'Tell the truth and shame the devil,' her father had always said.

For the remainder of the afternoon, Kate helped Audrey prepare the dinner of lamb cutlets with vegetables and a type of potato called dauphinoise. Audrey explained that she wasn't often called upon to make fancy foods, but she liked to challenge herself. The potato dauphinoise had been popular back in the days of Monsieur Gotti and ever since, bulbs of garlic had been grown in the kitchen garden and stored alongside the onions in the vegetable store. Before the bell rang for upstairs service, Kate sat with the sisters to eat their meal. As with everything she had eaten since her arrival, the food was delicious, but she had little appetite. The image of the clipper wouldn't leave her thoughts. When Rosemary took the dessert of baked apples upstairs, Kate followed and added coal to the fires in the hall and the drawing room where the family planned to congregate after dinner for board games. Returning to the kitchen, she helped Audrey and Rosemary clean and wash up. But she refused the offer of taking dessert in the parlour before the fire.

'If there's nothing else wanting doing, I think I might turn in,' she said when Audrey made a pot of cocoa to take through to have with the apples.

'That'd be a shame,' Rosemary said. 'I was going to put the wireless on. I was hoping you might dance with me. Aud never wants to dance.'

'Perhaps another evening,' Kate said. She smiled but could feel her eyelids gradually closing.

'Leave Katherine be,' Audrey said, placing just two plates of baked apples on the tray. 'It's six o'clock for the fires tomorrow,' she reminded Kate. 'We'll have tea and toast for breakfast. The family have a quicker breakfast of porridge and toast so that we can change and be ready to go to church at half past nine.'

'Church?' Kate said.

'Of course,' Audrey said, her eyebrows dipping.

'Yes,' Kate said. 'Of course. Church. Half past nine. I'll say goodnight then.'

'Good night,' Audrey said. 'God bless.'

Kate took the stone steps quickly, racing to escape the cold of the stairwell. She undressed, turned out the light and slipped into bed. Since her father's funeral, the closest she had been to the pews at St Mary's was passing the door on her way to the churchyard. Her mother still went to church with her neighbours. She seemed to find comfort in it. But any faith Kate had

had was now stripped raw. What kind of God would take a man from the world when he had only just begun to reap the rewards of the life for which he had worked so hard?

Kate turned onto her side. It would be hypocritical to attend church. But how would she ever get out of it?

Closing her eyes, Kate was almost asleep when an image of the clipper presented itself to her. She heard the call of men high up on the rigging and was sure she smelled the salty sea. She opened her eyes and looked into the dying flames of the fire. The image of the clipper had been so real today. But why had she seen it? She had never seen the history of an object outside her parents' home. Why that and why now? She turned onto her side. It was a pointless question to ask herself. Why did she see anything, ever? Until today, it had been possible to believe that this 'gift' was in fact vivid daydreams of a sort centred around her family and their history. But she had no knowledge of the clipper and its history, or that its timbers had been used in the construction of this house. So how had this come to her? She shook her head. The best she could hope was that today was a one off and a very strange coincidence. She couldn't be distracted. She had to work and prove herself worthy of becoming a housemaid. The here and now and her situation was far more pressing than images in her head.

Nestling further into the warm sheets, Kate tried to distract her thoughts by picturing other events from the day. She saw Bertie and Audrey in the kitchen. Bertie giving her a brief history of the house he loved so much. Bertie's moustache rising when she said she hoped Audrey wouldn't have his guts for garters. He was a man of many sides, was Mr Morrison. One minute quite proper and reserved, the next smiling and laughing and tucking into a scone. Kate let her eyes close again, picturing Bertie's cheeks growing pinker when he looked at her rather than the painting of the yew trees in the woods where they had met. Finally, she drifted away.

EIGHT

SUNDAY 27TH OCTOBER, 1935

'What do you mean, you're not coming to church?' Audrey said, looking in the mirror above the fireplace in the housekeeper's parlour, stabbing her hat with a pin to secure it to her hair.

'Please don't be cross,' Kate said to Audrey's reflection. 'It's just that... something... it's just that I haven't been going to church recently. Something happened and it doesn't feel right.'

'I'm not cross,' Audrey said, buttoning up her dark coat. 'Just surprised. I can't imagine anything happening that would stop me going to church.'

'Does that mean I don't have to go?' Rosemary said.

Audrey turned and frowned at her little sister who was standing beside the small table, pulling on her gloves. 'No,' she said. 'It does not mean you don't have to go. Now come on, we haven't got all day.'

Rosemary muttered under her breath as she secured her scarf at her neck.

'I'll make myself useful,' Kate said. 'Any jobs that you want me to do while you're gone, I'd be happy to get on with them.' Remembering the pile of vegetables on the kitchen table, she said, 'I could peel the vegetables for lunch. I'd like to do something worthwhile.'

Audrey seemed to mull it over for a moment. She unclasped her handbag and looked inside. 'It wouldn't do any harm, I suppose.'

'And would you like me to baste the joint? I saw you put it in the oven earlier.'

Audrey snapped her bag shut. 'Very well, but don't leave the door open too long and let the heat out. It needs to be cooked by one o'clock.'

'You can trust me,' Kate said. 'I must have helped my mother cook hundreds of Sunday lunches.'

'We'll be back just before half past eleven,' Audrey said. 'Oh, and you won't be alone. Doctor Kenmore doesn't come to church either. Don't be alarmed if you see him.'

'Why would I be alarmed?' Kate asked.

'He was wounded in the war,' Rosemary said, adjusting her hat. 'Some people are a bit scared when they see him. But you don't need to be. He's a very kind man.'

'Scared?' Kate said.

'Come along now, Rosemary,' Audrey said. 'I don't want to be late.'

'Why would I be scared?' Kate tried again.

'Pay her no mind,' Audrey said, shooing Rosemary through the door. 'He's got some scarring is all.'

Kate watched the sisters walk along the corridor, through the door at the end and up the steps to ground level. Perhaps she should have gone to church after all. With everything that had happened yesterday, she didn't relish the thought of being given a scare today.

In the kitchen, Kate set to work peeling the vegetables. Soon there were pans filled with carrots and cauliflower. And other pans with potatoes and parsnips ready to be parboiled when Audrey came back. She filled each pan with water and placed them back on the stove. She looked at the clock. It was still only half past ten. Another hour before the sisters and the rest of the family would be back. It would be too early to go upstairs to check on the fires she had set before breakfast. She would give it another half an hour so that the fires were roaring when everyone returned.

Kate rested against the sink. Following lunch, the family would visit the dower house at Caxton Hall where they would spend the afternoon and stay for their evening meal. They visited the dower house every Sunday so that the children could spend time with their grandparents and great-aunt, which was why the maids were given every Sunday afternoon off. Kate thought about her mother at Harry's house. The children would occupy her time. It would be lively and hopefully would leave less time for her to be melancholy.

Kate looked up to ground level to check on the weather.

'It's a beautiful day out there,' a man said. The voice was deep and heavily accented in a way Kate had only ever heard at the picture house – an American accent. Knowing who it would be, Rosemary's words rang in her ears. She stole herself before turning around, not knowing what to expect. What she saw left her momentarily unable to speak. The man standing in the doorway was impeccably dressed in a light suit. But his face... it was damaged. Half was unscathed and very handsome. The other half was terribly scarred. Jagged pink lines ran from his eye all the way to his chin. On the injured side, half of his eyebrow was missing, and his mouth dipped slightly.

'You must be Katherine,' he said.

She continued to stare. 'I-I...'

'Did nobody prepare you for my appearance?' he asked. He smiled, but only half of his mouth lifted.

'I... yes,' Katherine said.

'I'm not a big churchgoer,' Doctor Kenmore said, still smiling. 'And clearly, I have met a similar cynic. Would you be an atheist or perhaps agnostic?'

Kate shook her head. 'Sorry.'

'Don't be,' he said. 'My appearance can come as a shock. It was a souvenir from my time in France during the war. Most people get used to it after a while and no longer see it. Kenmore,' he said. 'Paul Kenmore.'

'Mrs Kenmore's husband,' Kate said.

'For my sins.' Doctor Kenmore laughed. It was such a warm laugh that Kate couldn't help but smile.

'Can I get you something?' she asked.

'A cup of coffee wouldn't go amiss,' he said. 'I usually come down and help myself on Sunday mornings when everyone is at church. It's a rarity to have the house to myself and a bit of peace and quiet.'

'Would you rather I left?' Kate said quickly.

'Not at all. It's nice to have a bit of company. Especially when it's company that doesn't charge around or chuck toy building bricks at me or want help with homework!'

Kate took the pot down from the dresser and filled it with coffee and water as she had seen Audrey do. She placed it on the range.

'Would you mind if I wait for it to be ready?' Doctor Kenmore asked.

'Not at all,' Kate said.

Doctor Kenmore took a tray from the dresser and placed a cup and saucer on it. He opened the refrigerator and took out a jug of cream. 'So,' he said. 'How have your first days here been?'

'Good, thank you,' Kate said. She should be respectful but answer only what was asked of her – at least, that's how she assumed she should behave with a member of the family she didn't know.

'Charlotte and Alice are taken with you,' Doctor Kenmore

said. 'They're very impressed with your work and how you've settled in. You have made quite the impression. According to my wife, the steelworks' loss is our gain.'

'Thank you,' Kate said, turning around to see Doctor Kenmore adding a sugar lump to his cup. 'I'm very grateful.'

Doctor Kenmore looked up. 'For what?'

'For the job and for giving me somewhere to stay.'

The pot rumbled. Steam escaped the spout. Kate took the pot from the range and placed it on the tray.

'Thank you,' Doctor Kenmore said. 'And would you mind if I share a thought with you?'

Kate shook her head.

'It's a two-way street.'

'Pardon?'

'This arrangement,' Doctor Kenmore said. He poured steaming coffee into his cup. 'In any big house, the family need the staff as much as the staff need a job. Without you and Audrey and Rosemary and Bertie and Elliot, we simply could not keep going. You are just as important to this house as any of the family.'

Kate stared at Doctor Kenmore as he added cream to his coffee. None of the managers at the steelworks would ever speak to an employee as though they were important. They were constantly reminded that they were lucky to have employment and that employment could be taken away at any moment.

'I know that hasn't always been the case in houses such as this,' Doctor Kenmore said. 'Staff were made to tug their forelocks and turn away if they crossed the path of a member of the family. It might still be that way in other houses, but the Mandevilles want everyone to feel valued. So you don't need to be grateful, Katherine. You work hard at your chores and deserve your salary and home. The family work hard in different ways. But it takes many parts to make a well-oiled machine. And each cog and piston is as important as the next.' Doctor Kenmore held up the coffee pot. 'Would you like one?'

Kate shook her head. 'Thank you. No.'

Doctor Kenmore placed the pot on the tray. 'There are a few things that you should know about this family that I doubt anyone will tell you,' he said. He leant back against the dresser, crossed one foot in front of the other and folded his arms. 'The Mandevilles have a social conscience. They treat people kindly and fairly. You've probably noticed that my wife is a tad unconventional.' He raised his good eyebrow.

Kate laughed. 'A little.'

'She has a fire in her belly about social reform,' he continued. 'She wants to make the world a better place and has her heart set on using Mandeville assets and land for the greater good. She doesn't talk about it much, but in her younger days, she and her aunt, Mrs Hart, were suffragettes.'

'Suffragettes?' Kate said. She could hear the wonder in her voice. Her father had spoken of the women who had taken direct action so that all women and men might have the vote. He had been in awe of them and respected them very much.

Doctor Kenmore nodded. 'And Edward and Alice – Mr and Mrs Mandeville – are about the kindest souls you could ever hope to meet. They helped Audrey and Rosemary out of the orphanage to give them a good life. Those girls weren't the first that the Mandevilles helped, and they won't be the last. I'm sure Alice won't mind me telling you this, as it's no secret, but she met Edward when she was a maid in this house. She was an orphan when she came to work here. So you see, she understands people. She understands how important it is to be kind and decent.'

Kate's mind swirled around what Doctor Kenmore was telling her. He pushed himself away from the dresser. 'I should take my coffee upstairs before it gets cold,' he said. 'Thanks for the company, Katherine. I'll let you get back to your day.' He picked up the tray and Kate watched him leave.

She listened to Doctor Kenmore's footsteps out in the corridor until there was silence. She stared at the door. A member of the family, who she had never met before, had spoken to her, and valued her as a fellow human being. And the Mandevilles were social reformers. Mrs Mandeville had been a maid! Now that she knew this, it made sense. As the Mandevilles had given Audrey and Rosemary the chance of a future, so they had given her this chance of a job in their household. And it probably explained why they were so different to how she imagined a grand family might be. A small part of her had been uncertain what her father might think of her taking up a job in a big house, waiting on a titled family. But he would have been proud of this. Proud to know that she was working for a family who were trying to deliver the same change of which he had always spoken so passionately. To make the world a better place for everyone.

Kate realised that she had been so surprised by what Doctor Kenmore had told her, that she had forgotten to think about his face. He didn't seem at all cowed by what had happened to him in the war. Perhaps it was because he was American. They always seemed so confident in the pictures.

Taking up a cloth, Kate wiped the table down with renewed vigour. This new knowledge of the Mandevilles made her want to work even harder to keep her position. At the sound of the door opening in the basement corridor, she placed the cloth on the side of the sink. Audrey appeared in the doorway. Unpinning her hat, she looked over the pans. 'I'll get the batter for the Yorkshires going,' she said. 'Would you get the heat on for those potatoes and parsnips please, Katherine? I'll be back in a few minutes.' She joined Rosemary in the corridor, and they left to change from their Sunday best into their work dresses and aprons. Kate smiled to herself. No criticism was praise indeed from Audrey. And now that she knew more of Audrey's history, it made sense that she was wary and wanted everything done just so for the family who had helped her and her sister.

When the family's lunch had been served and cleared away, Kate joined Audrey and Rosemary to eat their meal in the housekeeper's parlour. With the sisters settling in for an afternoon of knitting and reading magazines and the concert on the radio, Kate excused herself. In her room, she changed quickly, shrugged on her coat, pulled on her beret, and grabbed her handbag.

Waving to the sisters on her way past the parlour, Kate opened the door at the end of the basement corridor and made her way up the steps. She paused at the top. Closing her eyes, she breathed in deeply. Fresh, crisp air filled her lungs. She smiled. The late autumn sunlight lit the world behind her eyelids. For the first time in so many months, she felt... calm.

She stepped onto the path, the gravel crunching beneath her shoes. If somebody had told her last Sunday that she would have a job and somewhere to stay in less than a week, she would have called them mad. She smiled again. The only outstanding business was moving the last items from her parents' house to their neighbours before the new people moved in next weekend. Kate's smile slipped. The curtains and odd sticks of furniture to be left had no meaning. Not like the kitchen table. She had known it all her life. It was the table she had played beneath as a small child, learned to bake on, sat at to do her homework and to read the newspapers with her father. If she could take just one item, it would be that table. But the new people had already paid Mother for it to stay in the house.

Breathing in deeply again, Kate followed the path around to the front of the house. It was far too nice a day to spend what was left of it in the basement. Picking up her pace, she headed down the drive briefly before leaving the path and heading into the woodland. It was already quite dark amongst the trees, but it wouldn't take long to get to where she had decided to go.

Twigs crunched beneath her shoes and Kate breathed in the fusty scent of damp earth. Above her the leaves were turning from their summer green to autumn shades of orange and yellow. After a short while, she found the little gate and squeezed between the collapsing wood and the wall and eased past the holly bush.

A different feeling rose in her chest when she knelt before her father's grave than she had experienced before. 'Hello, Dad,' she said. The sadness was there. It always would be. But she could hear a lighter tone in her voice. It was the first time she had visited his grave with good news to tell. She rearranged the flowers and told him about her new job and what she had learned of the Mandevilles that morning and how good and kind they were.

When she stood, Kate brushed the dry mud from her knees. 'I'm sorry it's a short visit but it'll be dark soon. I'll come back as soon as I can.' She kissed her palm and placed it on the wooden cross. 'I miss you, Dad,' she said. The light tone had left her voice. And she felt like she always did when she had to leave her father alone. She closed her eyes and pressed her hand to the cross for a moment longer.

With the light failing, Kate made her way through the woods as quickly as she could. She had a much better idea where she was going now and was relieved to see two familiar trees ahead. She stopped at the yews and looked up into the branches, trying to work out where each branch began and ended to form the cage-type shape.

'You seem determined to spend a night lost in these woods,'

a voice said. The voice was now familiar and Kate couldn't help smiling.

She wanted to make a quip about knights in shining armour, but instead said, 'I'd rather not make a habit of it.'

Turning around, she found Bertie standing just behind her. 'What brings you here again?' he asked.

'I just wanted a bit of air,' Kate said.

'I can't blame you after being cooped up in the kitchen all day?' Bertie said. He rocked back on his heels and looked up through the branches. 'If it was earlier, I could give you a tour around the grounds, but it will be getting dark soon. We could take a turn around the walled garden, if you'd like to. It doesn't look its best this time of year but it's still very pleasant.'

'I'd like that,' Kate said. 'If it's not too much trouble.'

'No trouble at all,' Bertie said. He nodded to a gap in the trees. 'This way.'

Kate walked beside Bertie. He held back a branch for her to pass and she thanked him.

'This is my favourite time of day to be in the woods,' he said quietly. 'It's so peaceful.'

'Except when strange women wander around looking for the way out,' Kate said.

She felt Bertie look down at her. He laughed. 'Indeed. Except for then.'

They were soon out on the path and Bertie led the way along the wall to an open gate. Kate stepped through and her breath caught in her throat. With its rows of carefully secured canes and earth dug over in preparation for planting in the spring, it looked just like the garden at the cottage, but on a far larger scale. The greenhouses and potting sheds had red brick bases and ran the entire length of the wall at the far end of the garden. Her father would have loved this. To have such a garden would have been his idea of heaven.

'Katherine... Katherine...'

Kate heard her name. It took a moment to rouse herself. 'Sorry,' she said.

'Here.' She felt Bertie take hold of her elbow and guide her to a bench. He sat beside her.

Kate stared at the grass before her feet. It felt wrong to keep so much from Bertie. 'I'm afraid I haven't been entirely truthful with you,' she said.

'Oh?' Bertie said.

Kate took a deep breath. 'I did lose my job in Sheffield, that's true. But the house... my parents' house... there's nobody there. My mother moved to live with my brother. The day you found me in the wood. Because... because...'

'Please,' Bertie said. 'Don't go on if whatever you have to say is too painful.'

Kate shook her head. Still looking at her feet, she said, 'I have to. It doesn't feel right that I haven't told you everything.' She breathed in deeply again. 'My father died. In the summer. He had been ill for quite a while but had kept it from us all. I was so determined not to lose my job in Sheffield that I didn't come to visit him when he took ill for the last time. I always tried to please him, and I knew how proud he was of me getting on so well at the steelworks. He said he would get better... I lost my job and my father on the same day. Without having the chance to say goodbye. Or to thank him for everything he did for me. Now my mother has had to sell their home because she can't afford to keep it on. And my father is buried at St Mary's.'

Bertie had stayed quiet throughout her admission. And he stayed quiet for just a while longer. He removed his cap and placed it on the bench beside him.

'Katherine,' he said. 'I am so very sorry. I had no idea.'

'Why would you?' she said. 'When you came to the house, I was careful that you didn't see inside. I was embarrassed.'

'Please,' Bertie said softly. 'Don't ever feel embarrassed with me. I know that everyone has a bit of a laugh behind my back because I seem so formal. And proper. But really, I am not as sure of myself as I might appear. And not nearly as proper. It's a bit of a show. And...' He paused. 'And I know a little of what you are experiencing. Captain Mandeville wasn't the only man from this house that was lost in the war.'

Finally, Kate found the courage to look at him.

'I was seven years old,' Bertie said. 'It was almost twenty years ago now, but I remember the moment my mother told me my father had been killed as if it was yesterday.' He stared ahead, as though parting the veil of time to peer through. Kate wanted to reach and take his hand. But she couldn't. He was her employer, of sorts.

'It's my turn to say sorry,' she said. 'I'm sorry that you lost your father when you were so young. I'm lucky that my father came home from the war and that I had him for so much of my life.'

'I'm very glad you did,' Bertie said. 'And I was fortunate, too. The Mandevilles took me under their wing. They paid for my education and Mr Mandeville has been like a father to me. I've known Doctor Kenmore for most of my life, too, and he has been a sort of tutor in how to be a good man. They are all so kind, but...'

'But they are not your father,' Kate said.

Bertie shook his head.

'Doctor Kenmore seems like a very good man,' she said.

'He is,' Bertie said. 'He came here to convalesce when Hill House was a hospital. That's how he met Charlotte – Mrs Kenmore now. He made a point of teaching me how to play chess.' Bertie smiled. 'Doctor and Mrs Kenmore are the most marvellous couple. They always try to do good. My hope is that one day I will be fortunate to find my match as they have.'

'I'm sure you will,' Kate said. Bertie smiled at her and something inside Kate hoped that he was pleased with how she smiled back at him.

She looked out over the garden. 'My father would have loved it here,' she said. 'He had an allotment when I was young and in recent years was never happier than when he was in his garden at the cottage. He was so proud of what he was able to achieve.'

'I'd like to hear more about your father,' Bertie said. 'If you'd like to talk of him, that is. He was clearly a good man to have raised such a hardworking and diligent daughter.'

'Thank you,' Kate said.

Bertie looked up to the darkening sky. 'Perhaps I should see you back to the house,' he said. 'I might stay for a cup of tea, if that wouldn't be too much trouble.'

'It would be no trouble,' Kate said. 'No trouble at all.'

NINE

In the kitchen, Kate put the kettle on to boil. Bertie took four cups and saucers down from the dresser. He placed two on the table and two on a tray since Audrey and Rosemary had said they would have their tea in the parlour as they didn't want to miss the concert. He took the milk jug from the refrigerator and poured a little into each cup.

When the tea was ready, Bertie left with two cups on the tray for the sisters. Kate watched him go, carrying the tray with great care. She heard him deliver the tea and Rosemary tease him about something. His voice rumbled in reply although she couldn't hear what he said. Whatever it was, it would be kind and gentle. She smiled. Taking the biscuit barrel down from the shelf, she clutched it to her stomach.

Kate was mulling over whether they might invite Bertie to stay for his supper – it was just some bread and cheese with pork pie, which they planned to have in the parlour – when a light shone up at ground level. She craned to see through the top of the window. The lights grew closer, accompanied by the sound of an engine and tyres in the gravel. Kate placed the biscuit barrel on the table. Out in the hall, she met Bertie, Audrey and Rosemary, who had heard the car approaching, too.

Bertie turned to Audrey. 'We're not expecting anyone, are we?'

Audrey shook her head.

Kate joined the sisters at the parlour door.

'Who do you think it is?' Rosemary asked, straining to see to the top of the steps when Bertie opened the door and made his way up.

'How should I know?' Audrey said with a tut in her voice.

Soon a pair of shoes appeared, descending the stairs. Then came a second pair and a third. Bertie was the first through the door, followed by two men Kate didn't recognise: a young man and a much older man.

'Tommy,' Audrey said. 'What on Earth are you doing here?'

The young man made to speak, but he looked so weak that it seemed he might fall over. He stumbled. Bertie and the older man moved to support him. They helped him into the parlour and settled him in a chair beside the fire. Kate stood in the doorway and watched. This young man with auburn hair, oiled back, was Mr and Mrs Mandeville's oldest son, who should by rights be at university. He was so very pale, his eyes hollow, his cheeks gaunt as though he had not eaten in days. He had clearly not shaved in days either as auburn stubble darkened his chin and cheeks. He looked like he might be handsome in more normal circumstances.

'I'm so sorry,' he said. He sat back, the side of his face pressed into the chair. Audrey took a blanket from the back of the other chair and placed it around him.

'You're shivering,' she said. She pressed her hand to his forehead before looking over her shoulder. 'What's happened to him?' she said to Bertie and the other man. Bertie nodded for Audrey to follow them back out into the corridor.

'Rosie,' she said to her sister. 'Get some more coals on that fire and stay with Tommy. I'll make some beef tea for him.'

Kate followed Audrey, Bertie and the older man into the kitchen. Audrey made directly for the sink. 'What has happened to him?' she asked as she filled the kettle.

'He telephoned,' the older man said. Kate recognised his broad accent instantly. It was a Sheffield accent. 'I was bringing in the coal,' he continued, 'and heard it ring in Mr Mandeville's office. Good job I did. Master Thomas telephoned from the stationmaster's office. He'd come back on the train and wanted collecting.'

This must be Elliot, the groom and chauffeur who carried the coal around the house in the dead of night, Kate thought. She looked at him, and at the lines life had etched into his slim face. He was much older than Bertie. Possibly in his sixties. Possibly older. It was difficult to tell. But from the way he had supported Tommy when he was about to collapse, he was clearly incredibly fit and appeared to possess the strength of a much younger man. He also had the bearing of a man half his age. He stood straight, with his shoulders back.

Audrey placed the kettle on the range.

'Did he say why he had come back?' Bertie asked.

'No,' Elliot said. 'I helped him into the car. At first, he was talking. He wasn't making much sense, mind. And the closer we got to Hill House, the worse he got. Like he had taken a turn. By the time we got here he was as you see him.'

'You don't think it's influenza, do you?' Bertie asked.

'No,' Audrey said. She took a pot from the refrigerator and spooned a mound of thick brown jelly into a cup. 'He's got no temperature. If anything, he was cold.' The kettle came to the boil and Audrey poured steaming water onto the jelly, filling the kitchen with the smell of beef. She gave it a good stir. 'I can't see why he's shivering if he has no fever.' She picked up the cup and saucer. 'Let's take this to him and see what we can find out.'

Kate followed the others back through to the parlour. The fire blazed in the hearth and Rosemary crouched before Tommy, holding his hands. She got up so that Audrey could take her place. 'There now, Tommy,' Audrey said. 'Whatever has happened to you?'

Still with his eyes closed, Tommy shook his head slightly. 'I just started to feel ill,' he said.

'How long have you been feeling poorly?' Audrey tried again.

Tommy swallowed. 'A few days,' he said quietly, still without opening his eyes. Audrey placed the cup and saucer on the small table. She looked up. 'Bertie, I think we should telephone for his mother to come home. Rosemary and I can stay with Tommy, and I'll get him to take something of the beef tea when it's cooled.'

Bertie nodded. 'Elliot,' he said. 'Could you set off now for the dower house? I'll go to the office and telephone so they know to expect you.'

Without a word, Elliot set off at pace along the corridor, up the steps and through the door to the outside. Bertie disappeared in the other direction, heading for the steps up to the staff passageway.

Kate stood and watched the sisters taking care of Tommy. They knelt before him, Rosemary holding his hand and patting it reassuringly, Audrey blowing across the cup to cool the beef tea. 'There now, Tommy,' Rosemary cooed. 'You'll be right as ninepence in no time. And your mother will be here soon.'

Tommy groaned and Rosemary turned to her sister, her face full of concern. Audrey smiled at Rosemary, clearly trying to reassure her. She held the tea to Tommy's mouth and a dribble of the liquid sat on his lips.

Kate could hardly take her eyes from Tommy. There was something so familiar in his face. She felt as though she knew him somehow. Yet she had never met him. She wanted to rush to him and wipe the liquid from his lips and take care of him. He seemed so vulnerable.

Unnerved by her feelings, she turned away. 'I'll lay out the supper on the kitchen table,' she said. 'In case anyone is hungry.'

Audrey looked up at her. She smiled at Kate in the same way she had smiled at her little sister. 'That's a grand idea,' she said.

In the kitchen, Kate filled the kettle at the sink. She looked up out of the window. It was after five o'clock and the world outside was dark. In her mind, Kate pictured the gaunt and sallow face of that poor young man. Perhaps she felt as though she knew him as he reminded her of other members of his family. How he had managed to make his way all the way from Cambridge in such a state was a miracle. It was fortunate for Tommy that he had arrived when he had, and that Elliot had been able to collect him from the railway station and bring him home.

Kate placed the kettle on the range and set about laying tea out on the table. There was no telling how many of the family might come back together and they might not have had time to enjoy their evening meal, so Kate took down a dozen cups and saucers from the dresser. She cut the large pork pie into slices and placed two loaves of bread on boards. She took the biscuit barrel and tin of scones down from the shelf. From the refrigerator, she retrieved butter and cheese and a jug of milk. It didn't seem enough somehow, so she set a pot of water onto the range and added half a dozen eggs to boil. She stood back and looked at the hastily prepared meal. If more was needed, there were two tins of ham in the pantry that could be opened. And there were plenty of apples in the cold store. Covering the food with clean tea towels from the drawer, she glanced towards the door, wondering what to do next. The decision was taken away from her by the sound of voices and footsteps hurrying along the basement corridor. She recognised Mrs Mandeville, Doctor Kenmore and Mrs Kenmore as they rushed past. The sound of many voices came from the parlour and, within a few minutes, Audrey and Rosemary returned to the kitchen.

'How is he?' Kate said quietly.

Audrey looked over her shoulder. 'The same. But Doctor Kenmore is seeing to him now. Mrs Kenmore used to be a nurse so Tommy couldn't be in better hands. As soon as the telephone call was made, one of the Caxton Hall chauffeurs drove them over. The rest of the family will come back with Elliot.'

'At least he has his mother with him,' Rosemary said. 'What a relief that must be.'

Kate watched Audrey take her sister's hand and pat it again.

'Can I get you both a cup of tea?' Kate asked.

'That's very kind, thank you,' Audrey said.

The sisters sat at the table, Audrey reassuring Rosemary. Kate was glad to be busy making the tea. All she could think was that Audrey and Rosemary had never had a mother. Never had the love of a parent.

'How is he?' a man's voice asked. Kate recognised it instantly. She poured water into the teapot and, in the reflection of the kettle, saw Bertie.

'I couldn't really tell,' Audrey said. 'I've not seen anything like it before. He has no fever but behaves as though he has.'

'Tommy will be all right, won't he, Bertie?' Rosemary said.

'Doctor Kenmore will know what to do for the best,' Bertie said.

Another person joined Bertie in the doorway. 'I could do with a hand, Bertie,' Doctor Kenmore said, and Bertie followed him to the parlour.

Kate joined Audrey and Rosemary in staring at the open door. Soon, the sound of footsteps came again, slower this time.

Heavier. Doctor Kenmore and Bertie passed slowly, one on either side of Tommy. His arms were about each of their necks. Both men supported one of Tommy's legs and his head rested on Bertie's shoulder. They were closely followed by Mrs Mandeville and Mrs Kenmore, each with a look of worry etched into their faces.

Kate and the sisters stared after them. The basement corridor was silent once more.

'Oh, Aud,' Rosemary said. She sobbed and her sister patted her back.

'There now,' Audrey said. 'Tommy will be fine. You just see.' But to Kate, Audrey looked just as unsure as her sister. 'We've known him since he was a little boy,' Audrey said to Kate. 'That's why Rosie is taking on so. But Master Tommy is strong. Always has been. He was a robust little chap. Do you remember when he had measles and we helped look after him?' she said to her sister. Rosemary nodded, staring at the table. 'He was up and about before anyone said he would be. Running rings around us all and escaping to his dens down in the woods.'

Rosemary smiled sadly but her bottom lip began to tremble. 'I couldn't bear to lose him, Aud,' Rosemary said, a tear slipping down her cheek.

'There now, Rosie, it won't come to that.' Audrey looked at Kate again. 'They've always been very good friends. Tommy is a bit like a little brother to her. Although we would never say as much to the family. That would be presuming too much familiarity.'

'I understand,' Kate said and hoped that her smile was reassuring. 'When you share a house, it's only natural to begin to feel fond of the people you live with. We are all human. And Rosemary,' she said, 'I'm sure Audrey is right. I'm sure Tommy will feel better soon. Home is the best place to be when you don't feel quite yourself.'

With her free hand, Audrey pushed her spectacles up the bridge of her nose and mouthed a 'Thank you' to Kate.

Together they sat quietly until footsteps sounded in the corridor and Bertie appeared in the door.

'How is he?' Rosemary asked before anyone else had the chance to speak.

'He's sleeping,' Bertie said. 'Doctor Kenmore can't find anything too wrong with him. He thinks he might be exhausted from his first few weeks at university. It can happen apparently. Mrs Mandeville and Mrs Kenmore are in his room with him. He really is being very well looked after.'

The news seemed to rouse Audrey. She stood up and smoothed down her apron. 'Are the rest of the family home?' she asked.

'Just arrived,' Bertie said. 'And I think they might be a little hungry. They came straightaway so missed their dinner.'

'Right,' Audrey said. 'Katherine has done a fine job of preparing a supper. Do you think that will do for the family?'

'I think they would be very grateful,' Bertie said.

Audrey began to load the food onto the trolley. 'Katherine,' she said. 'Would you mind helping me? I'll take it up. I think our Rosie is a bit distracted. Rosie, you keep yourself busy. Make a fresh beef tea for Tommy and prepare a tray for Mrs Mandeville and Mrs Kenmore.'

'Can I be of any use?' Bertie asked.

'Tea,' Audrey said. 'Make lots of tea. And a jug of milk for the children.'

Bertie took off his jacket and hung it on the back of a chair. In just his shirtsleeves, he helped prepare supper for the family.

Kate followed Audrey, helping her load then unload the food from the dumb waiter and onto the trolley upstairs. The sound of voices came from the dining room, and they stopped just outside.

'Is there anything special I should do?' Kate asked.

Audrey shook her head. 'We'll just lay it out on the side-board and they'll help themselves.'

Kate smoothed down her apron.

The family seated around the table sat quietly. Even the children, who had been so lively when Kate had met them at breakfast.

'Good evening, Audrey,' Mr Mandeville said. He looked like an older version of Tommy. 'And this must be Katherine,' he added. 'It's very nice to meet you.'

'And you, Mr Mandeville,' Kate said.

'We're taking a tray up for Mrs Mandeville and Mrs Kenmore,' Audrey said.

'Thank you,' Doctor Kenmore said.

'How's Tommy?' Audrey asked.

'Sleeping,' Doctor Kenmore said. 'And thank you for rustling up this supper for us.'

Kate concentrated on taking dishes from the trolley and placing them on the sideboard. The atmosphere in the room felt heavy and she didn't want to look at any member of the family and intrude on their worry.

Down in the kitchen, Kate joined Audrey, Rosemary and Bertie in eating their supper. But she had no real appetite and touched little of the bread and cheese she put on her plate.

With supper cleared and the washing up dried and put away, Kate refused the sisters' offer to join them when they went through to the parlour. She was on her way up the corridor to head to bed when she felt a presence behind her. 'It's been quite a day, hasn't it?' Bertie said.

Kate turned to face him and tried to smile. 'It has,' she said.

'I just wanted to say ...' Bertie started and then faltered. 'What you told me in the garden. About your father. I really am very sorry.'

'Thank you,' Kate said.

'I hope what's happening with Tommy isn't reminding you somehow. You seem very sad.'

Kate wanted to say something to reassure him. But when she looked up at him, she couldn't tell an untruth. 'It has. A little.'

'Is there anything I can do to help you?'

Kate smiled again. 'You're very kind. But a good night's sleep will see me right.'

Bertie nodded. 'That sounds like a grand idea. I should be getting back to my cottage.' He seemed to falter for a moment, as though there was something else he wanted to say. 'Good night, Katherine. Hopefully I'll see you tomorrow. And please try not to worry, I'm sure Tommy will be his old self again very soon.'

Lying in bed, Kate stared into the darkness. How was it that Bertie Morrison seemed able to make her talk of things she had thought she would rather keep to herself? He was so kind, with such compassion. He had set to helping them all in the kitchen without being asked to and with no fuss or ceremony. And he had been right. Seeing Tommy so unwell had stirred feelings in her. She had never seen her father unwell. He had managed to keep it from them all. And in that final illness, it had been only Mother and Harry who had tended him. She had been spared from seeing him desperately ill. Perhaps that was why she felt such heaviness in her heart. It was the only explanation for why Tommy's illness was affecting her so. She didn't know him. Before this night, she had never met him. She hadn't said a single word to him. But in picturing his face, she knew that it wasn't a resemblance to other members of his family that made it seem as though they had a connection. It was possible that seeing everyone so concerned had brought this feeling out in her. It was one explanation. But it didn't feel like the right one.

Kate turned onto her side. She slipped her hand inside the neck of her nightdress and clutched her St Christopher. The gold was warm from her skin. Imagining Bertie and his reassuring presence made some of the anxiousness slip away. She closed her eyes and kept her hand to her St Christopher.

TEN

'I hope you don't think it would be too much of an inconvenience,' Mrs Mandeville said to Kate. They were in the kitchen clearing away breakfast while Mrs Kenmore walked the children to school.

Kate wiped her hands on her apron, her mind whirring about the request. 'You want me to make costumes?' she said. 'For the children?'

'Only if it's not too much bother,' Mrs Mandeville said, putting the butter into the refrigerator. 'I'm afraid my brother-in-law has been filling the children's heads with the Halloween celebrations he enjoyed as a boy in America. We usually bob for apples and carve a few turnips into lanterns. Elliot can be relied on to scare the children with stories of his Irish mother's experiences of All Hallows Eve. That's normally the extent of it.' She closed the refrigerator door. 'But the children saw some photographs in one of the magazines Doctor Kenmore's mother sends over from America. The children in the photographs were dressed in all manner of costumes to celebrate Halloween and they are given sweets and toffees. Now they will not stop pleading to be allowed to dress up for Halloween. Charlotte and I have said no so many times, but they have worn us down.'

Mrs Mandeville took up a loaf of bread and wrapped it in a clean tea towel. 'Since you worked at the draper's and said how much you enjoyed dressmaking, I thought I would ask. You are quite welcome to say no if it's too much. I thought for a while last night that we might have to cancel the party for the children. But since Tommy is feeling much more himself this morning, we don't have to worry about him, which is a relief. I think he wore himself out with all the excitement of university. I'm sure he will return to Cambridge in the next few days.' Mrs Mandeville smiled at Kate.

Before the sensible voice in her Kate's head had the chance to talk her out if it, she said, 'All right, I'll do my best to make costumes for the children.'

'Oh, that's fabulous,' Mrs Mandeville said. 'You are a dear. But please don't worry about making anything fit for the stage at the London Palladium. If the best we can achieve is a tabard and some kind of hat or mask for each of them, they'll be thrilled. And we've given you precious little time.'

Mrs Mandeville took a magazine from where she had placed it on the dresser and laid it out on the table. 'Sit yourself down,' she instructed. 'Let's make some plans.'

Kate sat beside Mrs Mandeville, the magazine open to reveal photographs of children at a Halloween party in Los Angeles dressed as bunny rabbits, cowboys, Pierrots, clowns and pirates. There were entertainers, too. Jugglers and a puppet show. It all seemed so glamorous. Kate could hardly imagine a party for children involving anything more than a balloon or two, a ham sandwich and a plate of fairy cakes.

They discussed the costumes that would be most suited to each of the young residents of Hill House and that would not be too taxing to make. It was decided that little Oscar should be a dog, Charlie a pirate and Louisa a clown. Mrs Mandeville was certain that although she was fifteen, Daphne would not want to be left out. So, she would be a Pierrot. They agreed that the costumes selected would be kept a surprise until the day of the party.

Mrs Mandeville handed Kate a slip of paper. It contained the measurements for each child from when their school uniforms had been fitted at the end of the summer. 'Hopefully this will give you something to be going on with,' she said. 'We can measure them properly when they get back from school. They will have only grown a little in the last few months.' She closed the magazine. 'Are you sure this isn't too much? You can tell me if it is.'

Kate thought through the requirements for each costume. She thought about the need to show willing to secure her place here. But even more than that, she thought about the utter joy of putting her dressmaking skills to use. 'Three days should be enough. It's almost a day for each costume.'

'That's wonderful.' Mrs Mandeville smiled. 'Audrey said she can excuse you some of your duties for the next couple of days. The house won't fall down because a floor isn't mopped for a day or two.'

It was arranged that Mrs Kenmore would drive Kate into town later that morning to pick up all the fabric she needed.

'Elliot can help you bring down anything you require from the lumber room,' Mrs Mandeville said. 'There's definitely a sewing machine up there. Edward thinks there might even be a trunk of costumes from when he, Tom and Charlotte were little. But they would be full of moth holes by now!'

'Thank you,' Kate said. 'And I'll do my best to do all my chores as well as make the costumes.'

Mrs Mandeville placed her hand over Kate's. 'Please, Katherine, don't worry too much. It would be good if you could make up the fires in the rooms in the mornings. But none of us will care about a bit of dust or a few footprints on the tiled floors or crumbs on the carpet. We live in a home. Not a show house.'

ELEVEN

Kate waited in the hall, clutching her handbag. She had dressed in her brown jumper and brown pleated skirt and had used the opportunity of returning to her room to collect the letter she had written to her mother. She placed it on the post tray and looked at her reflection in the mirror above the grand fireplace. She adjusted her beret and smoothed down her overcoat.

'Sorry to keep you waiting!' a voice called.

Kate looked up to see Mrs Kenmore rushing down the stairs. As always, she was just a little dishevelled, her fair hair escaping the silver clip holding it back from her face. She was the sort of woman whose constant enthusiasm made her always appear attractive, even though her overcoat was open and her slacks a little creased.

'Are we ready?' she said to Kate, beaming broadly. She tied a knitted scarf twice about her neck.

Kate nodded and followed Mrs Kenmore through the vestibule and out of the house. A small black car sat on the drive and Kate got in the passenger side. She had barely sat in the seat when Mrs Kenmore started the engine, and they roared away down the drive. They passed through the gates and out onto the road.

'So, how are you getting on, Katherine?' Mrs Kenmore asked.

'Very well, thank you,' Kate said. 'Everybody has been very kind.'

Kate noticed Mrs Kenmore frown slightly. She glanced at Kate. 'Would you mind awfully calling me Charlotte?' she said. 'Oh, I know that in the house we try to keep to Mother's preferences on formality. But I find it so unnatural. I may have married my husband and had to take his surname, but I still have my own given name. It's rather rum that we women are expected to lose some of our identity when we marry. Don't you think?'

Kate clutched her handbag a little tighter. 'I'm not sure—'

Mrs Kenmore laughed. 'Sorry,' she said. 'If my mother were here, she would scold me for my overfamiliarity making you uncomfortable. I might have reached the age of two score years, but my mother still feels the need to pull me up on my behaviour.' She raised her eyebrows. 'I know she despairs at the freedoms I give Louisa, but I'm of the opinion that a child must be able to be their own person and tread their own path in life. I am a terrible rebel, Kate. I'm afraid I am a disobedient daughter and frightfully wanton raiser of children!'

She nudged Kate as she navigated the car down the road, making Kate smile.

'So, Katherine,' Mrs Kenmore said as they passed the duck-pond in the village. 'I hear that before you came to work with us, you worked at a steelworks in Sheffield, but you lost your job.'

'That's right,' Kate said.

'What is going on in this country?' Mrs Kenmore said, a note of anger in her voice. 'It's a bloody disgrace. Good people. Hardworking people like you, unable to keep their jobs. And through no fault of their own. And when they need help they are cast aside even though they have paid their taxes. Means testing! I ask you! How can you means test a household when there is little to nothing coming in. All those people having to march on London, cap in hand, begging the government to help them. It's an utter disgrace.'

Kate looked at the side of Mrs Kenmore's face. Her words were the words that Kate's father had used when reading the newspapers. Before meeting the Mandevilles, Kate had assumed that people of their class would hardly give a thought to the plight of the ordinary workers. But Mrs Kenmore and her aunt, Mrs Hart, had been suffragettes. And Mrs Mandeville had been a housemaid, who now used her position to help those in need.

'After the war,' Mrs Kenmore said, 'I begged my father and Edward to sell land at a reasonable rate to the council so that they could build decent homes for working people to rent. Oh, I understand there was a need to make money to keep Hill House going. The repairs and the upkeep. But it feels like such a missed opportunity. The Wilkinson estate is beautiful but only people of independent means or those who can afford to pay a mortgage are able to enjoy it.'

Kate stared out through the windscreen. Had her parents been able to rent their house at a reasonable rate, then her mother would still have her home. With the pension she had from Father's company, a rent would have been affordable. It was the mortgage and the repayments that she could not afford. All those years of saving and going without had ended in shattered dreams.

Kate gripped the strap of her handbag as Mrs Kenmore took a turn just after the Post Office.

'I'm sorry,' Mrs Kenmore said. 'Have I touched a nerve?'

'Pardon?' Kate said.

Mrs Kenmore paused at a junction in two country lanes. 'I

can go on when I have the bit between my teeth. Perhaps you would rather not talk about what brought you to Hill House.'

'I agree with every word you've said, Mrs Kenmore,' Kate said, blood warming her cheeks. 'I've seen so many people lose their jobs. I'm fortunate to have found another so quickly. But there are men and women I worked with who stand to lose everything with no wages coming in. And children to feed. And bills to pay with no money. And...' She paused. 'I know something about people living on the Wilkinson estate.' She paused again. She had already told Bertie about her family's recent situation. It could do no harm to tell Mrs Kenmore.

As Mrs Kenmore drove across the junction, Kate said, 'My parents bought a house on the Wilkinson estate. One of the little cottages. It was their dream to own a home and they saved for years. But... but my father died a few months ago and since my mother can't afford to pay the mortgage on her own, she had to sell the house to go and live with my brother.'

Mrs Kenmore's hands tightened around the steering wheel. 'I am so sorry for your loss, Katherine. And this is precisely my point.' She took one of her hands from the wheel and slammed it back down. 'Why should your mother lose her home? Why is there no help for her? And if no help, then a home available for her to rent so that she does not have to leave the area and all she knows. Isn't it enough that she has lost her husband?'

As Mrs Kenmore drove along the road, houses began to take the place of trees. They were soon in a small town. 'I've often thought about standing for election for the local council,' Mrs Kenmore said. 'And Paul is in full support. But it doesn't seem enough somehow. Westminster, that's where the real decisions are made. That's where you can effect real change.' She turned to Kate and smiled conspiratorially. 'What about you?' she said. 'Would you vote for me?'

Kate didn't have to think twice. 'Of course. And all the women I know would vote for you. You speak so much sense.'

'But under what colour?' Mrs Kenmore said. 'My family has always been Tory. Would I have to cross the floor to join the Labour party to get the votes of you and your friends?'

Kate thought again. 'I hope the women I know would listen to what you have to say and what you promise to do rather than what banner you stand beneath.'

Mrs Kenmore laughed. 'You are marvellous, Katherine,' she said. 'And if I ever need a campaign manager, I shall be sure to come knocking at your door.'

The blood rose to Kate's cheeks again. But this time it was driven by a little swell of pride rather than anger. It was wonderful to talk of politics again with someone as passionate as her father.

They soon came to the small centre of the town, with shops on either side of the road. Mrs Kenmore brought the car to a stop at the kerb outside a draper's shop. 'It's not as big as the draper's in Northampton,' Mrs Kenmore said. 'But I hope it has everything you need.'

'Thank you, Mrs Kenmore. I'm sure it will do just fine.'

Mrs Kenmore placed her hand on Kate's arm. 'Charlotte,' she said. 'I insist you call me Charlotte. Especially if you are to be my campaign manager. And you must call my husband Paul. He much prefers it, too.'

TWELVE

Kate stepped through the door of the draper's and the bell rang above her head. A shop girl greeted her and helped her navigate her way through the shelves of fabric. Kate selected a soft purple satin – just right for a clown's costume – and the years slipped away. She was back in the draper's in Northampton, running her hand over silks and satins, voiles and lace, helping customers make the perfect choice for a dress or blouse or an outfit for a special occasion.

Soon there was a pile of bolts on the cutting table, which matched Kate's list for the children's costumes. The shop girl said that she would have all the fabric cut, folded and wrapped in less than an hour. Thanking her, Kate stepped back out onto the small high street.

It was a cold but bright morning. Kate tucked her scarf into her overcoat and walked along, looking into the windows of each shop, sharing the pavement with women popping into and out of the butcher's, greengrocer's, fishmonger's, bakery, the Co-op and the haberdasher's. She looked up to the clock above a jeweller's shop. Eleven o'clock. There was another half an hour until she was due to meet Mrs Kenmore back at the car. Having never been to this small town before, Kate decided to take a walk the length of the high street. As well as the shops, the town was well-served by a tea shop, two pubs, a fish and chip shop and even a small cinema – The Grand. Kate smiled as she passed. It wasn't very grand at all, not in scale at least. Carrying on, she left the shops and passed a congregational hall and more serious-looking grey stone buildings housing a bank, a solicitor's and other businesses. As the town centre began to give way to houses, Kate was about to turn back but came to a stop. There was a sign beside the door on the last official-looking building in the row.

Caslington Spiritualist Church
Services every Wednesday and Sunday at 7pm
All welcome
Enquire within.

The door stood open. Kate peered inside. An aspidistra sat on a dark wooden stand in the small lobby and a staircase led up to the first floor. She recalled the images of the clipper with the men shouting from the rigging. And all the times she had seen the history of an item simply by placing her hand on it. She faltered on the pavement. Not for the first time, she was tempted to step inside a spiritualist church. In Sheffield, she had passed one regularly on her nights out with the girls from the boarding house. They had giggled about going inside to speak to the 'other side'. She had always put them off, saying it was silliness. In truth, she was scared of what might be revealed and what the reaction of her friends would be. What if someone in the church saw something in her that showed her ability to connect with the history of an item was more than simply an elaborate dream? That it could, in fact, be the spirits of long dead people coming back to show the history of an object. It seemed ludicrous and each time she thought it, she talked herself out of that explanation and into the explanation that they were vivid dreams. But the clipper. She had no knowledge of it and according to Bertie, nobody had died on it. So why had she seen it?

'Katherine!'

Kate spun around. Mrs Kenmore was standing outside the Labour Party office on the opposite side of the road. She waved at Kate and crossed.

'Ah, the Spiritualist Church,' Mrs Kenmore said. 'Are you interested in joining their congregation?'

'No, not really,' Kate said. 'I was just looking.'

Mrs Kenmore looked up at the sign. 'Sally and Mrs Randal come here every Wednesday evening,' she said.

'Bertie's mother and grandmother?' Kate said.

Mrs Kenmore nodded. 'Ever since they lost William they have been coming. If it brings them comfort, then it does nobody any harm.'

'And does Bertie come with them?'

'Oh, no,' Mrs Kenmore said, shaking her head. 'To be honest, Bertie doesn't talk about his father, not to anybody. He was ever such a small chap when William died. He didn't speak for weeks afterwards. We had to coax him out of it so gently. It's so awful that he has nowhere to go to mourn. No grave to visit. The only thing he has left of his father is his name on the war memorial outside St Mary's.' She looked at Kate and immediately added, 'Oh, Katherine, I am so sorry. Your father...'

'It's all right,' Kate said. 'Please don't apologise, Mrs—'

Mrs Kenmore held up her hand. 'Charlotte, please, I insist.'

Kate smiled. 'Please don't apologise, Charlotte.'

. . .

Charlotte helped Kate collect the fabric and a bag of yarn from the draper's and signed the paperwork for the bill to be sent to Hill House. They loaded the neatly wrapped and tied parcels onto the back seat of the car. All the way through the town and country roads, Charlotte chatted about politics. She seemed to have a real fire in her belly about the provision of social housing. Kate was happy to listen to Charlotte talk about the Beacontree Estate somewhere just outside London. It was the largest estate of social housing, with parks and gas and electricity and gardens for every house. If Charlotte had her way, she said, she would see to it that some of the land around Hill House was developed to provide affordable housing with gardens and parks and shops and a library. Kate nodded and agreed with all that she said. It sounded like a sort of heaven on Earth. And Kate was happy for Charlotte to talk. Every so often, her thoughts drifted away to what Charlotte had said about Bertie. That he never spoke of his father to anyone. But he had spoken to her. He had shared his sadness at the loss of his father as she had shared her sadness at the loss of hers.

Charlotte pulled into the driveway and brought the car to a stop outside the front door. She helped Kate take the parcels from the backseat and they carried their unwieldy load towards the house.

'So,' Charlotte said as she used her elbow to push the door open. 'Do you think we'll ever have our very own Beacontree Estate here on Hill House land?'

Kate wiped her shoes on the doormat in the vestibule. 'I'm sure that if anyone can make it happen, it will be you. I'm sure you could do anything you put your mind to.'

Charlotte laughed and pushed the door to after them. 'Keep talking like that and you'll definitely have to take up the role of my parliamentary campaign manager!'

They had barely stepped into the hall when Mrs Mandeville appeared from the morning room. 'My goodness,' she said. 'That's a lot of parcels. How exciting. Bring them in here.'

Kate followed Charlotte into the room. Charlotte dropped her parcels onto one of the sofas and sank into the cushions beside them. 'I could do with a cup of tea,' she said. 'What say I go and make us a pot?'

'That sounds like a fabulous idea,' Mrs Mandeville said.

Charlotte kicked off her shoes. One dropped to the floor with a thud. 'Alice,' she said, 'I've asked Katherine to call me Charlotte. Can we forego formality for now? We're going to have so much to do with each other sorting all this Halloween malarkey and I really can't abide the Mrs this and Mrs that.'

Alice smiled. 'How do you feel about that, Katherine? Would you feel comfortable calling us by our first names?'

Kate placed her parcels on the chair. 'Would you be happy with that?'

'It would be a relief,' Alice said.

'Right!' Charlotte jumped to her feet and stooped to collect her shoes. 'Tea for three coming up!' She whistled as she made her way up the hall.

'Now,' Alice said to Kate, clapping her hands. 'How will this do for a workroom? You'll need a place to do your sewing and set everything up.' She tucked a strand of hair behind her ear and looked around the morning room. 'We can move those tables from the windows to here in front of the fire so that you are warm. You can use the sofas and armchairs to lay out the costumes as you are making them. There are plenty of lamps we can rearrange if you need extra light. How does that all sound?'

'Perfect,' Kate said. 'And thank you for thinking of everything.'

'My pleasure,' Alice said. 'Right, how about we move this furniture now so we can get cracking? Pop your coat on the chair.'

Kate shrugged off her coat and helped Alice begin the

process of rearranging the room. They moved the sofas and armchairs away from the fire and together carried the two tables from the windows and placed them on the rug before the fire. They were just moving a chair from the desk and rearranging some lamps when Charlotte appeared with a tray of tea things. They all sat down, and Alice poured the tea before they enthusiastically began opening the parcels.

'It's like Christmas!' Charlotte said and held up a length of red satin intended for the trousers of Louisa's clown costume.

They soon had all the parcels open. Alice and Charlotte helped Kate sort the fabrics into separate piles for each costume, which they placed neatly on available surfaces: tables, chairs, sofas. Alice smoothed down a length of satin. 'The children will be home from school at half past three. We can get their exact measurements then.'

A knock at the door made the three women look up.

'Come in!' Alice called.

The door opened and Kate had to hide a smile.

'Elliot's gone up to the attic, as you asked, Mrs Mandeville,' Bertie said.

'Fabulous,' Alice said and got to her feet. Kate stood too.

'Have a good rummage,' Alice said to Kate. 'There's definitely a sewing machine up there somewhere.'

'There are trunks and cases of all sorts of things,' Charlotte said, crossing her legs and taking a cigarette from a box on the table. 'Frocks and costume jewellery. Borrow anything you like, but you might want to be careful of the moths!' She took up a lighter and lit the tip of her cigarette.

Kate followed Bertie from the room. He closed the door behind them.

'How are you?' he asked as she walked beside him to the door at the back of the hall. 'I've been a bit worried about you after everything we spoke about last night in the garden.'

Kate looked up at him. 'I think talking to you helped,' she

said. 'I haven't spoken to anyone about what happened with my father.'

They stopped just short of the bells high up on the wall. Bertie swept his fringe away from his face and smiled. 'I'm glad that talking to me helped,' he said.

They carried on and up the steps winding to the top of the house. In the attic, they passed the bedrooms and bathroom and, for the first time, the door to the far end of the attic corridor stood open.

With sunlight coming through the windows in the slanted ceiling, the dark side of the attic seemed less foreboding. Following Bertie, Kate looked at the bare walls and floorboards without carpet or rugs. The doors to other rooms stood open but they, too, were empty of furniture and decoration. 'Why is this side not made up?' Kate asked, her voice echoing in the empty space.

'None of the rooms in the attic were usable for years,' Bertie said. He glanced upwards. 'When the roof was fixed, we had some of the rooms decorated and furnished. But since there aren't the staff to occupy all the rooms, it didn't make sense to spend money when it wasn't needed. If there are ever any more staff, we can soon have the rooms decorated and furnished. At least the ceilings are sound now.'

Kate wrapped her arms around herself. She could see her breath in the cold air.

'I'm sorry,' Bertie said. 'There's no heating on this side. Would you like to get a coat?'

Kate shook her head. 'I'm fine. Thank you.' She looked about her. 'Was the refurbishment of this attic the kind of thing you manage as the estate manager?' she asked.

'I oversee all work anywhere on the estate.' Bertie stopped at an open door. 'Here we are,' he said.

The room they entered was quite unlike the other rooms they had passed in the attic. This room was anything but empty.

Cases and trunks and valises were piled all about the room. There were rails of clothes and there was furniture. So much furniture. Tables, chairs, sideboards and wardrobes. Paintings leant against the walls and trunks. Some items were covered by sheets. The room went back a long way and seemed to bend around a corner. The windows were shuttered with the only light coming from a series of lightbulbs.

'What is this place?' Kate asked.

'The lumber room,' Bertie said. 'It's where anything old is stored.' He stepped further into the room. 'Elliot is in here somewhere.'

'Back here,' a voice came. Elliot appeared from the very back of the room. 'I found it,' he said. 'The sewing machine.' He made his way through a clear path in the cases and furniture.

'I don't think you were properly introduced last night,' Bertie said. 'Katherine, this is Elliot. Elliot, this is Katherine, the new housemaid.'

Elliot gave a brief nod. 'If you give me a hand,' he said to Bertie, 'we can get it down the stairs. It's attached to a metal base. While we're up here, we could do with looking for that old nightstand Mrs Kenmore was wanting. It was back there somewhere last I saw it.' Without another word, he turned and made his way towards the back of the room again.

'If you find anything you want,' Bertie said to Kate. 'Just leave it outside the door and Elliot and I can take it down to the morning room later.'

Bertie began to pick his way along the path to the back of the room and Kate set about searching for anything useful. Lifting sheets, she coughed as she released a shower of dust. Rails contained uniforms of blue and gold and fine dress suits, all in adult sizes so of no use for the children's costumes. They were so beautifully tailored that it would be criminal to cut any up just to dress the children for a party. There came the sound of furniture moving. Kate glanced up. Bertie and Elliot had disappeared in the bend at the very back of the room. She carried on rummaging through cases and trunks, which contained even more adult clothes and scarves and hats as well as blankets and eiderdowns. In the drawer of a dresser, she found a box of costume jewellery and in another, a photograph album made of the softest red leather. She paused, stood back and looked around. Alice might be convinced there was a trunk of old children's dressing-up clothes somewhere but finding it would be like finding the pea hidden beneath the princess's stack of mattresses. With the sound of movement and scraping still coming from the back of the room, Kate eased through the cases to a particularly large object covered with a sheet. She took hold of the corner and pulled it free. As she gathered up the sheet and placed it on a chest of drawers, she looked at what had been beneath: a beautiful rocking horse. It stood before a full-length mirror with a trunk beside it. Not a grown-up trunk in brown or black, but a jolly blue trunk with a domed top that looked like a treasure chest in a fairy tale. Kate ran her hand down the horse's woollen mane and touched its slightly flared nostrils. It was the kind of toy any child would be thrilled to find beside the tree on Christmas morning. She touched the leather of the reins and saw a name on the bridle across its nose.

'Pegasus,' she said quietly. 'Hello, Pegasus.'

Kate looked down at the horse's white flanks and saw that wings had been painted on either side. She caught sight of her reflection in the mirror with the horse beside her. For the first time at Hill House, she saw a full version of herself. Not as a maid but in her brown jumper and skirt. She fingered the pleats she had worked on so diligently to make sure each was precisely the same width. Had she not worked at the draper's and developed her skills at dressmaking, Alice would not have given her the opportunity to make costumes for the children. And as grateful as she was for the job as a housemaid, it was thrilling to be called on to put her dressmaking skills to use. Crouching before the trunk, Kate flipped the silver clasps, and pushed the lid open so that it rested against Pegasus' wooden rockers. She was instantly met with a riot of colour from within. She had found it! Alice's trunk of children's dressing up clothes. There was a musty smell too, as though the trunk had been closed for many years. An airing and a quick wash in a bathtub of warm water and carbolic soap would set that right. Kate pulled out the first item, a little pink ballerina's dress. It was far too small for any of the children. Then came a little black and white suit that looked like it was to dress as a cat. Further down she went and found little waistcoats and neck scarves, skirts and blouses. It soon became clear that everything in the trunk was far too small to be of any use. And just like the adult clothes, they were beautifully tailored and far too fine to cut up to use in the costumes she was making. Removing the final item of clothing – a hooped petticoat – Kate found all manner of small toy knives and swords in the bottom of the trunk. One looked particularly promising and might just do to complete the pirate costume. Kate took hold of the handle. Immediately, there was a flash of light in the mirror. Kate looked up. She was no longer alone. A small boy charged at the mirror. The cutlass in her hand was somehow now in his hand. He wore an eye patch and had a black hat decorated with a skull and crossbones. He brandished the cutlass and posed before the mirror, his little chest puffed out, clearly proud of his reflection. He spun around and raised the cutlass. As he made to bring it down on Pegasus' head, the boy disappeared.

The cutlass fell from Kate's grasp. She scrabbled to her feet. She had not touched Pegasus, yet the horse was rocking wildly. She stumbled back from the mirror. Hers was the only reflection. There was no small, proud boy.

A commotion came from the back of the room. Bertie and Elliot appeared carrying the sewing machine between them. They stopped beside Kate.

'Ah, you've found Pegasus,' Bertie said, a broad grin on his face. 'I haven't seen him in years. He belonged to Mr Mandeville's aunt, Mrs Hart. I'll ask Mrs Mandeville if she'd like us to bring him down, too. Oscar might enjoy him in the nursery.'

Kate didn't reply. All she could do was stare at Bertie. She felt another pair of eyes looking at her. Elliot's eyes were fixed on her as though he was asking a question. He held her gaze for just a moment, his head slightly cocked to one side.

'C'mon,' he said before Bertie had the chance to speak again. Elliot nudged the sewing machine stand at Bertie so that he had to move towards the door. 'I've work to be getting on with. I can't wait around here all day.'

Kate watched them manoeuvre their heavy burden through the door. She glanced at the trunk and at the dressing up clothes scattered about the rocking horse. She should really put everything back as she had found it, but one look at the cutlass lying on the dusty floorboards before the mirror made her race from the lumber room, closing the door securely behind her.

Bertie and Elliot were soon at the head of the twisting staircase, preoccupied with navigating their way down. Kate used the distraction to dip into her bedroom.

Wrapping one arm around her waist, she covered her face with her other hand and closed her eyes. What was happening to her? These visions were coming at a rate she had never experienced before. Was her mind troubled by the change in her living arrangements and her new job? It would be easy to convince herself that an unease at her altered circumstances lay behind all that was happening. But she knew that wasn't true.

In her mind's eye, she pictured the face of the child in the mirror. Immediately, she opened her eyes and grasped the bedstead for support. The image was too awful. Because the look on that child's face had not been normal. She knew well enough what a child should look like. With her niece and nephew, she was experienced in the emotions and reactions of a child, whether it was happy or tired or needed its mother to console it when it fell and knocked its knee. But that boy... She shook her head. She didn't want to see his face again. But even with her eyes open, it would not leave her. The way he had planned to bring the cutlass down on poor Pegasus showed that he wanted to do that plaything real harm. But most unsettling of all was how he had looked at her. Because he had looked at her. As he held the cutlass aloft, he had sneered. And he had stared at her. As though daring her to watch him and witness what he was about to do. He had looked... evil. And he had felt so real that Kate was sure that had she looked around she would have seen his physical form standing in the lumber room, glaring at the mirror.

Kate stumbled to the window. She lifted the sash and leant out, breathing in the cold air.

THIRTEEN

'There you are,' Alice said when Kate entered the morning room.

'I'm sorry,' Kate said. 'I hope I haven't kept you waiting.'

'Not at all,' Alice said. 'Charlotte has gone to visit her mother and aunt. She'll collect the children from school later.' She paused and turned around, her palm upturned as though presenting the room. 'How did we do? Bertie and Elliot set up the sewing machine before the fire. Elliot gave it a bit of a clean and oiled the mechanisms. I've laid out the fabrics on the table.'

Kate took in all the details. 'It's perfect,' she said. 'I can start the rough cut of the fabric into manageable sizes before I have the measurements, if you're happy for me to do that.'

'That's wonderful,' Alice said. 'I'll be down in the kitchen if you need me. Audrey and I will be working on the grocery list.' Opening the door to leave, Alice paused. 'And thank you, Katherine,' she said. 'We are all so grateful that you've agreed to do this. It really is going above and beyond.'

Alone in the room, Kate pulled out the chair and sat at the sewing machine. Everything had been arranged so well for her. There was a basket of spools of thread, a case of needles, a pin cushion, tailor's chalk, a tape measure, and a pair of scissors. On the tables around her were the neat piles of fabric for each costume. Before her was the sewing machine on its stand. It was dark and decorated with a pattern of flowers. Everything was to hand, and she had everything she needed.

Kate took the edge of the red satin and rubbed the soft fabric between her fingers. The sewing machine sat there. Waiting. What if she touched it only to be presented with another image? What if she saw something as troubling as the look on that small boy's face when he brandished the cutlass?

Kate let the satin fall from her fingers. She took up a spool of thread from the basket and ran it around in her palm. She reached her hand out to touch the machine but pulled it away again. She closed her eyes and took a deep breath. She reached again...

'Would you look at it in here!'

Kate's heart slammed into her ribs. She dropped the spool of thread. The door to the morning room that had been opened a crack was now pushed wide.

'Mrs Mandeville asked me to bring you this,' Rosemary said, entering and placing a tray of jangling tea things on the low table before the sofas. She made immediately to the machine and looked over it with something that looked like wonder.

'You're a dark horse, Katherine,' she said, nudging Kate's shoulder. 'You're a dressmaker, so we're told.'

'I... I wouldn't exactly say that,' Kate said. 'It's more of a hobby.'

Rosemary took hold of the handle of the machine and turned it. Kate winced. But Rosemary clearly saw nothing apart from the handle moving the mechanism up and down. No ships in a storm. No child charging at a rocking horse.

'Will you show me how to use it?' Rosemary asked. 'Once you're done making the outfits for the children?'

'I suppose I could,' Kate said. 'If Mrs Mandeville says it's all right.'

Rosemary let go of the handle. She nodded to the tray. 'There's a bit of bread and cheese for your lunch, as well as the tea.'

'I'm sorry,' Kate said awkwardly. 'That you've had the trouble of running around after me. I should be helping you and Audrey, not adding to what you have to do. Is Audrey terribly cross that I'm not doing what I should?'

Rosemary shrugged. 'Not really. You'd know if she was. Anyway,' she said, picking up a spool of thread. 'Mrs Mandeville says we've no need to do your chores while you're doing your sewing. So don't worry, the dust and filth will be waiting for you!' Rosemary dropped the spool back into the basket. She looked over the fabric. 'Perhaps me and Aud can get a new frock out of this, too.' She winked at Kate.

'Maybe you will.' Kate smiled.

'I'd best be getting on,' Rosemary said. Before she closed the door behind her, Kate reached and placed her hand on the sewing machine, wanting the reassurance of another person's company. The metal was warm from the heat of the fire. That was it. No images unfolded in Kate's mind.

As Rosemary closed the door, Kate sighed. She turned the handle of the machine, placed her foot on the treadle and worked it up and down. She touched the spools of thread, the pins and the needles. When nothing untoward happened, she sighed again. There was too much work to be done to sit idle any longer.

Kate set about spreading out the lengths of fabric on the table and cutting them into manageable sizes. When she had all the fabric prepared, she poured a cup of tea and ate a slice of the bread and cheese. If Alice agreed, she would ask for the sewing machine to be taken down to their parlour when the costumes were finished so she could show the sisters how to use it. She had just taken a final mouthful of tea when there was a knock on the door. It opened slowly.

'Mind if I come in?' Bertie said, holding the door as though unsure of whether he should enter.

'Not at all.' Kate smiled and placed her cup back in its saucer.

Bertie looked around the room. 'You've been busy,' he said.

'I'm just about ready to start cutting properly and sewing once I have the children's measurements.'

'Ah, yes,' Bertie said. He forced his hands into his trouser pockets and rocked back on his heels. It seemed to Kate as though he wanted to say more, but something was stopping him.

'Did you want me for any particular reason?' she asked.

Bertie took his hands from his pockets. He drummed the fingertips of his right hand on a table. 'In the evening,' he said. 'In the evening, do you have to stop sewing? Because of the light?'

'Was there something else you want me to do this evening?'

'No... no, not at all.' He drummed his fingertips again. 'I wondered... It's your day off tomorrow, isn't it?'

Kate thought back to the arrangements she had made with Alice. 'Yes, it is, I think.'

'And do you have plans?' Bertie asked.

'Not particularly,' Kate said. 'But I'll probably spend the best part of the day in here making the costumes.'

'I don't think you'd be expected to forego your day off,' he said.

'I know,' Kate said. 'But I would rather work on the costumes. There's not much time to finish them and I actually enjoy sewing. I haven't made anything in quite a while.'

Bertie chewed his bottom lip and nodded. He seemed to be looking anywhere but at her. 'But you won't be sewing all day. Not in the evening, at least. Because of the light?'

'I shouldn't imagine so,' Kate said.

Bertie nodded again. He swept his fringe away from his face. 'It's just... there's a new picture on at The Grand in Caslington. I wondered... you said you liked going to the pictures. Would you like to... tomorrow evening... no, probably not.' His cheeks flushed to a deep pink.

A little thrill rose in Kate's chest. 'Are you asking me to go to the pictures with you?'

Finally, Bertie looked at her from beneath his fringe. 'I am,' he said. 'If you would like to. But please don't feel compelled.'

Kate could feel the broad grin on her face. 'I don't feel compelled,' she said. 'I would love to go to the pictures with you.'

Her smile was matched by Bertie's. 'That's wonderful,' he said. 'Really wonderful.' He swept his fringe back from his face and couldn't seem to stop smiling. 'Would half past six suit you? The picture starts at seven.'

'Perfect,' Kate said.

Kate was still smiling when a commotion in the hallway signalled the return of Charlotte and the children. Taking the tape measure and a pad and pencil, she joined Alice and Charlotte in the dining room to measure the children. There was much excitement about what each costume would be.

'Oh, please tell us, do, Mama,' Daphne said as she held out her arms for Kate to measure while Charlie and Oscar pursued each other around the dining table and Louisa tried to coax her pet cat from beneath the sideboard with a piece of one of the salmon paste sandwiches that Rosemary had brought up for them to have as tea, along with a seed cake.

'I could tell you,' Alice said. 'But it wouldn't be a surprise then, would it? But if you want to know...'

'No!' Daphne laughed. 'I want the surprise!'

Kate enjoyed the laughter and merriment. And she had a

good reason to be happy. A trip to the pictures was a treat she had missed.

After measuring all the children, Kate was invited to join them for tea. She sat between Daphne and Louisa. The cousins involved her in their conversation about their day at school and the plans for the Halloween party. Alice spent a great deal of her time attempting to keep Oscar from spilling food down himself and on the table and Charlotte helped Charlie in the construction of a tower made from napkins.

The children were mid conversation about the board game they should play that afternoon when Alice suddenly go to her feet. 'Sweetheart!' she said. 'Should you be out of bed?'

Kate had her back to the door and turned to see Tommy standing in the doorway. He was wearing blue striped pyjamas with a robe over them.

'I felt a bit better,' he said. 'I knew you would be having tea at this time and wanted to join you.'

Alice rushed to her son and placed the back of her hand to his forehead. 'You still have no temperature. And you have more colour in your face.' She took hold of his hands. 'And you've stopped shaking.'

'I feel better than I have in days,' he said.

Charlotte joined Alice. She took her nephew's hand in hers and pressed two fingers to his wrist. She made him look into her eyes.

'A huge improvement,' Charlotte said. 'Like Paul said, it was likely exhaustion brought about by the excitement of starting university. It's a big change in your life.'

'Uncle Paul said I should get out of bed when I felt ready,' Tommy said. 'Would you mind if I join you for tea? I'm a bit bored of looking at the walls in my room.'

'Of course!' Alice said. She seated her son between herself and Daphne. She poured him a cup of tea and placed a plate of sandwiches and cake before him.

Kate looked along the table at Tommy. His face wasn't ashen as it had been when he collapsed into the chair in the parlour. It was almost as ruddy as his younger siblings and cousin. He was able to support his own body weight without help from anyone else and to speak lucidly rather than whisper words on a shallow breath. The only clue that he had been at all unwell was the fact that he was dressed in pyjamas and his dark red hair was flat at the back from resting against pillows.

'Tommy,' Alice said. 'You haven't been properly introduced to Katherine. Katherine is working for us now and has agreed to make costumes for the children for the Halloween party.'

Tommy looked past his sister. 'It's a pleasure to meet you properly, Katherine,' he said. 'I have a vague recollection of meeting you last night. But I'm afraid I wasn't looking my best.' He smiled and the children laughed.

'It's a pleasure to meet you, too,' Kate said. This young man had certainly inherited his mother's warmth, as well as her looks. There was still something so familiar about him that she couldn't place.

Alice pushed the plate further towards her son. 'Eat up,' she said. 'I won't send you back to Cambridge until I know you have built up your strength.'

Tommy took a sandwich from the plate and ate it in just a couple of bites. 'I was thinking,' he said. 'I'll probably go back after the party. It's only a couple of days and I wouldn't want to miss all the fun.'

'That sounds like a stellar idea,' Charlotte said. 'Bobbing for apples just wouldn't be the same without you!'

'No,' Charlie said. 'Because he is rubbish at it.'

'Hey now, that's unfair,' Tommy said. 'It's only because you cheat!' He laughed and tucked into another sandwich.

FOURTEEN

Following Tommy's arrival, Kate excused herself to return to the morning room. She found all she needed to operate the sewing machine in a small wooden drawer in the stand. She wasted no time in preparing bobbins for the threads she planned to use. Taking a needle from a paper sleeve, she placed it into the mechanism of the machine. She took up a small offcut of material and ran it through the machine. It all worked perfectly. She set to cutting out the pieces of each costume. She had no patterns to use so would have to judge each piece by eye. As agreed with Alice, each costume would be simple with ties, tabs and drawstrings rather than buttons and hooks.

Kate spread a length of the red satin on one of the tables and purple satin on another. With tailor's chalk, she marked out the design for the trousers and smock of the clown costume. The scissors made a reassuring clunk as she moved the flat edge across the tabletop while the fabric slipped easily through the cutting edges.

Preparation for the first costume complete, Kate collected a bag of yarn and headed down the back steps.

· · ·

'Can I help?' Kate asked, placing the bag of yarn on a chair, and pointing to the pans on the stove, steam rattling their lids.

Audrey looked her up and down. 'You're not dressed for kitchen work.' She took up a board of peelings and tipped them into a bowl by the sink. They would be transferred to the pig bin out by the door later.

'I wanted to thank you,' Kate said, handing another board of peelings to Audrey. 'For saying that you could spare me to make the costumes for the children.'

Audrey scraped the peelings into the bowl. 'It's best we direct our labour where it's needed most.' She pushed her spectacles back up her nose with the side of her hand. 'You can lay the table. It's cottage pie tonight.'

Kate took the plates down from the dresser. 'I wondered,' she said, 'whether you might have some old cereal packaging? I'm making pompoms and need circles of card.'

'Pompoms!' Rosemary entered the kitchen and looked into the bag of yarn. 'How do you make *pompoms?*'

'I can show you, if you like,' Kate said, placing cutlery on the table. 'We could make them after dinner.' She glanced into the bag of yarn. 'I'll just pop back up and get my scissors.'

Up in the passageway Kate paused beneath the bells. All was quiet. She let herself through the door into the deserted hallway. She had been waiting most of the afternoon for everyone to be up in their rooms preparing for dinner, leaving less chance of her being caught. She may be allowed into every room downstairs to clean but that didn't mean she was allowed to snoop around willy-nilly and pry into what was none of her business. Justifying what she was about to do by telling herself that she was only going to look at what was on display for all to see - she could have looked at any of the items when she was dusting but had had no reason to pay them any mind before - she paused outside the library. There was no sound from within. She pushed open the door, ready to say that she was checking on the fire, if anyone was inside and wondered what she was doing. Quickly, she moved from shelf to shelf, studying the faces in the photographs in frames. Most were photographs of the Mandevilles either formally posed or in more casual times, in the garden and even some at the seaside. She looked carefully at each face but didn't see the person she was looking for. Closing the door gently behind her, she went next to the drawing room, then the billiard room. She checked dozens of photographs on shelves, desks, bureaus, mantelpieces and arranged on side tables beside lamps. Finally, she opened the door to the morning room and checked all the photographs in there too. By the end, she felt she knew the faces of so many Mandevilles but the one face she had been hoping to see wasn't amongst them. It was the face of the boy in the mirror. Even now, the memory of the anger in his eyes sent a chill down her spine. If she had found him in a holiday snap or a posed portrait, she would have known that he was real and could have asked who he was. From there, she might have been able to find some sort of reason for why she had seen him, what history connected him to this house and why he was shown to her when she took the toy cutlass in her hand. But as with the clipper, she was left with no explanation for what she was seeing and whether there might be a reason behind it. Or whether she was in fact, losing her mind.

FIFTEEN

'Are you not hungry?' Rosemary said when Kate balanced her knife and fork on her plate, the cottage pie only half eaten, and the vegetables barely touched.

'I don't seem to have much of an appetite,' she said. 'Sorry, Audrey. It was delicious.'

'I'll put a plate over the top of it,' Audrey said. 'In case you want it later.'

Rosemary wiped a slice of bread around her plate to mop up the rich gravy. 'What's happened to you?' she said to Kate. 'You were all right earlier and you've gone all... quiet now.'

Kate smoothed out the pleats of her skirt. 'I'm just tired.'

'Come on,' Audrey said to her sister, getting to her feet. 'Hand that plate over. There'll be no pattern left at that rate.'

There was something in Audrey's tone that told Kate she was trying to protect her from Rosemary's prying. And she was grateful for it.

Rosemary popped a final piece of bread into her mouth. 'Can we still make *pompoms* later?' she asked.

'Yes,' Kate said. 'We can still make pompoms later.' She had a job to do and couldn't let anything get in the way of it.

.   .   .

After serving and clearing away the family's dinner, Audrey and Rosemary joined Kate in the parlour. She cut out half a dozen circles from a cereal package and showed the sisters how to wrap the yarn around two of the circles pressed together. Then how to cut the yarn and secure it with a length to make a pompom. Rosemary was thrilled with her new skill and was soon comfortably ensconced in a chair by the fire, happily wrapping yarn around pieces of cereal packaging. Audrey left to make a jug of cocoa and when she returned, she had Kate's dinner on the tray. 'I warmed it up for you,' she said, placing it on the table. 'You need to keep your strength up for all the work you have to do over the next few days.'

Kate thanked her. And Audrey was right, she had to keep her strength up. Besides, there was no good reason for wasting food. She sat at the table and took up the cutlery. Audrey joined Rosemary in sitting in a chair by the hearth. Kate ate her food, trying to distract her thoughts.

Rosemary snipped around the yarn wrapped around the card and tied a length around the middle. Securing it tightly, she released the circles and held the black pompom aloft. 'Ta da!' she said, dangling it on its long thread. 'What colour would you like me to make next?'

It didn't take long to make all the pompoms needed for the costumes. Piling them into the bag with the remaining yarn, Audrey and Rosemary returned to the kitchen. They wanted to get ahead of themselves with bread making for the next two days and would spend the next hour before bed making themselves useful. Kate cleared the parlour, tidying away the cruet and mats, wiping down the table, and shaking out the cushions on the chairs. She flicked though the pages of a magazine before abandoning it on the arm of a chair. She walked around the room, circling the table.

'Hello.'

The sudden voice gave Kate a start and she turned sharply.

'Sorry,' Tommy said, standing in the doorway. 'To disturb you.'

'Did you want something?' Kate said. 'Perhaps from the kitchen?'

He shook his head. 'I just wanted a bit of exercise. I've been cooped up in my room. I stopped in to thank Rosemary and Audrey for looking after me last night. I wanted to thank you, too. I didn't mean to startle anyone.'

'I didn't really do anything,' Kate said. 'But I'm glad you're feeling better.'

Tommy had changed from his pyjamas and dressing gown into smart trousers with a white shirt and a red sweater. His hair was clean and parted to the side and he was freshly shaven. But he wore no shoes, just socks.

'Would you mind?' he said, pointing to one of the chairs at the table. 'It would be nice to have a change of scenery. And it's rather dark to be taking a walk outside.' He grinned. He had his mother's charm and Kate felt sure he could win anyone over.

'Of course,' she said. 'I can leave if you would like some peace and quiet.'

He shook his head. 'I'd rather you stayed.' He pulled out a chair. Kate sat down and he took a seat at the table beside her.

'The squibs are delighted that you are making Halloween costumes for them. It's all they talk about!'

'The squibs?' Kate said.

'Sorry,' Tommy laughed. 'My younger siblings and cousin. There are so many that I find it useful to have a collective noun for them.' He took a handful of pompoms from the bag and laughed as he juggled them. Kate watched him. Tommy was slender and hadn't yet filled out in the way men do. Freckles danced across his nose and his hair looked slightly wild when he leapt from the chair, only just catching one of the pompoms when it threatened to fall to the floor.

'My juggling skills would seem to be a bit rusty,' Tommy said. He placed the pompoms back in the bag and sat in the chair again. 'Am I making a nuisance of myself?'

'Not at all,' Kate said.

Tommy took an apple from the bowl of fruit kept on the table. 'May I?' he asked.

Kate nodded.

Taking a bite of the apple, he chewed slowly before swallowing. 'May I ask you something?' he said.

Kate nodded again.

Tommy tapped the apple against his cheek when he spoke. 'Would we have met somewhere before?' he asked. 'It's just that you seem so familiar to me.'

'I don't think so,' Kate said. 'I've only just come to live here after a few years in Sheffield.'

Tommy pressed the apple to his cheek. 'I don't mean to stare, it's just that I can't quite fathom it. I thought last night as soon as I saw you that I knew you. I wondered whether it might have been part of an hallucination since I was just a little under par!' He laughed and then focused on her again. 'But this afternoon, at tea, I thought it again.'

'Perhaps we've seen each other in the village,' Kate said.

Tommy took another bite of apple and chewed slowly. 'Perhaps,' he said.

But Tommy looked as uncertain about that explanation as Kate. Sitting here together, he felt as familiar as he had yesterday.

Tommy pushed his chair away from the table and crossed the room. Throwing the apple core into the flames of the fire, he said with excitement, 'There it is!'

He knelt down, reaching between one of the armchairs and

the wall. When he stood, he held up a small metal item. He threw it into the air and caught it again. 'My penknife,' he said. 'I thought I'd left it in Cambridge. It must have fallen out of my pocket last night when Bertie and Elliot brought me in here.' He smiled as he pushed it into his pocket.

He sat back at the table. Kate was well aware of how attached young men were to their penknives. Harry had carried his everywhere after their father gave it to him on his thirteenth birthday.

Kate straightened out a crease in the tablecloth. She only gradually became aware of the silence. She looked up to find the colour had drained from Tommy's face.

'I... I don't feel so well,' Tommy said. 'I'm sorry.'

'Should I get someone?' Kate asked.

There was a pause. 'Tommy?' she said.

He lifted his head. Slowly. He swayed slightly, but his eyes were open. Wide open. And his pupils were large so that it was almost impossible to see where the black centre ended, and the green of his eyes began. 'I do know you,' he said. He spoke in a measured way. Quite unlike the energetic way he had spoken just moments before. 'But... but something is stopping me seeing you. I need to help... but I can't... something is in the way... I-I...'

Kate tried to laugh. Having an older brother meant she knew just how young men liked japes. Perhaps Tommy was playing at being ill again to get a reaction from her. 'Are you playing a trick on me, Tommy?' she asked.

Tommy's gaze didn't flinch. 'You,' he said. 'You can see. You can see and I need your help. I need you to see for both of us. We need you to do that.'

Kate got to her feet. 'Please, Tommy,' she said. 'Please stop this. You're scaring me.' She was thinking about whether she should ring the bell to summon someone when Tommy fell forward. She had to move quickly to stop him from tumbling to

the floor. He groaned and collapsed on her. Kate took his full
weight.

'Tommy. Tommy, what is it?' she said.

Before she had the chance to call out, the sound of running
footsteps came from the corridor. Someone rushed into the
room behind her. 'He's ill again,' she said with no clue who she
was talking to. 'Tommy is unwell.' She braced, straining to keep
Tommy upright. Suddenly, the weight was taken from her.
Someone was standing beside her.

'Tommy,' Bertie said. 'Tommy, what has happened?'

Getting to her feet, Kate took a step back.

Bertie knelt before Tommy, Tommy's head resting on his
shoulder. Bertie turned to Kate. 'What happened to him,
Katherine?' he asked.

'I don't know. We were talking. He came down to thank us
for looking after him last night.'

'What else?' Bertie gently pushed Tommy back in the chair
so that Tommy's chin fell onto his own chest. Bertie pressed his
palm to Tommy's forehead.

'He ate an apple.'

Bertie placed his hands on Tommy's knees as though to
reassure him. 'Anything else?'

'He found his penknife. It had fallen on the floor.'

'Anything else?'

Kate faltered. 'He said things.'

'What?'

'It was nonsense. I think he was hallucinating.'

'What, Katherine? What did he say?' Bertie's voice was
sharper, more urgent than she had heard it before.

'He was saying that he can't see... The rest of it doesn't
make any sense.'

'Please, Katherine,' Bertie said urgently again. 'Tell me
exactly what he said.'

Kate looked at Tommy's face, drained of all colour, and then to Bertie. 'He said that he can't see. Something is in his way. And that I need to see for both of us... I told you it didn't make any sense.'

Bertie looked to Tommy. 'He said that *you* need to see for *him*?'

'I said it was nonsense.'

'What else did he say?'

'That he needed to help me and then that I needed to help him.'

'And did he look different? Was there anything in how he looked?'

'What is going on here, Bertie?'

'Please, Katherine. For now, just tell me what you saw.'

'It was his eyes,' Kate said. 'Tommy's pupils were big. And he was staring. He was looking at me, but it looked like he was looking through me.'

Bertie scooped his fringe away from his face. 'Was anyone else here?'

Kate shook her head. 'Just us.'

Bertie looked up at her. She felt him search her face as though trying to find an answer in it. 'I'm telling the truth,' she said.

Bertie turned back to Tommy. 'I believe you.' he said. 'Would you please go and get Elliot? I want to get Tommy back to his room, but I don't want to worry the family.'

'Shouldn't I get Doctor Kenmore? If Tommy is ill again, he needs a doctor.'

'I don't think Doctor Kenmore can help with this.'

'What do you mean?'

Bertie got to his feet. He looked down at Kate. 'There's someone else better able to help Tommy.'

'Is it a special doctor?' Kate asked.

Bertie stared at her for a moment. It felt to Kate as though he wanted to say something else. 'Not a doctor,' he said. 'But someone who can help Tommy. Please, go and get Elliot. He'll be in the stable. And Katherine—' He looked at her with so much concern again. 'Do your best not to let Audrey and Rosemary know what is happening. I don't want to worry them again and Rosemary is likely to get very upset.'

Out in the corridor, Kate toyed with leaving straightaway. But she knew that the sisters would come to find her to say good night.

She stopped at the open door to the kitchen, the smell of bread filling the room. 'It looks like you've been busy,' she said, trying to sound normal.

Audrey and Rosemary were tipping the last of the loaves onto a cooling rack. 'We're almost done in here,' Audrey said.

Kate forced a smile. 'I've tidied the parlour. The guard is over the fire, so there's nothing to do in there.'

'Thank you, Katherine,' Audrey said. 'We'll go straight up when we're finished.'

Rosemary placed a tea towel over some buns. 'Will we make some more pompoms tomorrow night?' she said.

'If you'd like to.' Kate forced a smile again.

After saying their good nights, Kate carried on up the corridor. At the top of the steps, she turned right in the passageway, passing the bells on the wall. She couldn't leave by the back door. The sisters would see her. Gently, she eased open the door to the hall. All was quiet. The family had either all gone to bed or were busy in the rooms behind closed doors. She hurried across the hall, through the vestibule and let herself out of the front door. She ran along the front of the house in the direction of the stables.

SIXTEEN

Kate crossed the cobbled yard, guided by an orange light glowing from a window at the far end of the stable block. Pushing open a small door, she stepped inside, where she was met with the smell of stone and the tang of fresh hay. From what she could see, only two stalls were occupied. In one, a small pony chewed at feed in a bag suspended from the wall. In another, two grey donkeys were curled up on a comfortable-looking bed of hay. They didn't respond when she ran towards the orange light coming from the open doorway at the end of the stables.

She knocked on the open door.

'Come in,' Elliot said gruffly.

She stepped inside the room. Elliot was sitting at a table before a warming fire, surrounded by shelves of saddles and what Kate assumed to be other riding equipment. A Jack Russell dog slept soundly on a rug before the fire.

Elliot got to his feet and stubbed his cigarette out in an ashtray. 'He can't hear you,' he said, nodding to the dog. 'He's deaf.'

'It's Tommy,' Kate said, her voice full of breath from running. 'He's ill again.'

Almost before she had finished speaking, Elliot grabbed his jacket from a hook beside the door. He pulled it on as he led the way at speed through the stables. They came to the donkeys' stall and Kate stumbled on a cobble. She reached out to steady herself, grabbing the end of the wooden divider between stalls. Instantly, a flash stopped her. Gone were the donkeys, replaced by a dappled horse with a mane cut short. There was a woman. In the stall with the horse, stroking its neck. Sadness surrounded her. Kate spun around. Another woman watched through the window, as though seeing the woman in the stall but not seeing Kate. As quickly as the vision had appeared, it disappeared. The donkeys took the place of the dappled horse. Kate put her hand to her chest, struggling to catch her breath. Elliot stood before the door. He didn't say anything. He just stared at her. But Kate felt that he looked at her differently. She had no idea what happened to her when she had one of her visions. What might he have seen?

'We should go,' he said, leading the way out of the stables and across the yard, guided only by the pale light from the moon. The whole time she was beside him, Kate felt Elliot glancing at her in that strange way.

At the back of the house, she looked down to the window of the basement kitchen. The lights were out. 'Audrey and Rosemary have gone to bed,' she whispered. 'We won't need to worry them.'

They took the steps down. Kate knocked gently on the door and Bertie soon arrived to let them in. They followed him back into the parlour where Tommy still sat in the chair at the table, his chin resting on his chest. Bertie looked down at him with such tenderness and worry in his eyes.

'The lad's bad again?' Elliot said quietly.

'He recovered during the day,' Bertie said. 'He was almost

back to normal. But this evening... he's just as bad as he was last night.'

'Do you know what brought it on?' Elliot asked.

Bertie looked at Kate. 'He came down to thank the sisters and Katherine for taking care of him. And that's when it happened. That's right, isn't it, Katherine?'

She nodded. 'He was normal and juggling with pompoms. He ate an apple and was very talkative. And all of a sudden...'

'We should get him to his room,' Elliot said. 'There's nothing to be gained from making him sit there.' All the while he spoke, Kate felt him stare at her still. Did he think there was something she wasn't telling them? Did he think she was somehow involved?

Elliot stepped forward. Crouching, he positioned himself so that Tommy's arm was across his shoulders. Bertie took up position on the other side of Tommy, mirroring Elliot's actions. Together, they gently lifted Tommy from the chair. Tommy's head rested on Elliot's shoulder.

'We'll go up the back stairs,' Bertie said. 'We're less likely to disturb anyone. We don't want to wake the children. They have school in the morning. Katherine, would you lead the way and open the doors for us?'

Kate went first into the hall, Bertie and Elliot following, carrying Tommy between them. The only noise was their soft soles on the flagged floor. At the top of the stone steps, she led them along the dark passageway to the back staircase. She flicked the light switch and had just started to lead the way up when Tommy groaned. Kate stopped. She looked back. Elliot and Bertie paused. Tommy groaned again. Elliot whispered something to Tommy, his low voice rumbling. Kate couldn't hear what was said but it seemed enough to settle Tommy. Bertie nodded to Kate, and she continued up the stairs. Coming to the first floor, she checked that Bertie and Elliot were close to her. She switched off the light and gently pushed the door open to the carpeted landing. All was dark. All was silent. Kate led the way to the room that she knew to be Tommy's. It was far away from any of the other bedrooms and in the old bachelors' corridor. Once inside, she turned on the lamp on the nightstand. Bertie and Elliot placed Tommy on the bed. He was shaking again. Elliot pulled a blanket from the end of the bed and tucked it around Tommy.

Kate felt gentle pressure on her arm. She looked down. Bertie's hand was on her elbow. He nodded to the door. She followed him into the near darkness of the carpeted corridor.

'What's happening, Bertie?' Kate whispered.

Bertie pressed his finger to his lips and indicated for her to follow him along the corridor and back to the narrow door and the stone stairwell. He closed the door behind them. They were instantly plunged into darkness. Kate heard him feel along the wall and a bare bulb sprang to life above them. The sudden light made Kate blink.

Bertie looked at her. 'Thank you for your help,' he said. 'I hope you weren't too alarmed.'

'I was glad to help,' Kate said. 'But what is happening to Tommy? Are you sure we shouldn't get Doctor Kenmore?'

Bertie glanced to the floor. When he looked back to Kate, his brow was creased. 'Doctor Kenmore is a great man. And a brilliant doctor. But he is at a loss for what is happening with Tommy. There's someone else who might be able to help. Another person with medical training. And who loves Tommy.'

'Who?'

Bertie swept his fringe away from his eyes. 'Please, Katherine, will you leave it with me for now?'

He looked so earnest.

'All right,' she said.

'And you,' he said. 'How are you? Those things that Tommy said must have unnerved you.'

'Do you think it's because he was hallucinating? It was making him say strange things?'

'I should think it's something like that.' Bertie looked back at the door. 'I should go to see how Tommy is.'

'Of course,' Kate said. 'Do you think he'll be all right?'

Bertie smiled at her. 'I'm sure he will. Now you go to bed. I'll sort out everything. Trust me.'

Kate stood in her room, her back pressed to the door. She concentrated on bringing her heartbeat under control. Breathing in slowly and exhaling. Slowly in and slowly out. All the questions she had been unable to ask earlier crowded her mind with nowhere to go. Tommy had been so very pale and taken ill so suddenly. And those things he had said. How was she to see for him and why had his eyes grown so large and strange? He was unwell. That was the explanation. There was no sense to be found in what he said as there was no sense in it at all. Thankfully another person trained in medicine was coming to look after him.

Peeling herself away from the door, Kate undressed quickly. She piled her clothes on the chair, pulled on her nightdress, and crawled under the covers. Checking her alarm clock, she turned out the light and burrowed further into the sheets and eider-down. She tried to distract her thoughts by planning the costumes and what she would make first in the morning. But all thoughts of the costumes were pushed aside by the face of the child in the mirror and the scene that had played out in the stable when Elliot had looked at her as though she had lost her mind. Who were those people that she had seen? The two women. And the child. The child... the very thought of his face made her shudder. He had looked so evil. There was no other word for it. She'd had enough of a memory of his reflection when she made her way to her room to make sure that the door along the corridor was closed and locked and covered by the curtain. And she had never been more reassured to hear anything as she was when she heard Rosemary's gentle snoring coming from the room next door.

Kate closed her eyes. She took hold of her St Christopher and held it tight as she fell into a restless sleep.

SEVENTEEN

TUESDAY 29TH OCTOBER, 1935

'I feel awful about this,' Alice said, placing a tray on a clear space on one of the tables in the morning room. 'You shouldn't have to be working on your day off.'

Kate took her foot from the treadle of the sewing machine. 'It really is no trouble,' she said. 'I've no plans for the day.' She stroked the red satin she had been working through the machine. 'And this is a pleasure to me.'

'Well,' Alice said. 'I will certainly make sure there is extra in your pay packet this week.' She looked around the room and smiled. 'You have been so busy! The children are going to be thrilled.' She took up the white tabard decorated with black patches that Kate had begun that morning and already finished. It was to be Oscar's dog costume. She had also made a hat of sorts with two floppy ears and a strap to secure it under his chin. All that was left to make was a tail to attach to the tabard as Alice had said that he could wear a pair of his black shorts beneath.

Kate almost didn't want to ask, but all night and all morning, she had thought of little else but the events of the previous evening. 'I hope you don't mind,' she said. 'But I wondered how Tommy is this morning?'

Alice's face darkened a little. 'He's not so good again,' she said. 'I was worried that he was overdoing it yesterday by getting up and about. Charlotte checked on him this morning and said he just needs to get some rest. He has exhaustion. If I have anything to do with it, I'll make sure that he stays in that bed for a good few days. But' – she shrugged – 'he has a mind of his own and I doubt he will listen to me. Like all young men of that age, he thinks he is old enough to know best.'

'I hope he gets better soon,' Kate said.

'Thank you.' Alice tapped the teapot on the tray. 'Stop for your breakfast, at least,' she said. 'Audrey said you haven't been down to the kitchen at all this morning.'

'I will,' Kate said. 'Just as soon as I've finished these.'

'See that you do.' Alice smiled.

Alone again, Kate ran the leg of the clown trousers for Louisa through the machine. They were a baggy, almost shape-less design which would be secured at the waist with a matching purple ribbon. When she had finished the leg, she snipped the cotton attaching the fabric to the machine. Placing it aside, the clock out in the hall chimed in time with the rumble in her stomach. She got up and sat at the table. By rights, she should be the one fetching and carrying. The lady of the house bringing her a tray was turning the world on its head. But it seemed that the whole world had been turned on its head since her arrival at Hill House. Kate lifted a silver lid and found a bowl of steaming porridge. She took the bowl and a spoon from the tray and ate her breakfast.

She would have liked to ask Alice whether the person had arrived to help as Bertie said they would. But did Alice even know that Kate had seen Tommy last night and had helped take him to his room? Would it be indiscreet to ask or reveal her involvement, such as it was? Kate poured a cup of tea. It was probably best to stay out of what was happening as it really was none of her business. Her business was to make these costumes. That was it. And it was why she had risen early from bed to make up the downstairs fires then begin sewing by lamplight and well before daybreak. She hadn't been able to sleep. The memory of the boy in the mirror and the women in the stable had come to her almost as soon as she closed her eyes.

Kate took her tea to the window. A thin haze of fog hovered over the grass running down to the gates at the end of the drive. In the cold light of the day, it was almost possible to believe that some of the stranger events hadn't happened.

She looked to the trees neighbouring the drive and then to the spire of St Mary's. It was her day off, but she had to work to stand a chance of finishing the costumes. She would visit her father at the next opportunity. He would understand the need for her to work hard to prove herself in the hope of securing the permanent role of housemaid.

Kate was about to return to work but was distracted by the sight of a car turning into the gates. It progressed up the drive and Kate recognised it as the car Charlotte had driven the day before. As it grew closer, she saw that it was not Charlotte at the wheel, but Elliot. He brought the car to a stop and got out to open the back door closest to the house. A woman stepped out. Elliot offered her his arm, but she shook her head, relying instead on the cane she placed in the gravel. Kate watched the woman emerge. She wore a long coat of the most magnificent peacock blue. The silk scarf at her neck was a riot of lighter blues and purples. Even from this distance, Kate could see that it was a paisley design. The woman's hair was grey, almost silver, and she wore it piled neatly as women of that age did. But she looked different to any woman Kate had seen of that age. There was a stylishness about her. A dignity. And that extended to how she approached the house. Even though she used the stick, she planted its silver tip with assurance. Kate's gaze travelled up from the gravel and found that in the time she had been admiring this woman, the woman had been looking at her. The woman smiled and nodded. Kate turned quickly away from the window, almost spilling her tea over herself. She placed the cup on the table.

A knock at the door made her stand up straight and smooth down her apron. She took a moment to compose herself and opened the door.

'Miss Durrant,' the woman in the blue coat said. She spoke with such familiarity that Kate didn't know how to respond. There was friendliness in her eyes as well as her smile. She removed her gloves and pushed them into her pocket. 'Where are my manners?' she said. 'We haven't been introduced. You must be wondering who on Earth I am!' The woman still smiled when she took Kate's hands in hers. 'I am Mrs Hart,' she said. 'Sir Charles' sister and Tommy's great-aunt.' She squeezed Kate's hands and looked past her. 'My, you have been busy!' she said. 'Charlotte told me all about what you are doing for the children and their party when she came to tea yesterday. And I can see that you have made a jolly good start.'

'Thank you,' Kate said, feeling her cheeks warm.

Still holding Kate's hands, Mrs Hart said, 'Bertie told me all about you on the telephone and Elliot has filled in some other details.'

Kate looked past Mrs Hart to Elliot. He was standing in the hallway, his eyes dipped to the floor.

'Don't worry,' Mrs Hart said. 'It's all good.'

Kate could sense Mrs Hart still looking at her.

'As I understand it, Tommy has taken a turn again and you have helped in looking after him.'

'I really haven't done anything,' Kate said. She felt her fingers squeezed again.

'Sometimes we help in ways we are not aware of at the time,' Mrs Hart said. Before Kate could think how to respond,

Mrs Hart added, 'Right, I should go to see how my great-nephew is. Some good homecooked meals and fresh air is what that boy needs, I am sure of it. And I should let you get back to your sewing, Miss Durrant. I would hate to get in the way.' She squeezed Kate's fingers one last time before letting her hands slip.

Mrs Hart swept from the room in the same way that she had entered. She was the kind of woman whose presence was felt long after they had been in a place.

Elliot reached and closed the door behind Mrs Hart. But as he pulled it to, he looked at Kate in the same way he had looked at her in the stables.

Kate stared at the closed door, listening to the tap of the silver tip of the cane as it crossed the tiles of the hallway.

So, that was Mrs Hart. The suffragette. What activity had Mrs Hart had been involved in twenty years earlier? Could it have been throwing rocks through windows, or chaining herself to railings, or protesting outside Parliament? Kate rubbed her palms together. Mrs Hart's hands had been so warm. And she had looked at Kate so deeply. It had almost felt as though she had seen something in Kate's face. But not like Elliot. Elliot seemed to look at her in a suspicious way, whereas Mrs Hart looked at her with a smile and with... warmth, as though she somehow knew her. And Mrs Hart's hands... Kate rubbed her palms together again. They had been more than warm. It almost felt as though there was an energy in them. Kate let her arms drop to her sides. She was tired. And her imagination was running away with her. Mrs Hart had warm hands. And she had looked at Kate in a kindly way. That was it. Kate turned around and headed to the sewing machine.

It was only just after half past eleven when Kate finished the tabard to match the trousers that she had already sewn together and hemmed. She lay the clown costume out on a chair beside the dog costume. A cup of tea. That's what she needed. And when she was finished, she would come back to stitch the pompoms onto the purple and red tabard. Collecting the tray, Kate left the morning room and made her way downstairs. She was surprised to find the kitchen deserted. Putting the kettle on the range, she washed the crockery from her breakfast. The kettle whistled as it came to the boil.

'Oh, lovely,' Rosemary said from the doorway. 'I'm spitting feathers here.'

Kate looked up. 'What have you got there?' she asked.

Rosemary nodded to the bulging laundry bag in her arms. 'Just about every item of clothing Tommy owns.'

Kate took a second cup and saucer down from the dresser. 'Why?'

'Mrs Hart is a stickler for cleanliness. She took one look at the pile of clothes on the chair in Tommy's room and called for me to take up a laundry bag. She even took clothes from his wardrobe! Give me a minute,' she said. 'I'll put this with the laundry hamper by the back door. It's being collected later.'

Kate poured the steaming water into the teapot.

Rosemary reappeared and they sat at the table waiting for the tea to brew.

'Why does Mrs Hart want Tommy's clothes to be washed?' Kate asked.

'She used to be a nurse,' Rosemary said and put a teaspoon of sugar into Kate's cup and then one into her own. 'She ran this place when it was a hospital in the war, so I'm told. And she likes everything just so. She said that the clothes boys bring back from school or university are in such a state, they could walk into the laundry copper by themselves! She said when Tommy is better, she wants him in all clean clothes. With no germs and no grimy collars!'

Kate poured milk into the cups. Mrs Hart was the perfect

person for Bertie to call on to take care of Tommy. There could be nobody better placed than a devoted aunt with medical training to restore health to an ailing nephew. 'She seems like a very nice person,' Kate said.

'She really is,' Rosemary said. 'She's kind and generous and has always treated me and our Aud like we are part of the family. Mind,' she added, widening her eyes, 'I wouldn't want to cross her. She is what they call "formidable"!'

Kate laughed.

'Oh, ta,' Rosemary said when Kate poured the tea. She pulled a cup and saucer towards her. 'It's funny though,' she continued, stirring her tea, 'some of this family have a way of looking at you, like they know what you're thinking. Mrs Hart, in particular.'

Kate stirred her own tea and thought about how Mrs Hart had received her in the morning room. 'Why is that, do you think?' she asked.

Rosemary shrugged. 'I suppose knowing us well means they know how to get the best work from us. Our Aud is always saying how we have fallen on our feet here. I shouldn't think staff are treated so well in every household.' She took a sip of her tea. 'Aud's gone into town with Mrs Mandeville. There are some special things wanted for the party, and they decided to go and pick them out themselves. Fancy a biccie?' Rosemary collected the biscuit barrel and Kate joined her in a piece of buttery shortbread. She was almost tempted to tell Rosemary about the trip to the cinema with Bertie. But Rosemary would make more of it then necessary. She was also a terrible gossip so would likely tell everyone. And Kate wanted it to be something just for her. For now, at least.

EIGHTEEN

The pressure of her foot operating the treadle, the rhythmic rattle of the needle, and the whir of the sewing machine mechanism became Kate's constant companion for the remainder of the morning and well past her normal lunchtime. At almost two o'clock, Kate snipped the thread on the waistcoat she had made for the pirate's costume. She shook it out and held it against herself. Even if she did say so herself, it had come out better than she had anticipated. Before stitching the two breast sections to the back, she had taken the scissors and snipped the bottom of the whole garment into jagged points. It would be worn with a pair of Charlie's normal trousers that Alice had said could be sacrificed as he had almost outgrown them, and the knees were threadbare. Kate had a plan to fashion an eyepatch from a piece of black fabric and ribbon and a headscarf from a length of red satin. Charlotte said they could complete the look with pieces of her costume jewellery and a kohl pencil she rarely used.

Draping the pirate waistcoat over the back of the sofa, where she had already laid out the clown and dog costumes. Kate stood back and studied them. She really had achieved more than she thought she would in the short time she had worked on her project. With the exception of a few accessories, they were ready for the children. Tidying up her sewing area and scooping away the scraps and debris, Kate collected the wastepaper basket and headed out into the hall. With plans to make a quick sandwich, she passed through the door into the passageway and became aware of voices coming from the basement kitchen. Making her way down the steps, placing her foot in the grooves worn into the stone by centuries of staff passing this way, Kate could hear they were the voices of a man and a woman. She stopped and was about to turn around and head back up the steps.

'Who's out there?' the woman called from the kitchen.

Kate stopped. She placed the wastepaper basket on the floor, smoothed down her apron and presented herself at the door.

'Miss Durrant!' Mrs Hart said. 'How delightful to see you.' She was standing at the range, an apron covering her dress, and stirring what looked like a pan of soup. There was a loaf of bread on a board on the table, with a plate of cheese and ham, and jug of lemonade. Sitting at a chair was Tommy. He wore not the pyjamas of an invalid, but a blue sweater over his shirt. His hair was clean and brushed neatly and his face glowed with rude health.

'Good afternoon, Mrs Hart. Tommy,' Kate said.

Tommy jumped from his seat and pulled out a chair. 'Please, Miss Durrant,' he said. 'Won't you join us?'

Kate sat down.

Mrs Hart looked over her shoulder. 'Doesn't Tommy look well?' she said to Kate.

'Very well,' Kate said, unable to take her eyes from Tommy who stood beside her. He couldn't be more different from the desperately ill Tommy of last night, his head lolling against Elliot's shoulder as Elliot and Bertie carried him to his room.

Kate glanced towards the range and saw Mrs Hart still looking over her shoulder. She smiled at Kate and nodded, before turning back to tend the pan.

'I don't believe in malingering,' Mrs Hart said. 'If someone is well enough to get out of bed then the best thing for them is a bath, fresh clothes, and a walk outside. We plan to take a turn around the gardens after lunch, don't we, Tommy?'

Tommy poured a glass of lemonade and placed it in front of Kate. 'I can't wait,' he said. 'I feel as fit as a fiddle. And I can't bear being cooped up.' He took the seat beside Kate. 'I have to thank you once again, Miss Durrant,' he said. 'You helped me yet again last night when I took a turn. Honestly, I don't know what keeps coming over me.'

'You are exhausted, my darling,' Mrs Hart said. She took the pan from the range. Kate saw that Mrs Hart's walking stick was balanced against the table and she used the back of the chair to support herself. Tommy got to his feet.

'It's all right, darling,' Mrs Hart said. 'I can manage.' She placed the pan on the table. Tommy took three bowls from the dresser.

'You will join us, won't you?' Mrs Hart said to Kate. 'There's plenty to go around.'

'I don't want to be a nuisance.'

'A nuisance!' Mrs Hart said, taking up a ladle. 'You, my dear Miss Durrant, could never be a nuisance. We have you to thank for helping Tommy.'

'I don't really think I have helped,' Kate said.

'Oh yes, you have,' Mrs Hart said. 'In more ways than you know.' She ladled the soup into the bowls. 'Might I ask you something, Miss Durrant?'

Kate nodded.

'Would you mind terribly if Tommy and I call you by your given name? I believe it is Katherine. Using your surname just seems so formal. And a bit cold.'

Kate nodded. 'I'd actually prefer it.' She smiled.

'I thought that might be the case.' Mrs Hart put the pan back on the range and sat opposite Kate and Tommy. Unfurling a napkin and placing it in her lap, she said, 'Minestrone. I hope you like it.' She offered the board of bread to Kate.

'Thank you,' Kate said. She took a slice of the bread and buttered it. 'It all looks delicious.'

Mrs Hart cut a chunk of cheese and placed it on the edge of Kate's plate. 'It will be. But I can't take any credit for its creation. Audrey prepared it for me this morning and I simply heated it through.' She took a spoonful of the steaming soup, blew across the top and tasted it. 'Delicious,' she said.

Kate collected her spoon and dipped it into the bowl. She took a taste and closed her eyes. 'It's wonderful,' she said.

Tommy hungrily tucked into his meal like a man who hadn't eaten in a week.

'It's the soup that roused the spirits of all the men we treated here during the war,' Mrs Hart said, smiling at her great-nephew. 'It was a particular favourite of everyone. Did you know we had a hospital at Hill House during the war, Katherine?'

Kate cut a nub of the cheese Mrs Hart had given to her and placed it on her bread. She nodded. 'Rosemary told me.'

Mrs Hart ate another mouthful of the soup. She closed her eyes. 'Nourishment for the soul,' she sighed. 'And do you know, Audrey makes it to the same recipe as Mrs Randal. All those young servicemen we looked after here have Mrs Randal to thank for their recuperation. Sir Charles, Lady Mandeville and I are fortunate that she came to the dower house with us and graces us with her wonderful cooking every day.' She rested her spoon against the side of her bowl. 'And Katherine, did you know that Mrs Randal is Bertie's grandmother?'

Kate paused with her spoon to her mouth. Mrs Hart gave her one of her knowing little smiles. Kate placed her spoon back in her bowl. 'I did,' she said. 'Rosemary told me.' She could feel her earlobes burn at the thought of the trip to the pictures with Bertie that she had kept a secret.

'It seems like Rosemary has told you a great deal about the family,' Mrs Hart said, a laugh in her voice.

'I'm sorry,' Kate said quickly. 'She's not indiscreet. She's just trying to help me understand who everyone is.'

Mrs Hart laughed and shook her head. 'Please don't worry yourself,' she said. 'I'm having a little joke with you. We adore Rosemary and we all know that she loves to chatter and gossip. But that girl doesn't have a malicious bone in her body. Everything she says about this family and household is driven by love.'

Relieved that she had not somehow got Rosemary into bother, Kate picked up her spoon again. She had just taken a mouthful of soup when Mrs Hart said, 'And speaking of Bertie, I do hope you enjoy your trip to the pictures tonight. You've worked so hard and deserve a treat.'

Kate swallowed hard. She could feel the glow in her cheeks to match the warmth in her earlobes.

Mrs Hart took another spoonful of soup. 'Bertie is very much looking forward to it,' she said, with that little laugh in her voice again.

Tommy took a hunk of bread from the board and a huge slice of ham. 'Might I go, too?' he said. 'It's been an age since I went to the pictures.'

Mrs Hart smiled at him. 'Oh no, darling,' she said. 'There's such a thing as too many cooks.'

'Beg pardon,' Tommy said, buttering his bread.

'Your company will be needed here,' Mrs Hart said tactfully. 'I'm certain your mother would like to spend some time with you now that you are feeling much better.'

Tommy seemed to think about it for a moment. 'Of course,' he said. 'I can always go to the pictures another evening. I don't plan to go back to Cambridge until after the party.'

'And I will stay here, too,' Mrs Hart said. 'I feel like I might be needed. Rosemary has made up my old bedroom for me.'

'But I am so much better,' Tommy said. 'Please don't feel you need to stay on my account.'

'I see,' Mrs Hart said with mock offence, dabbing her mouth with her napkin. 'I am not wanted in my old home!'

Tommy laughed, his mouth full of bread. 'You know I don't mean that.'

'And you know I am toying with you,' Mrs Hart said. 'But there might be other people here who need me.' As she placed her napkin back in her lap, she looked directly at Kate.

Kate ate her soup, with the bread and cheese, and drank her lemonade. She spoke when spoken to. But she didn't talk beyond that. It seemed that whatever she said to Mrs Hart, that shrewd woman was able to read her thoughts or the meaning behind her words. Even when Mrs Hart was turned from her to talk to her great-nephew, Kate felt as though she could see her. As though she was still watching her. It wasn't horrible or intrusive. It felt reassuring in some way. As though someone was looking out for her. And it also wasn't possible. Mrs Hart was clearly clever and astute, but she did not have eyes in the back of her head. Tommy seemed not to notice at all. He ate his lunch with gusto. When the soup was finished, he took a tin of rock cakes down from the dresser and ate three in quick succession. While Tommy ate, Mrs Hart looked on as though satisfied with his progress.

When lunch came to an end, Kate offered to tidy away and wash up the pans and crockery.

'Oh, no.' Mrs Hart smiled. 'Tommy and I will see to this. You have enough to be getting on with.'

'Thank you,' Kate said. 'And thank you for the soup.'

'It was our pleasure,' Mrs Hart said. 'And you enjoy the pictures tonight.'

NINETEEN

The afternoon simply flew by and Kate could barely hide a smile as she raced through her work. Never had she fed so much fabric through a sewing machine in a few short hours or pinned hems or cut out pieces to stitch together so quickly.

When the clock out in the hall struck half past five, Kate tidied the sewing equipment away into baskets and drawers and bags. She looked at the three complete costumes laid out on the back of the sofa. The pirate costume now had an eye patch and a red headscarf, a black tail stuffed with offcuts from the fabric hung from the dog tabard, and the clown costume was complete with its trousers and pompoms running down the front of the smock. Switching off the light, Kate ran through the plans for the final costume, which she would have plenty of time to complete tomorrow.

Back in her room, Kate changed out of her work clothes and into a lilac-coloured dress she had made over a week of evenings in Sheffield. She had worn it for her niece's christening, and it was a particular favourite. She peered into her washbag at her few items of cosmetics. She took out the lipstick, hesitated and then dropped it back into the bag. She hadn't worn lipstick or rouge in her whole time here. And she didn't want to look like a different person tonight. She grinned at her reflection in the mirror. She wanted to look like the person Bertie had invited to the pictures. Taking a beautiful pink silk scarf from a drawer, she tied it at her neck. It was the scarf she saved for special occasions.

Kate descended the back staircase dressed in her overcoat, with her handbag balanced in the crook of her arm. Once in the hall, she pushed open the door to the morning room. Bertie stood before the sofa with the costumes arranged along the back. His smile when he saw Kate was so broad that she could hardly believe it was for her.

'Katherine,' he said, stepping towards her. 'You look lovely.'

'And you look very smart,' Kate said. Gone were his tweeds; in their place, he wore a dark suit with a crisp white shirt and dark green tie with a gleaming gold tie pin. His hair was parted neatly to the side, and he smelled of cologne. He had an overcoat over his arm.

'They're looking splendid,' Bertie said, nodding to the costumes.

'Thank you,' Kate said. 'I've enjoyed myself. And I've tried my best to keep up with as many of my chores as I can.'

'Audrey said as much,' Bertie said. 'She even sounded impressed. And impressing Audrey is not an easy thing to do.' He held his open palm to the door. 'Shall we?'

Out in the hall, Bertie suggested they leave by the office corridor. 'There will be too many prying eyes if we go through the basement corridor,' he said quietly.

'Audrey and Rosemary?' Kate said.

'Have you told them about our trip tonight?' Bertie asked.

Kate shook her head. 'No.'

'Good.' He smiled.

Kate followed Bertie through to the corridor and into a small room with rows of coat hooks and umbrella stands. He opened the door to the outside. It was already dark, and their shoes crunched on the gravel as Bertie closed the door behind them and shrugged on his overcoat.

The black car that Charlotte had driven into town and that Mrs Hart had travelled in with Elliot was parked up at the side of the house.

'We're not going in your truck?' Kate asked.

'It didn't seem appropriate,' Bertie said. He opened the door and Kate slipped into the passenger seat. She watched him walk around the front of the car. In his dark suit and overcoat, he seemed broader somehow, as though he had filled out. And he appeared to walk a little taller and speak in a more confident way. He got in beside Kate. Kate looked at him as he started the engine, and he looked back at her. They both smiled.

The journey into town was quick with little other traffic on the roads. Bertie asked Kate about the costumes and Kate asked Bertie about the plans for the party.

'It's always the same,' Bertie said. 'The day before Halloween – so tomorrow – the children will insist on Elliot telling them tales about the origins of Halloween in Ireland. They are tales that Elliot's mother passed down to him. He lights a fire in the stable yard, and they all sit around it to hear his stories.. He generally goes a bit far and scares the children, but they seem to enjoy it.' Bertie navigated the car around a bend. 'And then on Halloween, after school, they have party games and food and a jolly good time.'

'Does Tommy join in?'

'Usually,' Bertie said. 'And now he's decided to stay at home for a few days, I'm sure he will be keen not to miss out.'

'He seems so much better,' Kate said, picturing the young

man tucking into soup and bread and cake. 'I joined him and Mrs Hart for lunch and he seemed to be back to normal. You were right to ask Mrs Hart to come to look after him.'

'She's a wonderful nurse,' Bertie said. 'And she knows Tommy so well.' He glanced across at Kate. 'Has Tommy said anything else unusual to you?'

She shook her head. 'I imagine he said those things because he was ill. He probably didn't know what he was saying.'

'You're probably right,' Bertie said.

'Mrs Hart thanked me today for helping with Tommy,' Kate said. 'She seems to think that I had something to do with making him better. When I tried to explain that it was nothing to do with me, she didn't believe me.'

Bertie manoeuvred the car into a space on the high street. 'That sounds like Mrs Hart.' He smiled. 'She can be quite forceful when she has her mind set on something.'

They joined the queue outside The Grand, illuminated by the bright light flooding from the foyer. When it was their turn at the ticket booth, Bertie insisted on paying for them both, even though Kate had her hand on her purse, saying that she would be glad to pay for her own ticket.

'My treat,' Bertie said as they pushed through the turnstile.

Inside, The Grand did its very best to live up to its name. Tall columns like those Kate had seen in the architecture of ancient civilisations in her schoolbooks reached to the ceiling. The deep blue carpet was decorated with a pattern of gold laurel wreaths and the walls were painted in gold. A shallow but wide set of stairs rose to meet a vast blue curtain decorated with golden fringe. Bertie guided Kate through the crowd thronging the foyer to the refreshment kiosk. 'Those, please,' he said, pointing to a shelf. The woman, dressed in a blue and gold striped dress, took down a box. She passed it to Bertie. After paying, Bertie turned to Kate.

'These are for you,' he said, handing the box to her.

Kate looked down at the chocolates. 'A whole Dairy Box for me? I can't let you do this.'

Bertie swept his fringe away from his face. 'Yes, you can,' he said.

A bell rang, silencing Kate's protest. Two ushers pulled back the vast blue curtain and organ music started up beyond. As one, the crowd from the foyer began to make their way up the stairs. Clutching her box of chocolates, Kate made sure to stay close to Bertie. They found their seats and he helped her remove her coat before he removed his and they sat down. The organist was positioned to the side of the screen, which was covered by another blue curtain.

'What's the picture?' Kate asked, over the loud and enthusiastic organ music. 'I forgot to ask.'

Bertie thought for a moment. 'I don't know,' he said with a laugh. 'I just know it changed today.'

Kate opened the box and peeled back the paper. She offered the chocolates to Bertie, but he insisted she take one first. Consulting the pictures on the box, she chose a nutty one. She chewed it slowly. When she looked at Bertie, he was smiling.

'Good?' he asked.

'Very good,' she said.

Bertie took a chocolate and nodded his appreciation as he chewed. Kate selected another chocolate and offered him the box again.

Soon the lights dimmed. Kate placed the box in her lap. The organist picked up the tempo of the music. Bertie leant into Kate. 'He's keen!' he said. Kate fought to hold in a laugh. Suddenly the music took a sinister turn. Bertie feigned shock and Kate had to suppress a laugh again.

'What have you brought me to see?' she said. 'I hope it's not a frightening picture!'

Bertie shrugged and smiled.

Kate settled back in her seat. The curtains at the front of the auditorium parted and the chatter of the audience subsided. A few people coughed. A late arriving couple apologised, clutching their coats as people stood to let them through to their seats. After a final dramatic flourish, the organ music subsided. It was replaced by gentler music accompanying the *Gainsborough Picture* lady on screen. In her old-fashioned feathered hat and sitting in her frame, she smiled out and nodded in the direction of the audience. The lady faded and was replaced by a gentleman in a white bowtie looking very serious. Even before his name appeared on the screen, with the name of the film, *The Clairvoyant*, Kate recognised him. She leant into Bertie.

'It's Claude Rains,' she whispered.

'Claude who?' Bertie said.

'Claude Rains. He was in *The Invisible Man*. Did you see it?'

Bertie shook his head.

'And look,' Kate said, pointing to another name on the screen. 'Fay Wray. She was in *King Kong*. You must have seen *King Kong*.'

Bertie shook his head again. 'I can see I'm going to have to come to the pictures more often with you, if I'm to keep up with your knowledge.'

Before Kate could answer, someone shushed them from behind. 'Sorry,' Bertie whispered over his shoulder. Looking at Kate he grimaced and nodded to the screen. Kate glanced at Claude Rains and Fay Wray disembarking a ship, but only briefly. When she was sure Bertie's attention was on the film, she turned her attention to him. In the darkness, she was sure he didn't know he was being watched. The light of the screen lit his face. He had his elbow on the armrest between them and as he watched, he hooked his forefinger over his moustache and top lip and rested his chin on his thumb. His eyes flicked this way and that as they followed the action on the screen. Kate so wanted to place her elbow on the armrest beside Bertie's, but she didn't want to disturb him. It would also be quite a bold thing to touch a man she barely knew. She placed her hands over the box of chocolates and looked up at the screen.

The cold night air greeted Kate and Bertie as they left The Grand. A pool of light shone on the pavement when they joined their fellow picture-goers outside. Kate clutched her box of chocolates and Bertie pulled on his gloves. 'Did you enjoy that?' he asked.

Kate nodded. 'Do you really think that there are people who can tell the future like that?'

Bertie thought for a moment. Kate had come to expect his pause in replying to a question since any response he gave was always considered. 'It's difficult to tell, isn't it?' he said. 'At the beginning Claude Rains' character was a fraud. He was so convincing that his audiences didn't realise he wasn't telling their futures but guessing at them. It was only when he met Christine that something changed so he could truly tell the future. As though she released a skill in him.'

'And do you believe such a thing could happen?' Kate asked.

Bertie buttoned up his overcoat. 'I don't disbelieve it. But to believe it, you would need to see proof. I don't like to dismiss anything as impossible unless I have evidence to say it is.' He glanced up the street. 'Are you hungry?' he asked.

'A bit,' Kate said. 'It's been a while since lunch.'

Bertie held out his hand to take her chocolates. 'I'll put them in the car for safekeeping,' he said.

. . .

Walking slowly up the road, they passed from the pool of yellow light of one streetlamp to another, still discussing the film. Kate was surprised that Bertie would even consider fortune telling to be possible. Since Charlotte had said he wouldn't join his mother and grandmother at the spiritualist church, Kate had assumed that he wouldn't believe anything of the sort.

'Have you experienced anything like clairvoyance?' Kate asked.

Bertie swept his fringe from his face. 'Not exactly,' he said. 'And not personally. There was an incident one night many years ago when the Mandevilles and some of their guests played with a spirit board.'

'Oh, tell me about it,' Kate said, her interest piqued.

'There's not much to tell.' Bertie shrugged. 'I wasn't there at the time. But it was enough to scare some of the people in the room and for Mrs Hart to have the board banished from the house. What about you?' he asked. 'Have you had any unexplainable unusual experiences?'

Kate's mind immediately went to the strange things she saw. The flashes of what might be the histories of objects. Bertie might be open to the idea of the existence of clairvoyance if presented with enough evidence. But what she experienced was not clairvoyance. She could not predict the future. And she had never spoken of what she saw outside her family. She shook her head. 'No,' she said. 'Nothing. Not really.'

The smell of fish frying grew stronger the closer they got to the fish and chip shop. The windows dripped with condensation. They joined the end of a short queue of people inside and both ordered a bag of chips.

'Are you sure you wouldn't like a piece of haddock?' Bertie asked, after insisting on paying again.

'Just chips is perfect,' Kate said.

They both added lots of salt and vinegar and since they

were the only remaining customers, they took a seat on the bench in the window to eat their newspaper-wrapped supper.

Bertie smiled at Kate as they blew on the hot chips. He popped one in his mouth and chewed slowly.

'You said "not really",' Bertie said.

Kate covered her mouth. 'Pardon me?' she said, through a mouthful of warm vinegary potato.

Bertie took a bite of another chip. 'When I asked whether you had had any unexplainable unusual experiences.'

Kate swallowed the chip that suddenly felt like a lump of raw potato in her throat. 'It was nothing,' she said.

'You know you can trust me, don't you?' Bertie said. 'If anything ever alarms you or unsettles you – particularly at Hill House – you can always come to me.'

Kate stared at the grease blooming and darkening the newspaper holding her chips. She thought of the boy in the mirror and the women in the stables and the ship with its creaking rigging. Bertie couldn't possibly know anything of this side of her. And yet... She looked up into his face. He no longer ate his chips but smiled at her. The sort of smile you might give to someone to reassure them, and he nodded slightly. He gently nudged her with his elbow. 'Eat your chips,' he said. 'Before they go cold.'

Bertie's elbow rested against Kate's arm. His touch was reassuring somehow. It felt safe. 'Thank you,' she said. And Bertie nodded to her chips again.

TWENTY

It didn't take much to convince Kate that they should stop at The White Lion in the village.

'A nightcap?' Bertie said. 'To wash the grease down.'

He brought the car to a stop beside the village green. Bright orange light glowed from the windows of the pub and reflected in the still water of the duckpond. When Bertie opened the door, warmth escaped into the cold night air and the bright light was momentarily startling. In the bar to the right, Kate saw lots of men playing cards and laughing loudly, thick cigarette smoke like a spectre hovering above their heads.

'This way,' Bertie said. He took Kate's elbow and directed her into a bar to the left. It was much quieter than the bar on the other side of the pub, with low ceilings and dark beams. The two other couples in the bar looked up when they entered. Bertie pointed to a table beside the fireplace, which was decorated with highly polished horse brasses. A fire roared in the open brick hearth.

'What will you have?' Bertie asked.

'A small stout, please,' Kate said, shrugging off her coat and placing it on the back of her chair.

She watched Bertie place the order at the bar with the land-lady. He soon returned to the table with a pint and a half of stout. He put his coat over the back of his chair and sat opposite Kate.

He picked up his drink. 'Cheers,' he said, tapping his glass to Kate's.

Kate took a sip. For a moment, Bertie's moustache was deco-rated with a line of foam from the top of his drink. He wiped it away with his fingers and placed his glass back on the table. 'They keep a good pint here,' he said.

'Do you come here often?' Kate asked.

'Once or twice a week.' He paused and a grin made his nose twitch. 'But the company isn't usually so refined.'

Kate laughed. 'I don't think I'm at all refined.'

Bertie's nose twitched again. 'Well, you are compared to the farmhands I usually take a pint with.'

Kate took another sip of her drink. The light from the fire picked out the gold of Bertie's tie pin. '*That's* refined,' she said, nodding to the pin but pointing to where it might sit on her own chest.

Bertie ran his finger along the gold. 'It was my father's,' he said. 'A twenty-first birthday present. All my family pitched in to buy it for him.'

'He must have been very smart,' Kate said.

'He was. From what I remember.' Bertie paused. Staring into his drink, he said, 'But I was so young when he died that I wonder whether I have memories of him or it's what I have seen in photographs or learned from what other people have told me.'

Kate so wanted to reach and take his hand. 'I'm sorry,' she said. 'Truly.'

'Thank you,' Bertie said.

He looked so sad. Kate didn't know whether it would make him feel any better, but she put her hand to her throat and slipped her St Christopher from her collar so that it sat on her dress. 'My father gave this to me,' she said. 'When I went away to Sheffield. It was his good luck gift to me.'

'The patron saint of travellers,' Bertie said.

Kate nodded. She rubbed the figure of St Christopher bearing the lamb on his shoulders.

'I wish I'd met him,' Bertie said. 'Your father sounds like he cared for you very much.'

'I wish you could have met him, too,' Kate said. 'He was a wonderful father. As I'm sure your father was.' She paused, hoping she hadn't gone too far.

'And did he have a good sense of humour?' Bertie asked, taking a sip of his drink.

'He did. He was serious and sensible when he had to be, but he loved telling jokes and making everyone laugh. He had this way of putting everyone around him at ease by being funny.' Kate smiled. 'Why do you ask?'

'Because I see that in you.' Bertie took another sip of his drink. 'You try hard to be serious, but I can see that you are masking a silliness.'

'A silliness?' Kate said, not knowing whether to be offended.

Bertie laughed. It was soft and low. 'Poor choice of words,' he said. 'Not silliness, exactly. A playfulness. A sense of humour. I think you're trying to hide it behind being sensible because of your new job.'

'Perhaps I am,' Kate said. 'Is that a bad thing?'

Bertie shook his head. 'I like light-heartedness in others. I'm afraid that I am too serious sometimes.'

The light from the fire lit Bertie's eyes. Alice had said that he had an old soul. As Kate looked into his eyes, it seemed there was a depth of life, a depth of feeling, that she had never seen in the eyes of anyone before.

'I'm sorry you had to leave your home,' Bertie said. 'That

must be hard. I've only ever lived at Hill House. I should feel lost if I ever had to move away.'

'It's not as bad as it might be,' Kate said. 'My parents' house on the Wilkinson Estate wasn't really my home. I only ever stayed as a guest. The house in Northampton was more my home. Before I went to Sheffield.' She looked into her glass. 'There are a few things still in my parents' house that came from Northampton. I actually need to move them out this weekend. My parents' old neighbours have agreed to look after them for now. Some of the things belonged to my father and it feels important that I should keep them.'

'I can help you move them, if you like,' Bertie said. He took another sip of his drink before dipping to look into her eyes. 'What's wrong?' he asked.

'Pardon?' Kate said.

'You seem sad all of a sudden.'

'It's just... There's a table. Just an ordinary kitchen table. Nothing fancy or valuable. But it was the table we used my whole life. My mother sold some furniture to the new owners. And that was one of the items she sold.' Kate shook her head. 'It's silly, really.'

'That's a shame,' Bertie said. 'That you couldn't keep it.'

'I'm being sentimental,' Kate said. 'It really is just an old table. But it reminds me of my father.' She placed her hand to her St Christopher. 'We're lucky that we have these tokens to remember our fathers by. I'm sure some aren't so lucky.'

'We are, Katherine,' Bertie said. He smiled at her.

Kate twisted her glass on the table. 'Kate,' she said. 'You can call me, Kate. If you'd like to.'

'I would,' Bertie said. He put his glass to his lips but couldn't hide a grin.

. . .

Kate refused Bertie's offer of another drink. As much as she would have liked to stay longer, she also had a busy morning ahead with the final costume to make. Bertie drove slowly up the drive and brought the car to a stop at the side of the house.

He turned off the engine. 'I'll walk you into the house,' he said.

'There's really no need,' Kate said. 'You should get home, too.'

'I'd like to.' Bertie made his way around the car and opened the passenger door for her. They walked slowly around the side of the house, with only the light from the moon showing their way. An owl hooted in the woods close by. Their shoes crunched in the gravel. A frost had begun to settle and sparkle on the grass.

They stopped at the steps leading down to the basement kitchen.

'I'll leave you here,' Bertie said softly. 'You have your key, don't you?' His warm breath was a cloud in the cold night air.

Kate nodded. 'Thank you,' she said quietly.

'And thank you,' Bertie said. 'You have been wonderful company. And I need to continue my education in films and actors. Perhaps we can go to another picture next week.'

'I'd like that,' Kate said. She tucked her hair behind her ear and tried to force herself to head down the steps to the door. Her feet refused to move. All she could do was look at Bertie while he looked at her. Finally, he took a deep breath. 'I suppose I should say goodnight,' he said.

'I suppose you should,' Kate said.

With a smile, Bertie said, 'Goodnight, Kate.'

Up in her room, Kate dropped her handbag and kicked off her shoes. She shrugged off her coat and let it fall to the floor. She tumbled onto the bed and stared up at the ceiling. Almost immediately, she was on her feet again. Pacing to the window and back to the door, she caught a glimpse of herself in the mirror above the fireplace. Someone had kindly been in to light a small fire. Her cheeks were pink from coming in from the cold to the relative warmth. She walked to the window again and looked down the drive. On their way from The White Lion, Bertie had pointed out the cottage where he lived. It was the cottage his grandmother and his parents had lived in. Try as hard as she might, Kate couldn't see lights from any of the cottage windows. She was just a bit too far away.

Leaving the window, she collected her coat and hung it behind the door. She changed into her nightdress and slipped into the warm bed. Whoever had lit the fire had also very thoughtfully put a hot water bottle between her sheets. She moved the stone bottle to the end of the bed, turned out the light and snuggled down under her blankets. She could feel herself smiling, which made her smile even more. So many thoughts and images wanted her to think about them at the same time. Watching Bertie in the darkness of The Grand. Sitting beside him at the fish and chip shop, their arms touching. Talking about their fathers in his local pub where he had been pleased to take her for all to see.

Kate turned onto her side. She breathed out deeply and pressed her toes to the hot water bottle. He had said her name. The name her friends called her. Kate. It had sounded so nice in his voice. So normal and reassuring. Closing her eyes, Kate nestled even further into the warmth.

TWENTY-ONE

WEDNESDAY 30TH OCTOBER, 1935

It was dark when Kate woke the next morning and dark when she made up the fires in the downstairs rooms. It was still dark when she sat down at the sewing machine to start work on the final costume.

As she worked, a glow began to light the room. She looked over her shoulder to see the pink sky of the morning just breaking.

Red sky at night, shepherd's delight.
Red sky in the morning, shepherd's warning.

Smiling at the memory of her father looking out of the window each morning to see what job the weather would allow in his garden, Kate got up to turn out the lamps. She sat back at the sewing machine and pressed the treadle, easing a seam of the Pierrot costume through the needle.

She was so skilled at using the machine that her mind frequently drifted away to the trip to the pictures. Bertie had been the perfect gentleman. The perfect companion. The thought of going to the pictures with him again made her cover her mouth and smile into her hand.

The picture they had seen had made her think, too. The clairvoyant of the title had been a charlatan, his accomplice feeding him information about individuals so that it appeared he could tell a person's past or future as part of his music hall act. When really his predictions were based on intelligence he had been given. Hadn't that been her family's explanation for her party trick? Her family would certainly have thought her mad if she tried to say she sometimes knew nothing of an object until it was placed in her hands. That her touch would see the history come through from the object as an image. But these visions since she had arrived at Hill House... she couldn't explain why they were happening here and why they were so different. They were sudden, sharp in focus and affected all her senses.

Kate shook her head, what was she trying to tell herself? That Hill House had somehow unlocked something in her? That her gift was developing simply by being here? In the picture, the clairvoyant's true skill had been awakened by a person he met. Only through his closeness to her could he truly predict the future. If Kate let her mind carry her on the path it was trying to take her, it would attempt to convince her that a house was awakening her skills.

She shook her head again. Unlike the clairvoyant in the picture, she couldn't tell the future. She saw only the past of an object. What purpose was there in that? What benefit? And why did it happen to her? They were questions she had asked herself so many times since she was a very small child. She could go to the spiritualist church and ask if they saw something in her to explain her skill. Bertie's mother and grandmother must believe in what they were able to tell if they had visited for at least a decade. The thought led her back to Bertie. She hid a smile behind her hand again. There were no answers to the questions in her mind, so there was little point dwelling on them anymore this morning.

At almost eleven o'clock, Kate sat back in her chair. Raising her arms above her head, she grasped her hands and moved them from side to side, stretching her spine and crunching each back-bone into place. Taking up the scissors, she snipped the thread on the final seam of the tabard. Turning it the right way round, she shook it out and held it against herself. The baggy trousers were already draped over the back of the sofa with the other costumes. All she had to do was hem the trousers and stitch the black pompoms onto the tabard. She would be done by early afternoon.

'I thought you'd done a flit in the middle of the night!' Rosemary said when Kate pushed open the kitchen door. 'Your room was already empty when I got up.'

The sisters were sitting at the kitchen table having their morning tea. 'I wanted to get ahead of myself,' Kate said, taking a cup and saucer down from the dresser. 'I want to finish the costumes this afternoon.' She sat at the table and picked up the teapot.

'You're a dark horse, Katherine Durrant.' Rosemary smiled at Kate over the rim of her teacup.

'Stop it,' Audrey said to her sister. 'Have you had breakfast, Katherine?'

Kate shook her head. She picked up the jug and added a splash of milk to her cup.

'Well, we'll sort that out,' Audrey said. 'You can't be expected to work on an empty stomach.'

'I don't want to be any trouble,' Kate said.

'Why would it be trouble?' Audrey said. 'My job is to feed the household.'

Kate knew better than to argue with Audrey, especially when it came to her duties. 'Thank you,' she said.

Audrey got to her feet and brushed down her apron.

Kate added sugar to her tea and stirred it. While Audrey busied herself at the refrigerator, Rosemary stared at Kate, still grinning over the top of her teacup. Finally, she placed it into the saucer.

'Where was my invitation?' she said. 'That's what I'd like to know.'

'Excuse me?' Kate said.

'To the pictures last night.'

'Oh,' Kate said. She could feel the colour begin to rise in her cheeks. 'Sorry.'

Audrey closed the refrigerator door with a thud. 'It wasn't your day off,' she said to her sister. 'You can't go off gallivanting when it's not your day off.'

Rosemary still stared at Kate, smiling.

'It was Tommy,' Audrey said, cracking two eggs into a pan. 'He told us that you'd gone to the pictures.' She looked over her shoulder at Rosemary. 'And you can stop with your gossiping.'

Rosemary picked up her cup and took another sip. 'Bertie came in earlier, for his morning tea,' she said. 'Like a dog with two tails, he was.'

'Rosemary!' Audrey said.

'It's not gossiping.' Rosemary put her cup down in its saucer, making the spoon rattle. 'I'm only saying what I've seen and heard.'

Audrey wiped her hands on a tea towel. 'The furniture in the library isn't going to dust itself, is it? I want that done before lunch.'

'Before lunch?' Rosemary said. 'That's hardly any time.'

'Then you'd best get on with it.' Audrey turned back to the

range. Rosemary gave her sister a look that said, in that moment, she really didn't like her very much. She pushed her chair away from the table.

'I'll see you later,' Rosemary said to Kate before leaving the kitchen and stomping away up the hall like a little girl who'd had a telling off from her mother. Almost as soon as she had left, there was a knock at the kitchen door.

Audrey and Kate both looked up.

'I've this,' Elliot said, showing them a small parcel. 'For Master Thomas, it says. Postman just gave it to me on the drive.'

'He's out at the moment,' Audrey said. 'He's gone into town with Mrs Hart to get something for his mother. I'd say leave it on the post tray in the hall. He'll see it when he gets home.'

'Right,' Elliot said.

'Will you want a cup of tea?' Audrey asked.

'No. I've my work to get on with. But thank you all the same.' He touched the peak of his cap and closed the door behind him.

Kate collected her cup and the tea things and placed them in the sink. 'Thank you,' she said to Audrey.

'For what?' Audrey asked.

'For stopping Rosemary saying whatever it is that she was going to say.'

'My little sister is too fond of sticking her nose into the business of others,' Audrey said, flicking hot oil onto the tops of the two eggs. 'You and I are a few years older than her and know when to let alone. Pay her no mind and don't feel you have to explain yourself to her.' She took a loaf of bread from the bread bin and placed it on a board. 'But know that her heart is in the right place. We both care for Bertie very much. We've known him since we were children. But she does like to tease him, like she would if he was our brother.'

Kate smiled. 'I know what that's like. I'm afraid I was just as troublesome to my brother.'

Audrey stopped flicking the oil. Resting the spoon against the side of the pan, she looked at Kate. 'I know you have been separated from your family,' she said. 'But I do hope that with me and Rosemary, you feel you have found somewhere akin to a home. You're a good worker. And I speak as I find.' She smiled. It was the first time Kate had seen her smile.

'Thank you,' Kate said. 'I really do appreciate how welcome you and Rosemary have made me.'

Audrey batted her compliment away. 'Sit yourself down,' she said. 'I'll see to those pots later. We need to make sure you have a good feed.'

Audrey was true to her word and gave Kate a very good feed. There were fried eggs, two slices of ham, fried bread and butter, washed down with a pot of tea. Audrey began the preparation of a soup for lunch while Kate ate. They chatted about the house. Audrey didn't mention the trip to the pictures. But it was all Kate could think about. Rosemary had said that Bertie was like a dog with two tails when he had his morning tea. Kate hooked her forefinger over her top lip as she chewed, to hide the smile which simply would not go. With so much work left on the final costume, she had to push thoughts of the pictures away so that she could concentrate. But here and now, in the kitchen with Audrey and chatting about chores in a way that Kate didn't really have to concentrate on, she pictured Bertie's arm on the armrest between them in The Grand, the condensation on the window of the fish and chip shop as they sat next to each other on the bench, Bertie's elbow touching hers, the warm fire in the pub with glasses of stout and talk of their fathers, the cold night air as he walked her around the side of the house, his breath a warm cloud. And how she wished he would kiss her.

'Katherine... Katherine...'

'Sorry,' Kate said, bringing herself back into the moment. In the kitchen. At the table.

'I was talking to you,' Audrey said. 'It was like you weren't listening or couldn't hear me. Are you ailing?' she asked, staring at Kate through the thick glass of her spectacles.

'Pardon?' Kate said, trying to regain control of herself.

'I hope you're not coming down with whatever it was Tommy had.' Audrey said. 'I should imagine it's because you're tired. You really should get more sleep.'

'I have,' Kate said. 'I mean, I have been sleeping.'

'That's not what I heard last night.' Audrey turned back to the stove and stirred something in a pan. 'Such a commotion from up your end of the corridor. And it was past midnight. I looked at the clock on my nightstand.'

Midnight? Kate thought. It wasn't even eleven o'clock when she had settled into the warmth of the hot water bottle. 'Perhaps it was Rosemary,' she said.

'What would Rosemary be doing up at gone midnight?' Audrey stirred the contents of the pan. 'Besides, I asked her earlier and she said she was fast asleep all night.'

'But I wasn't up at that time either,' Kate said.

Audrey glanced over her shoulder. 'I daresay you got up to use the lav in the middle of the night and have forgotten about it.'

Kate was about to say that no, she hadn't. But stopped herself. 'That must have been it,' she said, trying to sound convincing. She had never been one for walking in her sleep and was hardly likely to start at her age. But something inside her made her want to confirm Audrey's suspicions. Because all she could see in her mind's eye was the face of the awful boy who had wanted to hurt Pegasus. The boy who she was sure had glared at her.

Taking the salt down from the shelf, Audrey added a pinch to the pan. 'I don't know what you were doing. It sounded like that door at the end was going to come away from its hinges for a moment. And then it stopped. Had you gone to the wrong door?'

She waited for an answer, but all Kate could do was stare at Audrey's dark hair pulled back into a bun. 'Well?' Audrey tried again.

'Yes... yes... that must have been it.'

'I was going to put on my slippers to come out to see what all the fuss was about. But when the noise stopped, I thought you must have realised your mistake and found the bathroom in the dark.' Audrey returned to her cooking, clearly satisfied that the late-night goings on in their corridor had been explained.

TWENTY-TWO

Sitting back at the sewing machine, Kate hemmed the trousers of the Pierrot costume and the edges of the tabard. It was a task she preferred to do by hand, which meant there was no noise. No rattle of the machine to drown out her thoughts. She focused on the stitches, making each one the same length and size as its neighbour. And she had almost completed the last side of the tabard when finally, the thought would not be silenced. What had made that noise out in the corridor last night? If it hadn't been Audrey or Rosemary rattling the door at the end of the corridor and it hadn't been her, who was it? Her brain sought to find a logical explanation. Wind. There had been a storm that rattled the door. But last night had been still. There was something wrong with the door that made it move for no reason. But that didn't make any sense. And then it came again. The image she had been trying so hard to push away. The face of the angry child in the mirror. Only in her mind, it was even more awful than she remembered. Contorted and out of control. What was she trying to say to herself? That the child had somehow jumped from the mirror, charged down the corridor and thrown itself at the door in an attempt to get through. To get into the first occupied room. Her room. A sharp stab made her wince. A drop of blood bloomed on her finger. She quickly put her finger in her mouth and set the tabard aside. It wasn't enough that her mind was plagued by the image of the child, now events were conspiring to stain the tabard and see her ruin her work of the morning.

Getting up, she took a handkerchief from the pocket of her apron and wrapped it around her finger. She looked out of the window. It was a clear day. The sun shone and there was a glow over the drive and the lawn.

A knock at the door made her turn around. 'Come in,' she said.

The door opened and the thoughts that had plagued her suddenly seemed less important.

'Hello,' Bertie said.

Kate took a step towards the door. 'Hello,' she said, knowing that she was smiling.

'How are you today?' he asked.

'Very well,' she said. 'And you?'

'Perfect.' He smiled.

Kate hadn't realised but Bertie had one hand behind his back. When he brought it forward, she saw that he was holding a familiar box. 'You forgot these,' Bertie said. 'They were on the back seat of the car.'

'Thank you,' Kate said. But when she reached to take the box of chocolates, Bertie looked down at her hand and frowned.

'You've hurt yourself,' he said.

'It's nothing, really,' she said. 'I just pricked my finger on a needle.'

'Let me take a look,' Bertie said.

He placed the chocolates on the table and took Kate's hand in his. Kate watched as he gently unwrapped the handkerchief and placed it on the table with the chocolates. He examined her finger so earnestly, and while he checked her over, she studied his face. His fair hair had fallen forwards, and the side of his moustache rose as he considered the small spot of blood on her finger.

'I should get the first aid kit,' he said.

'There really is no need,' Kate said. 'It's only a little prick.'

Bertie glanced to the tabard draped over the sewing machine table. 'You don't want to bleed on your handiwork,' he said.

'You're right,' Kate said. 'I wouldn't want to do that.'

'I'll be just a minute,' he said. 'The tin is in the office.'

Bertie left in such a rush that anyone would have been forgiven for thinking he was about to tend a patient with a broken limb. True to his word, he returned before Kate had the chance to move. He brought with him a tin, which he placed on the table. Opening it, he removed a square of gauze and a roll of adhesive dressing tape. Kate watched as he took a small pair of scissors from the tin. He cut a piece from the gauze and a length of tape, which he stuck to the very edge of his thumb. Gently, so very gently, he took Kate's hand in his again. He placed the gauze over the almost non-existent wound. She stared at his face as he peeled the tape from his thumb and wrapped it around her finger, pressing it with great care to her skin. He nodded at his dressing. When he glanced up, Kate didn't look away.

'Thank you,' she said.

'You're very welcome,' Bertie said. He still held her hand, his fingers warm on hers.

For a moment Kate thought about what Audrey had told her about the door. Hadn't Bertie said last night that she could talk to him about anything that troubled her? Particularly about Hill House. 'May I ask you a question?' she said.

Bertie nodded. 'Of course.'

Kate chose her words carefully. 'It's probably nothing,' she said. 'But Audrey was sure she heard noises last night coming from the door up in the attic that separates our side from the lumber room side. She might have been dreaming. Or it could have been the wind rattling the door, but—'

'Would you like me to check that the door is secure and locked?' Bertie asked.

'If it's no trouble,' Kate said.

'No trouble at all,' Bertie said. 'It's my job to make sure everyone in the house is safe.' His chest heaved as he let out a breath. 'I enjoyed last night very much,' he said.

'I did, too,' Kate said.

Bertie's fingers tightened around hers. 'I should probably let you get back to your work.'

'You probably should,' Kate said.

She gave Bertie's hand a squeeze. He sighed and shook his head, smiling all the while.

'Will you come to the pictures with me next week?' he asked.

'There's nothing I would rather do on my evening off,' she said, knowing that she was smiling as broadly as Bertie.

'I really must get on,' Bertie said. 'And I must let you get on so that everything is ready for the children tomorrow.'

His hand slipped from hers. 'Enjoy the rest of the chocolates,' he said. 'And let me know if there's any help you need with the costumes. Or anything else.'

'I will,' Kate said.

Bertie walked slowly across the room. When he reached the door, he paused and looked back. It seemed that he might be just as reluctant to leave as Kate was to see him go. He raised his hand.

'I'll see you later, Kate,' he said and closed the door gently behind him.

His footstep had barely crossed the hall when Kate fell back into one of the armchairs. She clasped her hands, recalling Bertie's warm fingers. How gentle he had been. How careful he was with her. And how kind. She looked up to the ceiling and smiled.

TWENTY-THREE

'How are you getting on?' Audrey said, when Kate joined her in the kitchen.

'I sewed the final pompoms onto the last costume and now everything is ready.' Kate looked past Audrey to a pan bubbling on the range. She took a deep breath of the sticky brown liquid. 'Sugar?' she asked.

'I always make cinder toffee for the children for Halloween. They like to eat it sitting around the fire in the stable yard when Elliot tries to frighten them half to death with his stories.'

'Are they really that frightening?' Kate asked.

Audrey kept the sticky liquid moving with a wooden spoon. 'Elliot's mother was Irish. You can't normally get a word out of him about his family – or anything really – but on Halloween he will tell the stories his mother told him as child. About how the spirits come out on All Hallows' Eve, and the mischievous fairies, and how the veil between the living and dead is at its thinnest.' She shuddered. 'I don't scare easily but his stories set my nerves on edge.' She lowered her voice. 'Mary, who used to work here, told me that Elliot's mother more than told stories. Apparently, she had special... gifts.

Fortune telling and communing with spirits.' Audrey shuddered again.

A bell rang out in the hall rang. Audrey frowned. 'Our Rosemary has gone out with Mrs Mandeville and Mrs Kenmore to collect foliage from the woods to decorate the stable yard.' She looked from the pan to the basement corridor.

'Would you like me to go?' Kate asked. Since the costumes were finished, she should show willing to work in any way she could.

'Thank you,' Audrey said. 'I should imagine it will only be someone wanting tea.'

Up in the passageway, Kate looked at the bells, waiting for one to ring again. She didn't have to wait long. Above her head, the coiled spring attached to the bell for the morning room danced, making the bell chime. Quickly, Kate passed through the passageway into the hall. But in the morning room, she found... nobody. It had definitely been the bell for the morning room, she was sure of it. She looked around. Everything was as she had left it. Costumes neatly arranged over the back of the sofa. All the leftover fabric folded, and pins, needles and scissors tidied away. It didn't look at all like anybody had been in there. Kate stopped short of checking to see whether anyone was hiding behind the curtains to play a trick on her and settled instead on going back to check the bells.

On her way out, she paused to plump a cushion that was quite flat. It was on the armchair nearest the door. She must have crushed it when she collapsed into the chair after Bertie applied the dressing to her finger. She took the pale green cushion in her arms and instantly a flash stopped her. She saw the cushion, not in her arms, but behind a seated woman. It was the woman she had seen in the stables. But now, she was sitting on one of the sofas. In a dress that looked like the ones women wore in the historical films Kate loved so much. She was not alone. There were two other women, one kneeling on a rug before the fireplace and another sitting in an armchair. Before Kate could see their faces, the scene changed. She was still in the morning room. But she was alone. And then she wasn't. The now-familiar woman ran through the door to the window. She was followed by a man. She pointed to something out of the window and the man looked. Almost instantly, his focus turned to the woman. He looked at her so warmly. With love. Such a love that Kate had never seen. As though his eyes burned into the woman, so full of yearning. The scene changed. Kate was no longer in the morning room, but in a bedroom. A masculine room with books on shelves, trophies, and riding boots. It was night-time and a fire burned brightly in the hearth and the room was lit only by lamps. The couple from the morning room stood in the middle of the room. Kissing. Kissing so passionately. He kissed her neck, her shoulders. Slipped her dress down. She struggled to help him. They kissed again. They...

'Kate... Kate?'

With a flash, Kate was no longer in the bedroom. She was in the morning room. Her breath came thick and hot. In her mind's eye, all she could see was the couple. Her legs gave way. She fell into the armchair. Dropping the cushion to the floor, she stared straight ahead. Someone crouched before her.

'Kate ... Kate ...?'

The voice was familiar. She looked up to its owner. Bertie stared at her with so much concern that she could have cried.

'What's happened, Kate?' he said gently. 'I came to tell you the door upstairs is secure. I thought you'd be pleased to hear it.'

She couldn't form a single word. She gasped for breath.

'Are you unwell?' Bertie tried.

Kate shook her head. How could she ever explain to him what had just happened? She stared at the cushion on the rug. Why did it have to be Bertie that found her like this?

'Please, Kate,' he said. 'Please tell me what's happened to you.'

Kate wrapped her arms around herself. Still staring at the rug. Still not looking Bertie.

'Stay here,' he said. 'Please, Kate, stay here while I go to get someone.'

Still with her arms around herself, Kate heard Bertie leave. Once she was sure that he was gone, she looked towards the door. She tried to slow her breathing, filling her lungs full of air before exhaling slowly. What she had seen in that room played in her mind over and over again. But instead of the couple, she saw herself and Bertie. She grasped the edge of the chair and sat forwards. It didn't matter what she did, the image would not change. She imagined Bertie kissing her neck and shoulders and pushing down her dress. The breath caught in her throat again. She had never done anything like that... a man had never kissed her like that. There had been a couple of chaps in Sheffield who had stolen a kiss at the end of the night at a dance. But nothing like... *that*. And she had never seen two people do such things before. But she could feel it. Feel it in her heart as the blood pumped so fast, she felt she might faint. And she felt it through her body. Like a charge.

The door flew open.

'Katherine,' Mrs Hart said. She rested her cane against the arm of the chair and placed her palm on Kate's forehead.

'No fever,' Mrs Hart said. 'But you're trembling.' She placed her finger beneath Kate's chin and gently tipped her face up. Kate had no choice but to look at Mrs Hart, who held up a finger. 'Follow this, please,' she said. Kate moved her eyes from side to side, following Mrs Hart's finger. Mrs Hart nodded. 'And can you stand up, Katherine?' she asked.

Without responding, Kate rose from the chair so that she stood before Mrs Hart.

'Would you mind going down to the kitchen,' she said over her shoulder, 'and asking Audrey to make some beef tea? Oh,' she added, 'and please say it's for me. I'm sure Katherine doesn't need all and sundry in the house knowing her business.'

Kate briefly let her gaze rise. She hadn't realised that Bertie had come back. But there he was, his hand on the door. Watching.

'Of course,' he said quietly. 'I'll bring it up.'

'Thank you, Bertie,' Mrs Hart said. 'Would you mind closing the door on your way out?'

With one hand, Mrs Hart took hold of her cane and with the other, she grasped Kate's hand. Guiding Kate to the sofa free of costumes, she had her sit down and sat beside her. Mrs Hart rested her cane against the arm of the sofa and took Kate's hands in hers. They were positioned so that they faced each other. As much as Kate kept her focus on her own lap, there was no escaping the fact that Mrs Hart's eyes were on her, searching. Finally, and trying as hard as she might, Kate was unable to keep from looking at Mrs Hart.

'There,' Mrs Hart said, her eyes soft and kind, 'Now that you can bear to look at me, we can talk.' She gave Kate's hands a gentle squeeze. 'You are not ill, are you, Katherine?'

Kate shook her head.

'Sometimes we need a diversion from our thoughts,' Mrs Hart said. 'Would you mind if I told you a story?'

Kate shook her head again. She would listen to Mrs Hart's stories all day if it meant she didn't have to speak. Because what could she possibly say to explain her behaviour?

'I have always been fond of stories about old houses,' Mrs Hart said. 'You see, I find it fascinating to think of all the people who have lived in a house. Small houses, large houses, grand houses, castles, and palaces; they all hold the stories of the people who have called them home. Take the dower house where I live now with my brother and his wife. It is a beautiful house built on the land of Caxton Hall. It was built specifically to house the dowager. Imagine! It is a house built for a single person to call home, but it is a house far larger and far grander even than Hill House.' Her eyes widened, making Kate smile. 'But for me, there is also a sadness about it. It is a house built for a widow. It is not restricted to Caxton Hall. Any grand house like it will have its dower house, to house the woman who had once been mistress of the great Hall. On the death of her husband, she must leave her home to make room for her son to inherit his father's title and his wife to become mistress of the grand house. Not only must she leave her home, but she must relinquish the title bestowed on her in marriage. It is no longer hers. It was transient and on the death of her husband, passes to her daughter-in-law. So, you see, for me, a dower house – as grand as it might be – feels tinged with a melancholy. Thanks to the current Lady Caxton, we can live there in more comfort than most can enjoy. It is peaceful and tranquil. It got rather noisy here for Lady Mandeville – she has always lived on her nerves and as much as I would be happy to live amongst the children, she finds it... overwhelming. I like to keep her company, especially as Sir Charles is away on ministerial business in London for much of each week. And we have lots of visitors with the children constantly coming over for tea! But at night, when I sit alone, I feel that I can almost hear the voices of the house talking to me. Not in words necessarily, but in feelings. In things that I sense. Have you ever had the sensation when you walk into a room that there is a presence there? As though someone left the moment you entered but you can still feel their energy.'

Mrs Hart's eyes remained fixed on Kate's.

'I don't... I don't know...' Kate said.

Seemingly unperturbed by Kate's response, Mrs Hart continued. 'You know, I often fancy that every house has a... how to put it? A soul, if you will. With so many lives having passed through it, how could the walls not somehow soak up some of the energy... some of the essence... some of the history of each person who has crossed its threshold or called it home? I think most people would be oblivious to the other lives of the house. They go along with their lives, not hearing what the house has to tell us. But then there are special people. People who are open to the voices. Who can hear what a house has to say. And do you know what else I think?' Mrs Hart lowered her voice. 'I think there are those that are even more special. There are those who can see what has passed in the house before and hear what the house has to tell us about its future. Who are brought into the house to help. Some even come back more than once when they are needed, because they love this house and have loved the people in it. Because don't we all need help sometimes, Katherine?'

Kate stared at Mrs Hart, unable to speak. It was as though Mrs Hart was somehow inside her head, reading her mind.

'The last incumbent of the dower house at Caxton Hall – Lady Caxton – was a marvellous woman. I feel her presence there every day. In life, she was such a great friend. And why should she not be there even when she has passed? Her daughter, Emma, the current Lady Caxton, has inherited all of her late mother's qualities. She is generous and loyal and fiercely believes in doing the right thing. And she shares her late mother's feelings about her own brother.'

Mrs Hart's face altered. A hardness deepened the fine lines in her face. 'Emma feels the same about her brother, George Caxton, as their mother did. It broke Lady Mandeville's heart to cut him off but had she not, he would have ruined his family. His father Lord Caxton knew it, too, and made sure that Emma inherited Caxton Hall and not George. Even his mother, Lady Caxton, could see George for what he was.' She paused. 'I never used to believe that there were people who could be without redemption. In my whole life, I have believed that people should be given the opportunity to atone for their behaviour. Even crimes. But through George Caxton, we have all come to know that there are people who are evil. They delight in tormenting others. There are some people whose presence taints a house and who will do all they can to destroy that house and the family that lives within it. Even when they are not here.' Mrs Hart squeezed Kate's hands tightly. The intensity with which she looked into Kate's eyes, made Kate want to turn away. At the same time, she felt compelled to continue to look. It was as though Mrs Hart was still talking to her but without the need for words. And then, as suddenly as Mrs Hart had grasped Kate in her spell, it was broken. She smiled. Letting go of Kate's hands, she patted them.

'Sorry,' Mrs Hart said, shaking her head. 'That wasn't a very good story, was it? By rights, a story should have a beginning, a middle and an end. I have just given you the beginning and the middle. But Katherine, it is my true belief that we must all write our own ending. Anyway.' She clapped her hands to her knees. 'I talk too much. In my experience, it is those who rarely speak, or those who speak quietly, that have the most to say. And who we should listen to most carefully.'

The door opened. Bertie entered, carrying a teacup with steam swirling above it.

'Thank you, Bertie,' Mrs Hart said. 'Pop the tea on the table, that's it.' She took up her cane. Leaning on the silver handle, she rose to her feet. 'Give me your arm please, Bertie,' she said. 'I'd like to go and see how Audrey's toffee is coming along. I might even sample a piece. I am a fiend for a sugary treat! And I think Katherine could do with some time alone to drink her tea and gather her thoughts.'

'How are you feeling, Kate?' Bertie asked, placing the tea on the table closest to her.

'Katherine is feeling so much better,' Mrs Hart said. 'Aren't you, dear?'

Kate nodded.

Bertie offered his arm to Mrs Hart. She took it and smiled at

Kate. 'Drink your tea while it's hot. Now come along, Bertie.
I'm sure I can smell that toffee and hear it calling to me. Oh, and
Katherine, you will be joining us in the stable yard for Elliot's
stories, won't you? Seven o'clock sharp!'

Alone, Kate took up the cup. She blew across the top and
took a sip of the hot beef tea. She didn't know what else to do.
What had Mrs Hart's story meant? If, indeed, it meant anything
at all. Did she expect Kate to find some meaning in it? It hadn't
really been a story at all. It had seemed like a lesson in the
Mandevilles and their cousins across the valley at Caxton Hall.
And if, as Mrs Hart had said, Kate should write her own ending
to the story, how should she know what to write when the
beginning and middle didn't make any sense? She didn't know
this George Caxton and his sister, the current Lady Caxton,
and was hardly likely to meet them. She didn't keep the
company of aristocrats. She only knew the Mandevilles because
she worked for them. She wasn't part of their story. Unless she
could include her visions. They seemed to want to tell her the
history of this house, but they couldn't. Because she didn't
know it.

Kate placed the cup back in its saucer and looked into the
coals glowing in the fireplace. It was clear that the quiet man
who Mrs Hart spoke of was Bertie. He only ever spoke sense
and about things that mattered. Perhaps, after all, Mrs Hart had
simply wanted to play matchmaker and sing the praises of good
and diligent men like Bertie Morrison. It must be Bertie who
had been brought in to help the house. And he saw to its future,
too, with the planning and work as the estate manager. He had
lived here his whole life and was as much a part of Hill House
as the fine furniture and as much a part of this family as anyone
born into it. All Mrs Hart had said about this George Caxton
must have been to warn her away from men like him.
Dangerous men. Men who were not to be trusted.

Kate got to her feet. She rested her arms on the mantelpiece.

Balancing her forehead on her wrists, she looked down into the fire. She couldn't be sure of much of the reason behind Mrs Hart's words or their meaning, but one thing she was sure of in all of this was what she had felt when she imagined those lovers in the bedroom. A thrill raced through her again. It touched every part of her body, making it come alive. Because what she had imagined them doing, she had simultaneously imagined doing with Bertie. Poor Bertie. How would he feel if he knew the thoughts in her head? Had he ever done such a thing with another woman?

Recoiling from the heat of the fire, Kate collected the cup and saucer.

The hall was mercifully cool as was the stone passageway. Kate had been planning to return the cup to the kitchen but stopped at the top of the stone stairs. Voices raised in good spirits came from the kitchen. She could make out Audrey, Mrs Hart and Bertie. She couldn't hear what they said but recognised the pitch of each voice.

She faltered in the passageway and was more than a little relieved and surprised when a bell rang above her head. 'I'll go,' she called before anyone could come from the kitchen. Placing the teacup and saucer on the top step, she ran along the passageway and up the back stairs.

At the first floor, she emerged onto the carpeted landing. Since Rosemary was responsible for making up the fires for the family and seeing to their rooms, Kate hadn't been on this floor many times. But Rosemary had given her a quick tour of the corridor and explained which bedroom lay behind each closed door.

Kate came to the room whose bell had rung down in the passageway. She knocked. 'Hello,' she said. 'You rang.'

There was no response.

'Hello,' she said, just a little louder. She pressed her ear to the door. There was no noise from within. Turning the handle, she pushed open the door. Still standing on the threshold, Kate put her hand to her mouth. Bookshelves lined one wall of the room. Sporting trophies took pride of place on the mantelshelf. There was a washstand with hairbrushes, a bowl and jug, a box of collars that had fallen out of fashion at least twenty years ago. An ashtray sat on the arm of the comfortable looking chair. A pair of long boots stood beside the fireplace. On the bed was a small well-used leather suitcase. And next to the bed was a roll-top desk. Kate had never seen this room before this moment. But she knew it. It was the room of the couple. She closed her eyes and saw them again, standing on the rug in the centre of this room. Embracing. Then in the bed. Covers kicked away. Him, with his arms around her naked body. Them, looking at their reflection and smiling at each other. Her, turning to him and kissing him.

The heat of the room wrapped around Kate. The heat of them. The heat they had made. She opened her eyes and placed her hand to her chest. Her heart beat rapidly. But in the light of day, this room... it was cold. This room that had once belonged to a man who was no stranger to her. Unlike the woman, Kate knew him. She had dusted the frame of his portrait in the hall. The man she had seen in her visions and who had once called this room his own, was Captain Thomas Mandeville.

Kate looked around the room. If what she had seen in her vision had once happened, could it be because the events that had occurred between Captain Mandeville and his lover were now held in the walls of this house? In its fabric. In its soul.

'Hello, Katherine.'

Kate's heart slammed into her ribs.

'I'm so sorry,' Tommy said. 'I didn't mean to startle you.'

Kate steadied herself. 'I just wasn't expecting... Did you ring the bell in here?'

Tommy shook his head. 'Not me,' he said.

'Then perhaps one of the children?'

He shook his head again. 'The squibs are all at school.' He crossed the room and took hold of the handle beside the fireplace. He turned it and it spun around. There was no tension in it. No resistance. 'Hasn't worked for as long as I've known it,' Tommy said.

Kate managed to bring her breathing just about under control. 'It must have been a bell in another room,' she said, although she knew full well that it had been the bell in this room. 'I'm sorry to have disturbed you,' she said, backing away towards the door.

Tommy smiled brightly, his face full of life. 'It's no trouble at all,' he said. 'I say,' he added, with real excitement. 'Did you enjoy the film last night with Bertie? I haven't seen him today to ask.'

Kate thought back to the trip to The Grand. How far away that all seemed now. How normal in the face of... everything. She backed away still further but wasn't looking where she was going. She stumbled into a small side table. A photograph in a frame rocked. Tommy leapt to catch it before it could tumble to the floor.

'I'm so sorry,' Kate said.

Tommy smiled. 'Don't be. I should imagine my uncle rather enjoyed going on a bit of a trip there!' He laughed at his own joke. 'I'm named for him, you know, my Uncle Thomas. Pa's older brother. I wish I could have met him, but I was born years after he died. I hope I can be at least half the man he was.' He looked down at the photograph, his eyes filling with pride for a man he had never known. 'I come in here sometimes to think about him. To read his books and soak up something of him. I want to be able to live up to his name.'

'I should leave,' Kate said. 'I've disturbed you for long enough.'

If Tommy heard, he didn't answer. As Kate took another step back, crossing the threshold into the hall, Tommy appeared to lose his footing. He stumbled and sat heavily on the bed.

'Tommy?' Kate said. 'Tommy, what is it?'

He clutched the photograph, staring into it, seemingly transfixed by the image of his uncle. He began to tremble.

Kate stepped back onto the bedroom and knelt before him. 'Do you feel ill again? Tommy, are you ill again?'

Tommy slowly shook his head.

Kate tried to take the frame from his hands, but he held it firmly. As suddenly as he had begun trembling Tommy became still. He tensed. And he began to sway. He was behaving as he had in the housekeeper's parlour when they were last alone.

'I see him, sometimes,' Tommy said. He spoke so quietly and so softly. It was his voice, but it sounded different somehow. 'I know you understand.' He looked at Kate. Just like the evening in the parlour, his eyes were wide, his pupils dark and larger than they ought to be.

Kate searched her mind for how to respond. She did understand that he might see his uncle sometimes, but to say as much would make her sound quite mad.

Tommy nodded. 'It's you,' he said. 'You will help. You will. And I am sorry. I should be the one to help you. Guide you.'

'What do you mean?' Kate said. 'I'm here to work. To do a job as a housemaid.'

Tommy shook his head. 'You are here because we need your help. You have a gift that can help.' He smiled, so warmly. 'You are a special visitor. Ah, and you have seen other special visitors.' He smiled. 'Yes, you have seen them. In your dreams.'

'What are you saying, Tommy?' Kate said. 'I don't understand any of this.'

He seemed to think for a few moments. Then his brow furrowed, and he shook his head. 'I can't see,' he said. 'I can see what has been before, but not what I am to do now. He is getting in the way. He is making me ill. He doesn't want me here. He doesn't want me anywhere.'

Again, Tommy began to tremble. Kate placed her hand over his. 'Please, Tommy,' she said. 'Please wake up.' She glanced at the handle beside the fireplace. It should be attached to pulleys and mechanisms running behind the walls of the house and ending with a wire agitating a spring to make it dance up on the wall in the passageway. She should be able to use it to summon someone to come to help.

'I don't need anyone else,' Tommy said so quietly that it was little more than a whisper. 'It is you that I need. You. *One in, one out.* It's the way it always has been, it's the way it always will be.'

Tommy's hands dropped to his knees so that the framed photograph rested on his legs. He blinked. Blinked again. Colour bloomed in his face and all Kate could do was stare at the transformation.

'He's very handsome, isn't he?' Tommy said. 'I hope I've inherited some of that, too.' He smiled at Kate as though oblivious to what had just occurred between them. He held the frame up to his face. 'What do you think? Is there a resemblance?'

Tommy's face was once again flushed with health. The man in the photograph was captured in shades of greys. He wore a military uniform. Not the grand uniform of the portrait below the stairs but the everyday uniform of a cavalry officer. And he looked more normal somehow. More like the man she had seen in this room with the woman. Who had opened her eyes to things that she had never before considered could happen between a man and a woman.

Kate got to her feet. 'Do you think someone is trying to hurt you?' she said. She couldn't very well just ignore what he had said.

'I jolly well hope not.' Tommy laughed, placing the frame back on the desk. 'Whatever made you say that?'

'Nothing... I should go,' Kate said. 'I'm wanted. I have work...'

She could hear Tommy call after her but was already running along the landing. She threw open the door to the hidden stairwell. Slamming it behind her, she ran up the twisting staircase. At the top, she raced past the other rooms and into her bedroom.

TWENTY-FOUR

With her back to the door, Kate struggled to catch her breath. She paced around what little space there was, walking to the other side of the bed and back again. What was she to make of the conversations she'd had with the Mandevilles today and the activity around her in the house? Mrs Hart clearly expected her to find meaning in her half-story, telling her to listen. To what? The house? Well, the house had somehow managed to ring a bell to summon her to Captain Mandeville's bedroom, where Tommy had once again said she was there to help. But with *what*? And he said she had a gift. What kind of gift? Because it couldn't be the gift of telling the history of an object since nobody knew about that.

She held her right hand to her head and wrapped her left arm around her waist. According to Tommy, she was a special guest. But she was not a guest, special or otherwise. She was a housemaid who had to prove herself during a trial period otherwise she would be out on her ear with no job and no home.

Kate stopped pacing. Tommy was clearly delirious and still in the throes of the illness that came and went, apparently with no logic. There could be no other explanation for the odd things he had said. When she had asked him if someone was trying to harm him, he had laughed. But all that he had said made it sound like he was asking her to believe he was somehow being controlled by someone wanting to do him harm.

Kate started to pace again. She could put most of Tommy's behaviour and the odd things he had said down to the delirium. But one thing would not be silenced. He had said that she had seen other special visitors. The only people she had seen since her arrival at Hill House were members of the family and members of their household. Unless... she stopped and braced against the mantelshelf. She *had* seen other people. But they were the people from her visions. The sailors on the clipper. The awful child. The two women in the stables. One of whom she had also seen with Captain Mandeville in his bedroom... The instant she pictured Captain Mandeville and his lover, her thoughts raced again to Bertie.

Kate's reflection in the mirror above the mantelshelf showed that her face glowed, as though she had sat too close to the fire for an evening. She closed her eyes, and there he was. With his fair hair and moustache. His quiet kindness. She clasped her hands, feeling the ridge of the adhesive dressing, remembering the touch of Bertie's warm hands as he tended to her. Hadn't he said that she could talk to him about anything? That she should go to him if anything unsettled or alarmed her, particularly at Hill House.

Since her arrival, her visions had been bolder, more vivid, more lifelike. Was it the history of Hill House that she was sensing? Was she really telling herself that someone or something at Hill House had awakened a part of her gifts that she had never known? And if it had, then shouldn't she at least try to find out whether the people she saw in her visions were real? Everyone was convinced that Tommy was ill. But what if there really was someone trying to hurt him? And what if it was one of the people she had seen in her visions?

Kate stared at her dark eyes in the mirror. She had tried to find the awful boy in the photographs around the house, but he was in none of them. If either of the women she had seen had been in the photographs she felt sure she would have remembered.

Turning, Kate grasped the bedframe. It was solid. And real. And, apparently, didn't have a story it wanted to tell her. There was no flash of the history of the countless maids who must have slept in this bed over the years. No riddle they wanted her to solve. Letting go of the frame, she stood up straight. She had to drag her thoughts back to the here and now. In this house, her time was not her own. She was an employee. She would be missed. Since she had finished making the costumes, the family would expect her to take up her normal duties.

Smoothing down her hair and straightening her apron, Kate opened her bedroom door. And stopped. The curtain just beyond the bathroom shuddered in the cold breeze blowing in from the uncarpeted, undecorated and unheated corridor. The door that should have been locked, stood wide open. Part of her wanted to run down to the warmth of the kitchen, to the company of others and away from the image of the door rattling in the dead of night and the possibility that it was the boy from the mirror trying to get through. But something compelled her to look through to the rough walls, the bare floorboards and the emptiness. Closing her eyes, she breathed in deeply to calm her thoughts. And that's when she saw it. The lumber room and the album of photographs she had seen in the drawer of a dresser.

TWENTY-FIVE

Putting her fear aside, Kate made straight for the door. With no fires in the deserted rooms, cold air surrounded her. She wrapped her arms around herself and pressed on, her footsteps loud on the floorboards and echoing from the bare walls. She thought about the boy in the mirror and shook away the image. She would not be put off. Coming to the lumber room, she marched inside without slowing her pace. She switched on the light and stopped in the middle of the room.

Amidst the furniture and before the mirror sat Pegasus. He was perfectly still with not a sign of movement in his rockers. The children's dressing up clothes she had left strewn across the floor had been cleared away and the lid of the trunk closed. Kate stole a glance into the mirror. All that it reflected back was a perfect image of the room. There was no boy. Nothing to be scared of. The curtained door had no doubt been left open as Elliot had been in to move more furniture downstairs.

Kate began lifting sheet after sheet until she found the dresser. She opened the drawer and removed the red leather-bound album. For a moment, she considered placing the album on the table to look through it and put it back into the drawer once she was finished. But one look at the dust on the floor around the dresser told her that nobody had bothered with either it or its contents in years. The album wouldn't be missed if she borrowed it and returned it later.

Kate turned out the light and hurried down the corridor. She closed the dividing door and pulled the curtain across. Whoever had been up here had taken the key with them. She would let Audrey know so that it could be locked before bedtime.

Back in her room, Kate placed the album on the bed. She opened the cover and began to carefully turn the pages. Each sheet of thick cream paper held photographs secured with tiny white paper corners. The glue had dried so that some of the corners had become detached, making photographs sit at unusual angles. Kate did her best not to disturb them as she looked into the faces in the pictures. There were picnics and parties and even trips to the seaside. She recognised many of the Mandevilles and from their clothes she judged most of the photographs to have been taken a decade or so earlier. She recognised many of the rooms as the rooms of Hill House and paid close attention to the faces of the children within the groups. These were not studio photographs, but snaps caught by a camera at home, recording the life of a family. She came to a page whose backdrops she didn't recognise. It was a garden and from the houses behind, it was clearly a garden in a town. The first photograph was of a tall man standing proudly with a young girl smiling for the camera, neither of whom she recognised. The next photograph was of a boy and a woman. Kate looked closer. The child had a mass of curls. She judged him to be about ten years old. He stood beside a woman who had her arm around him as he leaned into her. Kate felt her heart thump. Her hands trembled as she eased the photograph from

its paper corners to study it even closer. The woman had her
short hair styled so that it sat in a precise line with her chin. She
smiled broadly and Kate recognised her. She was the woman
she had seen looking through the window of the stables. And
the boy! She was almost sure she knew who it was, but she had
to find someone who would know for sure. Closing the album,
she pushed it under the bed before slipping the photograph into
the pocket of her apron.

TWENTY-SIX

Down in the kitchen, Kate found Audrey busy kneading dough on the flour-dusted table, the scent of cinder toffee hanging deliciously in the air.

'Who was it?' Audrey asked.

'I beg your pardon?' Kate said.

Audrey looked up from the dough. She pushed her glasses up her nose with the heal of her hand. 'The bell. Who was it?'

'I don't know...' Kate said.

Audrey gave her a strange look.

'I went to the room, but nobody was there.' It didn't feel like enough of an explanation for how long she had been away, so Kate added quickly. 'While I was upstairs, I went to find something for the children's costumes.' She hated to lie to Audrey, but she had to say something.

'Well now you're back I could do with a hand. Rosemary is off decorating the stable yard with Mrs Mandeville and Mrs Kenmore.' Audrey turned her attention back to her dough. 'Get the tins out, would you. I'm making three dozen bread rolls for this evening.'

Kate took the tins from the dresser and placed them on the table.

'The stew might want a stir,' Audrey said.

Kate took the lids from two huge pans on the range, releasing a rich meaty smell. She stirred both and replaced the lids. 'What else can I do?' she asked.

'Get some clean towels from the drawer and line those baskets, please,' Audrey said nodding to the baskets on the dresser. 'We'll put the bread in them later to take over to the stable yard.'

Kate chose two blue and white checked towels. She shook them out and pressed them into the baskets. When she could contain herself no longer, she dipped her hand into the pocket of her apron and pulled out the photograph.

'Do you know who these people are?' she said, holding the photograph out to Audrey. Audrey glanced at the photograph before wiping her hands on her apron and taking it from Kate to get a better look.

'Where on Earth did you find this?' she asked, smiling at the photograph.

'In the lumber room,' Kate said. 'When I was looking for things for the costumes.' Another white lie.

'That's Tommy,' Audrey said, still smiling. 'I'd say it was taken not long after me and Rosemary started coming here.' She smiled again. 'Oh, but he was a tearaway then. Always into mischief. It's hard to believe he grew up to be such a studious young man.'

'And who is that with him?' Kate asked. She tried to make it sound like she was being chatty.

'That's Margot Evangeline!' Audrey said as though Kate should know who she was. Kate shrugged, trying to seem slightly disinterested but really wanting to know all Audrey had to tell.

'She's an author,' Audrey explained. 'And a great friend of

Mrs Kenmore. Her real name is Helen Potter. Actually, it's Helen Painter now that she's married. She comes to stay every summer with her husband, their daughter Lilian, and their son Philip. I think that must be in their back garden in London.'

'She and Tommy look very close,' Kate said.

'They are. She saved his life.'

'Saved his life?' Kate repeated. Audrey had said it in such a matter-of-fact way that Kate was at a loss at how else to respond. 'How?'

Audrey stared down into the faces caught in a moment, standing on the lawn and before shrubs in full bloom. 'It was a terrible time,' Audrey said softly. 'A terrible thing that man did to this family.'

For a moment Kate thought that Audrey might stop speaking. She had already chastised her little sister for gossiping. Before Kate could think of what to say, Audrey said, 'It's as well you know. It's no secret in any case. It was a cousin of the family. For some reason, when Tommy was a small boy, he kidnapped him.' Audrey's voice trailed away. It looked to Kate as though she was reliving the memory. 'It was Miss Potter that rescued him. But not before George Caxton stabbed the police inspector who was investigating. Inspector Painter was lucky to survive. It was a happy day when he and Miss Potter married the next year. They had the wedding in St Mary's and the wedding breakfast here. It was such a happy, happy day.'

Kate's mind stuck on the name of Tommy's attacker. 'Caxton?' she said, 'George Caxton, the family's cousin.'

'That's him,' Audrey sniffed as though smelling milk gone sour. 'We have Miss Potter to thank for Tommy still being with us. That's why they are so close...' Audrey straightened and handed the photograph back to Kate. 'See that you put it back where you found it,' she said.

'I will,' Kate promised.

Audrey began kneading the dough again. As she stretched it

out and let it fall back to the table, she began to give Kate a list of jobs that needed to be done before the storytelling of the evening. Kate made a mental note of everything she was to do: bring the sack of turnips out and place it beside the back door; sort enough crockery, cutlery and glassware into baskets, but not the good china – there were plenty of stoneware plates in the store that had once been used by the staff, if any of it was dropped on the cobbles it wouldn't matter if it smashed; and help Rosemary clean down the kitchen when the cooking was finished.

'Elliot will come across later to collect everything,' Audrey said, stretching the dough again. 'So have it by the back door waiting for him.'

'I will,' Kate said. She made straight for the store along the corridor.

Taking the plates and bowls and glasses from cupboards and down from shelves was just the repetitive job Kate needed. From what Audrey had said, it was clear now that her visions were the same as they had always been. They occurred to tell her the history of an item. When and how they occurred had never made sense. Hill House was no more communicating with her than her parents' house had.

Even as she thought it, Kate shook her head. Anyone else would think that a mad thing to say, but to her, it made sense – as much as being able to tell the history of an item by touching it could ever make sense. What she was seeing were people who had been important to the house. The timber from the clipper formed the very fabric of Hill House. Captain Mandeville and those he knew had played such a key role in this house and still did, with Tommy's admiration for his uncle. Miss Potter had saved Tommy. There could be nothing more important than that. What she was seeing were events connected to the heir of the house. What she was seeing was the past that had shaped Tommy. The only person she couldn't place was the awful boy, but he might have been a child at a birthday party who had once been spiteful to Tommy. Dressed as he had been, as a pirate, it seemed logical.

Kate closed the crockery cupboard and began taking glasses down from a shelf. A name kept coming to her: George Caxton. It was a name that had been mentioned a number of times today. No wonder he was hated by the Mandevilles and had been disinherited by his own family. What kind of man would kidnap a child and want to murder him? It was no wonder that Tommy had slipped into a strange state when he was ill and said odd things. He had lived through a terrible event which surely resurfaced when he was delirious, as though he was reaching out for help and imaging someone still wanting to do him harm. Poor Tommy. Poor dear Tommy.

With the crockery, cutlery and glassware in baskets by the back door, Kate turned her attention to colleting the sack of turnips from the cold store.

The aroma of baking bread met her when she returned to the kitchen, where she helped clear down the table, wash up and pack the cinder toffee and toffee apples. 'Doctor Kenmore insists on the apples,' Audrey said. 'Apparently, he used to have them every Halloween when he was a child.'

Kate finished putting away the last of the baking tins. 'Where would I find the key for the attic door?' she asked Audrey.

'The key for the attic door?' Audrey said, dusting the tops of the cooling buns with a handful of flour. 'What are you wanting that for?'

'To lock the door,' Kate said.

'Lock it?'

Kate nodded. 'It was open when I went up before.'

'Open?' Audrey said.

'Yes, open.' Kate hung the tea towel over the handle of one of the ovens to dry. 'I thought Elliot might have been up there looking for something again.'

Audrey shook her head. 'He can't have.'

'Why?' Kate said.

Audrey wiped the flour from her hands onto her apron. She reached into the pocket of her dress and produced a jangling chatelaine of keys attached to the chain at her waist. 'Because I have the key for the door. And nobody has borrowed it all day.'

'Perhaps they accidentally left it open when they last went up there and someone else went up today.'

Audrey shook her head slowly as though thinking. 'I checked the door this morning. I always check the door in the morning.' She thought again. 'At least, I think I did.'

'Perhaps you didn't,' Kate said. 'But if you give me the key, I can make sure it's locked now.'

Still shaking her head, Audrey unfastened the key from the chatelaine and handed it to Kate. 'Perhaps I was mistaken,' she said. 'Make sure it's properly locked. And you've had no break today, have you?'

'Not really,' Kate said.

'Then take a short one. Be back down here at six o'clock sharp to help me carry the food across. Oh, and you can change out of your work clothes. And don't forget your coat.'

'I won't. And thank you, Audrey,' Kate said.

TWENTY-SEVEN

It was just after half past five when Kate stepped onto the attic landing and almost dark outside the slanted windows. She switched on the light. The corridor was just as she had left it. Passing the bedrooms and the bathroom, she pulled back the curtain, placed the key in the lock and turned it. She tried the handle twice. It was secure. Elliot must have a second key to get in and out. It was the only explanation that made sense. As she had realised over the course of the day, there were quite logical explanations to be found for some of the things that might be thought strange at Hill House.

In her bedroom, Kate slipped the photograph from her pocket and placed it back inside the album. She would keep it in her room for now in case any other vision meant she wanted to work out who she saw. She changed from her working clothes into her brown skirt and jumper and collected her coat on her way out.

Making her way down the back stairs she looked up at the bells in the passageway. Bells ringing in empty rooms was hardly surprising. The house was old, and it was quite likely that the mechanisms inside the walls had become twisted and signalled that help was needed in the wrong rooms.

In the kitchen, she handed the key back to Audrey, who placed it in her pocket.

'You locked the door properly?' Audrey said.

'I checked it twice,' Kate said and helped Audrey load the food into baskets. Elliot had already collected everything Kate had prepared earlier; he had also taken the stew to keep warm over on the small stove in the stables.

Once they were ready, they pulled on their coats and, with a basket of bread in the crook of her arm, Kate followed Audrey up the basement stairs to the outside. It was dark with a sharp chill in the air. Audrey shrugged her shoulders to her ears. 'It feels like the season is turning. It'll be winter soon.'

Kate paused. She placed the basket on the ground briefly to tie her scarf tighter at her collar, before rushing to catch up with Audrey.

TWENTY-EIGHT

Stepping into the stable yard was like stepping into fairy land. Kate paused to take it all in. Foliage had been strung along each wall, above the doors of the stables, and around every window. It was deep and dense like festoons of bunting and the waxy leaves shone in the light of dozens of candles placed in jam jars on the cobbles of the yard. Some jars had even been suspended by wire amongst the branches. In the centre of the stable yard a fire blazed orange in a brazier of sorts, although it was low and wide. Upturned logs had been placed around it, along with bales of hay covered with blankets and a couple of chairs. A table at the far end held some of the turnips from the sack Kate had taken from the store, along with various knives and cutting implements. Another table just outside the stable doors held bottles of pop and beer, glasses, crockery and cutlery and the covered bowls of food brought over from the house. Kate followed Audrey and placed the basket of rolls on the table.

Outside the light from the fire and candles, shadows lengthened on the walls and darkened the corners of the yard. Beyond the buildings and towards the woods, all was darkness. But within the glow of the fire and with the light from the candles, the stable yard felt like a welcome beacon in the approaching winter darkness.

'Doesn't this look splendid!' Mrs Hart said, approaching Kate and Audrey.

'It's beautiful,' Kate said.

'I'll go inside and check on the stew, if you don't mind?' Audrey said after placing her basket on the table.

'Should I come with you?' Kate asked.

Audrey shook her head. 'I'll not need any help now other than tidying up later.'

'You will ask if there's anything we can do to help, won't you?' Mrs Hart said.

Audrey said that she would before disappearing inside.

'I think that means you're off the hook for the rest of the evening and are free to enjoy yourself, Katherine.' Mrs Hart smiled. She took a deep lungful of the fresh night air. 'I always think the air smells at its cleanest at this time of year.' She buttoned her coat to her neck. 'I do like this part of this evening,' she said. 'When we have the place to ourselves and before everyone arrives. Oh, I enjoy seeing the children having fun and hearing Elliot's tales, but I like the stillness of the early part of the night. Before all the noise and commotion. And being outside like this, with nature all around, feels rather spiritual. Like we are connecting with the way our ancestors used to live.'

Kate nodded. Mrs Hart's company and her words were soothing. Perhaps it was because she had been a nurse and knew how to reassure people.

'I believe we think too hard about things a lot of the time,' Mrs Hart said. 'We forget to just *be*. To sit with our thoughts and feelings and let them rest with us.'

'I'm guilty of thinking too hard about things much of the time,' Kate said.

'We all are, Katherine.' Mrs Hart smiled. 'Now, shall we get a drink? I think I'll have an ale, I'm quite partial to a drop? What about you, Katherine?'

'Would you like me to pour?' Kate asked, remembering her position in the household.

'Let me,' Mrs Hart said. 'I spent much of my life fending for myself, and I think I remember how to wield a bottle opener.' She winked and took up a bottle and the opener. 'There are no airs and graces tonight, Katherine. And nobody will stand on ceremony. You should relax and enjoy yourself. We are all the same meat and gristle beneath our skin.'

Kate couldn't help but laugh. Mrs Hart was like nobody she had ever met. She had taken the time earlier to reassure her and give her advice. And here she was about to serve her a beer. There was clearly still some of the suffragette in her.

Mrs Hart opened an ale and shared it between two glasses, handing one to Kate and taking the other for herself.

'Down the hatch,' she said, chinking her glass to Kate's.

'Down the hatch,' Kate laughed.

They both took a sip. 'Oh, that's rather good,' Mrs Hart said. 'Elliot brews it in a little shed out the back there.'

'It's delicious,' Kate said. 'Very rich.'

'I think it might be a tad stronger than usual.' Mrs Hart raised her eyebrows and took another sip.

They stood for a few minutes breathing in the night air and sipping their ale. Every so often, Kate glanced at Mrs Hart. She seemed content to be in Kate's company. Kate wished her parents and Harry could see how well she had done in the last week. They would be tickled and so very thrilled for her.

The companiable silence came to an abrupt end with the sound of loud voices and many footsteps running along the gravel path.

'I am afraid our peace is about to be shattered,' Mrs Hart said. 'Brace yourself, Katherine.'

As one, the Mandeville children raced through the gates

ahead of Alice, Charlotte, Edward and Paul, who brought up the rear. Everyone was dressed in their winter coats. The children charged into the yard, scattering as they came. Two ran to the fire, the other two to look at the decorations and candles. They all wore masks, decorated with paint and crepe paper, milk bottle tops and paper straws. Each had what Kate imagined was supposed to be a terribly frightening look on its face. She laughed as she had to dodge out of the way of a child with paper straw fangs and green crepe paper like hair, trailing to his shoulders. He was intent on looking over the food on offer.

'Off with you!' Mrs Hart laughed. 'Refreshments are for later! Oh, my dear Lord, Katherine, isn't that child absolutely frightening! Is it a goblin masquerading as a small boy, I wonder?'

'I'm the spirit of the woods,' the child shouted.

'I don't doubt you are,' Mrs Hart said. 'Isn't he terrifying, Katherine?'

'He is the most monstrous creature I have ever seen,' Kate said, feigning horror.

The child scrunched up his hands and made a roar before running away to look at the fire. From his size, Kate guessed it to be Oscar.

'Hey!' a gruff voice shouted. 'What's all this about?'

All activity stopped and everyone turned to a figure standing in the doorway of the stables, lit only by a cigarette that he took from his mouth. He blew a plume of smoke into the air above his head. 'Who said you could come and trouble the peace of my stable yard like this?' There was no answer. 'Well?'

Kate looked at the adults. They were all smiling. Mrs Hart leant into Kate. 'This is part of Elliot's performance,' she whispered. 'He does it every year. The children love it.'

'You did,' one of the bolder children shouted at Elliot.

'I did?' Elliot said. 'I did? Well, if I did say you could come here, then I expected you to be quieter about it.'

'Tell us a story!' another child shouted.

Elliot stepped forward so that it was easier to see him. He looked into the fire then up to the sky. 'It's too early,' he said. 'When the embers glow and the moon is further along its path, it will be time.' He retreated inside the stables. Immediately the door closed behind him, the shrieking of the children started up again.

'Children! Children!' Alice called over the screams. 'We must make our lanterns before we can have our stories. Come.' She waved towards the table with the turnips. It seemed an irresistible pull for the children who crowded around the table while Alice and Charlotte supervised, with many warnings of missing fingertips from the haphazard use of a knife. Rosemary appeared from the stables and joined in to help with the children.

Edward and Paul left the fire and instead of joining their wives, joined Mrs Hart and Kate at the refreshment table.

Paul lifted one of the covers to reveal a tray of toffee covered apples. He smiled like a young child might. 'Audrey has outdone herself,' he said. He made to take one, but Mrs Hart tapped his hand.

'I told the children they had to wait until later and so must you!' She replaced the cover. Paul pouted. 'Spoilsport,' he said with a smile.

'How's the plonk?' Edward asked, nodding to the glasses in Mrs Hart and Kate's hands.

'You won't be disappointed,' Mrs Hart said.

Edward picked up a bottle and showed it to Paul.

'Please,' Paul said. 'If we're allowed,' he added with a laugh in his voice as he looked at Mrs Hart. He glanced at Kate's hand. 'What have you done there?' he asked, his voice a little more serious.

Kate turned her hand over. 'It was nothing, really. Just an accident with a sewing needle.'

'Would you like me to take a look at it?' he asked.

'No need,' Mrs Hart said, leaning into Kate. 'Bertie is taking good care of Katherine.'

Edward paused with the bottle opener over the cap of the bottle. He looked to Paul and they both smiled. 'Glad to hear it,' Edward said. 'About time he found someone to take care of.'

Paul grinned. 'Indeed, it is.'

Edward eased the cap from the bottle and poured two glasses, handing one to Paul. 'What shall we toast to?' Paul asked.

'Old friends,' Mrs Hart said. 'And new.'

They encouraged Kate to hold up her glass so she could join in the toast. She took a mouthful of her ale and smiled. It seemed that any mention of Bertie's name was enough now to make her smile even when she tried not to.

'And here is the man of the moment!' Edward said. He had removed the cap from another bottle of beer before the newcomer had even joined them.

'Have I missed something?' Bertie asked. Edward handed him a glass of beer and Bertie thanked him.

'I hear you're after my job,' Paul said with a laugh in his voice.

Bertie appeared confused as he took a sip of the beer.

'Ignore Paul, he's being silly,' Mrs Hart said. 'I was just telling them that you are responsible for dressing Katherine's wound so professionally.'

'It really was just a prick,' Kate said. 'I wouldn't say it was a wound.'

'But all cuts must be cleaned and dressed,' Bertie said. 'To stop infection.'

'You can't argue with that,' Paul said. 'And Bertie is nothing if not thorough in everything.' He held up his glass. 'Cheers, Bertie.'

'Shall we take these to the fire?' Edward asked Paul.

Paul and Bertie agreed. Mrs Hart asked whether she might join them to take the weight off her feet and they enthusiastically agreed. Kate couldn't imagine anyone not wanting Mrs Hart to be in their group.

'And you, Katherine?' Mrs Hart said. 'Will you join us?'

'If you don't mind,' Kate said. 'I'd like to look around at all the decorations.'

'Of course,' Mrs Hart said. Paul offered his arm to Mrs Hart, and they moved off to sit beside the fire, the men on the upturned logs and Mrs Hart on one of the chairs.

Kate retreated to the far corner of the yard. She touched the fresh foliage. She hid a smile, thinking of how she had met Bertie beneath the boughs of that great yew tree in the woods. From the relative privacy of the shadows, she watched the party at the fire, enjoying each other's company. Chatter and laughter came from the table where the lanterns were being made. She hoped that she hadn't offended Bertie when she said that her injury was simply a prick. Surrounded by people he knew and clearly liked, he didn't seem in the least troubled. His eyes glittered in the light of the flames. He drank his beer, laughing along with the rest of his party at something one of them said. When he looked up, Kate retreated further into the shadows, wanting to watch him unobserved. And watch him she did, with all the feelings of that afternoon. A glow rose in her. She wanted to touch him. Even just to hold his hand would be enough. Or would it? She stared at the cobbles, embarrassed by her own thoughts. Should she be embarrassed? Were those things she imagined truly what other people did? How they touched. How they kissed. How they... Smiling, she turned away, and chewed her bottom lip.

When she turned back, it was to see two other people arriving to join the party beside the fire. Tommy and a woman she didn't recognise. The woman nodded hello to Paul and Edward, embraced Mrs Hart and then Bertie.

Kate took a step back into the shadows. The woman took the chair beside Mrs Hart. She was too far away for Kate to see her distinctly. She was clearly known to the family since she slipped into their conversation easily. She laughed at something Bertie said and it was all Kate could do to keep hidden in the shadows. If there had been a way to leave the yard without being seen, she would have done it. A different feeling overtook the glow in her. If she had been able to put a face to it, she would have said it wore a mask like that goblin mask worn by Oscar. It was full of what she could only name as envy. That woman had touched Bertie in a way that Kate never had. And was never likely to.

The door to the stables opened. When Audrey stepped out and saw Kate lurking in the shadows, she approached her.

'How's it going?' Kate asked.

'Fine,' Audrey said. 'The stew's done. I'm just keeping it warm until everyone is ready to eat.' She looked towards the fire. 'Mary's here then,' she said.

'That's Mary?' Kate asked.

Audrey nodded.

Kate thought for a moment, before saying, 'And is she Bertie's sweetheart?'

Audrey laughed. 'Whatever made you say that?'

'Nothing. I just wondered. They seem close.'

'They are,' Audrey said. 'They've known each other since Bertie was a very little boy. Mary is at least ten years older than him.' She looked at Kate and laughed again. 'Come on,' she said, 'I'll introduce you.'

'You won't say I said anything, will you?' Kate said.

'Don't worry, I'll not say a thing to embarrass you.'

Kate followed Audrey across the yard and was relieved to see that she had stopped laughing. They reached the fire and Audrey had just introduced Kate to Mary – who was as lovely and friendly as everyone had said – when Charlotte called out from the lantern table. 'Look, everyone!'

A whole army of carved vegetables was lined up on the table, each with jagged teeth and eyes and a candle glowing inside. There was a round of congratulations from beside the fire before Tommy asked whether it was time to eat.

Audrey and Rosemary disappeared inside the stable and Kate went to the table to uncover the bread rolls. The sisters emerged with pans of stew that filled the air with a savoury scent.

Soon everyone had a bowl of steaming stew and a fluffy bread roll. They all joined together to sit on the various seats around the fire. There was much chatter and appreciation for the wonderful meal.

With the plates cleared away, the cinder toffee and toffee apples were brought to the fireside. Before they could be handed around, the last member of the party appeared in the doorway to the stables. He looked towards the fire.

Silence fell. Even the children were quiet. Kate looked around the faces, half lit by the fire and half in shadow. This was clearly a well-rehearsed event and she realised that she was the only person who had not attended before. The trays of sweet treats were handed around as Elliot sat in a free chair. Each person took something, so Kate took a piece of cinder toffee.

'Now,' Elliot said. 'If anyone here is of a nervous disposition, I suggest they leave. I shan't spare anyone's sensibilities. And I won't be held responsible for any nightmares.' Elliot paused. When there was no reply, he said, 'Good, I can see you all have the backbone and stomach for it.' He paused. 'See those, over there.' He pointed to the table of candlelit vegetables. 'You will need those tomorrow night. Jack-o'-lanterns they are. And since you make them every year, you should know why.' Elliot launched into a story about a man named Jack who tricked the Devil many times over so that when he died, God refused to let him into heaven and the Devil refused to let him into hell. But, taking pity on him, the Devil gave him a piece of coal, which he put into a hollowed-out vegetable.

'Old Jack is forever destined to roam the world looking for help that he will never get,' Elliot said solemnly. 'Those lanterns are your reminder that you should be a good person, or you might end up wandering the world forever with nothing but a burning coal for company. And beware. Any tap on your window or rap on your door tomorrow night might just be Jack coming to trick you into letting him inside. Don't! If he can fool the Devil, imagine what he could do to you. And leave them lanterns outside to scare Jack off if he does come a-calling.'

Elliot delivered his story in such a deadpan way, with no emotion of any kind. Kate looked to the children. They sat enthralled. Louisa's toffee apple was halfway to her mouth with not a bite taken. Oscar's cinder toffee sat uneaten in his lap.

'And tomorrow night, like Jack, you need to be on your guard for the Devil,' Elliot said. 'For tomorrow night is All Hallows' Eve, when we cross from autumn into the darkness of winter. It is the time of year when the veil between the living and dead is at its thinnest. Tomorrow the spirits may cross into this realm, even the spirits of our ancestors. And the fairies. We don't know what they mean to do to us. Harm or good? But we need to do our best to scare away the evil spirits and welcome only those that mean us good.'

Elliot continued with another story. He spoke of a tradition called mumming, where people dressed in masks to obscure their identity and went to the houses of other people to trade entertainment for food, just as they wore their masks tonight so they could enjoy their toffee and sweet treats. Charlie looked at his toffee apple and took a large bite as though reassured that he had earned it through his mask making.

Elliot leant forward. The glow from the fire lit his face.

'Remember,' he said, 'tomorrow night, when you are enjoying your party, you must be on your guard. Keep your lanterns lit. Do not let any bad spirits cross into our world. If the spirit of one of your ancestors comes through, be sure it is them before you let them in. If they are true, they can protect you. But if it is one of the fairies masquerading as a good spirit...? Well...' He sat back in his chair. 'I will leave it to you to decide what that means and what they can do.' And with that, Elliot left the chair and walked slowly back to the stables.

Along with everyone else, Kate watched him go.

'Well,' Paul said. 'How were those stories, kids? Did they scare you?'

Charlie jumped to his feet. 'Not me!' he said.

Louisa followed her cousin. 'Or me!' she said.

Soon all the children were on their feet, saying that they weren't at all frightened by Elliot's stories, while tucking into their sweet treats, although Kate was sure that she saw each child gravitating towards a parent or sibling.

'He spins a good yarn, doesn't he?' Kate said, leaning into Audrey beside her.

'Do you think any of it's true?' Audrey asked, holding her hands out to the fire.

'I should imagine people dressed up because of superstitions but I should imagine most of it was said to scare the children.' Kate wasn't quite sure who was attempting to reassure who.

Audrey leant past Kate. 'Mary,' she said. 'Mary. Is any of what Elliot said true? You're a schoolteacher. You know about these things.'

'I wouldn't say I know everything!' Mary said. 'But Elliot's stories have an element of truth. Some of the older children at school have been studying it. The Irish used to celebrate a festival called *Samhain*, rather than Halloween. Much of what Elliot says stems from that. With all the emigres from Ireland to

America, they took elements of that festival and turned it into a lot of the Halloween we see today.'

'And the fairies?' Audrey said. 'Are they really evil?'

Mary smiled. 'You've nothing to worry about from the fairies, Audrey. You're good through and through.'

Audrey seemed to mull this over before heading back to the stables to begin the process of clearing up.

Gradually the festivities wound down as the children grew tired. Alice, Charlotte and Mrs Hart along with Paul and Edward rounded up the children and saw them back to the house. Kate helped collect up the crockery and with Audrey, Rosemary and Mary carried it back to the house while Elliot, Bertie and Tommy tidied away the tables and seats.

The women arrived back at the house to find that two lanterns had been placed on either side of the stone steps. Their ghoulish eyes and jagged teeth glowed in the light of the candles inside their bellies.

'At least we'll all be safe tonight, too,' Audrey said.

In the kitchen, Kate and Mary helped Audrey and Rosemary with the washing up.

'I hear you're in my old room,' Mary said to Kate.

'That's right,' Kate said, placing glasses back on a shelf of the dresser.

'I do miss it,' Mary said. She covered the leftover cinder toffee with a cloth. 'It was ever such a cosy room. Don't get me wrong, I love having the cottage that comes with my job. But with just me rattling around in it, it seems so big. Far too big for just one person.'

'You're not married then?' Kate asked.

'No,' Mary said. 'I'm not married.'

'Mary's wed to her job, Katherine,' Rosemary said. 'She's no time for a sweetheart! That's right, isn't it, Mary?'

'Something like that,' Mary said. She placed a cloth over the leftover toffee apples. 'You must visit for tea one day, Katherine. It would be so nice to get to know you better.'

'I'd like that,' Kate said. 'Thank you.' She placed another glass on the shelf. She had gone from no friends in the area to a handful of friends, even one she could call on for tea.

Tommy soon appeared at the kitchen door as agreed, to walk Mary back to the village. He accepted the offer of another piece of cinder toffee and another toffee apple.

After saying their goodbyes to Mary, Kate joined Audrey and Rosemary in retreating to the housekeeper's parlour. Over a pot of cocoa, the sisters planned the party tea that was needed for the children the next day. Kate sat with them but inside her own thoughts. There were days and there were *days*, her mother liked to say. And this had definitely been a *day*. Some days passed like most other days in life. But there were others that creaked under the weight of what happened within the space of twenty-four hours. It had been full of so many things that Kate's head spun. She reached her hands out to the fire, hoping that the letter had arrived with Mother. It would be nice to receive a letter in reply to hear how she was getting on with Harry and his family.

'Shall I make a fresh pot?' Kate asked.

'That would be lovely, thank you,' Audrey said. 'And put a kettle on for the hot water bottles if it's not too much trouble.'

'No trouble at all,' Kate said, collecting the cocoa pot.

'Oh, Katherine,' Rosemary said when Kate was halfway out of the door. 'There's a box of bits and bobs on the window ledge by the door out there. The laundry was collected today, and I always have to fish through the pockets of whatever's in the hamper before it goes. You find all manner of things left in pockets. You might want to have a look in case any of it's yours.'

Kate put a pan of milk on to heat before heading back out into the hall. She looked inside the box on the window ledge but saw nothing that belonged to her. There were a couple of clean, pressed handkerchiefs, some buttons, a paste brooch, and a handful of coins. But she did see one familiar item. Tommy's penknife. She could take it and return it to him when he got back from walking Mary home. He had seemed very keen on it and would no doubt be upset to find it missing.

Reaching into the box, Kate took hold of the knife. There was a flash. She was no longer in the hall. She was in a dark wood, in some kind of den made of bent branches. A man was in there, handing the penknife to the boy. The scene changed again. The boy was grown into a young man. He was in a small room surrounded by books. Alone and far away from home. He was ill. Desperately ill. The man loomed over him. But the man was not there. It seemed that his essence was there but not his physical being. The scene changed. The young man had collapsed. He was being helped by two men along a basement corridor. And then she saw the knife. Lost beside a fireplace in a parlour. The young man had been well when it was there. When he didn't have the penknife in his hand or in his pocket he was well again. Kate's grasp tightened around the penknife. The man charged at her. He was the man who had given the penknife to the young man when he was still a child. His face was contorted in rage, furious that she was able to see him. He raised his fist to strike her. She stumbled back and fell heavily.

'Kate! Kate!' she heard someone call.

The penknife fell from her hand.

She looked around. She was in the basement corridor, slumped against the wall beside the door leading to the outside. The box had tumbled to the floor. Handkerchiefs, buttons, brooch and coins scattered on the cold flags around her. The door to the outside stood open. Cold leached into the basement. Audrey and Rosemary hovered in the doorway of the parlour, their faces full of concern. Bertie crouched before her. It was his voice that had pulled her back from wherever it was that she had gone. She looked into his eyes and felt her face crumple.

Tears streaked down her face, and she shook her head at him. The sound of boiling milk spilling over the side of the pan and sizzling on the stove made Audrey run to the kitchen.

Bertie's arms were around Kate, pulling her close. 'I've got you,' he said, his voice soft in her ear. 'I should never have let it get this far.'

He lifted her from the floor and she rested her head on his shoulder.

'What has happened?' Rosemary asked. 'Katherine. Katherine, what has happened?'

'I'll look after her,' Bertie said. 'You and Audrey have no call to be concerned. Kate said to me earlier that she wasn't feeling quite well. You go back to your cocoa.'

Audrey came into Kate's field of vision again.

'Are you sure, Bertie?' Audrey asked.

'Perfectly,' Bertie said. 'Please don't worry. Kate will be well soon enough. I promise.'

Kate felt herself carried at pace along the corridor and up the steps into the passageway. She kept her face pressed into Bertie's neck.

'I've got you,' Bertie whispered over and over again. 'I've got you.'

TWENTY-NINE

Kate was placed gently onto something soft, her hair pushed back from her face. Bertie looked at her with such intensity. A frown creased his brow. His eyes looked this way and that as though searching for something in Kate's face.

'Are you with me? Are you here, Kate?' he asked. It was such an odd question, but Kate knew precisely what he meant.

'I am,' she said quietly.

Bertie's head fell forward, and he sighed. He took her hands in his. 'I know strange things have been happening to you since you arrived at Hill House, Kate.'

'I'm not going mad then?' she asked.

He shook his head. 'It's difficult to explain. I'm not sure how much I should say.' He glanced at the door. 'I need to leave you for a few minutes. I'll be back just as soon as I can.'

Kate nodded. It felt as though her head had become too heavy for her body to bear the weight. She heard the creak of a door closing and gave in to the urge to lay down. Her head came to rest on a cushion. She brought her legs up and curled into a ball. She fell into a sleep of some kind. Unsure of how long she had stayed like that, she heard voices.

'I think she's sleeping,' she heard Bertie say.

'From what you told me about what happened to her, I'd say it's not sleep. Whatever occurred has taken all the energy she had.'

'What is doing this to her?' Bertie said, his voice full of worry and tinged with frustration.

'I don't know,' Mrs Hart said.

'Do you feel anything?' Bertie asked.

Mrs Hart sighed. 'No, I don't. Other than that Katherine is a very special visitor. I've done my best to explain that Hill House is unlike any other house and that some of us have a special connection to it. But Bertie, darling, I am old. My connection to this house is on the wane. You must take up the mantle now.'

'I don't know what to do,' Bertie said. 'I can't even protect Kate. Just look at her. Look what something has done to her, while I have been trying to help. I should never have brought her here. But I had no idea when I met her that she was so special. I'm not ready to take on your role.'

Kate heard pacing across the floor and the dull beat of the tip of Mrs Hart's cane on carpet. 'You are not to blame for anything. And you are more ready to take on the role I have performed than you think you are. You know better than anyone that events here are not directed by us. But I have never seen the like,' Mrs Hart said. 'Nobody has been physically hurt before. This is outside of my understanding. Katherine has skills beyond those we have seen in anyone else. I think whatever is happening is not contained within the walls of this house. But it doesn't make sense.' The pacing stopped. 'We do know one person who might understand.'

There was a pause before Bertie said, 'I'll go and get him.'

Kate heard the door open and close. She felt the dip of the sofa as it took someone's weight. Her hair was brushed back from her face again. 'If you can hear me,' Mrs Hart said, 'we will do our very best to keep you safe. Trust us, if you can. You are here for a reason, darling. We will try to find out what that is and help you.'

Without the energy to open her eyes, or the strength to even acknowledge her presence, Kate slipped back into darkness.

THIRTY

'I knew something was going on with her.'

Kate began to come to at the sound of a familiar gruff voice. Opening her eyes, she gradually focused on a face on a level with hers. Elliot crouched before her, staring into her eyes.

'Are you back with us, Katherine?' Mrs Hart said. She was next to Kate on the sofa, still holding her hand.

'I think...' Kate wanted to say that she thought she was back but the words to form an entire sentence wouldn't come.

'What is to be done, Elliot?' Mrs Hart asked.

Elliot framed his face with his hand and scratched his chin. 'I think it's best we take her out of here. For now, at least. I need to think, and I do that best in my own space.'

Kate watched Elliot look over his shoulder. 'Will you help me move her?' he said.

Bertie stepped forward. Kate could have wept for the anxious look on his face. 'Of course,' he said. 'Whatever you think best.'

It seemed to cause Elliot no effort at all to lift her from the sofa. Mrs Hart placed Kate's arms around Elliot's neck. Kate rested her head on his shoulder, aware of everything going on around her but without the energy to speak or move.

Bertie went first into the hall and looked about. He beckoned for them to join him. He opened the door to the vestibule and then the front door and he and Mrs Hart followed Elliot out into the dark night. With the house secured, they took the gravel path to the stable yard, into the stable itself and then into the tack room at the end.

Kate felt herself placed into a chair at a table and a blanket put around her. She put her arms on the table and rested her head on her wrists. There came the smell of leather and sweet hay, like the smell of a summer meadow. Voices murmured around her like the buzz of bees, as if she had fallen asleep beneath the boughs of a tree on a warm summer's day. The tip of Mrs Hart's cane tapped on the stone floor. Kate heard Elliot offer her a chair, but she said she would stand. There came the sound of coals being shaken into a grate. The sizzle of flames.

'What is happening with Katherine?' Mrs Hart said.

There was a pause. 'What she can do goes further than we have seen here before,' Elliot said. 'I knew I saw it in her. I sensed it in her.'

'Does she know?' Mrs Hart asked.

'I should think she knows there is something different about her. But whatever it is, is untrained. Unharnessed.'

'Is she in danger?'

Another pause. 'All we can do is our best to help her,' Elliot said. 'I'll make her a brew.'

Kate listened to the noises of something being prepared. The crunch of stems and leaves beneath a knife. Water rushing. The chink of metal when something was placed onto a trivet. But nobody spoke.

Gradually, Kate opened her eyes. Slowly her vision adjusted. She took in three faces. Mrs Hart stood on the other side of the table, resting on her cane, looking at her kindly.

Elliot was beside Mrs Hart. He gripped the back of one of the chairs, leaning forward and staring at her. And Bertie, he stood beside the fire, with Elliot's Jack Russell asleep by his feet on the rug. Kate had never before seen a person's face so pained.

'There she is,' Mrs Hart said warmly.

Kate looked at her but couldn't speak.

'You'll be reet, lass,' Elliot said.

Kate moved her head ever so slightly to look at him. She knew enough of the Yorkshire dialect to know he was telling her she would be all right. But would she? She moved her head again, to look at Bertie. He tried to smile, but he didn't seem able. Kate clutched the blanket tighter around her neck.

Taking a pan from the fire, Elliot poured some liquid into a chipped cup and put it before Kate. 'Drink it,' he said. 'It's a tonic.'

Kate let go of the blanket and took the cup in both hands. Steam swirled about her. The smell of the drink in the cup was like nothing she had ever smelled. It was warm and smelled green and full of herbs. She took a sip. It tasted like an autumn walk through a forest. Earthy. Damp leaves. She took another sip.

She felt her gaze slacken. Her eyelids became heavy. The cup was taken from her hands, and she felt the blanket move so that it covered her again.

'I take it the lad is meant to be looking after her and guiding her,' Elliot said.

Finally, Bertie spoke. 'As far as I can tell,' he said. 'But whatever is making him ill is stopping him.'

'Best we keep her and the lad separate for now, then,' Elliot said. 'He's in no state to do what he must. And the lass here is suffering for it. They may just do each other more harm than good.'

From somewhere in the depths of the sleep that was trying

to take her, Kate became aware of who they were talking about. She forced her eyes open and sat up.

'Tommy,' she said. 'He's in danger. The man who... the man...'

'Who?' Mrs Hart said. 'What man?' There was a panic in her voice that Kate had never before heard. 'Katherine, what man?'

'The knife...' Kate said, mustering every ounce of energy to stay awake. 'Tommy's penknife... by the door. He mustn't get it. Please.'

'I saw it!' Bertie said. 'Kate dropped it.'

As Kate collapsed onto the table again, she heard shouting, doors slamming and footsteps slapping on the stone floor.

THIRTY-ONE

THURSDAY 31ST OCTOBER, 1935

The birds were already singing outside when Kate woke. With her cheek still pressed to the pillow she opened her eyes. Something was wrong. She sat up and looked around. In the faint morning light, she saw that she was in a large bedroom with a dark wardrobe, chest of drawers and a washstand. A small fire glowed in the grate and a towel warmed on a rail set up before the hearth. The curtains at the window were blue. The floorboards were bare. But from what she could see, the room was fastidiously clean. It smelled of furniture polish and... cologne. Kate clutched the eiderdown to her chin. She looked around again. There was nothing but a jug and matching washbowl and a pair of hairbrushes on the washstand. No cold cream. No lipstick. No vanity set. She looked down at herself. She was dressed in what she could only describe as a nightshirt. A man's nightshirt.

Kate hastily pushed the covers away and got out of the bed. She opened the wardrobe. There was a single rail. Of shirts and trousers and a suit or two. A row of shelves held sweaters and cufflinks and... before she could see anything else, she closed the wardrobe and became aware of a burning sensation in her thigh and buttock. She lifted the nightshirt. The relief at finding that she was still wearing her undergarments was replaced by confusion. A purple bruise ran down the side of her leg. And then she remembered. The box on the ledge in the basement. The man making her stumble. The penknife. The penknife! Tommy!

Without another thought, she yanked the door open. She was on a small landing with only one other door. She ran down the stairs and along the hallway, passing a parlour – completely empty of any furniture – and into a kitchen.

The single occupant hurriedly got up from his seat at the table.

'Kate,' Bertie said and pushed his fringe back from his face. 'How are you? You must be cold. I left a robe on the back of the bedroom door. Let me get it for you.' Bertie raced from the kitchen and Kate heard him run up the stairs.

She looked down at herself and placed one arm across her body and the other across her chest. It took only a few moments for the footsteps to come back down the stairs and for Bertie to appear in the kitchen. Kate was facing away from him.

'I'll help you put it on,' he said from behind. 'If that's all right with you?'

Kate held out one arm and then the other. Bertie eased the brown robe onto her shoulders. It was no sooner on her than Kate had drawn the two sides together and tied the cord at the front.

Bertie stepped from behind her and pulled out a chair at the table. Kate sat down. 'The penknife?' she said.

'It's safe,' Bertie said. 'And in a place where Tommy won't find it.'

Kate nodded.

'Can I get you a cup of tea?' Bertie asked.

Kate nodded again. 'Please.'

Bertie filled the kettle and put it on to boil. Kate took in the details of the kitchen. A stove in the chimney breast, an armchair before it. A sink below the window. A larder in the corner. A broom, mop and bucket beside the back door. A neatly folded tea towel hooked over the oven door. Bertie took tea things from the larder and placed them on the table.

Kate sat with her hands in her lap.

Bertie grasped the back of his chair. 'Mrs Hart came here with Elliot last night. She's the one that... she took...' He paused and pushed his fringe back from his face.

'She's the one that put the nightshirt on me?' Kate said.

'She was a nurse, so she knows what to... how to...'

'I know,' Kate said, helping him. 'Thank you for explaining.' She could breathe just a little easier knowing it was Mrs Hart and not Bertie who had undressed her.

The kettle rumbled to a boil. Bertie poured the steaming water onto the leaves in the pot and sat down. 'Do you remember much from last night?' he asked.

Kate shifted in her seat. The bruise on her leg caught on the hard seat of the kitchen chair and she winced.

'Are you hurt?' Bertie said.

'A little bruised.' She paused. When she spoke next, she stared at her lap. 'I know you saw what happened to me. In the basement. And I heard some of what you and Mrs Hart and Elliot spoke about.'

'So, you weren't asleep all the time?' Bertie asked.

'I was, after Elliot made me that drink. I don't remember anything after that until waking up.'

'Good,' Bertie said. 'That's good. You needed proper sleep and Elliot has special ways with things.'

Kate looked up. 'I don't understand any of this,' she said. 'But if I can rely on what I heard last night, you and Mrs Hart and Elliot might.'

Bertie drummed his fingers on the table. 'I will tell you all I can. But first, will you let me make you something to eat?'

'Will you answer a question first?'

'I will.'

'Why am I here? Why did you bring me here?'

He breathed out heavily. 'We needed to get you away. Just for a while. Just until we understand what is happening.'

'And will we understand?'

'You have my word that we will try.' He looked at her so earnestly that Kate was sure Bertie would do everything that was in his power to help her. 'Do you like bacon?' he asked.

After pouring the tea, Bertie moved around the kitchen, slicing bread and frying bacon. He joined Kate in eating a sandwich. He talked almost constantly, explaining how his grandmother had taught him to cook so that he could fend for himself if he ever had to live on his own. Before becoming a lady's maid, his mother had been a chambermaid and from a very young age had taught him all there was to know about cleaning and polishing.

Kate was almost able to forget the events of the previous evening. When they threatened to disturb her, it seemed that Bertie was able to say something to distract her thoughts.

Following breakfast, Bertie filled a jug with hot water for her to take to the bedroom. It wasn't until she was midway up the stairs that Kate remembered she had been sitting and eating breakfast wearing Bertie's nightclothes. She blushed. She blushed again when she stood in the middle of the bedroom and pulled the nightshirt over her head. She was almost naked in Bertie's bedroom. And after everything she had been picturing in the last few days. Filling the bowl with hot water from the jug, she used the fresh bar of soap Bertie had left out to hurriedly wash. She dried herself with the towel warmed by the fire and dressed quickly.

· · ·

Kate stepped into the kitchen and Bertie got up from the armchair. 'How do you feel?' he asked.

'Better, thank you,' Kate said.

'Would you feel up to seeing Mrs Hart and Elliot again?' Bertie asked. 'There are things we need to talk about.'

Kate nodded. 'I know.'

THIRTY-TWO

Kate walked beside Bertie along the drive, the details of Hill House coming into focus the closer they got. That house was full of souls she now knew. People she had come to care for.

The morning sun shone in the windows of the downstairs room where she had spent so many contented hours sewing costumes for the Mandeville children. Up in the attic and beyond what she could see, was the bedroom that was hers. That house had given her a room of her own when she hadn't had her own room in so many years. Hill House and the Mandevilles had given her a home when she didn't have one.

It was a house so full of kindness and love, yet what she had seen last night was without love or compassion of any kind. It was evil and it had already done Tommy harm. If she was going to help that young man, then she had to believe in all that was happening. That it was real. And she had to believe that she possessed some kind of ability that was just as real. She had lived with her strange skill for her whole life, without under-standing it. But it was now time to gain control of it and to stop whatever or whoever was trying to harm Tommy.

'How do you feel?' Bertie asked.

'I'm fine,' Kate said. 'Thank you.'

They entered the stables and found Mrs Hart and Elliot sitting at the table before the fire.

Mrs Hart got to her feet, using the edge of the table as a support. 'My darling Katherine,' she said. 'How are you? Did you have a restful sleep?'

'I did, thank you,' Kate said.

Mrs Hart looked from Kate to Bertie as though trying to read what had passed and what she should or should not say.

Elliot got his feet. He stood before Kate, looking down at her. He scratched his chin. 'There's been a change in her,' he said.

'Kate heard some of what we spoke about last night,' Bertie said. And then he stopped. 'But she is more than capable of speaking for herself. It's not for me to put words in her mouth.'

The way Elliot looked at Kate made her feel like he was reading something in her face. He pulled out a chair and Kate sat down. Mrs Hart, Elliot and Bertie joined her.

Kate brought her hands together and placed them on the table. It seemed impossible that she was about to say what she was going to say. But she had to. The people around this table were the only people who could help her untangle the mess of thoughts and experiences and hope to make any sense of it.

She looked around at each of them. 'I see things,' she said. 'I always have, ever since I was a little girl. When I touch an object, I can sometimes see the history of it. Flashes... pictures of its history. My family used to think it was a party trick. They explained it by saying that I remembered the history of an item from what I had overheard. But I've always known it's not that simple.' She looked at them all again. And they all looked at her, waiting, with not a glimmer of surprise or disbelief at what she had revealed.

'It's not everything I touch,' Kate continued. 'And until this week, it only ever happened in whatever house my parents lived in. But since I arrived at Hill House, it has started to happen here. And I don't know why.'

'What have you seen?' Mrs Hart asked.

Kate recounted her experiences, beginning with the ship she had seen when she touched the bannisters in the hall and then the two women in the stables when she touched the stall. When she told them of the lovers, she left out the precise detail of what she had seen them do. She didn't reveal what she knew of the identities of these people. For some reason, it felt like there were details that she should keep to herself. For now, at least. Finally, she explained the presence of the boy in the mirror in the lumber room, the awful look on his face, and how it seemed he wanted to harm Pegasus.

'And did you recognise the child?' Mrs Hart asked.

Kate shook her head. 'No. But it was after I saw him that strange things started to happen. The door rattling in the attic corridor in the dead of night as though someone was trying to get through. The bells ringing in empty rooms.'

'And you said last night that you had seen a man,' Mrs Hart said.

'When I held Tommy's penknife,' Kate said. 'I saw the man with Tommy in his room at university. It's like he's there, but not there. Almost like a... spirit.' A chill raced through Kate, but she would not be put off recounting the details. 'It feels like he is controlling Tommy. Somehow, he is making him ill whenever the penknife is in Tommy's possession. Last night, when I touched the penknife, I saw the moment he gave the knife to Tommy when he was still a child.'

'And did you see the man's face?' Mrs Hart asked. 'Do you know who he is?

Kate shook her head. 'All I know is that he means to do Tommy harm. Very great harm indeed.' She paused. 'Since I came to Hill House, what I see has changed. I don't simply see things now, I feel them. I felt the spray from that ship on my face, the warmth of the horses in the stables, the...' she stopped herself from speaking of the lovers. 'And then last night that man attacked me. I felt him push me against the wall.'

Bertie leapt from his chair. 'This is too much!' he said, his voice full of fury. 'What is Kate being exposed to? It's not safe. And do we even know how to protect her?'

Mrs Hart rose to her feet. 'Katherine, you must understand that this is not how we would normally manage such things at Hill House. We have... special visitors, as we like to call them, who might experience Hill House differently to other visitors. And you, it would seem, are our most special by far. From what I can see, you have been sent to help Tommy. We don't ordinarily discuss this side of Hill House with anybody. We are placing great trust in you. Hill House is placing great trust in you. And Katherine, has Tommy said anything unusual to you?'

Kate thought back to all the conversations she'd had with Tommy. 'Most of the time, he is absolutely normal and just like any young man of his age. And then sometimes he seems to slip into a strange trance-like state. I thought it was because he was ill and had a fever. But when he's like that, he says odd things, like he is supposed to help me but can't. I don't understand much of it. But he gets upset. And he said something about... *"one in, one out"*.'

Mrs Hart, Bertie and Elliot all made a noise. 'There is no more proof required,' Mrs Hart said.

'What does it mean? Kate asked.

'It means,' Mrs Hart said, 'that we are right to put our trust in you.'

'Where is the penknife?' Kate asked. 'Tommy mustn't touch it again. I feel... I know, that is how this man has been controlling him. It is this man who has made Tommy ill.'

'How can you be sure?' Mrs Hart asked.

'I don't have any proof to give you,' Kate said. 'But I feel it. And it seems all I can do now is trust how I feel.'

'She's right,' Elliot said. 'The lass has the intuition. We must trust her.'

Kate felt Elliot look at her and she knew that it was important that she look back at him. They stared at each other across the table for a few moments. Elliot nodded. 'She knows.'

'Knows what?' Mrs Hart asked.

Kate continued to look at Elliot. She would hold his gaze for as long as he held hers. As she looked into his eyes, she made a pact with herself to live up to her promise made as she walked beside Bertie along the drive: that she would do whatever was in her power to help this family and their household.

Elliot smiled as though he had read her thoughts. 'The lass knows that she must do what's best,' he said. 'And she is the one that can help. The rest of us, you, me and Albert, might have been here longer and think we know more because of what we have seen. But the lass has seen and knows more than we ever could. And she has found her courage.'

'We must all keep a close watch on Tommy,' Kate said. 'There's no knowing how else this man might be trying to harm him. And while we try to work out who it is and how to stop him, Tommy needs our protection.'

It was agreed that Kate would return to the main house and go about the day as though nothing had happened. She would prepare the costumes for the children's party and help with the arrangements. But they would all – Kate, Bertie, Mrs Hart and Elliot – keep a close watch on Tommy and any events around him. Bertie was sure that he would be able to enlist Tommy as his helper for the day. Tommy had always been keen to learn the business of the estate so Bertie would take him out to properly introduce him to the tenant farmers. Now that he was a young man – and the man who would one day be their landlord and set their rents and maintain their properties – the farmers would be sure to welcome the chance to talk to him.

It was agreed that Elliot would keep a watch outside the house and make regular forays into all areas of the house – from the basement to the attic – to check for anything untoward.

'I will watch Tommy like a hawk when he is inside the house,' Mrs Hart said. 'He has always been so fond of the Halloween festivities, and he will be sure to join in with the other children, even if he has grown into a young man.'

'Be sure that there are lanterns at every door,' Elliot said solemnly.

'Really?' Mrs Hart said. 'Isn't that simply a distraction for the children?'

The look on Elliot's face rarely altered. But in that moment, he appeared rather fierce. 'No,' he said. 'It is not.'

'I'm sorry,' Mrs Hart said quickly. 'That was rude of me. They are the superstitions of your mother's country and should be honoured.'

'No offence taken, ma'am,' Elliot said. 'But I wouldn't call them superstitions. They are practices that should be followed. Always.'

'Of course,' Mrs Hart said. 'I will have more lanterns prepared today.'

Kate couldn't remember having seen Mrs Hart look contrite before. She always seemed so confident and sure of herself. But it would seem that she trusted Elliot's take on this situation. It was also clear that she was prepared to follow his lead.

THIRTY-THREE

Kate accepted Elliot's offer to walk her back to the main house, while Bertie went to find Tommy, and Mrs Hart decided to remain before the fire in the stables with Elliot's Jack Russell.

The air was crisp with the hint of winter to come, and Kate walked in silence beside Elliot. They stopped at the top of the steps leading down to the basement.

'Do those really work?' Kate asked, pointing to the grimacing Jack-o'-lanterns on either side of the steps.

'My ancestors thought so,' Elliot said. 'And I'm minded to believe what they believed.'

Kate thought for a moment. There had been something she wanted to ask Elliot, but she hadn't wanted to pose the question in front of Mrs Hart. 'Bertie told me that some time back, a spirit board was used in the house,' she said. 'And it frightened the people who had been in the room at the time. He said that Mrs Hart had the board banished. Did you know about that?'

'Aye,' Elliot said. 'It was me who burned the board.'

'Could that board have opened something in this house, do you think? Making it possible for strange things to happen?'

'There's not a place on this Earth that sprits can't get

through to, if that's what you're asking me,' Elliot said. 'But some places and some people are more open to it.'

'And this is one of these places?' Kate asked.

'It's ancient land,' Elliot said. 'The trees in those woods go back thousands of years. Everything that has lived on this land has a spirit. But,' he added, 'sometimes it's not the spirits of the dead that we should be most concerned about.' He already spoke quietly but lowered his voice still further. 'We shouldn't always assume that it's the dead that want to hurt us. There are some men living whose hearts are black. Whose souls are beyond redemption. Maybe it's the dead who can help us against them.'

Kate tried to process everything Elliot was saying. In her visions she had seen people living and dead. The men on board the clipper would be long dead. Captain Mandeville had died. Miss Potter was alive. She didn't know about Captain Mandeville's lover or the boy in the mirror. 'And do you think that's what's happening here?' she asked. 'That it is someone living who is trying to harm Tommy?'

'Whether it's someone living or dead,' Elliot said, 'tonight is the night that Tommy could be at most risk. Whoever or whatever it is, is using dark arts to get to him. We have to be on guard. All night.'

Kate nodded. 'I understand.'

Elliot lifted his cap. 'I'll take my leave now,' he said. 'I'll be close by, if you need me.' He adjusted his cap and Kate watched him continue along the back of the house.

She took the steps down and paused to look in through the basement window. There, on the ledge inside, was the box of things she had knocked over last night. The handkerchiefs and coins looked so commonplace in the morning light. So innocent. And there, on that flag floor, just beside the parlour, was the spot where she had stumbled and fallen. She put her hand to her thigh, pressed and winced.

She had tried to be so brave with Mrs Hart, Elliot and Bertie, but looking at that spot now, some of that courage seemed to slip away. In the company of the others, she was able to be confident. But without them, all she had was herself. She had no one else to talk to. And she couldn't tell anyone even if she wanted to. Her silence would protect the Mandevilles.

Still staring at the flag where she had fallen, Kate tried to picture the face of the man who had pushed her. But all she saw was his anger. Fierce and red hot.

For her whole life, she had managed her gift, but what had happened in the last week was beyond anything she could ever have imagined. And she knew, she just knew, that there was more to come. But how could any of them fight something that was not physical, but a thought, a will-o'-the-wisp, an essence?

Kate tried the door. It was unlocked. Letting herself into the deserted basement, she made her way along the corridor, climbed the steps to the stone passageway, and quickly took the backstairs to her room. She quickly changed into her black dress and apron before hurrying downstairs to see to the fires in main rooms. Audrey would quite rightly be angry that she had failed in her duties, since a good part of the morning was already gone.

The long case clock struck nine o'clock as she passed into the hallway. Sunshine coming through the dome high up in the ceiling picked out the bronze floor tiles and the glittering marble of the statues on plinths. Kate paused below the staircase. There, on the wall, was the life-sized portrait of Thomas Mandeville, posed on a fine black horse with Hill House behind him. Closing her eyes, Kate summoned the faces of the other people she had seen in her visions. Captain Mandeville's lover and Miss Potter. Captain Mandeville had died to save his men. Miss Potter had risked her life to save Tommy. Had Captain Mandeville's lover also helped the Mandevilles in some way? Was Hill House bringing them to her to show that she too must find the strength and courage to help?

Kate looked into the library. A fire roared in the hearth. It was the same in the billiard room, dining room and drawing room. Someone had done her job for her. She was about to check the morning room when a set of double doors at the bottom of the staircase opened. Voices rang out.

'Katherine!' Alice said, crossing the hall to her. 'I've seen the costumes. You've outdone yourself!'

'It really was my pleasure,' Kate said, although the memory of sitting at the sewing machine for so many hours seemed distant now.

'I wish we had ordered costumes for ourselves, too!' Charlotte said, joining them in the middle of the hall.

Alice smiled. 'Now, Katherine, Audrey has said that she's happy for you to help me this morning. We need to set everything up for the party and Audrey and Rosemary will be busy in the kitchen.'

'Very good,' Kate said.

'I have some of Father's constituency correspondence to deal with,' Charlotte said, 'I'll be in the office, if anyone needs me.'

Kate followed Alice through the double doors, and was instantly lost for words. Two vast crystal chandeliers glittered high in the ceiling above them. Mirrors reflected daylight from the many tall doors lining the opposite wall, which were framed by blue curtains pooling on the floor. Gold mouldings decorated the walls and gold painted chairs had been lined up around the room. Kate could feel the wooden floor bounce slightly as she walked.

Alice turned to look at her. She had clearly read Kate's awe on her face. 'You haven't been in here before?' Alice asked.

Kate shook her head, craning to see the glittering crystal drops of the chandeliers. 'Audrey has never asked me to clean this room.'

'It is spectacular, isn't it?' Alice said. 'Apparently Lady

Mandeville's Christmas Eve balls in here were something to behold. I married Edward in the middle of the war so by then, the days of balls had come to an end. Well, if you don't count the parties we held for the soldiers we treated here when it was a hospital. Now we use the ballroom mainly for the children's birthday parties. It's the perfect space. They can run around and play games to their hearts' content.'

Kate thought back to her own birthday parties which involved half a dozen friends in the parlour with paste sandwiches, cake and a game of pass-the-parcel. This ballroom would be large enough for a good game of football, with full-sized goals at each end.

'Now,' Alice said, tapping her top lip with her finger. 'I thought we could arrange each costume over the back of a chair and bring the children in when they get home from school. I'll ask Rosemary to bring some sheets down so we can cover the costumes and reveal them all at the same time. How does that sound?'

'Perfect,' Kate said.

'If we do that first, then you could help me set up the tables with the games, which will free Rosemary up to help Audrey downstairs and then come upstairs to make more paperchains if we need them. After lunch, we need to make some more lanterns. Mrs Hart wants them at every door this year, so we have our work cut out!'

Kate had been waiting for an opportunity to ask after Tommy. It had to sound natural and as though she was dropping her question into conversation. 'Will Tommy be joining the party later?' she asked.

Alice laughed. 'Just try to stop him! The Halloween party has always been his favourite celebration of the year. He's gone out for the day with Bertie to visit some of the farms, but before he left, he said that he has come up with his own costume for this evening! Come on then, let's go and get your beautiful works of art.'

Kate helped Alice move the costumes from the morning room to the ballroom. They draped each garment over a chair so that it looked almost like four flat people were sitting in each corner of the room.

They had just finished when a familiar tip-tap came from the hall.

'What have we got here then?' Mrs Hart asked, joining them to look around the room.

'Hasn't Katherine done us proud?' Alice said.

'Indeed, she has,' Mrs Hart said. 'Katherine is putting her talents to good use for Hill House.' She slipped her arm through Alice's.

Charlotte appeared in the doorway. 'I hoped you'd still be here,' she said. 'Katherine, there's a telephone call for you.'

'For me?' Kate said.

Charlotte smiled and nodded. 'Come on, don't keep them waiting.'

Kate followed Charlotte through the hall and to the door below the stairs. 'I'll leave you to it,' Charlotte said. 'You can take it in Father's office. Give me a shout when you're finished. No rush, I'll be in the ballroom. I fancy a go at hanging some of those paperchains.'

Kate hurried to the office at the end. She hadn't given the telephone number for Hill House to anyone. She didn't even know the number. And nobody knew she was here.

She found the receiver beside the telephone on one of the desks. She picked it up.

'Hello?' she said.

'Katherine, sweetheart.'

Kate put her hand to her mouth. She almost sobbed.

'Katherine? Kate? Are you there? Can you hear me?'

'Yes, Mum,' Kate said quietly. 'I can hear you.'

'Oh, sweetheart. It's so lovely to hear your voice. I got your letter and Harry found the telephone number for Hill House for me. I don't want to be on the telephone long and have Harry and Enid get a big bill. I just wanted to check you're all right. Your news came out of the blue.'

'I'm fine, Mum. Honestly. The family here are very kind and it's a good job.'

'I'm so glad. The lady who answered the telephone was lovely and she said you're getting on very well.'

'I'm sorry I didn't tell you about losing my job before,' Kate said. 'I didn't want to worry you.'

'Now, you've nothing to be sorry for. I'm so proud of you for getting yourself sorted like this. You've always been such a hard worker. They are lucky to have you, you know.'

Kate laughed softly. 'Thanks, Mum.'

'I should go really. This is likely costing a pretty penny. And you've got your work to get back to, I should imagine. I've written you a nice long letter. I'll pop it in the post this morning. You'll write soon, won't you?'

'Of course, Mum. How are you are getting on with Harry and Enid?'

'We're just fine. There's never a dull moment with the children. But... I miss you, Katherine. After we've been together so much recently.'

Kate swallowed. 'I miss you too, Mum... And I've been visiting Dad's... I've been going to the churchyard.'

There was just a brief pause. 'You are such a good girl.'

Kate heard the tremble in her mother's voice. 'I'll see you as soon as I can,' Kate said. 'But I'll write in the meantime.'

'A good long letter?' her mother asked.

'A good long letter,' Kate said.

'I'll say bye for now then, sweetheart. Do your best.'

'I will. I promise. Bye, Mum. Look after yourself.'

'And you, sweetheart. Take care.'

Kate waited for the sound of the line disconnecting before placing the receiver in the cradle. She stared at the telephone. Putting her hand to her neck, she felt for her father's St Christopher. A tear formed in the corner of her eye. 'Do your best.' It's what her parents had always said to her. Whether it was when she was worried about a test at school, trying to learn the piano, or the first day in a new job. She held the St Christopher tighter still and wiped away the tear.

Kate returned to the ballroom where Charlotte was up on a stepladder with Alice handing her paperchains to decorate the room, supervised by Mrs Hart.

Charlotte stood on tip toes to drape a length of chains over a curtain pole. 'Good telephone call?' she asked Kate.

Kate nodded and said, 'Thank you.' She took hold of one end of the chains and while they worked, Alice ran through the remaining things to be done before the children returned from school. Once the paperchains were up, there were then bowls of water to be sorted for bobbing for apples, the table in the ballroom to be decorated, all the food to be brought up, a blindfold to be arranged for Blind Man's Bluff. And of course, the extra lanterns to be made.

With the paperchains in place, Kate went with Charlotte to the stable yard to bring in some of the festoons of foliage. When they returned, Mrs Hart helped place them along the edges of the floor around the room, bringing the outside world inside.

They stopped for lunch and joined Audrey and Rosemary in the kitchen. As she sat at the table, Kate tried to get a sense of whether Audrey and Rosemary were alarmed that she had been missing all night and whether Audrey was cross that she hadn't been there to make up the fires. If they had noticed her absence or been in any way angry, she felt sure she would have known. But they treated her like nothing unusual had happened.

'Did Emma arrange to have some lemons sent over from the Caxton orangery?' Charlotte asked, her finger hooked over her mouth as she chewed her flan.

'A crate arrived this morning,' Audrey said.

'Good old Emma,' Charlotte said. 'Shame her and her brood can't join us tonight. Raymond has a bit of a dicky tummy, and she doesn't want to pass it on to us.'

The women all laughed when Charlotte reminded them how competitive Edward and Paul were likely to be when it came to the three-legged race. 'They always say they let the children win,' Charlotte said. 'But it's not true. I don't think I've seen two more competitive men in my life!'

Then there was the memory of Paul at the last Halloween party, landing with a spectacular thud on the floor when he tried to overtake Charlie in the sack race.

Kate only vaguely listened. A phrase spun around in her head: *Do your best.* It's what she had always tried to do. She pictured Tommy and the man who had wanted to do him harm. She saw how ill Tommy had been due to the influence of the man. And somehow, the man had managed to hurt her. She could try to tell herself that she had stumbled back and fallen against the wall because she was alarmed by the vision. But she had felt his hands on her chest. Until now, he had only been able to influence objects around her, like the attic door. But his strength was growing. He had managed to physically push her because she was open to the visions. And if he was able to do that to her, what would he do to Tommy when he could? She had to do her best to put a stop to whatever plans this man had for Tommy.

. . .

It was decided that they would stay in the kitchen to carve the extra lanterns rather than making a mess in the ballroom. Audrey said that as they were at the table, they wouldn't be in her way at all. She could work around them, and it would be nice to have the company.

Rosemary collected a sack of turnips from the cold store and arranged an array of knives on the table. Each woman took a turnip from the sack, cut off the top and began the task of scoring the hard flesh inside so that it could be scraped out.

'These are so bloody tough,' Charlotte said. 'Whoever came up with this as a tradition needs their bumps feeling!' She wiped her fringe away from her face, still holding the knife. 'Why do we need so many of these, Aunt Leo?'

Mrs Hart was working diligently at her own turnip. 'I enjoy how they look at the doorways. They light up the dark night.'

'If you say so,' Charlotte said, setting to scraping at her turnip again. 'But we've never done so many before.'

'There's a first time for everything,' Mrs Hart said.

For an hour they worked at the table, the kitchen full of the scent of Audrey's beautiful cooking and baking, mixed with the earthy raw vegetable smell of the turnips. Audrey had them all put the scraped innards into a bowl, which she would make into a mash the next day.

Kate hacked away at her own turnips and made three lanterns. She carved and scored the most horrific face in each, making them as repellent as she could.

When the clock stuck half past two, Charlotte said she should get ready to collect the children from school. Kate helped Audrey and Rosemary tidy the table, putting away knives and scooping the insides of the turnips into bowls. Rosemary was given the job of taking the lanterns and placing them at all the doors to the house. The candles would be placed inside and lit at dusk.

'If nobody minds,' Mrs Hart said, 'I will go to my room to rest up for the party. What time would you like me in the ball-room, Alice?'

'Six o'clock,' Alice said. 'That's when the fun will start!'

On her way out of the door, Mrs Hart took Kate to one side. 'Can you spare me a minute?' she said.

Kate followed Mrs Hart from the kitchen and up the stone steps to the passageway. Mrs Hart took Kate's hands. 'Has anything happened today that I should be aware of?' she asked quietly.

'Nothing,' Kate said.

Mrs Hart frowned. 'I find this so frustrating,' she said. 'I can't feel anything. It's ordinarily me who is trying to help our visitors understand... It feels like all the responsibility is resting on your shoulders, and I don't know why.'

'I promise I will do everything in my power to make sure everyone is kept safe,' Kate said.

Mrs Hart looked deep into Kate's eyes. 'I know that you are more than up to the task you've been set. You are even stronger than you might think.' Releasing Kate's hands, she cupped Kate's cheek. 'Thank you, Katherine. For everything you are doing for my family.'

Mrs Hart turned and headed towards the door leading to the hall.

THIRTY-FOUR

'Brace yourselves,' Alice said to Kate, Audrey and Rosemary, who had joined her in the ballroom to await the sound of Charlotte's car pulling up on the gravel outside the house. The great front door opened, and the peace of the house was shattered by squeals and footsteps running across the tiles in the hall.

'Not so fast!' Charlotte called. 'One of you is going to fall and I shan't patch up any skinned knees as it will be your own fault.'

Charlotte's warning was in vain. Almost immediately it was issued, four children charged into the ballroom. Not just four children, but four very excitable children who made enough noise for eight or twelve children. Even Daphne, who was so much older than her brothers and cousin, was carried along by the excitement and joined with the others in wearing the masks they had made and worn to Elliot's storytelling. The only way to tell who was who was from their height and hair.

Charlotte appeared in the doorway, shrugging off her coat. 'They all insisted on putting those blasted masks on in the car,' she laughed. 'Every time I looked in the mirror, I thought the car had been invaded by the hounds of hell!'

The children looked at the foliage festoons brought over from the stable yard, at the paperchains, at the bowls full of apples ready to be bobbed for, at lanterns lined up like sentries on the table as decoration for the feast they would enjoy later, at everything that had been assembled over the course of the afternoon and arranged at the far end of the ballroom for when it was time for games later – four old flour sacks, scarves to be used to bind legs together or cover eyes, a bowl of hard boiled eggs and a pot of spoons.

The women laughed as they dodged the children running amongst them.

'Children! Children!' Alice called over the din. 'Come here... Come here! We have a very special surprise for you all.'

The promise of a surprise was enough to stop the children in their tracks and see them run to Alice and gather around her. 'Now,' she said. 'You know that Miss Durrant took your measurements the other day, well, she has worked so incredibly hard that she has finished the costumes for the party.'

Louisa lifted her mask. 'Really?' she asked.

Her cousin, Oscar, joined her. 'Really?' he said.

As had been arranged, Alice, Charlotte, Audrey and Rosemary took up position by the chairs covered in sheets. Kate stood on and watched. Each woman took hold of the sheet beside her. 'One... Two... Three!' Alice called. As one, they lifted the sheets. The children looked about them. Initially there was confusion, until Alice called out each child's name and pointed to the chair that contained their costume. They each ran to their chair and without exception, lifted the costume that was to be theirs and laughed and exclaimed with joy. Until Charlie told Oscar that as a pirate, he was in charge of his little brother and that Oscar would be the ship's dog and would have to do everything he was told, including sitting and begging for his supper. Oscar objected. He folded his arms across his little chest and stamped his feet.

'I don't want Charlie to be in charge of me,' he said. 'I shan't beg for my supper.'

'And you don't need to,' Alice soothed. 'Have you ever heard of a ship's dog? No, you haven't. There are only ship's cats. As a dog, you live on land and don't need to pay Charlie any mind. He will be off walking the plank while you have fun in your kennel and chase balls and are fed treats.'

Reassured that he wouldn't have to follow his older brother's instructions, Oscar exclaimed that he was happy to be a dog as it was man's best friend. He scooped up his costume again and smiled at the tail he would wear.

'What do you say to Miss Durrant?' Charlotte said.

All the children turned to Kate. There was a barrage of thanks and Kate smiled. 'You are all very welcome.' She couldn't have been more thrilled by their reactions as they explored the components of each costume.

'Careful,' Alice said. 'You don't want to damage or spoil them. Now, collect them carefully. *Carefully*, I said, Oscar! That's it. Drape your costume over your arm, darling. Now, ever so carefully take them to your bedrooms. Don't put them on yet. Leave them neatly on your beds. Rosemary will bring milk and biscuits up to the nursery and after that, you may change into your costumes. We'll light the candles in the lanterns when it starts to go dark and as soon as we have done that, we will start our party.'

There was a chorus of hoorays and as the children charged from the room, Daphne called, 'What time do you think it will be dark, Mama?'

'I would say around six o'clock, darling,' Alice said.

With the children running up the stairs, Alice turned to Kate. 'Thank you so much,' she said. 'They were thrilled.'

'I can't wait to see them all dressed up,' Charlotte said.

Audrey and Rosemary headed back downstairs to continue with preparations for the party tea. Kate was set the task of sweeping the hallway to clear the leaves that had blown in every time the door opened. As Alice and Charlotte headed upstairs, Charlotte called back. 'Meet us in the ballroom at six o'clock,' she said. 'And be ready for some fun and games!'

THIRTY-FIVE

With a broom kept just inside the passageway, Kate swept dried brown leaves from around the hallway into a pile at the bottom of the staircase. It was growing dark outside, and she worked with what little daylight found its way through the glass dome.

Sweeping the office corridor, she checked each door that led to the grounds at the back of the house, making sure there was a lantern waiting to be lit.

In the main rooms, she checked the fires and looked through the doors to the outside to see lanterns standing guard at each. It wasn't lost on her that what she had experienced so far since arriving at Hill House had come from inside the house itself. But it couldn't hurt to protect the Mandevilles from the outside too.

Sweeping the leaves into a pan, Kate opened the door to the vestibule and closed it behind her before opening the front door. Four lanterns sat in the gravel outside.

A Jack Russell appeared at her feet and Kate bent to scratch its ears.

'Evening,' called a familiar voice.

'How has your day been?' Kate asked.

'Uneventful,' Elliot said. 'Bertie and Tommy will be back within the half hour. They've stopped in at High Top farm as their last visit of the day. Old Bob always has his tea at half past five so will want them out before then.'

The dog began to sniff at one of the lanterns and Elliot gave it a signal to bring it to heel. He stared at Kate as he had in the stables. 'Have you sensed anything else today?' He asked it in that straightforward way of his.

'Nothing,' she said. 'Perhaps the threat has gone.'

Elliot didn't once break his gaze. 'Do you think it has?'

Kate shook her head. 'I think it's waiting. But I don't know what *it* is.'

'We'll find out soon enough,' Elliot said. 'I should go and feed the dog. But I'll be hereabouts all evening, should you need me.' He signalled to bring his dog to heel again and Kate watched them head for the stables.

Letting herself back inside the house, the clock in the hall chimed five o'clock. Kate made her way down to the kitchen and helped Audrey and Rosemary with the final preparations for the food, buttering bread for sandwiches, laying out cake on serving plates. When the food was ready to Audrey's satisfaction and covered in damp tea towels, Kate went back upstairs with Rosemary to transfer crockery, glassware and cutlery from the dining room to the ballroom. Kate waited for the sisters to mention her absence that morning but still they said nothing.

With twenty minutes to spare, Audrey said they should change – they weren't expected to wear their working dresses and aprons at the party. On the way up to their rooms, Kate took a quick detour, saying she would see the sisters upstairs. She ran into the empty ballroom and collected a turnip and a candle.

Up in her room, she quickly dressed in her jumper and skirt. She lit the candle from a flame in her fireplace and pushed it inside the turnip. The sisters were still in their rooms when she placed the lantern outside the locked door leading to the lumber room.

'What's that for?' Rosemary laughed when she emerged from her room.

'Just in case,' Kate tried to laugh.

Audrey soon joined them and as they made their way downstairs, Kate looked back to the glowing jagged teeth and eyes.

Voices met Kate and the sisters when they approached the open doors of the ballroom. There were so many and so much laughter that no voice could be heard distinctly. When they stepped into the ballroom, everyone turned to Kate.

'There she is!' Charlotte said.

Kate could hardly believe her eyes. The children were all dressed in their costumes, and they looked marvellous. Daphne ran to her. The white Pierrot tabard and trousers with black pompoms fitted her perfectly. 'Thank you so much,' she said. 'I love it, I really do. And Aunt Charlotte did my make up.' Daphne's face had been dusted with a pale powder. She had the slightest touch of red on her lips and a teardrop drawn in kohl on her cheek.

Louisa ran to join her cousin. She looked wonderful in her red and purple satin costume with her hair curled and her mouth outlined in a huge smile in kohl.

'Thank you!' she gushed, smiling up at Kate.

'You are very welcome,' Kate said.

The boys called their thanks for the pirate and dog costumes. They were far too busy chasing each other to stop. But she could see that they, too, had kohl embellishments. Charlie had pirate stubble draw on his chin and Oscar had a little black nose and some whiskers. He was particularly taken with his tail, which he twirled around, trying to use it as a whip to hit his brother.

'They look simply adorable,' Mrs Hart said. 'You have excelled yourself Katherine.' She put her arm through Kate's and leant in closer. 'Is everything all right?' she asked.

'It is,' Kate said.

'It looks like we haven't missed too much of the party then!' a voice called from the doorway. Paul was there with Edward, Bertie and Tommy.

The children ran to their fathers and after more appreciation of the costumes and the room decorations, it was decided that it was time to go around the doors to light the candles. The family was split into groups to go to the different areas, all with a box of small candles. 'You can count me out,' Tommy called as he ran up the stairs. 'I have a surprise for you all.'

Kate followed Audrey and Rosemary to the kitchen. But as they were about to head down the steps to the basement, a voice over her shoulder said, 'Katherine, might I have a word please?'

'I'll be just a minute,' she said to Audrey.

Kate stood with Bertie, listening until the sisters disappeared into the kitchen. She felt him close by her shoulder. In amongst everything that had been happening, she had been able to put her feelings for him to one side. But standing so close to him now, they bubbled to the surface.

'How are you, Kate?' he asked.

She turned to face him, 'I'm fine. How was Tommy today?'

'His usual self. Talking twenty to the dozen. Enthusiastic about everything. The farmers we visited were very taken with him and the young man he has become. They remember him as a cheeky little imp. They were impressed with his knowledge of the estate and the businesses.'

'And there was no sign of any illness?' Kate asked.

'None at all.'

'We need to keep a close eye on him tonight,' Kate said.

'I understand,' Bertie said. 'I'll go upstairs in a moment and make sure he is safe. And Kate, will you come to me with anything untoward or that troubles you, rather than going to Mrs Hart? She has worked so long and so hard for this house. It's time she took a rest. And I'd like her to enjoy herself this evening and not have any worry, if it can be avoided.'

'Of course,' Kate said.

'And how are you. Really?' he asked.

'I'm fine,' she said. 'I should go to help Audrey and Rosemary.'

'I'll see you at the party,' he said.

Kate watched Bertie walk through the door to the hallway before heading for the steps down to the kitchen.

THIRTY-SIX

By the time Kate and the sisters returned, bearing trays of sandwiches, pork pie, an assortment of cakes, toffee apples and cinder toffee, the ballroom was once again full. The gramophone had been brought from the billiard room and a jolly scratchy tune was coming from its trumpet. Paul's sister in Boston had sent a parcel of some of the latest popular records and the children seemed to be having great fun dancing to them.

Kate placed the tray of sandwiches she was carrying on the table. Charlotte rushed to put herself between the table and the children who immediately descended. 'Grownups first!' Charlotte said.

Alice helped Mrs Hart fill a plate and they sat at one of the decorated tables. Paul and Edward were next to the feast.

'What say you, Uncle Edward?' Paul said. 'Should we finish the pork pies and leave none for the children?'

'A splendid idea!' Edward said, making a play of pretending to sweep up all the pies. The children yelled loudly, and Paul and Edward agreed that they would leave some after all.

'Only a few, mind!' Paul said as he and Edward sat at the table with Mrs Hart and Alice.

Alice insisted that Audrey, Rosemary and Kate help themselves next. Kate took up a plate and chose two triangles of corned beef sandwich and a slice of pork pie and joined the sisters at the table beside the other grownups.

After filling her own plate, Charlotte let the children descend on the table. 'Savoury first!' she said to them. 'You can have your sweet treats after.'

Charlotte sat down with Kate and the others. She blew at her fringe. 'It's like herding cats!' she said before tucking into her food.

The children sat on the floor to eat, insisting on having lanterns around them. They were up and down to the food table continually and to change the music on the gramophone each time a record came to an end.

'You must be delighted with how the costumes turned out, Kate,' Charlotte said. 'The children couldn't be happier.'

'I had help,' Kate said, swallowing a mouthful of sandwich. 'Audrey and Rosemary helped make the pompoms.'

'Really! You'll have to show me how to make them. The children would love to learn too, I'm sure.'

The two grownup tables were side by side and soon everyone was chatting happily. While the children enjoyed their meal with glass after glass of sticky sweet lemonade, Edward had lined up a dozen bottles of Elliot's ale. He did rounds of the tables, keeping the adults' glasses topped up.

'Ta da!' a shout came from the doorway. Everyone turned to see Tommy run into the room. He held his arms wide. 'What do you think?'

There was a roar of laughter from everyone in the room. 'What on Earth are you?' Alice said through joyful tears.

'Why,' he said, 'I am Captain Dog Pirate, of course. Terror of the seas and any kennel in one thousand leagues.' He wore an old pair of trousers, ripped and tattered below the knees as Charlie's were. He wore a white shirt with similarly torn sleeves and a waistcoat over the top. He had tied a red scarf around his auburn curls and had drawn an elaborate moustache on his face but paired it with some animal whiskers and a sort of dog's nose to match Charlie's.

Charlie and Oscar ran to him. 'You are half Charlie and half me,' Oscar said.

'That's right, me hearties!' Tommy said. While he somehow managed to pick up both brothers beneath his arms, Bertie entered the ballroom. He took the free seat beside Kate as Tommy ran to the end of the ballroom and dropped his brothers to the floor, making them both laugh hysterically. 'You're getting too big for that,' Tommy said, puffing out his cheeks. 'Maybe it's all the toffee apples you've been eating.' He ran back to the food table with his little brothers close at his heels and took up the tray of toffee apples. 'So, I'll take these. They are all *mine* now.'

'You'll have to fight me for them first,' Paul laughed.

Tommy placed the tray back on the table. 'I'll have you walk the plank!' he said to his uncle. He held up his arm and looked at his hand as though looking for something. 'Blast,' he said. 'I'll have to get it later.' He turned back to Paul. 'We'll get back to the plank walking presently,' he said.

Paul laughed. 'I shall look forward to it.' He got up from the table and handed Tommy a glass of ale. 'But a pirate needs his ration of grog first.'

'Indeed, he does,' Tommy said. He chinked glasses with his uncle. After taking a large slug of the beer, he wiped his mouth on the back of his hand.

Alice told Tommy and Bertie to have something to eat. Tommy didn't need to be told twice. He filled a plate and sat on the floor with his siblings and cousin rather than the grownups. They were delighted with his company, and they laughed and joked, poking fun and teasing each other. Midway through a sandwich, Tommy feigned horror at something Oscar had said. Abandoning his plate, he grabbed his little brother and rolled around the floor with him, wrestling then tickling him, so Oscar giggled uncontrollably.

Kate looked to the women around the tables. They all watched Tommy, smiling. The mood in the room had been jolly before he arrived but it lifted further with him in it. Tommy was the very centre of his family's life. He was adored and so clearly loved by everyone. And in that moment, he looked so healthy and so full of life that it was possible to believe that the events of recent days hadn't happened at all.

A movement out in the hall caught Kate's attention. She looked up to see Elliot standing at the bottom of the stairs. When he saw her look at him, he nodded.

The atmosphere lifted still further when the games commenced. The ballroom turned out to be the perfect venue with the length of the room. There was so much fun to be had with the sack races, the egg and spoon race and bobbing for apples so that almost everyone had wet hair. The children's faces glowed, as did Paul and Edward's as they involved themselves in every game and were as competitive as promised, desperate to beat their children. Charlotte joined in, too, matching her brother and husband in the competitive stakes. Alice sat with Mrs Hart, and they cheered the children on. When Oscar fell over and grazed his knee, he sought out his mother for comfort. A quick kiss and he was off again, playing with his siblings and cousin.

Eventually there was a break in games to top up on refreshments. Once it was over, it was decided that the three-legged race should be next.

'Hey,' Paul shouted as Charlotte tied his leg to Edward's. 'Bertie. Katherine. Come and join in.'

'Oh, no, thank you,' Kate said.

'Don't be spoilsports,' Edward said and pushed his spectacles up his nose. 'Pair up and come and race me and Paul here. Or are you scared you'll lose?'

Charlotte held up a blue scarf. 'Come on, you two. Have some fun.'

Bertie turned to Kate. 'I think we might have to,' he said. 'I don't think they are going to take no for an answer.'

All eyes turned to her expectantly. She was on the verge of saying no when almost in spite of herself, she got to her feet.

'That's the spirit!' Edward said.

Audrey and Rosemary were already on their feet, rushing to Charlotte to have their legs tied while Kate and Bertie still lingered at the table.

Bertie slipped off his jacket and placed it over the back of the chair. They walked together across the room and stood waiting for Charlotte to finish with the sisters.

'Right,' Charlotte said, after securing the sisters' legs and pulling on the scarf to make sure it was tight. 'Come here, you two.'

It felt to Kate like her breath was caught in her chest. Bertie stood beside her, with so little distance between them. Charlotte took up the scarf and threaded it around their ankles. With one hard yank, Kate's leg, all the way from her ankle, up to her thigh, was touching Bertie's. His warmth seeped into her. Her breath that had been stuck in her chest tried to escape like a flock of birds taking flight. Charlotte crossed one end of the scarf over the other, yanked again and pulled it tight. She tapped the front of it. 'You won't get out of that in a hurry,' she said. Leaving them, Charlotte began giving directions to the competitors. Kate didn't hear a word of it. Bertie slipped his arm around her back and put his hand on the dip in her waist. His touch was warm and gentle. The birds flew directly at her ribs again.

'Are you all right?' Bertie whispered.

Kate nodded.

'We should go to the start line,' he said.

Gingerly, Kate put her arm around Bertie's back. She placed her hand on his side. His waistcoat had ridden up slightly and her hand was on the cotton of his shirt. She felt his muscles move beneath her hand as he stepped away, taking her with him.

She hardly heard any of the words spoken. Her full attention was on the sensation of Bertie's leg pressing against hers, the feel of his fingers pressing into the dip in her waist, her arm around his back and the tightness of his muscles beneath the thin cotton.

'Got that?' Charlotte called. She had clearly given the competitors some instructions, but Kate could think of nothing apart from Bertie pulling her closer to him as the race was about to begin.

'Are you ready?' he asked. 'We'll set off on our outside legs and then bring our joined legs forward.'

She nodded. Before she knew what was happening, Charlotte shouted, and they were off. Kate ran forward on her outside leg. Bertie was so strong and so fast that it was all she could do to hang on to him. At some points she was sure that he was lifting her off the ground. There was a wall of noise and cheers and whoops of encouragement. Then there was laughter and a bit of gentle jeering. Audrey and Rosemary were soon ahead. But try as hard as she might, Kate could not run as fast as Bertie. Almost as soon as the race had begun, it came rapidly to an end with Audrey and Rosemary touching the wall at the far and of the ballroom. Kate and Bertie weren't far behind and collapsed onto the wall, gasping for breath. Still there were cheers and laughter. Twisting around, Kate saw Paul and Edward in a heap on the floor some way back. They were embroiled in a very heated but good-natured argument about who had stumbled, taking the other one tumbling with them. But even as she looked and laughed as the others did, all she could think about was Bertie's arm around her. Audrey and Rosemary were already kneeling down, unfastening the scarf.

'Well played,' Bertie said to the sisters.

'Yes, congratulations,' Kate said.

She looked up at Bertie. 'And well played to you, too, Kate,' he said quietly, his cheeks pink.

'I'm sorry I couldn't run faster,' Kate said.

'It's not about the winning,' he said.

'Come on, you two,' one of the children shouted. 'We need that scarf for another game of Blind Man's Bluff!'

Kate felt Bertie grasp her side just a little tighter. 'We should go and sit down,' he said. 'So I can untie us.'

Slowly they walked back up the ballroom, their legs still touching, Bertie's hand on her waist. Kate pressed her fingers a little further into Bertie's side and the birds returned to fly against her ribs as she looked down at their feet walking side by side.

Coming to the table, they retook their seats. Bertie moved his chair closer to hers and leant forward to untie the scarf. His fingers brushed her calf. As though in response, every drop of blood in her body rushed to that point. She was suddenly in that room again, watching the lovers, imagining it was her with Bertie. She gripped the edge of the chair.

Bertie looked up at her. His fringe had fallen into his eyes. 'Is something wrong?' he asked.

All she could do was make a noise to indicate that she was fine.

Unravelling the final knot, Bertie got up and handed the scarf to Charlotte. When he sat down, he didn't move his chair away and he didn't put his jacket back on. They were sitting so close that their arms were touching. And with Bertie in just his shirt sleeves. Kate looked around the room; she had to focus to take the heat out of cheeks and to try to calm the beat of her heart.

The children began another game of Blind Man's Bluff. With its chaotic running about and dodging and hiding, it seemed to be a particular favourite. Bertie laughed at something one of the children did and his arm rubbed Kate's. She took a calming breath. She could have moved away but instead, looked to the children's game. It was easy to identify each of them by the costumes. As ever, Paul and Edward were in the midst of their offspring. Audrey and Rosemary had joined the game with Alice and Mrs Hart sitting on and laughing while Charlotte seemed to be refereeing proceedings. She stopped and looked round. 'Where's Tommy?' she said. 'He needs to take his turn.'

'He went to his room to get something when you were all busy with the three-legged race,' Alice said. 'He'll be back soon.'

Dread sent an ice-cold chill through Kate. She leant into Bertie. 'Elliot was in the hall earlier,' she said. 'I'll see if he's still there and if he's seen Tommy.'

'I'll stay here,' Bertie said. 'So that it doesn't seem off that we've both left.'

Behind Kate, the ballroom was so full of life, so noisy and vibrant. The hall was silent, apart from her footsteps on the tiles echoing in the emptiness. Lanterns glowed on the mantelpiece giving off the scent of singed vegetable.

Elliot stepped from beneath the staircase. 'I watched the lad go up not more than ten minutes since. I asked where he was off to and he said he'd forgotten something and was going to fetch it.'

'Something feels different,' Kate said quietly. 'Something feels off. Will you come with me to find him?'

They went through the doorway at the back of the hall and along the passageway. When they arrived at the stone staircase, they were practically running. Kate could sense that Elliot felt what she did. That something was very wrong. They didn't pause at the doorway to the first floor but rushed along the landing. The voices of the party at the bottom of the staircase floated up as they picked up their pace again, running to the room at the far end of the house in the bachelors' wing.

Elliot knocked on the door. When he received no response, he opened it. The room was only dimly by a lamp on the nightstand. Clothes were strewn across the bed, no doubt from Tommy's impromptu costume making. Nothing was instantly amiss. Kate ran further into the room with Elliot behind her. They came to an abrupt halt. There, beneath the window on the far side of the room, Tommy was curled into a ball, shaking almost uncontrollably, his arms covering his head. Elliot bent and helped him onto the bed.

Kate pressed her palm to Tommy's forehead. His skin was cool, with no temperature. He was so very pale and sweat glistened on his forehead. The kohl beard, nose and whiskers had smudged across his face. He was behaving as though he was in the throes of a fever again. Kate pulled the eiderdown up, but Tommy continued to shake.

'He has control over him again,' Kate said. 'But Tommy doesn't have the penknife.'

Tommy squirmed beneath the covers, threatening to knock the items from his bed to the floor. Kate collected the clothing and placed it on the chest of drawers. She took other items from the bottom of the bed: a book, the kohl pencil Tommy had used on his face, a sheet of ripped brown paper and a box from an unwrapped parcel. She grabbed an item poking from beneath the eiderdown. There was a flash. A small child was curled into a ball. A man with his back to Kate yelled at the child. He was furious. He raised his fist as though to strike the child. The child cowered from him. The man turned. She saw his face. It was the man who had attacked her.

Kate dropped the object. The boy and man disappeared. She was once again in Tommy's room, a child's toy cutlass at her feet. 'It's that,' she said. 'That cutlass was in the trunk in the lumber room. When I held it last time, I saw the boy in the mirror. Just then I saw the man who attacked me last night. He was shouting at Tommy.'

Elliot grasped the cutlass so that his knuckles were white. 'I'll take this,' he said. 'Will you wait here with the lad? I'll come back when I've sorted this.'

Elliot left, closing the door behind him. Kate sat on the bed beside Tommy. She tucked the eiderdown around him. He was still shaking, his eyes closed. She took a cloth from the wash-stand, dipped it in the water in the jug and used it to clean the kohl from his face. She cupped his cheek. She should have been watching him in the ballroom rather than playing games with Bertie. She had allowed herself to be distracted. Tommy began to tremble violently, so Kate doubled the eiderdown over and tucked it tighter around him.

Eventually, the door opened. Elliot entered but he was not alone.

'How is he?' Bertie whispered.

Elliot closed the door softly and Bertie joined Kate, looking down at Tommy.

'He should be getting better since Elliot took the cutlass away. But he hasn't changed.' She looked up at Bertie. 'How did you explain us all disappearing so suddenly?'

'I said you had taken yourself to your room because the toffee hadn't agreed with you and you wanted to sleep.' All the while he spoke, Bertie stared at Tommy. 'The party wound up after you left, and the children have been taken to bed. They were exhausted. Everyone else has gone to the billiard room. They had a quick chat about coming to find Tommy, but Paul reminded them that he's a grown man and should probably be left alone.'

'Wasn't Mrs Hart suspicious?' Kate asked.

'Of course. But I told her there was nothing for her to worry about.' Bertie scooped his fringe away from his face. He indicated for Kate to leave Tommy's side. Along with Elliot, they stood away from the bed and beside the window.

'Elliot told me you had one of your turns when you held the toy cutlass,' Bertie said. 'Can you tell me what you saw?'

'Like I said to Elliot, it was Tommy as a small boy with a man threatening him. It was the same man that was in the den in the woods and gave him the penknife. And the man who attacked me in the basement.'

Tommy groaned and kicked out. 'The cutlass is nowhere near him,' Kate said. 'Neither is the penknife. And still that man I see seems to have control over him. There's a connection to that boy in the mirror in the lumber room. But I don't know what it is.'

Bertie turned to Elliot, a troubled look on his face. 'It can't be him doing this to Tommy.'

Elliot ran his thumb along his top lip. 'If it is him, he is using skills I have never seen before. I've heard of them, but I've not seen them.' He nodded to the bed. 'He's harnessing powers to do that. Dangerous powers. We must fight fire with fire.'

'What are you saying?' Bertie asked.

'She has skills that go further than what you've done through your connection to this house. And what Mrs Hart and Tommy have done. Her abilities reach beyond these walls and what it can do. She knows she has gifts.'

Kate looked from Bertie to Elliot. 'I'll do anything,' she said. 'If it will help Tommy.'

'Will you?' Elliot said. 'Anything?'

THIRTY-SEVEN

It was decided that they should move Tommy. With the penknife and cutlass nowhere to be seen, there had to be something else causing his delirium.

'We'll take him up the back steps,' Elliot said.

'What back steps?' Kate asked.

'The old male staff quarters are directly above us,' Bertie said. 'Intentionally over the bachelors' rooms to keep all the single men on one side of the building.'

'You'll have to open the doors for us and lead the way,' Elliot said to Kate. 'There's no light on the back steps. It's barely been used in years.'

Elliot and Bertie took Tommy from the bed. Like so many times now, Kate watched them drape his arms around their necks. Kate opened the door and looked out. The corridor was empty. The lights out. She turned back and nodded. Bertie and Elliot joined her, and she closed the door.

With a flick of his chin Elliot indicated that she should go further along the corridor. Kate used the moonlight coming through the windows to make her way. At a bend in the corridor, she came immediately to a door.

'The ledge. Above the door,' Bertie whispered. 'The key's up there. It's locked to keep the children out.'

Kate reached up and felt along the ledge. She took the key down and turned it in the lock. Gently, she eased the door open. A musty smell rushed out on a blast of cold air. With no source of light inside, she had to feel her way along, using the little moonlight from the corridor. Directly in front of her a narrow stone staircase led up. Just one step inside, Kate had to wipe cobwebs from her face.

'Lock the door behind us,' Bertie whispered. He and Elliot eased past her and began to climb the stairs. Tommy groaned. Kate closed the door. After locking it, she pushed the key into the pocket of her skirt.

Kate gripped the handrail as she followed Bertie and Elliot, her soles crunching in debris underfoot. They made slow progress up the steep staircase and finally came to a small landing. Elliot indicated for her to go ahead. She made her way along a narrow corridor. Unlike the women's staff quarters, there were no windows in this part of the attic to let in moonlight. But there seemed to be a sliver of light coming from beneath a door.

'Here,' Elliot said.

Kate stopped at the door. She felt for the handle, pushed it open, and could hardly believe her eyes. A fire glowed in a small hearth. The room was warm and a kettle waited on a trivet beside the grate. The floorboards were bare, but a comfortable looking armchair sat before the fire with a small table beside it, containing a few books and a cup. The curtains at the window were open. Beneath the window was a neatly made bed. Elliot and Bertie followed her inside and gently placed Bertie on the bed. He immediately curled into a ball and Elliot pulled the eiderdown over him. Elliot took off his cap and put it on the nightstand.

'Whose room is this?' Kate whispered.

'You can speak freely up here,' Elliot said. 'The rooms in the bachelors' corridor below aren't occupied. There's nobody about to hear.'

'But whose room is it?' Kate tried again.

Elliot took a shovel from a bucket of coal and added a heap to the fire. 'We'll want to keep him warm,' he said.

'Sometimes it makes sense for Elliot to be here rather than in the stables,' Bertie said. 'He's the only other member of staff who knows and who understands how some things work at Hill House.'

Kate looked past Bertie to Elliot, as he added twists of paper to the fire.

'Elliot's been with the Mandevilles a long time,' Bertie said. 'He–'

'There's no call to protect her and me from the truth of it,' Elliot said. 'If she's to do what I'm to ask of her, she should know.' He took a cigarette from a box on the mantelshelf, struck a match and lit it, then threw the spent match into the fire. He rested his arm on the chimneybreast and looked into the flames. 'The stories I tell by the fireside,' he said. 'I learned them at the knee of my mother. I tell them not to entertain, but to warn. As my mother told them to warn me.' He drew deeply on his cigarette and blew out the smoke. 'My mother had a gift, although not the same as yours. I have no gift, but I'm open where others might be closed. I see what is there when others choose not to see it. And I have forgotten none of what my mother taught me. She made it her life's work to make sure I knew all that she did. The Mandevilles have been good to me, and I repay that by being what use I can with what I know.' He drew deeply on his cigarette again and turned to Kate. 'You must face it,' he said.

Kate looked to Bertie, but his expression was a blank. 'What must I face?' she asked.

'I have a suspicion that the person behind this has schooled himself in arts that no man has a right to know.'

Kate shook her head. 'I don't understand.'

'You must find it out for yourself. All I can do is show you how you might access it. But you have to want to use your gift if it's to work.'

'Who is it that you think is doing this to Tommy?' Kate said. 'Who can possibly have this power? And why is Tommy still like this? Now that the penknife and cutlass are away from him, why has he not recovered?'

'All I can tell you is that tonight, on *Samhain*, the veil between the worlds is at its thinnest,' Elliot said. 'There is naught but gossamer between this realm and the next.'

'Really,' Bertie said suddenly. 'This is too much. Kate comes into this house and a few days later we are asking her to do all this to save a member of its family.'

'It has to be her,' Elliot said. 'You know it does. Neither of us has the gift that can help him.'

Bertie looked down at Tommy. Kate watched him. Watched the worry appear on his face afresh. She looked at Tommy curled in the bed then turned to Elliot. 'Tell me what I have to do.'

Elliot flicked the stub of his cigarette into the fire. 'Come with me.'

Kate followed Elliot from the room and Bertie called after them. 'Take care of her, Elliot,' he said. 'Take bloody good care of her.'

Kate pressed her hand to the wall to steady herself while she followed Elliot in the dark. They seemed to be winding their way around the top of the house, their footsteps crunching in the debris covering the bare floorboards. Elliot walked quickly before coming to a stop and pushing open a door. 'In here,' he said.

Kate followed Elliot. With no warning, light flooded the

room. The shock of it made Kate cover her eyes. Parting her fingers, she peered through the gaps to see bare lightbulbs above. And she saw more than that. She saw boxes piled high. She saw old furniture and valises and trunks and rails of clothes covered with sheets. And she saw a rocking horse beside a child's trunk and before it a mirror. The lumber room. She prised her hand away from her face.

'Why have you brought me here?' she said.

Elliot picked up an old dining chair and placed it before the mirror. 'Sit here,' he said. 'I'd rather not,' Kate said. 'That's the mirror where I saw the child who wanted to harm Pegasus.'

'Sit here,' Elliot said again.

Kate did as Elliot asked and sat in the chair but looked to the floor.

'You need to look in the mirror,' Elliot said.

Kate gripped the seat of the chair. 'I'll look if you tell me why I have to,' she said.

'Very well,' Elliot said.

Kate looked up. But rather than look at herself, she watched Elliot's reflection.

'A mirror can show you more than yourself,' he said. 'It can show you another world, if you know how to look. And you have already seen more than you know.' He placed his hands on the back of the chair again and leant forwards. 'You need to look deeply. Look into yourself and beyond, until you no longer see yourself.'

'But how will I see anything if I'm not touching an object? My skill only works when I touch something.'

'Your gift is greater than that. You can see without touching. If you want to. Do you want to?'

'I can try,' Kate said.

'I will leave you alone. And you must be in absolute darkness.'

'Alone and in darkness?' Kate said, thinking back to the child in the mirror. 'I don't think I can.'

'You will look at yourself and into yourself. You will see beyond what you can see.'

Kate stared at the reflection of Elliot's face.

'Can you do this, Katherine?' he asked.

Kate pictured Tommy so pale and desperately ill with someone controlling him as though he was a puppet for them to toy with. She saw him being carried through the house as he couldn't support himself. She saw the fear in the eyes of his family when he was so ill that they didn't know what to do. What else might happen to him if this went unchallenged? Modern medicine had not been able to cure him. If they couldn't break this hold that someone had over him, what would happen to Tommy? And what kind of person would she be if she didn't do everything she could to help? She had to do her best.

'I can try,' she said. 'I will try.'

Elliot nodded. 'I will be outside the door. If you need me, call and I'll come.'

Elliot released the back of the chair. He moved away and Kate was left with the reflection of Pegasus behind her.

Her pulse quickened with every one of Elliot's footsteps towards the door. She gripped the edge of the seat tighter. She had to fight the urge to run. To get away from this room and flee to the room just a short distance away, next door to the rooms of the two sisters who were her friends. But as she thought of Audrey and Rosemary, she saw Tommy again. He was like a little brother to them. If anything happened to him, their lives would never be the same again.

The lights went out above her.

The lock of the door clicked.

Kate closed her eyes. She pictured the awful face of that boy in the mirror. He had wanted to hurt Pegasus. The rocking horse was an inanimate object. But it was a loved object. To the Mandeville children it had been real. Generations of children had adored that painted horse and imagined flying away to magical lands on its back. She let her mind wander. There were parties. Children laughing and so happy in the saddle of that horse. But there was a child. A child who wanted to hurt and maim. Anything that the Mandeville children had loved, he had hated and wanted to destroy. And he was proud. Oh, he was so proud. He would stand before a mirror imagining that he was a great military hero. He would revel in his reflection and take power from it – from looking on himself. Never had there been a more conceited child.

Still gripping the edge of the seat, Kate bent forward. That child had turned into a man who still felt the same. Who still hated. His reason for living was to destroy. All pleasure in his life came from harming others, proving that he was more power-ful. He was shouting furiously. A small child cowered from him. But Kate couldn't see the man's face. He was hiding from her. She looked around him. But he turned from her. He did not want to be seen. He did not want to be discovered. Not yet.

Kate screwed her eyes tight. But the man would not show himself. She rocked backwards and forwards slightly, as though to build momentum. And opened her eyes.

The room was dark. Pitch black. Darker than night. Darker than dark. Kate stared at where she thought her eyes might be. She stared directly ahead. Noises sounded around her. Floor-boards creaked. Joists settled. Rodents scratched inside walls. Still, she looked into the darkness. Still nothing would reveal itself. She stared harder into the mirror. A form began to take shape. She saw it in the mirror and saw it in her mind's eye. A man. Contained. Another helping him. Guiding him. He was a pupil to the tutor. What he was training for was beyond anything he had done before. He was learning to move through time and through space. In his dreams. In his imagination. His body might be contained but his mind...His mind was free to go where he had the skill to take it. It was he who had given the penknife to Tommy as a child. In a dark wood in a den. Even then he had been plotting and planning for what might come.

Kate tried to see the man again. Again, he hid his face. She saw the child with the cutlass. He charged at her so that she sat back in the chair. He was angry that she had seen him, angry that it was beginning to make sense. She saw the man kneeling alone on a cold floor. In what looked like a cell. A symbol was drawn on the floor. A symbol he had learned to use as guided by his tutor. An item sat in the middle of the symbol. She looked again at the man. And finally, she saw his face. It was the man who had attacked her in the basement. The man who had pushed her so that she fell against the wall. He rushed to his feet and threw himself at her. Kate fell back and with the chair, she clattered to the floor.

The door flew open. 'Katherine!' Elliot called.

The lights came on. Kate winced. Elliot ran into the room. 'What happened?' he asked. 'What did you see?'

'Him,' Katherine said, getting to her feet. 'The man who attacked me in the basement. He's able to come through the mirror. Not his body, he is using his mind. He is learning how to travel. How to move through time.' The words tumbled out. She wanted to share them before she forgot a single detail. Her body seemed charged with an energy that she had never before known. 'He gave Tommy the penknife when he was a child. That man was the child that I saw in the mirror. The cutlass was his. He seems able to control Tommy through anything he has touched or given to him. Elliot, I believe that he is evil. He is contained somewhere but he can come here in his mind. And there is something else. There is something else he was preparing to give to Tommy. That's why Tommy is still ill.'

Elliot righted the chair. 'We should go,' he said.

THIRTY-EIGHT

Kate and Elliot returned to the small room and Bertie joined them in the corridor. Elliot relayed what Kate had told him she had seen. She was happy for him to speak for her. It all seemed unreal. When Elliot had finished recounting the details. Bertie said, 'It can't be him. He's in a prison in Scotland.'

'He is capable of whatever he puts his mind to,' Elliot said. 'He escaped the hangman's noose when everyone knew it was him who pushed his accomplice onto the train tracks. And he has shown he is ruthless in getting to Tommy. We've been waiting for him to make his move and now he has.'

'It's George Caxton, isn't it?' Kate said, stitching together all she had heard of the man, all that she had seen of him and what he had tried to do to her. 'He kidnapped Tommy as a child and now he is trying to hurt him again.'

Elliot nodded. 'You had to see that for yourself. And now we know for sure that it's him.'

'But why? Kate said. 'Why would he want to harm a member of his own family?'

'He hates the Mandevilles.' Bertie said. 'He blames them for his father disinheriting him. Tommy is the Mandeville heir, so he's the focus. And he's named for his uncle Thomas who was Caxton's original target. If Caxton has his way, the Mandevilles will be wiped from the face of the Earth. He must have been planning this since Tommy was a child. That's just like Caxton. He is a bastard and a coward.'

A groan came from the room.

'I've no idea how he's still doing this,' Bertie said. 'I've checked every one of Tommy's pockets and there's nothing I don't recognise. All the clothes are clothes he has had for as long as I remember. Can't we just smash the mirror to get rid of Caxton?'

'We have to free the hold he has over Tommy first,' Elliot said. 'We can't risk him staying like that. Or getting worse.'

Kate returned to sit with Tommy. She held his hand and tried to sooth him when he moaned. Elliot smoked another cigarette. Pinching the knees of his trousers, Bertie crouched before Tommy and looked into his face. He shook his head. 'I am so sorry,' he whispered. 'I should be able to look after you.' He put his hand to Tommy's cheek. When his palm came into contact with Tommy's face, Kate saw a change come over Bertie. Almost instantly, his back straightened, his body becoming rigid. He closed his eyes and began to tremble ever so slightly. His lips parted. Still with his hand to Tommy's cheek, he seemed to stop breathing. All Kate could do was watch. She didn't dare move. Or speak. And then, as suddenly as the change had come over Bertie, he drew in a lungful of air. His body jerked back, and he opened his eyes. 'It can't be,' he said and leapt to his feet. 'Give me the key. Please, Kate, give me the key.'

She fumbled in her pocket and produced the key to the door leading to the bachelors' wing. Bertie ran from the room, his footsteps echoing all the way along the corridor and down the stairs. Kate stared after him. There was a sound like a cry. It was a man's voice. It was Bertie. Kate ran to the door and looked out. Soon, two figures emerged from the darkness. Bertie and a woman.

Kate stood back as Bertie followed the woman into the room. Once inside, Bertie all but fell into the woman's arms. She held him so close, like a mother might. Kate watched the woman's face. She was a woman in her middle years. From the flecks of grey in her hair and the fine lines round her eyes, Kate judged her to be a similar age to her mother. And there was something so very familiar about her.

When she pulled away, the woman still held Bertie's hands. She looked him up and down and smiled. 'Look at you,' she said. 'You are a man now. What happened to my little Bertie?'

'He's still here,' Bertie said with a tremble in his voice.

The woman placed her hand to his cheek and Bertie leant into it, closing his eyes. 'I've missed you so much,' he said.

'And I've missed you, my darling boy.' The woman let her hand fall from Bertie's face. She leant over Tommy and brushed his fringe from his face.

Bertie placed the key on the mantelshelf.

'Hello, Elliot,' the woman said. 'Please don't worry. I will explain everything in just a moment.' She crossed the room to Kate. 'You must be Miss Durrant,' she said.

Kate looked from Bertie to Elliot, hoping for an explanation of what was happening and why another person had joined them.

'This is Louisa, Kate,' Bertie said. 'She's a friend of Hill House. She understands the more... unusual side to the house.'

'You can't be here,' Elliot said suddenly and abruptly. 'What about Mrs Mandeville?'

Louisa glanced at the bed and lowered her voice. 'I want to let you all know that you are not to worry. When I last visited when Tommy was still a little boy, I made a pact with Alice. If ever I sensed anything was wrong with Tommy, I was not to wait for Alice to come to find me. She told me I should come straight in.'

'But that puts her position at such great risk,' Bertie said.

Louisa nodded to the bed. 'Alice is prepared for that. Her boy is more important to her than her position here.'

Kate searched the faces of the people in the room, lost for what they were talking about. The woman's face was kind. Warm. And then it hit her. Square in her chest. This woman was no stranger. 'If you'll excuse me,' Kate said. 'I need some air.'

Kate stepped out into the corridor. She made for the staircase and leant against the wall. Louisa was the woman she had seen with Captain Mandeville. This woman had been Captain Mandeville's lover when they were young.

'Katherine,' she heard the voice coming towards her. 'Katherine.' Hands sought out hers. In the faint light, Kate saw Louisa's face as a series of outlines and shadows.

'I know this is a lot to take in,' Louisa said. 'I was once in your position, trying to understand how this house could have brought me here to help the Mandevilles.'

'Is that really what's happening?' Kate said. 'I suspected it, but it seemed so ridiculous that a house can do that.'

'It only seems ridiculous because we've been taught there is a logical explanation for everything,' Louisa said softly. 'But there is so much more to the world than logic, Katherine, if we are open to it.' She squeezed Kate's hands. 'I'm sure this sounds ludicrous to you at the moment. But I promise that it will all make sense in time.'

'I know I have to help the Mandevilles, and I want to,' Kate whispered. 'But I'm scared. I am so afraid.'

'You are doing really well,' Louisa said. 'Better than you know.' Kate felt Louisa's hands slip away. And then arms were around her, holding her close. 'You are being so brave. Can you be brave for a little while longer?'

Kate felt as she did when her own mother held her. She nodded. 'You should know that I've seen you,' she whispered. 'In one of my visions. With Captain Mandeville.'

Louisa's arms tightened around her. 'You are not the first visitor who has seen me.'

'Was the other person Miss Potter?' Kate said.

'I'll try to answer your questions later. For now, we must focus on Tommy.'

'Is George Caxton really as dangerous as Elliot and Bertie say?' Kate asked.

Louisa took a step away and Kate could see the whites of her eyes as she stared at her. 'George Caxton is even more dangerous than anyone here can imagine. He will do anything – anything – to destroy the Mandevilles. He is a murderer, Katherine. Never let your guard down around him. Should it ever come to it, don't try to confront him on your own. Bertie and Elliot can help you. If I am able, I will help you too. And when he is well, Tommy will help you. That young man is your connection to this house. As Bertie was and is my connection.'

'I know,' Kate nodded. 'Tommy told me.'

'And only you can save him,' Louisa said.

Louisa took Kate's hand and Kate let herself be led back to the bedroom.

Bertie and Elliot joined them in the corridor, a little way from the bedroom, so there was just enough light to see each other's faces.

'He's using the dark arts he's been tutored in,' Elliot said. 'And using this time of year to open a channel to control Tommy.' He turned to Kate. 'You saw him in his cell and you saw what he is attempting to do. The normal rules of man cannot contain him. He has learned to move outside our realm. And his powers are getting stronger. But as much as he can take advantage of the time of year, so can we. Tonight, we can draw on the spirits of our departed loved ones to help us.'

Kate, Bertie and Louisa all looked at each other. Kate felt the uncertainty and fear like the charge in the air before a thunderstorm. And then she felt something else. 'Tommy!' she said.

She ran into the bedroom. The bed was empty, the covers kicked to the floor. Bertie searched the mantelshelf. 'The key is gone.' He made for the door, but Elliot blocked his path.

'Where's he gone, Katherine?' Elliot asked.

'I don't know,' she said.

'You do,' Elliot said. 'You are his connection to this house.'

'I don't have anything to hold to give me a clue,' she said.

'You no longer need anything,' Elliot said. 'You have your connection to Tommy. To this house. And you have your powers and the help of each of the departed loved ones we thought of when I said we needed their help.'

Kate looked around, hoping to find an answer for what she should do in the faces of the people in the room. But all she saw was them waiting for her to tell them where Tommy had gone. She closed her eyes and grasped the St Christopher at her neck.

There was no flash or vision like a picture book. She thought hard, so hard. With a rush of energy, so powerful that she was nearly knocked backwards, she saw bare feet and the sound of gravel under foot.

'He's outside, on the path. He's running.'

They all raced from the room, along the corridor and down the stairs leading to the door into the bachelor's corridor. It stood open. Bertie brought them all to a stop. 'We can't go chasing through the house,' he whispered. 'We'll wake everyone. And we need to find Tommy before anyone realises he is missing.'

Instead of taking them out onto the carpeted landing, he pulled the door closed and had them follow a turn in the stairs, to another flight of steps heading down. Bertie led them in absolute darkness, their shoes slapping on the cold stone. They reached the bottom and followed Bertie through another door.

It took a moment, but Kate realised they were in the deserted basement corridor. Moonlight shone through the windows high up in the walls and she saw that the door beside the dumbwaiter led not to a cupboard but to the staircase to the attic.

At the end of the corridor, Elliot eased the latch across the door to the outside and they all followed him up the stone steps. The candles in the lanterns at ground level still glowed, lighting their ghoulish features.

They hurried around the path, stopping just outside the stable yard and out of earshot of the house. 'Where to now?' Bertie asked Kate.

She closed her eyes. She heard breathing, heavy, laboured breathing. Feet stumbled over roots breaking through the surface of the ground, dried leaves crunching. 'The woods,' she said. 'He's in the woods.'

When they reached the line of trees, Louisa bent forwards, her hands on her knees to catch her breath. 'I should let you go without me,' she said. 'I'll slow you down.'

'No,' Elliot said. 'We go as one.'

'Which way, Kate?' Bertie said.

She closed her eyes. But all she saw was feet running and the sound of breath heavier and laboured. 'I don't know.'

Elliot took a step closer to her. 'Draw on the energy that we're bringing,' he said.

She closed her eyes. She imagined Bertie, Elliot and Louisa. Each one had an energy outside themselves. She couldn't see it, but she could feel it. She grasped her St Christopher. Trees. She saw trees. Running. Feet in dried leaves. Gnarled branches. Branches reaching down to the ground and up again. A cage. A hand reaching up, grasping some of the leaves.

'The yew trees,' she said. 'He's going for the yew trees. And he's picking some of the leaves.'

Elliot looked at Bertie. Kate saw the horror in his eyes. 'Run, Bertie,' Elliot said. 'Stop him. We'll follow.'

Bertie set off through the woods. He ran so fast that he disappeared and all that was left was the sound of crashing through branches.

Elliot led Kate and Louisa into the woods.

'It's not far,' Kate said to Louisa. 'Just a little further to go.'

They dodged branches, the moonlight guiding the way. Louisa panted, trying to catch her breath.

'No! Tommy, no!' Bertie cried.

Kate picked up her pace until she came to the branches reaching down to the ground. She almost ran into Bertie. He was sitting on the ground with Tommy before him. He held him from behind so that Tommy's arms were pressed to his sides. Tommy's head rested back against Bertie. Elliot and Louisa reached them and Elliot sank to the ground. He pressed Tommy's cheeks together and tried to look in his mouth. 'Did he eat any?'

Bertie panted, shaking his head. 'No, I saw him reach the tree and take the first handful. I smacked them out of his hand before he could put them in his mouth.'

'Why?' Kate said. 'Why would Tommy eat leaves from a tree?'

'It's poison. One handful is enough to kill a man,' Elliot said. 'This must be what that bastard had planned all along.' He looked up at Louisa and she nodded.

'What kind of twisted bastard builds a den with a child so that years later he can get him into those same woods to have him take his own life?' Elliot said.

'A dangerous one,' Louisa said.

Kate stared at Tommy. In the moonlight, he was greyer even than before. He was still so desperately ill, and deep under whatever spell had been cast over him. As Bertie, Elliot and Louisa discussed what was to be done next, Kate took a step back.

She placed her hand to her St Christopher and closed her eyes. She opened herself up. She was not alone. Around her, she felt the presence of a protective ring. She couldn't see faces but she knew she was surrounded by energies there to help her. She saw images of their essence. A shamrock. A black stallion. A tie pin. A St Christopher. Their love circled around the people now in the woods. With their protection she allowed herself to see into the darkness again. The blackness. The rotten core. There was a rage so strong. But it was contained as though behind glass. As though behind bars. Stopping what it had planned to do had taken some of its power. It could no longer stop her from seeing past it. The object placed on the diagram drawn onto the stone of the cell floor was a watch. It looked like a watch that had been worn for years. But it was new. And it was tainted. A box. Sent in the post. It was on the post tray in the hall. Tommy opened it. A gift from his classmates. Why had they given him a watch the same as his old watch? Ah, he thought with a smile. They knew he had always worried about losing it. The watch he wore had belonged to his uncle. His namesake. And it was the most precious thing he owned. His friends had brought him a doppelganger to wear so that he might not damage or lose what he so loved.

But it was not from his classmates.

Kate opened her eyes. 'The watch,' she said. 'It's not Tommy's. It's how Caxton is controlling him.'

Elliot grabbed Tommy's arm. He made to yank the watch from his wrist.

'No!' Bertie said. 'We can't have him wake up here. We'll get him back to his room. If he wakes in his own bed, he might not remember what has passed tonight.'

. . .

Gently, very gently, Bertie and Elliot carried Tommy back to the house. They left Kate and Louisa at the door beside the dumbwaiter to return Tommy to his room. Kate beckoned for Louisa to follow her to the parlour to wait.

Once inside, Louisa stood on the rug before the unlit fire, turning around as though to take in every detail. 'I remember this room so well,' she said. 'It's hardly changed in twenty years.' She stopped and looked at Kate. 'You saved him, Katherine,' she said. 'You saved Tommy.'

'We all saved him,' Kate said.

Louisa shook head. 'It was you. And you have no idea how important you are to this family now.'

'Why were you talking about Alice earlier?' Kate asked.

Louisa shook her head. 'There are some questions I can't answer,'

'Can't answer or won't answer?' Kate said.

Louisa laughed softly. Once again Kate was struck by the kindness in her face. Even in the grey moonlight there was warmth in her eyes. 'I can see why you were chosen,' Louisa said. 'You have spirit, Katherine. And you're loyal. You know you can't speak of any of what's happened tonight to the Mandevilles. And you can never talk about Alice in the way I did earlier or question why she is here. Great trust is being placed in you.'

'I know,' Kate said. 'Can I talk about Miss Potter?' she asked, feeling her way around what she could and couldn't do.

Louisa laughed again. 'Yes, you can talk about Nell. And you'll meet her soon. You are going to be such great friends.'

Kate shook her head. 'How do you know all this?'

'I might ask you how you know the history of an object simply by touching it,' Louisa said, her eyes wide. 'We each have our own reason for being here.'

Kate smiled. This most bizarre of conversations somehow made complete sense. 'How does it choose us?' she asked.

Louisa's smile faded. She looked to the floor and then to Kate. 'I hope this isn't too painful for me to ask. But before you came here, Katherine, did you suffer a loss so great that you felt you would never recover?'

Instinctively Kate reached for her St Christopher. She nodded.

'You needed Hill House and Hill House needed you,' Louisa said. 'It's simple when you think about it.' She wrapped her arms around Kate and held her close.

'What brought you here tonight, Louisa?' Kate asked. 'Where did you come from and how did you know to come? And why do you share a name with Charlotte's daughter?'

Louisa gave her a squeeze. 'You're persistent. I'll give you that. But I think I've answered enough questions and given you enough to think about for now.'

Kate closed her eyes and saw the black stallion. 'He was there with you tonight,' she whispered. 'Captain Mandeville. It's him you thought about when Elliot told us to see someone we loved.'

Kate felt Louisa nod. She didn't answer immediately and when she did, her voice caught in her throat. 'I felt him beside me,' Louisa said. 'In a way that I never have before.'

'He loves you so very much,' Kate said. 'He has shown me you together in this house.'

She felt Louisa nod again. When she pulled away, tears glistened in her eyes. 'Thank you,' Louisa whispered. 'Thank you for bringing him to me.' She smiled at Kate. 'You are so kind and gentle. I see so much of my eldest daughter in you.'

'I beg your pardon?' Kate said.

Any response Louisa might have given was lost when the parlour door opened.

'Elliot is looking after Tommy,' Bertie said. 'He's going to take care of everything.'

'Good,' Louisa said, wiping her eyes with the side of her hand. 'Then I should go.'

Kate had so many questions for Louisa. But it was clear they would have to wait for another day.

At the door leading to the outside steps, Kate watched Bertie and Louisa embrace. Again, Louisa held him as she might a child. She looked from Bertie to Kate and smiled before making her way up the steps. She waved when she reached the top and Bertie closed the door.

The house was once again silent.

Bertie took Kate's arm and guided her back into the parlour, closing the door behind them.

They stood looking at each other. Kate searched Bertie's eyes and thought to the tie pin she had seen in her vision. She wondered whether to say what she thought she should. Whether he would want to hear it.

'He was there tonight,' she said. 'Your father.'

Bertie nodded. 'I know.'

Kate watched a tear spill down Bertie's cheek. He put his arms around her, and pulled her close to him, one arm around her waist and the other across her back, his hand in her hair. He cradled her to him, and she slipped her arms around him, holding him as close as he held her.

'Thank you for bringing him to me,' he whispered into her hair. 'Thank you.'

THIRTY-NINE

FRIDAY 1ST NOVEMBER, 1935

When Kate woke, it was still dark outside. She had barely slept. She dressed in her black work dress and apron.

On her way down the back stairs, one thought occupied her mind. Tommy.

She collected the coal scuttle from the passageway and made up the fires in each of the downstairs rooms. When she had finished, she went into the ballroom to tidy and sweep the floor and mop up the spilled food and drink. There was so much to be cleaned that it was already eight o'clock when she carried the mop bucket out through the office corridor to pour the dirty water into the drain at the back of the house. She returned to collect the dustpan and broom to put them in the cupboard in the basement.

Even before she had walked along the passageway, she heard the voices coming from the kitchen. She took the steps down, placing her shoes in the familiar grooves worn into the stone. She paused outside the kitchen door, before stepping inside.

Almost every chair was occupied and the table laden with

breakfast. Alice and Charlotte and Audrey and Rosemary were
there, along with all the children dressed in their Halloween
costumes. Kate looked to the end of the table where Mrs
Hart sat.

'There she is!' Alice said. 'The woman of the moment! I
hope you had a jolly good sleep, Katherine. And managed to
sleep off the effects of the toffee. Bertie said you were a bit
unwell.'

'I'm sorry I left the party—' Kate started.

'Oh, pish,' Charlotte said. 'If you're poorly, you're poorly.
But would you just look at this lot, all dressed for Halloween
still like the party isn't over! They've convinced us to let them
go to school like that! I hope Mary doesn't mind. Come on,
shove up everyone, make room for Katherine.'

They began to move chairs around when someone entered
the room behind Kate.

'I couldn't find it!'

Kate spun around. She could have wept at the sight of the
person standing in the doorway.

'The oddest thing,' Tommy said. 'I can't find that cutlass
anywhere. It's vanished off the face of the Earth. I'm afraid that
you will have to go to school as an unarmed pirate, Charlie.
Morning, Katherine,' he added as he joined Mrs Hart at the end
of the table.

Kate sat at the space that had been made for her between
Alice and Charlotte. Audrey poured her a cup of tea and Kate
watched Tommy tuck into the plate of food before him. 'And do
you know what else was odd?' he said. 'When I woke up this
morning, I had bits of leaf stuck to the soles of my feet. And
they were all over my bedroom.'

'It's because you insist on going around without shoes on,'
Alice said. 'I don't know what you have against shoes.'

The hubbub of the family breakfast bubbled around Kate

and all she could do was look at every person at the table and not cry.

After breakfast, Alice asked Kate to run an errand for her, so Kate collected her coat and left the house by the back steps.

She walked around to the front of the house and stopped to look into the woods. She became aware of something nudging her feet. She stooped to stroke the ears of the Jack Russell.

'Morning,' Elliot said. 'It's a fine day for a walk.' He raised his cap and carried on along the path to the stable yard. The dog trotted away to join him.

Kate stared after Elliot. Was that it? Was that all he was going to say?

Walking down the drive, she began to wonder whether she had imagined everything last night. Whether it was she who had been in some kind of fever and had in fact dreamt it all. She slipped her hand into her collar and felt the St Christopher. It felt like it always had before last night. Like a bit of gold warmed by her skin. But she knew it was more than that now.

At the gates she tuned left onto the road. Before she got to the workers' cottages, she saw it. Bertie's truck parked up outside his house. She knocked on his door. It opened. Bertie was in just his shirtsleeves, rolled up to his elbows.

After Elliot's reaction to her, she wasn't sure what conversation would be welcome. She held out the letter she had been asked to deliver. 'Alice asked that you take this to Top Farm when you go later today.'

Bertie took the envelope from her and placed it on the hall-stand. 'Come in,' he said.

'I should probably be heading back.'

'You won't be missed for a few minutes,' Bertie said.

Kate stepped inside.

'I've got something to show you,' Bertie said. He pushed open the door to the front parlour. It had been empty when she last saw it. Now the familiarity of the little cottage and the contents of this room wrapped around her like a warm blanket. Her father's campaign bed stood before the fireplace, with Harry's camping stove, camping cup and the tin of pilchards on top. And there, in the middle of the room, was her parents' kitchen table.

Bertie stood behind her. 'Your old neighbour let me in yesterday to collect it all,' he said. 'Tommy helped me move it. I wanted it to be a surprise. And I got in touch with the people who have bought the house. They are ever so nice. They didn't mind at all that I wanted to buy the table back from them when I explained how special it was to you.'

'You bought it?' Kate said. 'For me?'

'I could see how upset it made you to have to part with it. You're welcome to keep these things here. I don't use this room for anything. But the strangest thing,' he said. 'When I brought the table in, I checked the drawers and found that.' He pointed to the mantelshelf. Kate had missed it at first. But now she saw it. A little tin soldier. The soldier that had been her father's. And that she hadn't seen for years.

Kate put her hand to her mouth.

'I'm sorry,' Bertie said. 'I didn't mean to upset you.'

She turned to face him. 'I'm not upset. But... last night. Did that all really happen?'

Bertie nodded.

Kate knew that any conversation about the other side of Hill House could wait for another day. And she knew that she was ready to do whatever was needed of her.

'Would you like me to drive you to your old house?' Bertie said. 'So you can say goodbye before the new people move in?'

Kate shook her head. 'That's not my home anymore,' she said. 'I have a new home.'

'Here?' Bertie said. 'At Hill House?'

She touched Bertie's hand. He leant and kissed her, holding her close. She wrapped her arms around him, and they kissed again.

EPILOGUE

EASTER SUNDAY, 1936

On a beautiful spring morning, the sun shines across a well-tended churchyard. The fresh grass almost glows. The first flowers of the year decorate the borders. Tiny wildflowers pepper the lawns.

A small group has gathered around a memorial recently installed. It is their first visit here together to see it. They lay flowers. They share stories. The two small children hold drawings up to the stone. There are tears, both happy and sad.

When most of the group depart for the tea they have kindly been invited to take at the big house at the end of the drive, a couple stay behind. Together, they ease behind a holly bush and through a gate in a low wall. They walk into the woods until they come to two trees. The trees are the oldest on the land. Their branches entwine so that they have become one. They were here before living memory and will be here long after. They are the trees of legend that can take life but also show the way to eternal life.

The man slips a knife from his pocket. He hands it to the woman. She cuts a small branch, and they return to the churchyard. He stands close beside her as she kneels to place the branch on the grass amongst the flowers her family has placed at her father's grave. The branch is a reminder that the departed are never more than a heartbeat away.

She stands and smiles as the man takes her hand. She knows that her hand will always be in his now.

A LETTER FROM THE AUTHOR

Dear reader,

I'd like to say a huge thank you for reading *The Mandeville Shadow*. I hope you enjoyed spending time with Kate and following the journey of the Mandevilles and their home, Hill House.

If you want to join other readers in hearing about my new releases and bonus content, you can sign up here:

www.stormpublishing.co/callie-langridge

If you enjoyed this book and could spare a few moments to leave a review, I would hugely appreciate it. Even a short review can make all the difference in encouraging a reader to discover my books for the first time. Thank you so much!

History is my passion and it has been a joy to continue the story of the Mandevilles into the changing world of the 1930s.

Thanks again for being part of this amazing journey with me. I love to hear from my readers through my social media channels, so please feel free to find me for a chat. I hope you'll stay in touch as I have so many more stories and ideas to share with you!

All the very best,

Callie Langridge

facebook.com/CallieLangridgeAuthor

x.com/CLangridgeWrite

instagram.com/CallieLangridge

ACKNOWLEDGEMENTS

I would like to thank everyone at Storm for getting this third instalment of the Mandeville series into the world. Special thanks to Kathryn for helping me make this book the best it can be.

So many fellow authors have continued to support me throughout the writing of this book. Thank you to my marvellous writing pals who have been with me for years – Zoe Antoniades, Sam Hanson, Susie Lynes and John Rogers. Thank you also to Clarissa Angus, Claire McGlasson, Emilie Olsson, Kate Riordan, Emma Robinson, Bev Thomas and Lisa Timoney for your support, laughs and productive retreats in creaking old houses (that might just have provided inspiration for some of the events in the Mandevilles' third adventure).

I am so grateful to Kim, Val and Virginia for their ongoing encouragement and never-ending patience and enthusiasm for my writing. And a very special thanks to Pete, always my cheerleader in chief.

Printed in Great Britain
by Amazon